Corruption of Innocence

Alan Ferrie

Published in 2014 by FeedARead.com Publishing

Copyright © Alan Ferrie.

First Edition

The author has asserted their moral right under the
Copyright, Designs and Patents Act, 1988, to be identified
as the author of this work.

All Rights reserved. No part of this publication may be reproduced, copied, stored in a retrieval system, or transmitted, in any form or by any means, without the prior written consent of the copyright holder, nor be otherwise circulated in any form of binding or cover other than that in which it is published and without a similar condition being imposed on the subsequent purchaser.

A CIP catalogue record for this title is available from the British Library.

This novel is a work of fiction. Names, characters, places, and incidents either are the product of the author's imagination or are used fictitiously, and any resemblance to persons, living or dead is entirely coincidental.

This novel would never have reached fruition without the unwavering support of my wife Sylvia; To Gerald, dear friend and brother-in-law, thank you for proof-reading the manuscript.

PROLOGUE
1978
It was after midnight when laughter from the staff common room roused him from a warm slumber. He wiped the sleep from his eyes, looked at the strip of light shining in under the door and bit his lip as the familiar sense of foreboding washed over him. He turned towards his friend, Tommy, and whispered. 'Are you awake?'

'Yeh. Sounds like they're back from the pub.'

'Pretend we're asleep.'

He turned and faced the window, pulled the bedclothes up tight under his chin and traced the raindrops running down the window in the light of the bright moon. He wished with all his heart that a guardian angel would swoop down, gather him up and whisk him away from this evil place, but he knew he would not come. He never did. No matter how hard he prayed.

A solitary tear fell from the corner of his eye, rolled down the side of his nose and rested on his top lip; he curled his tongue around the droplet and licked it away. The salty taste was a welcome lubrication to his dry mouth; he wished that there were more, but something inside him would not let him give in to floods of tears. That's what the bastards wanted. Tears only served as food for their sordid, sickening little games. It would only make the whole ordeal ten-times worse if they knew that he was hurting. He was determined that he would never give them that satisfaction. He pulled the bedclothes over his head, drew his skinny legs up to his chest and tried to blank out the wickedness emanating from down the corridor.

'They're coming! I can hear their voices along the corridor,' Tommy whispered.

'Shush! Pretend you're asleep.'

He screwed his eyes as tight as he could and said a silent prayer to himself, wishing against all the odds that the drunken revelry getting louder by the second would bypass their room and seek out someone else for their amusement.

Suddenly, it all went quiet. The squeak of the door handle turning and the door slowly opening sent a spasm of fear racing through every nerve end of his skinny body. He could smell the foul body odour mixed with beer and tobacco fumes contaminating the sweet scented air of the small bedroom. He knew the familiar stench belonged to Harry Critchley, the night warden of Whitehaven Children's Home.

A torch light searched the room then stopped on his head. He could see the beam of light on the bedside cabinet next to him. It moved slowly across the room and searched out Tommy. He prayed his friend didn't stir. The light blinked off, the room fell back into darkness and the door slowly closed. He breathed a sigh of relief. 'Looks like it's not our turn tonight,' he whispered, across to Tommy. There was no response. He guessed that Tommy was too scared to answer. Sometimes he clammed up for days . . . especially after . . .

He breathed a sigh of relief, and tried to settle down to sleep, safe in knowledge that it wasn't his turn tonight. Suddenly, the door crashed open and a swarm of bodies rushed into the room. He dived under the bedclothes and pulled them up as tight as he could. They were stripped back in one swift movement and a hand grabbed him around the neck. He kicked and bucked frantically, but he knew it was hopeless: they were too strong for him.

'Thought you got away with it tonight, didn't you? How could I pass you up? You're my favourite little chicken,' Harry Critchley whispered into his ear.

He almost retched as the man's putrid breath caught in his nostrils. He gasped for air as his head was buried into the pillow. He'd learnt a long time ago that it was hopeless trying to struggle; they would only hurt him even more. He lay motionless. Dissimulated. Like a corpse devoid of all feeling. Except the overwhelming feeling of revulsion. But the worse thing of all, the one single thing that festered deep inside him like a cancer was the feeling of disgust: with himself.

From the corner of his eye, he focused on a tattooed arm. A beautiful mermaid posing provocatively on a rock with the palm of her hand resting under her chin. Her long blonde hair curled down over her hips, her bright blue eyes smiled at him, and her pursed red lips reached out to kiss him. The vivid blue and green scales of her tail were a wonderful distraction from the agonising pain that was racing through his body.

CHAPTER 1

PRESENT DAY.

'It's getting late, where's Donna?' said Lee Carlin, to his wife Susan.
'She's out with, Haley.'
'Well it's past nine o'clock.'
'You know what those two are like when they're together, they lose all track of time. She'll be home soon. Don't fret.'
'All the same, I think I'll give Karen a ring. Tell her that I'll drive over and pick Donna up. It'll save her having to come out in the cold.'
Lee went out into the hallway and found the number on the speed dial. 'Hi, Karen. Thought I'd pop over and pick Donna up, if she's ready' Lee said, in a breezy tone. 'By the way, are we still on for Sunday lunch? Susan's looking forward to it, we both are.'
There was a pause.
'What do you mean she's not there? Susan said she was with Haley.'
Another pause.
'Let me get this straight, you're saying that Haley came straight home from school this afternoon and she says she hasn't seen Donna since lunchtime? Well where in the hell is she? Ok, thanks. I'll try her mobile and don't forget about Sunday.'
Five minutes later, Lee came back into the lounge with a disconcerted look on his face.
'What's the matter?' his wife asked, turning her attention away from the television.
'It's Donna. She's not at Haley's. She hasn't seen her all afternoon. I've tried ringing her mobile but it's switched off. I've even tried ringing around all her friends' parents and none of them have seen her.

Where on earth could she have got to? Do you think we ought to telephone the police?'

'She's only an hour late, love. She'll come breezing through the door any minute and wonder what all the fuss is about, you'll see. Sit down and relax, I'll put the kettle on.'

An hour later, Lee jumped up from the armchair. 'I can't have any more of this waiting,' he said anxiously, shaking his head. I'm phoning the police.'

*

DC Tanya Reid was sitting in the Carlin's lounge taking notes when her boss, DI John Loder arrived. She got up from the settee, met Loder out in the hallway and quietly briefed him with everything that she had so far.

'You take the wife upstairs and have a nose around the girl's bedroom. I'll have a word with the husband. By the way, what's his name?' Loder asked.

'Lee. Lee Carlin.'

'Right, let's get to it.'

Tanya led the way into the lounge and flashed a warm smile at Susan Carlin. 'Mrs Carlin shall you and I take a look upstairs in Donna's bedroom?' The woman nodded solemnly and led the way out into the hallway. 'I don't know what you hope to find?' she said, climbing the stairs.

Tanya didn't reply as she followed the woman up and along the plush-carpeted landing. She towered over Susan Carlin's short, five-foot slim frame as she led her into Donna's bedroom.

'What a lovely room,' Tanya said, trying to defuse the tension.

'Donna chose the colours and fabrics herself.'

'Did she!' Tanya enthused, looking at the flowery lace-edged curtains tied neatly back each side of the window. She thought the style and pattern a bit grown up for a thirteen year old.

'She's forever rearranging the furniture. Says she wants to be an interior designer when she leaves school. Says she's going to be more famous than that man on the TV, what's his name?' She mused. 'Oh yes, Lawrence Llewellyn, somebody or other. I can't remember,' she said, with a dismissive wave of her hand. She sat on the side of the bed and picked up a scruffy teddy bear from the pillow.

Tanya politely nosed around, careful not to untidy anything, at the same time looking for something, anything that might be out of ordinary. She slid the wardrobe doors apart and peered in. Hanging neatly on a rail was an assortment of trendy clothes. In the bottom was a box with a tangle of old toys and dolls. A neatly stacked CD rack stood next to a computer console with a bookcase above it. Nothing seemed out of place. Everything neat and tidy.

Tanya thought about her own daughter, Katie, and the perpetual chaos her bedroom was always kept in. That's what teenagers do leave their bedrooms looking like a bomb site, or so she thought.

'I have to say Mrs Carlin, Donna seems to be very organised for a boisterous teenager. I wish my daughter was the same, I'm forever arguing with her to clean up her act. But it always falls on death ears,' Tanya said, rolling her eyes.

'My Donna never gives us any cause for concern. She spends hours up here chatting to her friends on the Internet. Unhealthy, if you ask me. She should be out playing instead of sitting in front of that contraption, night after night.'

Tanya drifted across to the computer and switched it on. She turned and asked. 'Do you mind if I . . .?'

'No, love. You carry on,' she said, clutching the teddy bear to her chest.

She sat down in front of the console and booted-up the machine. Looking at the woman's reflection in the mirror on the wall in front of her, Tanya asked. 'How are things at home?'

'What do you mean?' She gave a confused look.

'There haven't been any little family tiffs? I know how frustrating teenagers can be.'

'No.'

'She wouldn't have had any reason to leave home: would she?'

'What are you getting at?'

'How does Donna get on with her father?'

'There is nothing untoward going on in this family, if that's what you're insinuating.' Her brow narrowed suspiciously, as she looked straight into the mirror at Tanya. 'My husband dotes on Donna. She's his whole life, there's nothing he wouldn't do for her. We're just a normal loving family. I take offence at your line of questioning.'

'I'm sure you'll appreciate that we do have to explore every avenue. What about school? Do you know if she was being bullied, or anything?' Tanya changed tack.

'No, Donna's a very popular girl, she has lots of friends. If anyone was giving her a hard time I'm certain that she would have confided in me.' Susan Carlin shook her head, not comprehending everything that was going on. 'All this, is so out of character for Donna. We always know where she is.'

The monitor prompted for a password, Tanya cursed under her breath. 'I don't suppose you know Donna's password, do you?'

'No. I'm afraid not. Those contraptions might as well be rocket science to me.'

Tanya keyed in the obvious ones that came to mind. Christian name. Surname. Initials. Nothing. 'What's Donna's date of birth?'

'Fourth of June ninety-three.'

Tanya keyed in the numbers. Nothing. She then went through the whole sequence again adding the year of birth to the end, but with no result. With a frustrated sigh, she switched off the computer, swivelled around on the stool and faced the woman.

'Does Donna take a bag to school with her? I can't see one anywhere around.' Tanya asked.

'Yes. She's got a navy, duffle-type bag with her.'

'I don't suppose you know if she took a change of clothes with her, do you?'

'No, she had no reason to. She told me she was going around to her friend, Haley's, after school. They were going to do homework together and watch a new pop video that Haley had been given,' Susan Carlin said, casting her eyes around the room inquisitively. 'Wait a minute! She asked me to iron her new hipsters and sweatshirt top. I left them, there!' She pointed to the end of the bed. 'Oh God! Where is she? Where's my baby?' She screamed, hysterically. Her bottom lip quivered as her eyes filled with tears.

Tanya sat on the bed next the woman and put a consoling arm around her shoulder. 'Come on, Susan. It's probably all very innocent. Donna could have met with a secret boyfriend, or something, and lost all track of time. Come on, it's too early to start filling your head with all this nonsense.'

Tanya reached across to the bedside cabinet, pulled a couple of tissues from a box and handed them to the woman. She wiped her eyes, and said, 'I'm sorry. You just think the worse, don't you? You hear about all these youngsters going missing, snatched off the street. You never think that it's going to happen to you.'

'Honestly, Susan. It's too early to start making assumptions. Now, give me a description of the clothes that Donna took with her.'

Susan Carlin's head seemed to shrink down between her shoulders as she began to speak. 'The hipsters are black and bell-bottomed, and the sweatshirt top is cream with a glittery FCUK motif across the chest.'

'And what did she wear going to school?'

'Her uniform. Navy blazer, pleated skirt, white cotton blouse, black tights and shoes.'

'That's great, Susan. Now where does her friend, Haley live?'

'It's not far, over on the Flower Estate, off of Old Oak Road. I'll get the address for you,' she said, getting to her feet.

'Come on, we'll go down together.'

Tanya cast Loder a surreptitious, tight-lipped shake of the head as they both entered the lounge. Loder was already on his feet. Lee Carlin was sitting on the settee staring down at the carpet. His wife went and sat next to him and linked her arm through his.

'Oh I forgot! I'll get Haley's address for you,' Susan Carlin said, getting up.

'That's okay, your husband already gave it to me,' Loder smiled.

Tanya made her way into the hall and phoned in Donna's particulars on her mobile to the duty officer back at the station. When she'd finished, she poked her head through the open lounge door and nodded to Loder.

'Right, we have everything we need for the moment. We've got every available patrol unit on the lookout for Donna. I want you to stay by the telephone, in case she rings. We'll be in touch later,' Loder said. 'I've left my card on the table, in case you need to get hold of me.'

Lee Carlin, jumped up from the settee, dashed out of the room and grabbed his coat off the wall-hanger by the street door. 'I can't sit around here doing sweet fuck-all. I'm going out in the car to look for her.'

'Lee!' His wife pleaded.

'It's okay. Let him go,' Loder said. 'You stay by the telephone, Mrs Carlin. We'll be back later.

Loder aimed his remote at his car as he strode out into the damp, chilly night air. The orange glow of the indicator lights blinking, as the central-locking released, illuminated the dimly lit street.

'What do you think, sir?' Tanya asked.

'Not sure. Too early to say,' Loder said, opening the car door. 'Let's go and have a word with Donna's friend, Haley. See what we can get out of her.'

Loder looked at the slip of paper with the girl's address on. She only lives about half a mile away. You might as well tail me up.'

'Okay, sir.'

As Tanya was about to get into her car, Loder shot off up the road. *Typical*, she thought to herself, rolling her eyes with infuriation as she sped off after him.

Four minutes later, with his hands buried deep into the pockets of his camel overcoat, Loder strode up the garden path to Haley's house, with Tanya in tow behind. His tall frame cast a long, menacing shadow in the dim street haze as he approached the street door and rang the bell.

'If you don't mind me saying, sir. It might be better if I talk to the girl. You'd only frighten the life out of her.'

'Are you saying that I lack any compassion?' Loder looked askance at Tanya.

'Let's just say that you're a little —'

The door opened just in the nick of time before an inquisition. Loder flashed his ID at the attractive, dark-haired woman poking her head around the door. The woman's eyes narrowed suspiciously at the two detectives, her mind racing as to what her husband had been up to this time. Before Loder had flashed his ID she knew they were Old Bill. It was in their demeanour; she could smell them a mile off.

'Can we come in for a moment? We need to have a word with Haley,' Tanya smiled.

'Why?' The woman sniffed.

'It's concerning her friend, Donna. She hasn't come home this evening and we thought that Haley might be able to help us,' Loder said, inviting himself into the house.

The two detectives followed the woman into the lounge where Haley and her father were sitting on a huge leather settee, watching TV together. The man stared up at the two detectives with a look of contempt on his face. He recognised Loder: he'd nicked him a few years ago for "Kiting" with stolen credit cards.

'Yeh,' the man sneered. 'What can I do for you, Inspector Loder?'

Loder recognised the face, but couldn't put a name to it. It was the shiny bald head that threw him. He was of a mind that the last time he had a run-in with this cocky bastard, he had a full mop of hair.

'Relax, Paul. It's Haley they want to see. Donna has gone missing,' his wife said, defusing the frosty atmosphere.

The pretty girl looked up at Loder, and then turned her eyes towards her mother, earnestly.

'It's okay. You're not in any trouble, Haley. We just need to ask you a few questions,' Tanya smiled, sitting down on the settee next to the terrified-looking little girl. She put her shoulder bag on the floor and took out her notepad. Then turned towards the girl, and said, 'When did you last see Donna, Haley?'

'Lunchtime, in the playground,' she replied, tentatively.

'Do you usually come home together after school?'

She nodded.

'Why didn't you come home together today? Was Donna going elsewhere, to another friend's house, maybe?'

Haley looked up at her mother and bit her lip nervously.

'Answer the lady, Haley,' her mother snapped, impatiently.

'You won't be in any trouble if you tell us,' Tanya said, reassuringly.

'Donna went to meet a boy she'd met in an Internet chat room.'

'What! Have you been messing about in chat rooms?' Her father went off on one.

'No. Not me, dad, honest.' She started to cry.

'Why don't you put the kettle on, Paul,' his wife said, before Loder had time to step in. It was an order not a question. She didn't want him scaring the life out of the girl; otherwise, she'd just go shtum. Karen knew her daughter all too well, and sensed that she knew a lot more than she was letting on.

The man got up from the settee and stomped out of the room in a huff.

'Where was Donna supposed to meet this boy, Haley?' Tanya asked, softly.

'Outside Shepherds Green Underground.'

'Do you know his name?'

'Jason,' Haley replied, wiping her eyes on the arm of her school blouse.

'You said that Donna met Jason in an Internet chat room?'

Haley nodded.

'Was it on your computer or Donna's?'

'Donna's.'

'Do you know the password to Donna's computer?' Loder, cut in.

'I think it's "Blue" the name of our favourite band. But she does change it quite often.'

'Were you there when Donna was online with Jason?' Tanya asked.

'Most of the time, but not all. We used to have a laugh together, stringing Jason along. We thought it was all a big joke, really. I didn't know she'd set up a meet with him 'til she told me this morning on the way to school.'

'Okay, Haley,' Tanya smiled. 'You've been a great help, but if you think of anything later that might be of help to us, tell your mum and she can get in touch, okay,' Tanya smiled warmly, brushing some strands of hair away from Haley's eyes with the back of her hand. She then got to her feet, picked up her bag, tucked the notepad down inside and followed Loder out of the room. As they made their way down the hallway, the husband came out of the kitchen holding a tray with mugs of tea on.

'Maybe another time,' Loder said, as he opened the street door.

Miffed, that his efforts had been ignored, he shouted into the lounge, 'Haley! Upstairs. Now!'

Tanya turned and looked over her shoulder at the mother, and then at Haley, as the girl bolted out of the room and up the stairs to her bedroom.

'Don't worry. He won't lay a finger on her. He's more frightened of me, than Haley is of him,' she winked. *Why do I believe that? Tanya thought as the woman shut the street door behind them.*

Sitting in Loder's car outside the house, he turned to Tanya, and mused, 'I've got an uneasy feeling about this.'

'Me too, sir. On the other hand, it could all be quite innocent. First boy to show an interest in her, it's all very flattering to an impressionable thirteen year old.'

'This Jason could also be a predator surfing internet chat rooms and currying favour with any number of young kids. Still, we'll have a better idea when we get into Donna's computer. Let's get back to the Carlin's house,' Loder said, starting the car.

When Tanya arrived at the Carlin's house, Loder was finishing a mug of coffee. Susan Carlin proffered a mug to Tanya and she wrapped both hands around it feeling the warmth radiating into her palms. 'Just what I need, thank you,' she said, taking a long swallow at the steaming, dark liquid. 'I take it, Inspector Loder has told you what we've learnt from Haley?'

Susan Carlin shook her head disconsolately. 'I can't believe Donna would do something like this.'

Loder got to his feet, and said. 'Right, let's have a look at her computer.'

The woman led them up stairs to Donna's bedroom. Tanya sat at the monitor while the other two looked on over her shoulder. She switched on the computer and waited impatiently for it to boot-up. When the screen prompted for a password, Tanya keyed in the word "Blue." All three of them looked on anxiously as she pressed the return key. The silence was almost palpable. Instantaneously, a desktop image of two lovers standing on the deck of a ship staring into a bright-red sunset appeared. All three breathed a sigh of relief. Tanya found Donna's email, opened her inbox and started to sift through her mail.

On the face of it, it all seemed very innocent. Two teenage kids swapping stories. Nothing untoward, just cheesy chat-up lines and the odd prying question of what she looked like, what clothes she liked to wear. Each message getting a little more subtle: more risqué. Until the penultimate one that jokily asked Donna in a roundabout way to send the sexiest picture she had of herself, so that he could keep it close to his heart when he went to sleep at night. The most recent message being the one confirming that he would meet her outside Shepherds Green Underground, and that they'd go for a pizza together. It was when Tanya went into "Sent mail" that things took a turn for the worse. In it were three pictures of Donna posing semi-naked on a bed.

Susan Carlin held her hands to her mouth in shock. She couldn't believe what she was seeing. 'Oh Christ! What on earth is she doing? That's not my little baby. Someone must have put her up to it,' she said vehemently 'She would *never* do something like this on her own. Must be that little bitch, Haley? She must have put her up to it.'

Tanya shut down the computer and swivelled around to face Loder. He looked uncomfortable as Susan Carlin buried her head into his chest and sobbed uncontrollably. Tanya got up and led her over to the bed, sat her down and handed her a bunch of tissues.

Loder then asked if Donna owned a camera. Susan Carlin pointed to a drawer under the computer desk. 'There should be one in there. We bought it for her birthday.'

Tanya went across, opened the drawer and pulled out a little digital camera. She switched it on and searched through all the photos stored in memory on the LCD, until she found the ones they had just seen on the computer. She looked at Loder and nodded.

'Right, disconnect the computer Tanya. We'll send it over to High Tech Forensics; see if they can trace the source of the emails.'

Tanya unplugged everything and wrapped the lead around the main tower. 'Here you are, sir, it's all yours.'

'Susan, can you open the front door for Inspector Loder, please.' Tanya motioned with her eyes to Loder to get the woman out of the room.

'Yes, if you could show me the way, please. This tower is a bit cumbersome,' he said, wrestling it in his arms. 'I don't want to knock anything over.'

The distraught woman nodded, dried her eyes and made her way downstairs with Loder behind. As he turned left out of the room, he looked back at Tanya, and she whispered, 'I need a couple of minutes.'

She closed the bedroom door, got out the camera and quickly found the pictures of Donna posing on the bed. She wanted to be sure that the photos were taken here in the bedroom. The background was the same, right down to the velour headboard and the sherbet coloured wall behind. Donna had either taken the photos herself with the camera in timer mode, or Haley had taken them, whichever, Haley would need to be interviewed again. Tanya was sure the girl knew a lot more than she already let on. She slipped the camera into her bag and went downstairs.

Loder was already loading the computer tower into the boot of his car when Tanya reached the bottom of the stairs. She poked her head around the lounge door, and asked, 'Have you managed to contact your husband, Susan?'

'Yes, he's on his way back.'

'Good. We'll be off, now. I'll ring you as soon as we know more.'

Tanya joined Loder by his car as he closed the boot.

'What were you up to, in the bedroom?' he asked.

'I was seeing if the photos of Donna could have been taken by herself.'

'And?'

'Yes, I think she angled the camera on the dressing table, switched it to timer mode and took them herself. The angle, the distance, the height and the background were about right. Unless Haley took them, of course.'

Loder nodded, pensively. 'Unless the girl turns up on her own accord, there's not a lot more we can do tonight. I'll get this computer over to the High Tech boys first thing, and we'll have a briefing, 8:00 a.m sharp.'

'If you don't mind, sir. I'd like to have a look through Donna's history Log, it would give us a better idea of what she was all about, what web sites she regularly visited.'

Loder got the gist of what Tanya saying, but in truth, she might as well have been talking in double-dutch for all he understood. Computer jargon was outside his vernacular. Numerous memos and circulars had crossed his desk requesting his attendance at in-house computer and IT classes, but he had always shied away from them. At his time of life he thought that he was a bit long-in-the-tooth to be going back to school. He was one of the old-firm; a hands-on police officer, working the streets and arresting violent criminals and murderers. Not someone who could sit behind a desk and stare at a computer monitor all day long; although he would be the first to admit that information technology was an integral part of police work these days. But not for him; leave it to the new generation of up and coming graduates and whiz kids.

CHAPTER 2

Donna sat on the dishevelled bed with her back against the wall, her knees tucked under her chin, and her hands wrapped tight around her bare legs. The room was sparse, apart from the iron-framed bed, a grubby duvet, smelly pillow, and a dirty tea-stained bedside cabinet. It was like a cell, cold and dank. The single light bulb gave the room a dull glow of despair. She was disorientated. Her head was spinning in a whirl of confusion, and thumped relentlessly behind her eyes.

She remembered going into a pub up in the West End somewhere. Everything else was a blur. Now she was cold and frightened and wanted to go home.

Why hadn't she listened to Haley? She'd warned her that meeting a stranger from the Internet was dodgy. But Jason sounded exciting and dishy and hit all the right notes. Now she wished she had heeded her friend's warning. She rested her head on her knees, closed her eyes and began to sob. A stream of tears trickled down her legs and pooled on the grubby sheet.

Upstairs on the ground floor of the large Victorian house, a teenage lad was sitting in the comfortably furnished lounge, with his feet up on a leather reclining armchair watching a huge wide-screen television. He laughed, as a fat girl with rings and studs pierced in every conceivable part of her ugly face and ears, attacked her partner on the *Jeremy Kyle* morning TV programme. She had so much metal sticking out of her that if she was left out in the rain she'd go rusty.

The door opened and a stocky-built, bulldog faced bald man wearing a navy, towelling robe walked in carrying two mugs of tea. He gave one to the boy, then walked over to the window and looked out through the net curtains onto the quiet street outside. 'Anyone see you coming in last night, Ryan?' The man said, without turning.

'No. I made sure it was all-quiet before I got her out of the car, Harry,' he said, laughing at the television again. 'Look at that fat ugly cow, I'd fucking kill her if she tried to hit me like that.'

'I hope you didn't let slip your real name?'

'Of course I didn't, I'm not that fucking stupid.'

'Good lad,' he said, turning and placing his hand on the boy's shoulder.

Ryan stared up at the man he looked upon as a father, pleased he had done well.

'Why don't you take her a mug of tea; see if she's alright? She'll probably be feeling a bit groggy after the Rohypnol you gave her last night.'

'Yeh, okay. In a minute. I want to watch Jeremy Kyle.'

'Now! The man's dark, baggy beady eyes bore down into the boy's soul, putting the fear of thunder into him.

Ryan jumped to his feet, picked up the mug of tea and made his way towards the door.

'I'll be down in a minute,' Harry Delaney called, as the boy left the room.

Donna heard the key turn in the lock and pulled the duvet up tight under her chin. Why was the door locked? Ryan breezed into the room without a care in the world, put the mug of tea on the bedside cabinet and sat down on the side of the bed.

'That was some night we had last night wasn't it, Donna?' he said, handing her the mug of tea.

Donna took the mug from his hand and searched her cloudy mind in a vain attempt to recount her steps of the night before. 'I don't remember much about it,' she said disconsolately, gulping down most of the tea in one go. Her mouth felt like sandpaper it was so dry.

'That's because you had too much to drink. I practically had to carry you out of the pub. That's why I brought you here. Couldn't let you go home in that state,' he smiled reassuringly, pulling the duvet down and snaking his hand up the inside of her thigh.

'Stop that, Jason!' Donna said, slapping his hand away.

'That's not what you said last night,' he said, reaching over to try and kiss her.

'What do you mean? And why was I locked in?' Donna squinted, trying desperately to recall how she came to be in this stinking place.

'Come on, Donna,' he said, pushing her legs apart.

'Hello! What's going on here?' Smiled, the unctuous, bulldog-looking figure standing in the open doorway in a towelling robe. 'Jason, what do you think you're doing? Get off the girl. Now!'

Ryan turned and shot off the bed like a recalcitrant child. It was all a charade.

'Now, who do we have here? What have you been up to, Jason? You dirty little bugger, that's no way to treat a guest.'

'I want to go home now, please.' Donna pleaded.

'Of course you do, darling. But we can't let you go in that state, can we? Why don't you come with me and we'll get you cleaned up,' He said caringly, holding out his hand.

She looked at the man's dark, hairy chest and fat belly peeking out under his robe where the cord had come loose and thought that he could have been related to a gorilla. Then she peered down lower and saw his "Thing" hanging down between his legs. Delaney sensed her anxiety and pulled his robe tight.

Frightened and confused, she looked at Jason leering at her, and decided that the better option if she was to get out of this place was to go with the older man. She jumped off the bed and ran towards the door. Delaney took her hand and led her up a dark passage. 'There, I knew you would see sense,' he said. Let's get you bathed and dressed, then we'll see about getting you home,' he said, with a lascivious smile. But there was nothing further from his mind than to let his beautiful little prize escape his clutches. Jason had come up tops this time.

To Harry Delaney, Donna was a glittering diamond mine just crying out to be cultivated. And, Harry Delaney would cultivate this little gem like any of his prized assets; fervently, and thoroughly, until there was no value left in it. Delaney had a stream of readily available clients who would give their high-teeth – and part with a fortune – to get a piece of this pretty little princess. And there was no better man than him, to relieve them of their cash. Business was business to Delaney, whether it be human, or otherwise.

CHAPTER 3

DC Reid had already been at her desk for over two hours when Loder and DS Frost buzzed themselves in through the double-doors and went straight into Loder's office. She looked up over her monitor and nodded when she heard her boss tap on the window for her to join them. She scooped up a flip-file from her desk and made her way out of the outer office that doubled as the incident room and into Loder's office.

She sat next to DS Frost, facing Loder on the opposite side of his desk and opened her file on her lap.

'Fire away, Tanya. What have you found?' Loder said, stretching his spine and clasping his hands behind his head.

'Not a great deal, really. I've been through all Donna's emails and there's nothing out of the ordinary apart from the messages between Jason and her. The rest are between friends discussing everyday things that teenagers do, homework, clothes, fashion, music, boys, etcetera. The only person Donna confided in with regard to Jason was her friend, Haley.

I've been in touch with the administrators of the internet chat room that Donna subscribed to - Teen Surf42 - and they said that the site is constantly monitored for tell-tale signs of paedophile activity and illegal infiltration. But if a couple decide to go into a private chat room between themselves, there's nothing they can do. As was the case with Donna and Jason. I also went through her address book, internet favourites and history logs, but there was nothing out of the ordinary.'

'I see,' Loder said, pensively. 'I've spoken to forensics this morning and they're confident that they'll be able to get into her hard-drive and find out the source of the emails,' Loder said.

'How long do they think it will take?' Tanya asked.

'They wouldn't commit themselves. I've told them it's a priority one.'

'I sent the tower over to them by courier first thing this morning. They should have it on the bench by now. Might be worth a call to chase them up though?'

'Good work, Tanya,' Loder beamed. Right, in the meantime we ought to be seen to be doing something positive. I want a routine search of all local parks, recreation grounds, towpaths and lay-bys. You know the form Tony. I'll leave that to you to organise, okay?'

'Onto it, boss,' he said, getting to his feet.

'Tanya I want you to get over to Shepherds Green Underground and see what CCTV they've got. If Donna went on a tube, with a bit of luck we should be able to follow her tracks and hopefully, get a positive ID on this Jason. Right, that's it for now. Let's get to work. I want a briefing scheduled for 4:00 p.m this afternoon, with the full team assembled. Okay, let's get to it. Oh, I almost forgot. Tanya, can you get a copy of Donna's mobile phone records. You never know they might throw up something.'

'Already onto it, sir.'

Loder made a face. Impressed with the way that she quietly, efficiently got on with things. Though sometimes her go-it-alone attitude towards the job got up people's noses. They thought that she wasn't always a team player. That she was looking for brownie points at every opportunity. But nothing was further from her mind. She just couldn't put up with the sexist juvenile banter from her male colleagues. There weren't any other women on the team, except Sheila, a civilian secretary, who typed up reports and fed data into the computer and she was only around when she was seconded from elsewhere. There was the odd WPC that she chatted to in the canteen, but no one she really confided in.

Tanya was on her way out when Loder came storming out of his office waving a sheet of paper in the air. 'I've got an address for the source of the emails. Mortimer Street, up in the West End.'

'That was quick. What happened, someone put a firework up the tech unit's arse,' DS Frost quipped.

'Right, let's get up there. Tony, leave what you're doing. Get one of the lads to organise the search,' Loder barked.

DS Frost dumped a procedure manual onto a young DC'S desk and fired off a volley of orders. Then he tailed up Tanya as she wrestled with her jacket and shoulder bag on her way out into the corridor.

Mortimer Street ran across the top end of Regent Street in London's West End. It was in the centre of the fashion and rag trade business. These days a lot of the old industry had moved out to the suburbs due to the exorbitant rents. Now trendy production and media companies had replaced a lot of the old wholesalers' showrooms and cutting rooms. A great many of the media start-ups were getting a very lucrative living on the back of the BBC, whose headquarters were around the corner in Portland Place.

Trying to find a parking space in the busy traffic was proving to be a logistical nightmare. Loder was getting visibly agitated at being caught up in the one-way system, which had sent them past their destination twice already. Moreover, being held up by a never-ending train of hanging garment rails being loaded onto delivery trucks was doing nothing for his self-restraint. Stuck behind yet another truck, he opened the door and was about to get out and deliver a volley to the driver when the heavy vehicle pulled away, revealing an empty parking meter bay.

'Quick, in there, Tony,' Loder said, jumping out of the car and commandeering the space so nobody else nipped in. It took DS Frost three attempts at reversing before he finally managed to manoeuvre the car into the tight space; reversing was never his forte.

They walked up to the end of Great Titchfield Street to the junction where Mortimer Street ran from right to left in the direction of Tottenham Court Road, which was about a half-mile away.

Tanya read the address on the slip of paper she had scribbled it down on. 'Over there, sir. Across the road and on the right, number thirty-four,' she pointed. They weaved their way across the road through the slow-moving traffic and peered through the frosted shop-front window. It had a transfer-pasted sign in it that read, "Internet Café."

Loder took the lead followed by DS Frost, while Tanya took up position inside the door to prevent anyone from leaving. Loder strode up to the counter at the end of the shop and waited while a young geeky-looking lad served coffee to a couple of foreign sounding young girls. DS Frost stood with his back to the counter and surveyed the establishment.

It was a modern, continental-looking café with half a dozen stainless steel-framed, glass-topped circular tables and chairs dotted around the rectangular counter. Along the right-hand wall were flat-screen monitors and keyboards, each one segregated by a thin partition. There were five terminals in use, all by young student types.

The lad behind the counter came across and smiled. The flash of Loder's warrant card wiped the smile instantly from his face. 'What can I do for you Inspector?' he hesitated.

'We're following a line of enquiry into a missing person and we've reason to believe the person in question received email messages sent from this establishment.'

'Most of the people that use the café open their own email accounts here.' The lad shrugged.

'Why would they do that?' DS Frost turned and asked.

'For all sorts of reasons,' he said, taking his frameless spectacles off and wiping them on his striped apron.

'Such as?' Loder asked.

'I don't know,' he shrugged. 'We get a lot of foreign students in here who attend the English language school just up the road. They use the computers to keep in touch with friends and family at home. There's a number of people who work in the area that don't have access to a computer. They pop in lunchtimes to pick up their email from their home computers. Some just come in for a coffee and a bite to eat and while away the time surfing the internet or playing on-line games.'

'We're looking for a young lad who we understand goes by the name of Jason. That's his email name.' The lad shrugged again. 'Could be anyone.'

'You don't know anybody named Jason that frequents the cafe?' DS Frost said.

'No. But I only do the day shift. Michael, does the late shift, he doesn't start until six, he might know.'

'Do all these terminals work on a network routed through a central server?' Tanya asked, walking towards the counter.

'Yes,' the lad replied. Caught off guard by the question.

'Then there'll be a log listing all the email accounts and back-up discs of all the data.'

'Of course,' the lad said, casting an approving eye over Tanya's body.

'How often is the system backed up?' she asked.

'Every night. The server performs the operation automatically in the early hours, when we're closed.'

'How long are the discs stored?' Tanya asked.

'They're rotated on a monthly basis. So there's four weeks full back up at any one time and at each month end a duplicate is made and stored for six months.'

'Very diligent,' Tanya said.

'We have to be. It's the law. I thought you would have known that,' he patronised.

'Don't get smart with me, laddie,' Loder growled. 'What's your name?'

'Eh . . . Nigel Beresford,' He said, combing his hands through his stiff, gelled-up hair, anxiously.

'Right, Nigel. Why don't you show my colleague here, where you keep all the backup discs.'

'They're out the back, if you'd like to come through.'

Tanya made her way behind the counter and followed Nigel through an open archway concealed by hanging, plastic blinds. The room behind was spacious with a kitchenette on one side and a workstation on the other. On it was the bulky server, three flat-screen monitors with keyboards, a printer and some other equipment that Tanya wasn't familiar with. Adjacent to the server, on the back wall, was a tall rack stacked full of CD's, all clearly labelled, date, time, month. Below them was a library of music and an assortment of DVD's.

Tanya perused the discs for a moment, then turned, and said. 'Is it possible to access the email address log?'

'Yes. But I would need to get authorisation from my boss, before I go accessing people's private correspondence. Data Protection Act, you see.'

Loder's voice caught Nigel by surprise as it resounded off of the stark walls around the room. 'And I can have you closed down while I send a team in here to take every single piece of equipment away for examination. Could take weeks. I don't think your boss would be too pleased with you, Nigel. Would he?'

The lad bit his lip nervously, trying to weigh up the situation. He knew full well who Jason was, and who he worked for; and what a nasty bastard he was. A few of the boys that worked the streets for the man down Soho, often came into the café for coffee, and some of the tales he had overheard left him cold. He knew who he was more scared of. He didn't have a choice.

Nigel sighed, and sat down in front of one of the monitors and began keying away. Loder and Tanya gathered around behind him and watched as his fingers deftly danced across the keyboard. In no time at all a list of addresses filled the screen. He scrolled down until he came to Jason's name; he then opened up the account listing all the mail that was channelled through that account.

Loder turned to Tanya and pulled a face, as if to say, what now. He knew how to send and receive an email, and write the odd memo, but that was about the extent of his grasp of 21st century technology.

He was old school, much more used to chasing villains around the streets of West London and slinging a few right-handers, when the need arose. Over the years, he had built a formidable reputation, both within the force and in the criminal underworld. He had a reputation for being hard but fair and as far as anyone knew; totally incorruptible.

Not so long ago he had handed damning evidence of police corruption that had come into his possession, to the DCS. The evidence implicated his immediate boss and his DS, resulting with both of them being sent out to grass and early retirements. Certain factions within the station had voiced their condemnation of his actions. As a result had given Loder a wide berth. They looked upon it as an act of betrayal. Loder couldn't give a flying fuck for their incestuous little circles of corruption, and if he ever came into possession of corruptible evidence again, he wouldn't hesitate for one second in taking the same course of action.

Loder abhorred corruption within the police force. He viewed officers that were on the take, trusted colleagues, who willingly held out their greedy hands for a few shekels, lower than a snake's belly. They were nothing more than the shit on the soles of his shoes, to be scraped off and discarded in the gutter. It went against everything he believed in. Everything that he had strived for his entire career.

Tanya pointed to the list on the screen, and asked. 'Can you print off copies of all the emails sent and received?'

'No problem,' Nigel said, without taking his eyes away from the screen. It might take a minute or two though.'

'We've got plenty of time,' Loder said, leaving the room.

The café was empty when Loder emerged through the blinds and out from behind the counter. 'Bit quiet, isn't it? Where's everyone gone, Tony?'

'Think they got wind of who we were and took a powder. I've got a list of names addresses, just in case. Did we get anything from the server?'

'Aye. Loder beamed. 'He's printing everything off for us.'

'Let's hope that it leads us somewhere. What do think about the lad behind the jump, Nigel? Do you think he knows more than he's letting on?'

Loder screwed his lips together and blew out a short burst of air. 'I'm not sure. He's certainly scared of something. If it's not us, then maybe he *is* hiding something.'

'Nigel-boy, strikes me as someone that doesn't let much get past him. This place is more than just an Internet café, it's a place where lots of people meet socially. Bet he's a right little "News of the World," and earwigs on a lot of conversations.'

'You may be right, Tony. But let's give him the benefit of the doubt: for the time being, at least. Besides we can always pull him in for questioning at a later date.'

'I suppose so,' DS Frost said, unconvinced. If it were left to him, he would pull the lad in now while they had him at a disadvantage and lean on him . . . hard.

As far as DS Frost was concerned, once they had lost the element of surprise and suspects had time to gather their thoughts, the chance that they would let slip under interrogation was much more unlikely. Strike while the iron's hot, was his mantra.

Tanya emerged through the blinds and walked out from behind the counter, carrying a bulky manila envelope.

'Got everything?' Loder asked.

'Yes, sir. It's all in here,' Tanya said, patting the bulky package.

'Right, let's get on our way.' He turned towards Nigel, who was standing in front of the blinds at the far end of the counter. 'We may need to talk to you at a later date. Not planning any trips abroad, are you, Nigel?'

'No. I'm here every day, six days a week,' he replied, sardonically, as the officers made their way towards the door.

'Oh, you might want to let your colleague know, the one who works the late shift, that we'll be back to talk to him, later,' DS Frost said, looking back, before closing the door behind him.

Nigel poured himself a mug of coffee and came around from behind the counter. He sat on a stool and watched as the three officers crossed the road and disappeared down Gt Titchfied Street.

He cupped the mug in both hands and took a long swallow. His mind was swimming with scenarios as to what to do for the best. He gathered his thoughts. Then made a conscious decision not to tell a living soul about the visit from the police: not even Jason himself – or Ryan, the name he knew him as. He didn't want to get involved in something that could cause him harm. He knew one thing, Ryan was a nasty piece of work, in his own right. And he was answerable to his boss, Harry Delaney, who was even worse. If he just kept shtum, maybe it would all just blow over.

Ryan had gone to ground, giving Soho and the West End a wide berth after being tipped the wink by a mate who had been in the Internet Café, at the time the police were sniffing around.

He had taken it upon himself to visit the café just one more time to pump Nigel for information and put the frighteners on him if need be. When he walked through the door, Nigel had turned a "Whiter Shade of Pale," as the song goes. That was all he needed to see, to know why the police had been there. Ryan made it clear, in no uncertain terms, as to what would happen to him, should he breathe a word to the police. And that it would be Delaney himself dishing out the punishment, not Ryan.

CHAPTER 4

It had now been forty-six hours since Donna's disappearance and the incident room was a hub of activity. Extra help had been drafted in to assist with the investigation and more computers had been set up on any empty desks.

Loder and DS Frost were in Loder's office preparing everything for the briefing, which was already behind schedule. Tanya knocked, poked her head around the door. 'We're ready for you out here, sir.'

'Okay, let's get to it,' Loder said, putting his palms on the desk and heaving his tall frame up.

He strode out into the incident room with DS Frost and Tanya behind, and took up position standing next to the window at the end of the murder board – as it was commonly known. Tanya sat at her desk behind Loder and DS Frost took up his place out front.

'Right, listen up everyone,' Loder said, holding his hand up. 'You all know why you are here. Most of you know me and what I expect from you. Those who don't, probably know me by reputation. Let me assure you that what you have heard is all true. I am, one difficult bastard to work for.' A wry smile spread across his face, softening the charged atmosphere. 'Right, listen carefully to what DS Frost has to say.' Loder nodded for him to begin.

'Donna Carlin aged 13 years disappeared on the 15th after meeting a lad, Jason, in an online chat room.' He pointed to a photo of Donna on the board. 'We know from her emails that she had been conversing with Jason for almost five weeks, before they met outside Shepherds Green Underground Station at 3:30 pm on Friday. We have Donna on CCTV walking up Uxbridge Road towards Shepherds Green Station,' he said, walking to the end of the murder board and inserting a disc into a DVD player.

Loder walked over to the TV and pointed at the grainy picture that showed Donna walking along Uxbridge Road in the busy afternoon shopping crowds. 'Look at Donna carefully. Memorise what she's wearing. The time on the bottom of the screen says 3:12 pm. Now, that means she must have skipped school early because they don't finish until 3:30 p.m. Donna attends Hammergrove County Comprehensive which is at the bottom of Bluefontein Road.' Loder produced a pair of half-moon gold-rimmed spectacles from the breast pocket of his shirt and slid them on. They looked incongruous perched on the end of his nose, given that he stood a good six-three tall. He pointed to a spot on a blown-up map of the area pinned to the board. 'We presume that she walked up Bluefontein Road and turned left onto Uxbridge Road. We've got her on CCTV walking past Shepherds Green Nick at 2:58 pm. Surprise! Surprise! Their CCTV was functioning, for a change,' Loder said, with a wry smirk. The team chuckled softly between themselves. Loder held his hand up and it went quiet again. 'So we can estimate that Donna must have left school sometime after 2:30 pm, but that needs to be confirmed. She must have changed out of her school uniform and into the trousers and top that she's wearing on the video, before leaving school.

Donna's mother has told us that she must have taken the clothes to school with her in the morning, because she had ironed them the night before and had left them laid out for her. Note that the trousers are black, hipster-type bellbottoms and her top is cream with a glittery FCUK motif across the front. Her duffle bag is navy and pink.

Now I don't need to tell you that some of these internet chat rooms are not what they seem. Paedophiles are known to surf these sites and they are a rich source for their perversions. However, we've been assured that this particular site was well monitored. But if couples decide to go into a private chat room, as was the case with Donna and Jason, then it's out of their jurisdiction, they can't do anything about it, basically. Cases have been known where paedophiles have actively groomed these kids on line and have openly met with them, and . . . I don't need to spell it out for you.

At the moment, we're keeping an open mind. We hope to know more when we've sorted through all the CCTV.' Loder slipped the spectacles back into his pocket and walked back over to the window.

DS Frost took up the position in front of the board. 'The Tech Unit came up with the address where the emails originated from. Unfortunately, they were all sent from a busy Internet Café in Mortimer Street – for those who are not familiar, Mortimer Street is up the West End, just off of the top end of Regent Street. We've interviewed both employees who work there, but they were unable to ID our Jason. It seems that they get a couple of hundred people through their doors each week and most of them have their own personal email addresses. But we did manage to retrieve copies of all of the mail sent between Donna and Jason. There are some photos that were sent as attachments by Donna. Some of them are quite innocent portrait shots, but as you can see,' DS Frost pointed to some pictures on the board. 'These ones are provocative poses of her lying semi-clothed on her bed. We have her digital camera and all the pictures are still stored in the memory. We're pretty certain that she took them herself, using the camera in timer mode.'

Loder cut in. 'What is a cause for concern is that there are no pictures of Jason,' he said, joining DS Frost in front of the board. 'Donna specifically asks on at least three occasions in her emails for a photo of Jason, but none was ever received. Why? If the banter between them was just an innocent flirtation, why was Jason reluctant to send Donna a picture of himself?'

'Maybe he's an ugly bastard,' a voice said, from the back of the room.

Muted laughter could be heard among a few of the new boys, the older ones knew better.

Loder shot a pointed look in the direction of where the quip came from. 'Who said that?'

'Sir,' said a dark-skinned lad, with a wide grin on his face.

'You're new to the team, aren't you?'

'Yes, sir.'

'I'll tell you this, just once, laddie. No one likes a smart-arse: least of all, *me*. Do you understand?'

'Yes, sir. Sorry, sir,' he replied sheepishly, wishing that he'd kept his mouth shut.

Loder picked up the thread and went on. 'Right, I want some of you on the street outside Shepherds Green Underground, distributing pictures of Donna and taking statements. A lot of people using the station are regular commuters, someone must have seen Donna, it's just a question of jogging their memories.

Also, I want a small team installed at Donna's school. I want all of her friends and teachers interviewed. We need to build up a picture of what Donna is *really* like. The rest of you I want ploughing through the CCTV footage.' Loder clapped his hands. 'Right, let's get to it,' he said striding out of the room. 'DC Reid, a word,' he barked, before disappearing into his office.

Tanya got up from behind her desk, grabbed a notepad and pen and followed Loder in.

'Close the door, Tanya,' Loder said.

She obliged, then sat on a chair in front of Loder's desk, crossed her legs and set her notepad on her lap, at the ready. 'Problem, sir?'

Tanya always addressed Loder as, sir. It wasn't so much out of respect, though she admired him immensely, as a consummate professional. If some of his tactics were a little draconian, even downright underhand at times. She looked upon him as a mentor from whom she had learnt an enormous amount in the two years she had been on the team.

'I want you to accompany me over to the Carlin's house and bring them up to scratch with everything. Having you with me rather than a team of gung-ho officers trampling around the place will, hopefully, have a calming influence; might open them up a bit,' Loder said.

'Do I sense a prick of compassion, sir?' Tanya said, with a wry smile.

'Don't get—'

The shrill of the telephone cut Loder short.

Saved by the bell, Tanya sighed.

'Loder,' he said laconically, into the receiver. 'I'm wanted upstairs,' he said, getting up and grabbing a file as he made his way out from behind his desk. 'Look, you get yourself over to the Carlin's and I'll meet you there.'

'Okay, sir,' Tanya said, following him out.

Loder suddenly turned, and said, 'So you think I'm lacking in the compassion department, do you, Tanya? Me! Empathetic, John. As if,' he winked, keying in his access code at the side of the double doors and disappearing into the corridor towards the staircase.

Striding along the corridor one floor above, Loder came to a halt outside his boss's office. He straightened his tie before knocking and going in. 'You wanted to see me?' he said, poking his head around the door.

'Come in, John,' said Detective Chief Inspector Anne Oakwood, in a throaty voice that could only have come from years of puffing cigarettes. 'Take a seat,' she said, getting to her feet.

Loder obliged. 'Problem, sir,' he said, settling into a high-backed deep chair. 'Forgive me, *ma'am*. I'm still getting used to the idea of having a woman as my boss,' he smiled, apologetically. *Great start to a working relationship.*

Although Loder knew Anne Oakwood in passing. Their paths had never crossed on a professional basis. He knew her to be competent, and tough, considering she stood no taller than five-three; and that was in heels. She had almost as many years on the clock as him, but he guessed that she was a few years younger. Perhaps mid-forties, not yet fifty. She had shoulder-length auburn hair that was swept behind her ears and tied in a scrunchy at the back and soft hazel eyes that belied her tough, no-nonsense disposition. Loder knew that she was known as Annie Oakley around the corridors of power. Unfairly, he thought, just because she was good at her job, and didn't suffer fools lightly. *Not unlike himself, really.*

'No need to apologise, I get mistaken for a man all the time,' she smiled, sitting back down. 'Maybe I ought to have my breasts surgically enhanced, see if that does the trick,' she said, looking down at her cream, silk blouse.

Loder crossed his legs, not knowing, quite where to look.

'Right, John. Shall we get to it?' she said, realising afterwards, the double entendre of the statement.

Loder raised an eyebrow, and couldn't help a little smile.

'Let me re-phrase that,' she said, closing her eyes with embarrassment and looking to the heavens for help. 'Shall we get to *work?*' A soft smile spread across her lips as her eyes caught his.

If he didn't know any better, he thought that he had just felt a slight flutter.

'Look, John,' she said, getting to her feet and walking across the room to the water dispenser. 'I want us both to know where we stand from the off.' She filled a small plastic beaker with water and drank some. Then walked back across the room and rested her bottom against the front of her desk, facing Loder. 'I'm aware of what went on between you and my predecessor and I want you know that I supported your action one-hundred percent. 'Had I been in the same position as you, I would have done exactly the same.'

'Kind of you to say, ma'am.'

'Corruption committed by senior officers – or anyone in the force – is a cancer that should be cut out: terminally, in my opinion. It infects everyone, not only the greedy scum seduced by the smell of money. It undermines everything we – you and I – have strived for, all these years. I know passing on that damning evidence, must have taken a lot of soul-searching.'

Loder felt a little flattered by her comments. Any doubts he might have harboured about this small, gutsy woman standing in front of him being his boss, were instantly dispelled. In fact, he found himself quite looking forward to them working together.

Anne Oakwood folded her arms in thought for a moment, before saying, 'I'm also aware that you passed up promotion to this office. So that makes me second or maybe third choice. I'm also aware exactly how you've operated in the past. A one-man crusade against the whole criminal underworld, but credit where credit's due, you get results. But if we're to have any kind of working relationship, we have to work together. I'll say this only once. If you undermine my position in this office, I'll nail your nuts to this desk. Do we understand each other?'

'Absolutely, ma'am.' Loder admired the woman's honesty, and knew instantly that they were both on the same wavelength.

'Now, where are we with the Donna Carlin case,' she said, steering the conversation back to why he was here in the first place.'

'Well, ma'am. We've—'

'Please, John,' she said, stopping him short. 'Will you stop calling me ma'am. It makes me sound like some old Dame. My name is Anne when we're in private and boss, or gov, or anything respectful that is, when we're out.'

Loder was warming to this woman by the minute. 'As I was saying, Anne.' He relaxed. 'We're gathering all the CCTV we can find, see what that throws up. I'm sending a team into Donna's school to take statements. We're also distributing pictures of Donna outside Shepherds Green Underground. I'm hoping that we'll get a break sooner rather than later. A routine search of all the usual places, parks, tow paths, waste ground, is already underway.'

'Good. Doesn't sound as if there's much more we can do at this stage. How are the girl's parents holding together?'

'DC Reid's on her way over to them now. I'm meeting her there when we're finished up here.'

'I want to be kept updated at all times. Are we clear on that, John?' she said, looking straight into his eyes.

'Absolutely . . . Anne.'

'As I've already said. Your reputation for keeping your cards close to your chest precedes you.' She rested her elbow in the palm of her hand and scratched the underside of her chin, pensively. 'And we don't want to get off on the wrong foot, do we?' she said, with a wry smile.

'Why don't you accompany me to the Carlin's house? It would bode well. Show that we're taking Donna's disappearance seriously.'

'Great idea, but I can't. Got a meeting upstairs,' she said, raising an eyebrow and looking to the ceiling, despondently. 'Can I hold on to this file for a while, I need to make some copies? I'll pop it down to you later.'

'That's okay. Right, if there's nothing else, I'll get on my way?' Loder said, easing himself up from the chair.

'No, you get on. We'll talk later,' Anne Oakwood said, walking him to the door.

CHAPTER 5

Set back from the road and hidden by a cluster of tall silver-birch trees on the fringes of Barnes Common, stood a large, red-bricked Victorian house. Behind the tall thick hedge and adjacent electric gates, was a horseshoe shingle drive wrapped around a lawn with bordering shrubs. Slate-grey stone steps led up to a gothic porch with a heavy, oak studded front door. At the foot of the steps, perched on parapets were two, large brass-framed glass lanterns, another hung in the arched porch. Many years ago, they probably would have had gas fuelling them. The garage adjoining the side of the building on the left, was a flat-roofed extension, not part of the original house.

The tall front gate buzzed and began sliding open as a black MPV with tinted windows pulled up outside, its thick tyres crunched on the shingle drive as it came to a stop in front of the garage. With a slow hum, the shutter lifted up and over into the roof space and the vehicle disappeared inside as the shutter closed back down behind it.

Harry Delaney swung the door open and heaved his heavy bulk down from the vehicle and then slid the passenger door aside. He poked his head inside and said, pointing a finger at the boisterous kids jumping around, 'I want you lot on your best behaviour tonight, is that clear?' No one took any notice as two of the kids began taking lumps out of each other. Ryan jumped over the front passenger seat, threw himself between them, and pulled them apart. 'That's exactly what I don't want,' Delaney spat, grabbing one of the lads by the scruff of the neck and pulling him out of the van. 'Did I not make myself clear?' he said, pulling the boy to within an inch of his clammy bulldog face.

'Yeh, Harry, I'm sorry,' the boy squinted with pain as Delaney tightened his grip on his neck. The boy caught a whiff of Delaney's putrid breath as he held him close to his face. It smelled like a sewer. The boy had to turn away to stop himself from retching.

'What's it all about?' Delaney said, loosening his grip on the boy.

'Nothing, Harry. It's sorted,' he replied, wiping flecks of Delaney's spit from the side of his face. But the look he shot at the other boy sent a message that said it was far from sorted.

Delaney shoved the boy back into the van. 'It had better be.' He stood aside. 'Right you lot, out of the van.'

Ryan got out first and the others followed behind. Delaney lined them up against the garage wall and then went along inspecting each one's appearance like a Regimental Sergeant Major. Satisfied that everything was in order he led them through a door, up some steps and into a huge modern kitchen. Delaney looked them up and down one more time. 'You know the rules boys and girls. Be nice. You two.' He pointed to a terrified looking Donna and a slim, blonde-haired boy with dull blue eyes, were once bright and alive with the freshness of youth. 'You stay with me.'

He was about to lead them out when a long, straggly haired man wearing rimless glasses and dressed in a navy, satin shirt, over a pair of tight, white shorts and flip-flops bounced into the room and across to the huge American fridge.

Jonnie James was an ageing pop promoter, who had made it big in the late sixties and early seventies. He sang catchy pop anthems dressed in outrageous camp costumes and make-up. His legendary long, permed, blonde hair was now thinning and dyed a hideous shade of honey. His popularity had long since faded into obscurity, but like most celebrities, once they had tasted the limelight and been centre of attention, they craved it . It was like a powerful drug and the more their popularity faded, the more they craved for it. But Jonnie James had kept his finger on the pulse by manipulating young talentless boy bands into thinking they were the next big thing, while systematically stripping them of every shred of self-esteem. To the unsuspecting public he was perceived as a generous man who gave the underprivileged a chance at stardom. He was the common-man's working class hero. But behind the façade, he was an evil man who had destroyed and abused kids all of his adult life.

Jonnie James looked along the line of kids and licked his lips lasciviously, and said, 'Wow! Boy, are we going to have some fun tonight.' He homed in on Donna like a heat-seeking missile. 'And who's this little sweetie,' he said, brushing some strands of hair off of her face. 'My, my, you're a pretty little thing,' he smiled. Donna stared blankly up at him and flinched as his hand trailed down the back of her ear. She had been sedated, just enough to offer no resistance.

'Right let's go,' Delaney said, leading them out of the kitchen, down a high-ceilinged hallway and into a huge lounge. The room had a tall, deep, bay window at one end and French windows to the other. On the far wall in the centre of the room stood a big, ornate fireplace under a tall mantle with a deep marble hearth and surround.

Like consummate professionals, far beyond their years, the kids melted into the crowd of specially selected guests. The assembled crowd read like a "who's who." They came from the world of politics, the media, the music industry, the clergy and even a high-court judge. It was an inner sanctum of members that went back many years and the only way in was by introduction. To the unsuspecting world outside, these people were respectable members of society. Pillars of the establishment. Secrecy was paramount.

Delaney went upstairs and into a room at the end of a long landing. In it were three leather Chesterfields around the walls and a rectangular Queen Anne coffee table in the centre. A crescent-shaped drinks cabinet was set in the corner. On the far wall was a large one-way mirror looking into a bedroom with an antique walnut, four-poster bed in the middle. It was draped with a rich, ruby satin sheet, cream satin pillows and a frilly valance surround. On one wall was a portrait of a nymph posing on a velvet chaise-lounge. On the other hung a pair of closed, heavy drapes framed with swags and tails. Set on a tripod in front of the coffee table was a video camera.

Delaney poured himself a beer, lit a cigarette, made himself comfortable on the Chesterfield and waited for the show to begin.

Tonight there was a new guest invited. A prominent member of Parliament who was a close adviser to the Prime Minister. Delaney always filmed the first-timers: it was his little bit of insurance. Over the years he had built up a formidable library that read like a "Who's Who." Should the need arise for some little favour to be done, he had more than enough ammunition to call upon. Had done so, on many occasions in the past. Delaney had no scruples when it came to getting something that he wanted and he wouldn't think twice about ruining someone's life or their career. To him, his clients' – as he liked to refer to them – sexual weaknesses were his bread and butter.

*

DS Frost and Tanya were pouring over the CCTV footage from Shepherds Green Underground when together, they both pointed to a grainy image of Donna walking up to a hooded figure outside the station entrance.

'Bingo!' DS Frost punched the air, got up from his chair and made his way into Loder's office. He poked his head around the door. 'We've just spotted Donna on tape, boss. Do you want to have a look?'

DS Frost still referred to CCTV footage as tape, even though, these days everything was mostly now stored on disc.

'At last!' Loder sighed, following his DS out into the busy incident room.

Both men stood over Tanya's shoulder watching the monitor as she searched back through the footage and pressed the play button. 'At least he looks to be a young lad, even though he's wearing that hooded top,' Tanya said.

'What age, would you put him at?' Loder asked.

'Not sure, sir. Mid-teens,' Tanya answered.

'Wish we could see his bloody face,' DS Frost barked at the screen as Donna and the hoodie walked out of camera shot together.

Tanya ejected the disc, put another in the machine and pressed the play button. All three of them stared intently at the screen, which showed a view of the ticket hall and the automatic barriers that let people through to the top of the escalators. It was the beginning of the rush hour and the hall was busy with commuters in a hurry to get home. DI Loder tapped his foot on the floor impatiently as they waited for Donna and the hooded figure to come into view.

'There, look!,' DS Frost pointed at the bottom corner of the screen. The couple walked through the hall, entered their tickets into the automatic barrier and passed through it one after the other. The hooded figure then turned around and held out his hand for Donna. 'Stop the tape!' Loder barked.

He too, was firmly entrenched in the past when it came to tapes and discs.

Tanya jumped and pressed the pause button.

'Can you get a close up of his face?' Loder said, slipping his specs on and leaning closer to the screen. Tanya zoomed in on the figure but his face was shadowed by his hood. Loder squinted at the screen trying to make a mental picture of the boy's face. 'Okay, play it,' he said, not taking his eyes away from the screen for an instant as the two images disappeared down the escalator.

DS Frost turned around and sorted through a pile of discs on the desk behind. 'Here try this one,' he said, passing it to, Tanya. 'It's a view of the eastbound platform.'

The two men leaned in closer over Tanya's shoulder as wavy horizontal lines sank slowly to the bottom the screen and disappeared, leaving a clear monochrome picture.

After a few minutes of nothing, Loder lost patience and asked Tanya to fast-forward the disc.

'There, look!' DS Frost said, pointing to two figures racing onto a train like madcap characters from an old silent movie.

Tanya stopped the disc, searched back a few frames and pressed play.

'Still can't see the lad's face under that hood,' Loder sighed, straightening his back and slipping his specs back into his shirt pocket. 'Right, we should be able to track that train from station to station. Have we got all the necessary footage here?'

DS Frost turned around and emptied a box of discs onto the desk. He quickly sorted them through and shook his head disconsolately.

'Tony, let's get over to London Transport's Central Monitoring Station, they should be able to help us out,' Loder said, marching out of the room. 'And bring that disc with you. Tanya you stay here and look through the rest of the footage,' he barked, without looking back.

When they had left the office, Tanya rubbed her tired eyes, went across to the water dispenser and filled a cup of chilled water. She then sat down at her own desk and switched on her monitor. Not looking forward to ploughing through all the footage herself, she pulled a young officer walking past, and said, 'Andy, could you make a start on those CCTV discs for me, please? If I watch much more I'll get square eyes.' She pleaded, her hands clasped praying up at him.

'Yeh, I don't mind. I could do with a break from sorting through piles of statements, anyway.'

'Thank you. I owe you one,' she said, relaxing back into her chair and sipping her water.

Without any thought as to why, she began a missing persons search on her computer. The list was much longer than she envisaged, so she narrowed the search to persons aged sixteen and under. The number was still into the hundreds, but she thought that she might as well have a look through, now that she'd started.

An hour and a half later, she stretched back tiredly and gave a long wide yawn. Her neck, shoulders and eyes were aching from the concentration and the glare of the monitor. It was no good, she would have to get her eyes tested when she found a spare moment, she thought: sometime never. Pleased as punch with herself that she had persevered, she lifted some printouts from the tray and sorted them into order.

She had found three young kids that had gone missing in similar circumstances in the last two years. The first, a fourteen year-old boy, had disappeared twenty-three months ago, after meeting another lad in a chat room. But the investigation led to the conclusion that the lad was exploring his homosexual leanings and had simply run away to be with his new friend. Nevertheless, the boy was a minor when he disappeared and there was no way of knowing if his chat room friend was whom he purported to be – a lonely fifteen year-old boy, with similar feelings of a sexual nature as his internet friend. The other person could just as easily have been a predator, praying on the vulnerable mind of a mixed-up kid: it wouldn't be the first time . . . Or the last.

The second, another lad the same age as the first, had gone missing eighteen months ago. He also was an active member in a number of chat rooms. But he was found washed up on the Chelsea Embankment. The boy had severe bruising to the neck, chest and arms. The pathologist's report stated that the injuries were received before he entered the water. And there were clear signs of sexual abuse. The investigation was still on going and as yet, no one had been convicted.

The third was the most interesting. A girl the same age as Donna had disappeared eleven months earlier in exactly the same circumstances. She had been swapping emails in a chat room and had met with the other person. Laura Davidson had never been seen since. There were no clues to her disappearance, other than a sighting on a CCTV camera walking along Hampstead High Street with a teenage lad.

Tanya bit her lip, pensively. Then tapping the picture of the missing girl with her finger, she thumbed down the page, found the senior investigating officer's name and contact number and called him up.

It was ages before a voice answered in a gruff, impatient tone. 'DI Baxter.'

'Morning, sir. My name's DC Reid from Hammergrove Nick. I was hoping that I could pop over to see you this morning.'

'Why?' Came the curt reply.

'It's in connection with your missing teenager, Laura Davidson. We've got a young girl the same age as Laura, who has gone missing under similar circumstances. I was hoping I could have a look at your case files; maybe pool our resources, sir?'

'I'm busy today, constable. I'll get one of my lads to fax everything over to you, if you like?'

'That'll be great. Thank you, sir.' He slammed the phone down. *Ignorant pig.*

CHAPTER 6

Loder and DS Frost entered the huge computer suite of the London Transport Surveillance Headquarters and were shown to a curved comfortable settee in a sectioned-off area in the corner of the room by a pretty WPC.

DS Frost looked agape at the crescent-shaped wall stacked from floor to ceiling with flat-screen monitors. The room was dark, like a cinema, but for the concealed lighting around the ceiling. Two rows of workstations stretched across the suite; on each one was a green, glass-shaded desk lamp.

Shirt-sleeved officers worked busily away at the workstations, not giving Loder or DS Frost a second glance. The huge suite was a quiet hive of efficient activity. There was a constant hum of electricity around the room. The air conditioning whispered in the background, keeping the suite at a comfortable ambience.

To DS Frost it was like watching a huge picture show. His eyes kept flitting from one screen to another as the locations changed and the cameras zoomed in and out at certain points. He was absolutely fascinated by it all. Loder, on the other hand, had seen it all before; though it wasn't as high-tech the last time he was here, he recalled.

The jury was still out, as far as he was concerned, as to whether the colossal amount of surveillance technology on our streets was absolutely necessary. He was in no doubt whatsoever that it had a part to play in today's modern police force, as he would hopefully find out in a few minutes time. But with all the CCTV they had on London's increasingly violent streets, the conviction rate from it didn't justify the huge cost: in his humble opinion. And as far as satellite surveillance went, it frightened the life out of him. To think that someone could zoom in and watch a person having a piss against a wall, for instance.

A smartly dressed man, wearing a clean-starched, white regulation police shirt with three stripes embroidered into his black, shoulder braids came over and met them. He was tall, slim, had close-cropped dark hair and a cool, confident air about him. One of the new generations of police officers. Undoubtedly, university educated. Loder eyed him suspiciously, trying his utmost to hide his contempt. He doubted that the man had ever mixed with the violent scum that he encountered day after day on the streets. And would bet a week's wages that the clean-cut lad had never set eyes on a decomposed corpse spread out on a pathologist's slab in his life, either.

Loder and DS Frost stood up as the Transport Police Sergeant approached them.

'Piers Waldergrave,' he said, shaking Loder's hand. 'What can I do for you, gentlemen?' he said, gesturing for them to take a seat.

'We've got a young girl that's gone missing, but we *have* got her on CCTV getting on a train at Shepherds Green Underground with a lad. What I want to know is, what station they get off at. Is it possible that you can sort through some of your old footage for us?' Loder asked.

'Of course. Did you bring the disc with you?'

DS Frost handed the sergeant the plastic DVD case.

'If you'd like to follow me, gentlemen,' the sergeant said, getting to his feet. 'There's a console over there we can use.' He pointed to an enclosed booth at the back of the room.

Built-in to an enclosed unit in the far wall above the booth was a bank of viewing monitors: all very state of the art. The sergeant slid the disc into the machine, pressed play and then took a couple of steps backwards to join the other two officers.

'We need to fast-forward the tape – sorry disc – a little way,' Loder said.

The officer slid the remote control out from a slot on the front of the equipment housing and pressed the search button.

'There she is!' DS Frost pointed at the screen.

The officer stopped the disc, searched back a few frames and then pressed play.

'There's our girl,' Loder said, walking up to the screen and pointing closely at the image of Donna as she got onto a train.

The sergeant noted the time and date from the bottom of the screen. As the train pulled away, he also noted the train number on the back of the last carriage.

'It shouldn't be too much of a problem to retrieve the information you require, gentlemen. But you'll have to be patient, it's not something we can do in five minutes, you understand?' said the sergeant.

'I can't stress enough, the urgency of this matter. Time is not on our side. We need to find this girl, and identify her companion ASAP.' Loder said, earnestly.

'I'll get a team onto it right away.'

'Appreciated,' Loder said, handing the sergeant his card. 'Ring me, when you have something.'

'Yes, sir. I'm going to need this for a while,' he said, ejecting the disc from the machine.

'No problem. Just get me a result.'

The sergeant grabbed the disc and put it back into its case. 'This way gentleman,' he gestured with a hand. 'If you'll follow me, I'll show you out.'

DS Frost stared around in awe at the expansive suite as they made their way towards the exit.

'Impressive, isn't it?' Sergeant Waldergrave beamed.

'Certainly is. Talk about big brother is watching. It's incredible.'

'It's part of 1.2 billion pound investment programme. We cover 25,000 cameras at the moment, and when the system is completed it will have the capacity to handle up to a further 250,000 cameras using the new asynchronous transfer mode technology. ATMT for short.'

'Won't be able to fart soon, without someone eavesdropping on it,' Loder remarked.

'We're far in advance of that already, sir.' Waldergrave gave a wry smile. 'I'll let you know as soon as we have something,' he said, opening the door for the two men.

*

Tanya was busy studying CCTV footage with DC Andy West. Andy had been on the team for about three months after being seconded from the robbery squad. Tanya quite liked working alongside him, because unlike most of their colleagues, he wasn't a chauvinistic sexist moron. Shelagh – a civilian administrator, assigned to the department on a permanent basis – handed Tanya a pile of facsimiles. She got up and carried them back to her own desk, sat down and started perusing the paperwork.

As she read through the file, it became obvious that the similarities between Donna's disappearance and Laura Davidson's case were too close for comfort. But it was when she read the email address that she was certain that they were looking for the same person. The address "Jason@yonder" had been traced to the same Internet café as Donna's Jason. Tanya had an unhealthy feeling about the whole thing, but she didn't want to speculate prematurely, not until they had spoken to Nigel back at the Internet café.

Loder and DS Frost came striding into the incident room and went straight into Loder's office. Tanya gathered all her paperwork together and made her way across to join them.

'I've got something here that you ought to see, sir,' she said, placing the pile of paperwork on the desk in front of Loder.

'What's this?' DS Frost sniffed, picking up the top sheet.

Tanya was used to handling chauvinistic pigs like Tony Frost. She had to deal with the likes of him every single day, and knew that he didn't mean anything personal by his demeanour: it was just the way he was, a belligerent buffoon. She had learned a long time ago to make her undoubted attractiveness work to her advantage when dealing with likes of DS Frost. After all, most men were just boys in long trousers and she could wrap most of them around her little finger if the need took her.

'They're copies of an ongoing investigation into the disappearance of a girl after meeting a lad in an Internet chat room. Her name is Laura Davidson and she's the same age as Donna. Laura went missing eleven months ago and no one has seen or heard of her since.'

'And?' Loder said, looking up.

'Well, sir, the source of all the forwarding email was traced to the same Internet café as ours. And you'll never guess the address name.'

'Jason!' DS Frost said, sifting through the papers.

'Correct.'

'Right, let's get back up to West End,' Loder said, getting up from behind his desk, grabbing his jacket from the hanger behind the door, and marching out of the room. 'You're driving Tony,' Loder shouted, as he pushed open the double doors and out of the office.

Tanya smiled. She knew DS Frost hated driving her boss around, because of his lack of patience with other drivers on the road made him nervous behind the wheel. And because of this, it made him drive erratically.

They drove around in circles for almost fifteen minutes trying to find somewhere to park. In the end, Loder told DS Frost to stop outside the Internet café and wait in the car while Tanya and he went in.

Once inside, Tanya waited by the door while Loder strode up to the counter. It was lunchtime and the place was buzzing. All the tables were occupied with office workers and students catching a bite to eat. All the computer terminals were busy as well.

Nigel almost dropped the mug of coffee and sandwich he was carrying when he heard Loder's voice. He finished serving a customer, turned around, and went over to where Loder was standing.

Loder could see the colour drain from his face as Nigel said, nervously, 'Inspector Loder, what can I do for you?'

'You haven't been entirely straight with me, have you, Nigel?' Loder said.

'I don't know what you mean.' He shrugged.

'Shall we go into the back?' Loder said, walking around behind the counter, through the plastic blinds, and into the back of the shop.

Nigel followed, tentatively.

'Right,' Loder said, turning around and looking down into Nigel's eyes. 'Shall we start again? Who is Jason?'

'I don't know, honestly, Inspector Loder. He could be any number of people that use this place day after day,' Nigel said, nearly pissing his pants.

'I've now got another missing girl on my hands Nigel. And guess where the source of all the emails came from?'

Nigel shook his head, trembling with fear.

'They were sent from this establishment by someone going by the name of Jason. Ring any bells, Nigel? Do you want to tell me something?'

'I can't help you, Inspector. Honestly, you took everything that's on file the last time you were here.'

'How long have you worked here, Nigel?'

'About nine months.'

Loder tightened his lips, deep in thought. 'And you've never been interviewed before, concerning the disappearance of this girl? Don't lie to me laddie, I can just as easily check.'

'Never, Inspector.' Nigel relaxed a little.

'I want you to check this email address for me.' Loder handed him a copy of one the emails.

Nigel looked at the sheet. 'It's an old address. We haven't used this ISP since I've been working here.'

'What do you mean?' Loder rested against the edge of a workbench. 'I'm listening,' he said, folding his arms.

'Since I've worked here we've always used Rycom. The ISP on this email is Yonder, so I can only assume that the company must have changed it before I started here.'

'I see,' Loder sighed.

'In any case, Inspector, if an email address lies dormant for more than 90 days, it's automatically deleted from the system.'

'You had better not be spinning me a line, Nigel' Loder said, pointing an accusing finger at him.

'Please believe me, Inspector, I wouldn't dare.'

'Okay, Nigel, we'll leave it there . . . for now,' Loder said, making his way back through to the front of the shop. Nigel followed behind, wiping his clammy hands down the front of his apron.

Loder emerged through the blinds and gave Tanya a shake of his head as he made his way towards the door. 'I hope you're not planning on changing jobs, Nigel. You wouldn't want me to have to come looking for you; would you?' Loder shot him a frightening look, as Tanya opened the door.

Breathing a sigh of relief, he watched Loder and Tanya walk across the road, get into a car and drive away.

'What was that all about, Nige?' said, a skinny, sickly-looking teenager launching himself up onto a stool at the counter.

'Nothing.'

'Didn't look like nothing. You're shaking. Look at your hands, Nige.'

'It's nothing to do with you, Kenny. Keep your nose out,' Nigel said, picking up a couple of empty coffee mugs from the counter.

'Bet Delaney would be interested to hear that the Old Bill were sniffing around,' Kenny said, with cynical sneer.

'You keep that zipped, Kenny.' Nigel ran his fingers across his lips. 'And I might let you have a free lunch.'

'Forgotten already, Nige. I'll have one of those chocolate coffee things?'

'Cappuccino, you mean?'

'That's it! I'll have a large one, and one of those cream cakes.' Kenny pointed to cream slice in the display cabinet.

As he prepared the cappuccino, Nigel contemplated the thought of handing his notice in and doing a runner, but knew that if the police didn't find him, Delaney was sure to. No, he would have to front it out for now, and then quietly disappear down to Devon, back to his parents' house.

'Get anything useful, boss?' DS Frost asked, pulling away from the kerb.

'Nothing. It appears that the email address is an old one. It's been deleted from the system.'

'High Tech Unit should be able to retrieve deleted data from the hard drive,' Tanya said.

Both men looked at Tanya uncomprehending.

'From what little I know about computers. When data has been deleted from the system it lays buried on the hard drive. Assuming the hardware hasn't been updated the Tech Unit should be able to open up the hard drive and retrieve all deleted data from the system,' Tanya said.

'If that's the case. Get a warrant organised and seize all the equipment from that place,Tanya.'

CHAPTER 7

Rocking and bucking on a thin mattress in the dark, Donna felt nauseas. Her eyelids felt like lead weights, and her head was all over the place. She tried to focus in the blackness but it was hopeless. Kicking away the duvet that covered her she tried to sit up. The overpowering smell of stale urine and sweat wafting up made her retch. Her stomach cramped and a vile-tasting acrid bile filled her mouth. Her head began to thump relentlessly against the top of her brow, as the foul liquid spilled out down her tee shirt.

The vehicle suddenly lurched forward and she fell back onto the mattress. Something was digging into her back. She rolled onto her side, felt behind her and picked up the object. Tentatively she held it with one hand, while tracing her fingers along the cold metal casing with the other. It was cylindrical in shape, and when she felt the circular glass top, thought that it must be a torch. She traced her hand along the casing again and found the switch.

Squinting in the bright light as it bounced off the sides of her confined cell, Donna's heart began to race as an overwhelming feeling of claustrophobia consumed her. Struggling up onto her elbows she tried to focus. Suddenly, she was thrown backwards, hitting her head against the hard metal casing of her cell as the vehicle came to an abrupt halt. She yelped with pain and the torch slipped from her hand and rolled off of the mattress. Quickly she scooped it up, turned it off and tucked it down the side of her. She lay back onto the mattress and waited. The silence, together with the darkness sent her whole body rigid with fear.

Suddenly the heavy vehicle lurched forward and gathered speed again. Donna closed her eyes and gave a sigh of relief. Her body felt heavy and cumbersome, as she hauled herself up into a sitting position and rested back against the cold, metal panel behind her. She switched the torch on and shone it around the confined space until the beam rested upon two, large plastic bottles of mineral water sitting in a metal rack fixed to the side of the cell above her knees.

Noticing a grab handle halfway up the left side of the cell, Donna leaned forward, got hold of it, and while reaching across with her other hand, lifted the heavy bottle free and dropped it between her legs. Exhausted, she fell backwards, hitting her head against the hard metal casing again. A sharp pain drummed against her skull making her retch violently again. She turned her head and let the acrid liquid dribble out onto her shoulder and down her arm.

She closed her eyes and wondered how she ever got herself into this nightmare. How could she have been so stupid as to let herself be taken in by that bastard, Jason? If she was honest with herself, she knew that all the warning signs were there, but she had chosen to ignore them: she was flattered by all the attention. The fact that someone older and more experienced could fancy her, had sent her head spinning into the clouds. Jason was such a charmer that she just couldn't resist him. She pushed the nightmare from her mind, reached forward and grabbed the bottle of water. She unscrewed the top and gulped down as much as she could take, before pausing for a breath and starting again. The water tasted clean and cool as the liquid found its way straight into her empty stomach.

The dizziness and nausea subsided, leaving just a dull ache across the top of her brow. Feeling ravenous, Donna picked up the torch and searched the claustrophobic box for something to eat. At the foot of the mattress was a plinth about 12 inches deep that stretched across the width of the cell. On it was fixed a mesh tray about 6 inches deep. In one corner was a hospital bedpan and in the other a selection of pre-packed sandwiches and a packet of biscuits. Donna kicked off the duvet and shuffled along on her bottom until she reached the end of the mattress.

Sitting cross-legged in front of the tray, she tore the polythene wrapping off one of the sandwiches and woofed down the two, ham and tomato wedges in no time at all. If she was to have any chance of freeing herself from this nightmare she knew she had to keep her strength up. She was about to open another sandwich when she felt the vehicle slowing down. Quickly, she shuffled back along the mattress, pulled the quilt over her and lay down. Remembering she'd forgotten the torch, she shuffled back, picked it up and dropped it in her lap while she shuffled back again.

She turned onto her side, brought her knees up to her chest, pulled the duvet tight up under her chin and waited. Suddenly, the vehicle groaned back to life as it gathered speed again. Her lips quivered, followed by floods of tears. 'Daddy.' She cried. 'Where are you? Please help me . . . I'm so sorry.'

*

Loder was in his office briefing his boss, DCI Oakwood, when a young DC knocked on the door and handed him a package that had been delivered by courier.

Curiously, he gave the bulky jiffy-bag the once over to see who had sent it. When he saw PS Waldergrave's name on the back his spirits were lifted. He opened his desk drawer, found a pair of scissors and snipped the bag open. Inside were two discs and a note telling Loder the reference points at which Donna and Jason appeared on them. Loder smiled. 'Let's have a look and see what we've got here,' he said, getting to his feet.

Out in the incident room, Loder called DS Frost over and handed him the discs. Loder and DCI Oakwood stood behind DS Frost as he sat in front of the monitor and inserted the first disc.

Loder handed him the note with the reference points on and DS Frost hit the search button until the counter reached the correct frame, then pressed play. All three of them leaned forward and waited.

'There, look,' DS Frost said, pointing on the image of Donna and a hooded figure getting on the train.

'Shit! They would have to sit with their backs to the camera, wouldn't they?' Loder said, clearly annoyed.

'Hold on a minute he's slipping his hood back,' DS Frost said.

Tanya came over and joined the other three as they all waited impatiently for the mystery figure to reveal his face. But after watching the film for a further 15 minutes, they were none the wiser. They had a side profile of the lad but they were sitting too far away from the camera to make out any distinctive features. Apart from his short blonde hair, thin face and small nose, that was all that they had.

They fast-forwarded the disc until they both got off the train. But even then, all they got was a side profile and the boy's hood was back on by that point.

'Put the other disc in, Tony,' Loder said. 'See what that throws up?'

DS Frost ejected the first disc and slid the second one into the DVD drive, hit the search button until the disc reached the correct reference point and pressed play. All three huddled around DS Frost's shoulders and looked on anxiously: praying for a breakthrough. It wasn't to be. The disc only showed a back view of Donna and Jason walking along the platform at Oxford Circus Station and then disappearing out of view.

Loder screwed his eyes in frustration. He wanted to let off a volley of expletives, but thought better of it, seeing that he was in the company of his new boss. 'Get them sent over to forensics, Tony. See if they can blow up any images of our, Jason. Never know, we might get lucky.'

'Onto it, gov,' DS Frost said, slipping the discs back into their sleeves.

DCI Oakwood looked at her watch. 'Care to join me for a drink and a sandwich across at the pub, John?' she asked.

'Aye, why not,' Loder sighed. 'On second thoughts, I'd better get over to the Carlin's house and let them know where we are with the investigation. Tanya, get your coat—'

'Why don't I come with you, John?' DCI Oakwood, cut Loder short. 'I could do with getting out of this place for an hour. Besides, a show of strength is always good for PR, don't you think?'

'Absolutely.' Loder said. 'In that case, Tanya, I want you to round up a few people and get up to Oxford Circus Station and distribute some pictures of Donna. Someone might remember seeing her.

'I'll just pop up and get my things. See you downstairs in five minutes,' DCI Oakwood said.

'Okay, fine,' Loder said, making his way back into his office. 'Oh, before I forget, Tony see what CCTV you can lay your hands on from around Oxford Street, Regent Street and perhaps Soho. There's a good chance that Jason and Donna may have headed down that way, it's exactly the sort of place he would have enticed Donna to. And it's only a stone's throw from the Internet café where the emails were sent from.'

*

Loder carried the drinks over from the bar. A white wine for his boss and pint of bitter for himself. He set them down at the table, unbuttoned his jacket and sat on a chair facing his boss.

'Donna's father is a bit of a hothead, don't you think?' DCI Oakwood said, taking a sip of wine.

'Well, it has been over a week since Donna went missing. You can't blame him for going off on one, he's out of his mind with worry. Under the same circumstances I'd be the same,' Loder said.

'I didn't know you had kids?'

'I haven't,' Loder said laconically, cutting her short.

It wasn't that he had anything to hide: it was just that his life away from the office wasn't up for discussion. Although Loder had a reputation within the force as being a hard taskmaster who didn't suffer fools easily, he liked to think that he had a sense of humour with the small circle of trusted friends he surrounded himself with. But his private life was just that: private.

Loder and his wife weren't against having children. In hindsight, it probably would have made them complete. But in the early days when he was an ambitious young DC climbing the greasy pole of success, he just never felt that the time was right. What with him working all the hours that god sent, and his wife a hard-working head of department at the local comprehensive school, they never seemed to find the time to have children. And before they both knew it, age had crept up on them both and when his wife was diagnosed with cancer, children were off of the agenda. She died nine months later.

Loder emptied almost a third of the contents of his glass in one swallow, and said, 'What about you, have you got kids?'

'Two boys. Grown up with children of their own now, of course.'

'You, a grandmother! I don't believe it,' Loder smiled.

'Are you patronising me, Loder?' She mocked.

He held his hands up in supplication. 'Would I? But I have to say, the years have been kind to you. Your husband is a very lucky man,' he placated.

'Are you coming on to me, Loder?'

'Would I dare?' Loder said, wishing he'd shut his mouth and kept the conversation on a professional footing.

'Well, that's very nice of you to say,' she flushed, taking another sip of wine to cool her down. 'Divorced.'

'Pardon, me.'

'I'm divorced. There isn't any "lucky man" as you put it. What about you?'

'Widowed. I lost my wife to cancer.'

'Sorry to hear that. How long?'

'Eighteen months, since. Same again?' Loder said, emptying his glass. Wishing to steer the conversation in a different direction.

'Yes, why not.'

Their glasses replenished. Loder sat back down.

'Do you think Donna's still alive?' DCI Oakwood said.

Loder shrugged. 'I don't know. My gut feeling is that she's been abducted, and not by Jason.'

'You think she's in the clutches of a paedophile ring, or something equally abhorrent?'

'Could be. Remember, we've got another girl of similar age to Donna that has gone missing under the same circumstances.'

'So you think we're looking for an organised child trafficking ring, then?'

Loder rubbed the back of his neck and stretched his shoulders. Pensively, he crossed his legs and brushed a few flecks of imaginary dust off of his trousers. 'I think we have to seriously consider the fact – yes.'

DCI Oakwood closed her eyes and slowly shook her head. 'Doesn't bear thinking about. Let's just hope that we get to Donna before any serious harm comes to her.'

Loder took a long swallow of his beer, and said, 'I think it's time we had a look through the sexual offenders register. Rattle a few cages and see if anyone starts squirming. I bet my life on it that someone on that register knows something about Donna's disappearance.'

'What do you think about a reconstruction? We could get a couple of child actors to impersonate Donna and Jason and take the same journey on the train,' DCI Oakwood said.

'We've got them on CCTV. Probably get the same result if we just show it on the local news.'

'You may be right, John. I'll get it organised when we get back to the office.'

DCI Oakwood picked up a menu from the table and quickly glanced through it. 'I'm going to order a sandwich, what about you,' she said, handing Loder the menu.

'I'll have the same as you,' he said, finishing his drink. 'You might like to fill that up for me while you're at the bar?' He said, looking up at his boss with a wry smile.

'How do I keep getting the feeling you're taking the piss out of me, Loder?'

'Insecurity, maybe?'

'Don't push it, Loder,' DCI Oakwood said, snatching the empty glass from him and walking to the bar.

Loder eyed Anne Oakwood as she walked away. Dressed in a fitted, black trouser suit that emphasised her slim shapely figure, Loder found himself being quite taken by her. *Forget it, she's your boss, you silly bastard.*

CHAPTER 8

Donna reached out, helplessly. 'Daddy, daddy,' she pleaded. Her soft hazel eyes full of hurt and confusion. A hand came from behind and went across her mouth stifling her pleas. Then slowly she faded into the distance. Her limbs thrashing out in defiance. 'Pleeease, daddy,' she cried, before disappearing into the darkness.

'Donna!' The piercing scream resonated around the bedroom walls. Drenched in sweat, exhausted and fighting for breath, Lee Carlin shot bolt upright from his pillow. His sheets were soaked from the ceaseless nightmare he had night after night.

Susan, his wife, was already awake – she'd not had a decent night's sleep since her daughter's disappearance. She just couldn't face up to the truth of what might have become of Donna: she just erased the thought from her mind. It was the only way that she could cope.

'Another nightmare? Come here,' she said softly, cradling her husband's head in her arms and wiping the sweat from his face with the sleeve of her pyjamas.

He brushed her arm away, threw the duvet off, got up, and sat on the side of the bed with his head in his hands. Susan shuffled across the bed, sat behind him with her legs tucked under her and gently massaged his neck and shoulders.

He shrugged her off, pulled off his boxer shorts, went into the en-suite and ran a shower. Closing his eyes and holding his head up to the cold spray, he tried to wash the nightmare from his mind. After a few minutes, he turned the temperature gauge up and soaped himself down in the comforting warm spray.

After towelling himself down, he went back into the bedroom and got dressed.

'What are you doing?' Susan asked.

'I'm going out to find Donna.'

'It's three-thirty in the morning. The streets will be deserted, what can you possibly hope to achieve?'

'Not up Soho, they're not.'

'Lee, come back to bed. You can't do anything at this time of the morning, besides, you've got to be up for work at six.'

'How can I think about work, you silly bitch. Knowing that some fucking filthy pervert has probably got his hands all over my baby—'

'Our baby!' His wife hit back, sitting back against the cushioned headboard. And you don't *know*, that someone has got hold of her.'

'Wise up, you stupid cow. You don't think she's playing happy homes with this fucking Jason, do you?'

'I don't know what to think,' she said, as the tears welled up in her eyes. And why do you keep taking everything out on me? I don't deserve to be the constant target of your filthy mouth. I don't know what's got into you lately.'

Lee felt the guilt wash over him. He knew that he shouldn't take out all his frustrations on his wife. She must be hurting just as much as him, but she was an easy target. With all the thoughts of what Donna must be going through, together with the feeling of helplessness, he just lashed out at Susan for no reason other than to vent his own pent up anger at not being able to do anything. He knew he was out of order, but he couldn't help himself.

'What do you want me to do? Donna's been missing for six weeks now, or have you forgotten that fact? I can't just sit around and do nothing,' he shouted, sitting on the side of the bed, struggling with his socks.

'Let the police do their job, Lee. All you're doing is getting peoples' backs up with your obsessive behaviour,' Susan implored.

'I am, am I? Well at least I'm doing something positive. That's more than what the fucking useless Old Bill are doing. Besides, they think Donna's already dead. They're just going through the motions until a body turns up. Case closed.'

'You think she's dead, as well, you bitch! I'm the only person who has any faith.' Lee spat the words out, poking himself in the chest.

'You bastard!' Susan cried. 'How dare you say that.'

'Yeh, well, that's what it seems like, to me.' Regretting his words the moment they left his mouth.

'And you think that walking the streets of the West End night after night, thrusting bad photocopies of Donna into people's hands, helps, do you?' his wife screamed, brushing away strands of damp hair from her face and wiping the tears from eyes.

'Well, it's better than doing nothing,' he said, slamming the bedroom door behind him as he stormed out.

'You *all* think that Donna's dead. But you're too cowardly to say it out loud. I know what everyone's thinking. You'll see, I'll bring her back.' His loud outburst lost stridency as he stomped along the landing and down the stairs. The windows rattled as Lee slammed the street door on his way out.

Susan Carlin sat up in bed with her knees tucked under her chin and her arms wrapped tightly around her legs. She closed her eyes to the silence of the room, and tried to wipe her husband's scathing rants from her mind. But it was true what he had said: she couldn't help thinking the worse had happened to their daughter. She hated herself for it, but it had been over six weeks since Donna had disappeared, and not one single person had come forward with any information as to her whereabouts. It was as if Donna had disappeared off of the face of the earth, and the longer it went on, the less likely it was that she would be found alive. The police had hinted as much, if not come right out and said it.

Susan Carlin felt so alone. Her world was falling apart around her. Everything that she held dear, the solid, loving family environment, her marriage, everything was coming apart at the seams.

She was convinced that her husband blamed her for everything. She was the brunt of all his frustration and anger. Nothing she did for him was right any more, he found fault with every single little thing. It was as if she didn't know him anymore. And when she had suggested that he should make an appointment to see the doctor, he had gone completely off the trolley and trashed their conservatory with his bare hands.

The anti-depressants that she had been prescribed just made the whole situation ten times worse. She managed to get through most days in a clouded haze; her head was on another planet most of the time. The more Lee took everything out on her, the more paranoid she got, and the more pills she swallowed. It was a vicious circle.

She closed her eyes and tried to erase everything from her mind. A colourful, vivid image of Donna appeared. Her husband was chasing her around their back garden. It was a beautiful summer's afternoon, the sky was a shimmering bluey-white. Pink, white and purple petunias were in full bloom around the borders. At the end of the garden stood thick, sturdy mature rose bushes with clusters of deep red and pink blooms; Susan breathed deeply, imagining the sweet fragrances tingling her nostrils.

Donna was four years old. Susan remembered the day as if it was yesterday. The episode was etched on her heart like a scar that wouldn't fade: always scratching away below the surface. Donna had fallen and grazed her knee. Susan had held her arms out to comfort her daughter, but she got to her feet, looked at her mother through tear-stained eyes and turned and ran into her father's arms. That's the way it had always been. Donna was her daddy's girl. She always went to him when she was troubled: never her. Susan loved Donna as any mother would a daughter, but it was never enough. It wasn't unconditional love with no boundaries. Susan always held something back. She couldn't express herself openly, not like her husband. Susan knew that Donna sensed her rejection from the moment the midwife had handed her to Susan. Donna had opened her eyes and seemed to stare straight through her.

Susan Carlin made soft whimpering sounds, like an injured puppy. Then floods of tears began to fall onto the duvet. 'Donna,' she cried. 'I'm so sorry.'

*

Lee Carlin drove along the A40, onto the Paddington flyover and onwards along the Marylebone Road. A big glass gyroscope balancing precariously on the top of the domed roof of The London Planetarium, illuminated the night like a beacon reaching out to the stars. Adjacent, was the long façade of Madam Tussauds – the famous waxworks. The edifice seemed, somehow, eerie with its concrete gargoyles and theatre masks spotlighted high up along its front.

Apart from an early morning supermarket delivery truck and a black, London taxi, Lee's car was the only vehicle waiting at the set of traffic lights. The journey into town had taken little more than twelve minutes on the empty road. The lights changed to green and Lee pulled away turning right into Portland Place. He followed the road to the end, passing the BBC Broadcasting House on his left, and then into Regent Street – if Lee only knew that he was less than a few hundred yards from the Internet café where Jason had initiated the evil cultivation of Donna.

The traffic began to get heavier as he drove down the sweeping curve of Regent Street with its tall elegant seventeenth and eighteenth century buildings – now mostly housing famous department stores.

After about half a mile, he descended onto Piccadilly Circus. Without really knowing where he was going, Lee turned up into Shaftsbury Avenue and before he knew where he was, he landed in the middle of Soho.

He parked on an empty meter bay in Wardour Street, locked the car and swept a panoramic look around. Until a few weeks ago, Lee hadn't set foot in Soho for over 25 years – not since seeing "The Jam" perform at the Marquee Club.

Gone were the seedy strip clubs on every street corner. Now, bright neon-signed "Gentleman's Lounges" with pictures of naked girls splashed across the entrance fronts, cast colourful patterns in the puddles on the wet roads left over from the earlier rain. To the uninitiated, it all purported a model of respectability: to the initiated, they were shit-holes that titillated the gullible, while relieving them of every penny they had in their wallets: nothing had changed.

Together with the plethora of seedy porno magazine shops and private cinemas advertising hard-core movies, Lee had found the whole atmosphere of the place intimidating. More so than he remembered. Perhaps it was because he was older and he had a different agenda now. And to think that Donna was last sighted not far from here sent a cold shiver down his spine.

Piles of black bin bags lined the pavements, some spilling over into the gutters of the near deserted streets. The whole place reeked of despair and depravity. Lee glanced at his watch. It was 4:25 a.m. He thought that there would have been more life around, but it was quiet, perhaps because it was midweek. Come the weekend the whole place would be rocking and rolling to all hours – the clubs didn't turn out until dawn these days.

It brought to mind the countless times that he and his mates had to walk the long journey home after leaving a disco in the early hours. The chance of getting a cab in those days was like winning the lottery: virtually impossible. The black taxis wouldn't entertain youngsters pissed out of their skulls, and private mini-cabs would charge a king's ransom.

Lee zipped his thin cotton bomber jacket right up to his neck and pulled up the short collar over his ears. There was a chilly breeze whipping around the streets. Slowly, aimlessly, he strolled along Wardour Street, stopping every so often to peer into the shop windows. Not for any particular reason, just to pass the time.

Perusing a menu displayed behind a glass cabinet on the wall outside an Italian Restaurant, Lee was startled by the clump of heavy shoes descending a bare wooden staircase. He shot an askance look at the short skinny guy with a tattoo of a snake creeping up the side of his neck. A multitude of studs and earrings hung off his lobes and out of his nose, as he emerged from an open doorway next to where Lee was standing.

The stranger looked up at Lee and cast him a baleful sneer as he passed around behind him. *Who the fuck, are you looking at.*

Lee turned and continued perusing the menu. Out of the corner of his eye, he watched with disdain as the shaven-headed figure scuttled away up the street.

Curiously, Lee looked in the open doorway and peered up the dimly lit staircase to the dark landing at the top. On the wall adjacent to the doorframe was an intercom with a list of girls' names. He read them one by one. Candy, Susie, Tammy, Lisa, Maria . . . *Donna*.

The shock of seeing his daughter's name staring out at him made him go so weak at the knees, he had to grab the doorframe for support. He stood motionless, trying to catch his breath, as his mind spun in turmoil. Then looking to the top of the stairs, he tentatively pressed the buzzer next to Donna's name: he had to know.

There was no answer. He pressed again, and wondered if the push was working because no sound was coming from the unit. Then a crackly sound cut the quiet night air. 'Come on up,' a croaky voice said. 'First floor.'

Lee stood riveted to the spot, not knowing what to do. He looked over his shoulder along the street to see if anyone was around. *Deserted*. He looked to the top of the landing and felt something inside drawing him in like a fish's favourite tit-bit wriggling tantalisingly from a hook. He was hooked.

Gingerly he made his way up the stairs. When he reached the top he looked to his left. Along the narrow landing were four, grubby doors badly in need of a lick of paint. He looked to his right – the same, except one door was ajar at the end. A light from inside the room cut a sharp angle across a threadbare mat that extended along the length of the landing.

Like a moth drawn to a light bulb, Lee walked slowly towards it. Not knowing what to do, he stopped outside the door like a naughty child waiting to be summoned into the headmaster's office.

'Are you going to stand out there all night?' came the throaty cockney voice from inside.

Lee crept in, quietly closing the door behind him. He stood in the middle of a tiny hallway and waited. Immediately in front of him was a bedroom. Through the open door, he could see a double bed. On it was a crumpled, single white sheet and a grubby-looking pillowcase, which must have been white at some stage in its long life. He strained his head left and then right to get a better look inside, but the room was bare apart from a couple of cheap bedside cabinets and a washbasin in the corner with a paper towel dispenser above it.

A tall, scantily dressed, painfully skinny girl emerged from a room on his left carrying a steaming mug of coffee. Her scrunched up, jet-black hair splayed out from top of her head like a spider plant. Suspiciously, she gave Lee the once over with eyes that could tell a thousand stories – mostly horror.

'Ain't seen you here before, love.'

Lee stayed silent. Averting his eyes to a stain on the thin rug on the floor.

'You left it a bit late, just left a club or something, have you? You're lucky I'm available, wouldn't have been, but for a client that's just left.'

Lee nodded. Dumbstruck. *Must have been the repugnant looking weasel that passed me outside.*

'First time, is it, darlin?' she said, turning into the bedroom. She knew from bitter experience that, Lee wasn't a regular punter. He looked like a frightened schoolboy. If she said, "Boo" to him, he would probably freak out, turn on his heels and run a mile, she thought to herself.

Lee couldn't steal himself away from gazing at the girl's thong and shapely arse through her short, black transparent nightie as she passed by him.

She put the mug of coffee down on the bedside cabinet, next to a glass ashtray overflowing with cigarette butts. She then sat on the bed with her back resting against the wall.

'Are you coming in, then? No need to be shy, I won't bite yer head off,' she said, reassuringly. Just like a mother would coax a child to a special treat.

Tentatively, Lee made his way into the room. Embarrassed by the girl's nakedness, and his own carnal desires, Lee stood by the side of the bed, his eyes firmly fixed on an empty packet of condoms on the floor under the bed.

'Why don't you come and sit down here,' she said, patting the mattress next to her leg. She then reached across to the bedside cabinet and picked up a packet of cigarettes and a lighter. She got one out, lit it, and sucked on it so hard that her cheeks almost imploded.

And when she finally exhaled, a cloud of smoke polluted the stuffy atmosphere, followed by a coughing fit that sounded like an old clapped out diesel engine struggling for life. She retched so badly that Lee thought her lungs were going to burst out onto the bed. Her second long drag, thankfully passed without her coughing half her insides up.

She offered Lee a cigarette. He took one, thankful of something to calm his nerves. He then sat on the side of the bed. She gave him a light and he drew on the cigarette deeply. Feeling awkward – like a spare prick at an orgy – he cast his eyes to the grubby floor. She reached out and tickled under his ear. Lee flinched. A flicker of a smile creased the furrowed crows' feet at the sides of his eyes.

'See, that's better,' archly, she said. 'It'll be thirty quid for French and sixty for full sex; either way, you wear a condom,' she said, in a matter-of-fact, business-like tone. Like a decorator pricing a painting job, one coat or two? Gloss is extra.

Lee turned and faced her. 'No, you don't understand.'

'Course I do, darlin,' she empathised. It was all an act – first-timers always needed a bit of sweet-talking for encouragement.

The girl couldn't have been more than a few years older than his Donna, he guessed, twenty years of age at most. But her sallow skin, hollow jowls and the dark lines under her sunken lifeless eyes, told a different story. She looked tired, haggard, like a woman far beyond her years. Lee, looked sympathetically into her eyes and sensed that the frail, under-nourished waif, had experienced more hurt in her short life than he had ever had in the whole of his 46 years on this planet.

'Come on, love. I haven't got all night,' she said, running out of patience, and taking his hand and guiding it to her breast.

Lee left it resting there for a moment, before coming to his senses and pulling away from under her hand.

'Come on. You know you want to.'

Lee sat wide-eyed at the sight of her small breasts sitting high and proud on her bony rib cage, her dark nipples were huge in comparison.

'Here feel,' she said, rolling her eyes temptingly, taking his hand again.

He felt her hard nipple in his palm. Feeling the warmth of her breast and the faint beat of her heart radiating through his hand, he let it rest there a little longer than he should have. *For fuck-sake what're you doing? This is someone's daughter.* A voice inside him screamed.

'You don't understand! I just want to talk,' he said taking his hand from her breast.

'Look darlin. You can play "Knick Knack Paddy Wack" on me arse, for all I care. But time is money.'

Lee lifted his bottom off of the bed, reached into the back pocket of his jeans and pulled out a small leather wallet. He opened it and sifted through some notes. Before he had time to get any money out, the girl had, deftly, relieved him of two twenty-pound notes.

'Now, you've been a naughty boy, haven't you? And mummy's going to have to spank you. That's what you want, isn't it?' She teased, sliding her hand along the inside of his leg and into his groin to the bulge of his penis.

Lee closed his eyes and felt his erection growing.

'My, my. You are a big boy, aren't you?' She said, unzipping his flies and sliding her hand inside.

Lee grabbed her wrist as she felt her way into his underpants. 'No, No! Please. You don't understand. I have a daughter . . . her name is Donna—'

'Oh, I think I get the gist, now,' she said, sitting up. 'You want me to call you daddy? She pouted, pulling aside her knickers and rubbing her vagina. Here I am, daddy. Look how wet my fanny is, and it's all for you. Please. Pretty please—'

'No! Stop!' Lee shouted, leaping to his feet fumbling with his zipper. 'What sort of monster do you think I am?' He spat, vehemently.

Standing with his back to the wall, Lee reached inside his jacket and pulled out a wad of paper. He unfolded a sheet, put the rest back into his jacket pocket, walked over to the bed and handed the sheet of paper to the girl.

She gave it a perfunctory glance. 'Yeh.' She shrugged.

'That's a picture of my daughter, Donna. She's been missing for six weeks. The last known sighting of her was up here, in Soho.'

'What's it got to do with me? I know fuck all,' the girl said, lighting another cigarette with a shaky hand and sucking the life out of it.

The deep retching sound of her coughing fit that followed when she expelled the smoke from her lungs, made Lee's eyes squint. And when she swallowed a mouthful of phlegm she had scraped up from her chest, Lee almost threw up.

'You ought to see a doctor about that cough,' Lee said.

'Tell me about it. A bit of a cough is the least of me problems.'

Lee guessed drugs. Heroin, by the angry looking needle marks and the deep purple, bruised veins on her arms.

'Look, what's your problem? It's nearly dawn and I want to get some fucking sleep. Do you want a shag, or not?' she yawned.

Lee sat back on the side of the bed and poured out the whole story, whether she wanted to hear it or not. Well, he was in credit to the tune of forty quid.

When he had finished pouring his heart out, he held his head in his hands and sobbed. The girl was at a loss as to how to handle the situation. She'd never had a grieving father sitting on her bed before.

She'd had one or two punters cry with frustration after she had relieved them of all their cash and they'd got a thirty-second shag in return. Most of her punters never lasted more than a few minutes anyway, before coming their load, especially the tourists. Guys with a drink in them were the worse punters. Egged on by their mates they would come up the stairs full of piss and bad manners, and chauvinistic bravado, but few of them could even get it up. And if they couldn't manage the job in ten minutes maximum, she would show them the door. Any shortcomings were handled by pressing a panic button by the side of the bed, which would alert all the other girls on the other floors and a resident minder that was employed on a permanent basis.

The girl lifted her legs over the side of the bed and sidled up next to Lee. Tentatively, she put a comforting arm around his shoulder, and he buried his head into the top of her breast. She stroked his hair. She felt sorry for him.

Why couldn't she have had a concerned father looking out for her: one like this man here. She knew the answer only too well. She never knew her real father. She also doubted whether her mother knew him, either.

All she had ever had when she was growing up was a succession of uncles. And one particular "uncle" thought that she came as part of the package when he ensconced himself in her mother's bed.

Her mother had turned a blind eye to his late night sorties into her daughter's bedroom. She guessed it was because her mother was out of her skull on drink and drugs most of the time and could never satisfy his sexual hunger. That was when he started turning his attentions towards *her*. And if he didn't get his own way, he would belt the life out of her mother: it was a catch twenty-two situation. She let him do those nasty things to her and in return, he didn't hurt her mother. That was the deal.

When she reached fifteen years of age, she was old enough, tall enough, and streetwise enough to confront him. And one night as he grunted and groaned on top of her. The weight of his big fat belly bearing down on her, together with the stinking smell of his sweaty body and his putrid breath assaulting her airways, it all became too much. And when he didn't take *No* for an answer, she reached out from under him, grabbed a solid glass orb off her bedside cabinet and smashed it across his head until he collapsed in a heap on top of her. After a struggle, she'd managed to push him off, rolling him onto the floor.

The orb was a souvenir from Margate. It was the only holiday she had ever had. When the orb was shaken, speckled snowflakes fell onto a little cottage. There was a snowstorm *that* night, alright.

She'd never forgot the look of abject horror on his face when he recovered consciousness, touched the side of his head and realised that there was blood pouring out of a gaping wound on the side of his temple. The look of pure hatred as he came towards her with his fists clenched. And when he laid into her, it was relentless. She had never known pain like it and was determined she wouldn't experience anything like it ever again.

The next morning when she came too in a bloody heap on her bedroom floor, she knew that she had to get out. It crossed her mind to go to the police. But something inside her told her that it would be a waste of time. When push came to shove, she knew that her mother would side with him. Her mother was a weak-willed mess and totally dependent upon him.

That morning, she cleaned herself up best she could, packed a bag and left. She had heard through the grapevine, sometime later, that her mother had died from drug and alcohol abuse. As for him, he had cleared the flat of anything of value – not that there was much – and had it on his toes. Donna last heard that he was doing an "eight stretch" for manslaughter.

Rough justice. Should have been life. After all, she was serving a life sentence: only her life would be short-lived. She was well aware that her drug addiction would kill her eventually. At least she'd be at peace then.

'Why don't you leave a couple of those photocopies with me and I'll ask around,' Donna said, sympathetically. Not that she held out any hope. The streets of the West End was awash with runaways, and most of them ended up as statistics buried in data files and discarded. She should know, she was a statistic.

Lee wiped his eyes and apologised for unloading all his grief on her fragile shoulders. The girl smiled. It was a genuine smile, full of compassion.

Lee got to his feet, reeled off half a dozen photocopies of Donna and placed them on the bed. 'Thanks,' he said. 'I'd better be getting on my way and let you get some sleep.'

Donna got up from the bed, kissed him affectionately on the cheek, and said, 'Don't worry, Donna will turn up: you'll see.'

Hearing it from this girl, a complete stranger, who somehow he felt closer to than his own wife, was a heart-warming experience. To think a young girl not much older than his own daughter, a prostitute with enough troubles of her own, would take the time to just sit and listen while he unloaded all his grief, his pent up emotion, his anger onto her, without sitting in judgement of him was like a sweet breath of fresh air.

Lee felt strangely unburdened, refreshed, as if a massive weight had been lifted from his shoulders. Now he could focus on the job in hand, his mission to find his daughter. And no matter what happened, he knew that he would not be deflected from his pursuit in finding Donna. Whatever the outcome.

Walking down Wardour Street, Lee passed an all-night café and went in. He ordered a coffee and some toast and then found a table in the corner by the window. He sat down and glanced up at the clock on the wall. It was 6:07 a.m. A wave of fatigue washed over him. He was knackered.

A sad-looking Italian girl, already dressed in her school uniform, brought the coffee and toast to the table without giving Lee a second look. The toast was hot with lashings of melted butter on top. He took a bite from one of the wedges and wiped the dribbles of butter away from the sides of his mouth with a paper tissue from a dispenser on the table.

He wiped a hole in the condensation on the window with his hand and gazed out into the street. A street-cleaning truck brushed noisily by, sucking up the dirt from the gutters with its rotary brushes and washing them down afterwards. An army of people dressed in overalls were milling around – early morning office cleaners, Lee guessed.

The traffic was starting to get busy and it wouldn't be long before all the parking meters were taken. He spooned sugar into his mug of coffee and drank some. It was hot and strong, just how he liked it.

His thoughts turned to the young girl he had just left upstairs in that disgusting room, and what might become of her. What could have possessed him to go up there, and worse, how on earth did he let himself get into a compromising situation with her. A girl, only a few years older than his own daughter. It frightened him, because he knew he was *that* close to letting it happen.

Sitting there with time to reflect, he began to doubt his own intentions. What had possessed him to come up here, to this cesspit of deceit and misery? Maybe his wife was right: he *was* just hindering the police investigation.

But there was something about this shit-hole that pulled him here night after night. Lee didn't know what it was, but there was a magnetism, a buzz, the whole area was alive and vibrant, especially late at night. Even midweek, people flooded into the pubs and restaurants after work. The atmosphere was electric. Especially on warm summer evenings when throngs of people spilled out onto streets drinking and making merry. Some would stay on to go to clubs, others drunkenly found their way to the station to catch the last train home.

He couldn't just sit about and do nothing. Just sit and wait for the inevitable bad news. He was well aware what everyone thought, but was reluctant to say. They all thought the police were looking for a body. Too much time had passed by and the police were no nearer to finding Donna now, than they were when she went missing. Together with the fact that he hadn't seen or heard anything from Loder or any of his underlings for ages, told its own story. It seemed to Lee that he was the only one that was one hundred percent certain that his Donna was alive. He felt at times that he was the only person looking out for her – him standing alone against the world. His so-called friends had even begun to give him a wide berth because of his self-obsession and single-mindedness. Until he knew for certain what had become of his daughter, he was determined to do whatever he possibly could to find her. Lee ate the last piece of toast, drank the bitter gunk from the bottom of his mug and left the cafe.

Outside, dawn had broken, bringing an orange glow behind the dark scudded clouds. A cold morning chill ate into Lee's thin cotton jacket sending a shiver around his shoulders. He zipped it up to the throat, buried his hands deep into the pockets and made his way back to his car.

He thought that he might as well go straight to work, it least it would take his mind off things. But he'd better go home first and make things right with his missus: he had said some terrible things to her last night. Words said in the heat of the moment, which he now deeply regretted. He knew that he took all his frustrations out on her, and he knew that it was wrong, but she always seemed to be in the firing line.

All said and done, he loved his wife, but he knew that their marriage was falling apart at the seams. Donna's disappearance just seemed to bring everything to a head. They had been having problems for a long time, but they both just dismissed it. Buried it. Brushed it aside. Neither of them was prepared to talk. Didn't know how to. Maybe it was just the complacency of married life.

Lee had known Susan since school days. She was the younger sister of a friend of his. When Lee had finished his apprenticeship, he joined a gang of older lads who drank in the same local pub as him. They were all electricians, well, a couple of them were, the rest never held a JIB ticket, not a legit one anyway. The gang were all working on the lump, earning bundles of cash, all of it "Nelson Eddie's." Lee was welcomed into the fold with open arms, because he was the only one who could read architects' drawings and decipher complex wiring diagrams.

Because Lee used to drive, he would call for Susan's brother in the mornings and take him to work. But her brother could never get his arse out of bed, so Lee frequently had to wait for him to get ready in morning. Susan would pad around the flat half asleep wearing just a flimsy nightshirt, completely unaware of the sex she exuded from every pore of her slim, shapely body. Lee could never take his eyes off her firm breasts that stood proudly under the flimsy nightshirt. And when he sat in the low armchair and she bent forward to hand him a mug of tea, he would see right down the inside of her top to her feet. He had to hold on to the mug of tea for dear-life to stop his erection from bursting through his jeans. Together, with her long, shiny, pitch-black hair cascading over the front of her shoulders that tickled the side of his face, he had to close his eyes and pause for breath. When she'd looked at him with her dreamy hazel eyes and smiled. 'Can I get you anything else?' It took every last bit of his resolve not to scoop her up and carry her upstairs to bed.

Susan was four years younger than Lee, and her brother always looked upon her as his "little sister." He had made it crystal clear that she was off limits to everyone: especially his testosterone charged mates, who only had one aim in life, getting their rocks off as quickly and as often as possible.

One Saturday night, Lee had espied Susan in a pub with a group of friends all having a good time. He couldn't take his eyes off her. She had looked stunning, and when she came over to say hello, he'd just got tongue-tied, he was so mesmerised by her beauty.

After he'd had a few too many beers, he'd mustered enough courage to go across and strike up a conversation with her. He'd had Susan in hysterics with his tales of what he and the lads had got up to at work. He gave her his phone number at the end of the night and thought no more about it.

No one was more surprised than he, when she had phoned the following day. The rest, they say, was history. They had been together for eight years before Susan gave Lee an ultimatum. Either he made an honest woman of her and married her, or she walked. She was pissed off with the lack of commitment from him.

It shook Lee rigid to contemplate life without her. So unbeknown to her he secretly booked a holiday on the Caribbean Island of St Lucia with a wedding thrown in as part of the package. When it was all planned right down to the last detail, he handed Susan the brochure and a wedding dress magazine. Then said to her that the hotel needed to know what flowers she would like for her wedding bouquet and if she wanted a steel band to play the wedding march. After the initial shock, Susan had been overwhelmed by it all. And when all their friends and families turned up at the resort it was all too much for her. She cried her eyes out.

Lee inserted his key into the lock and let himself in. He hung his jacket over the banister at the foot of the staircase, and poked his head around the front room door. *All quiet on the Western Front.* He then went down to the end of the hallway, through into the kitchen and filled the kettle.

Reaching into the cupboard for a mug, he happened to glance at the clock on the instrument panel at the top of the oven. It read 7:37 a.m. That was why it was so quiet, Susan had already left for work. She did an early morning office cleaning job five days a week with a friend. It didn't pay a lot but it was cash-in-hand and the money helped to swell the holiday fund.

Lee relaxed, knowing that Susan wasn't at home. But he knew he had a lot of apologising to do. He was a coward when it came to confrontation. *Like most men, when their backs' were against the wall.*

He popped a tea bag into a mug, filled the kettle and contemplated as to how he was going to approach the state of affairs with his wife while he waited for it to boil. He had said some nasty, unforgivable things to her; comments that she didn't deserve. *What a prick,* he said to himself.

To save time, Lee thought that he'd have a shower while his tea was cooling. Upstairs, on the way to the bathroom, he passed Donna's bedroom. The door was firmly closed: he couldn't bring himself to go inside. He hadn't been in there since she . . .

He undressed and threw his dirty underwear, socks and shirt into a wicker wash basket in the corner behind the door, then stepped into the shower cubicle. He turned the temperature gauge on and set the power to high, and instantly felt the force of the water spray beating down on his head, chest and stomach from the all-over body jets.

Lee closed his eyes and held his face up to the spray, trying to wash away the events of the last few hours. The stupid argument with Susan. The confrontation with the prostitute: of which he was deeply ashamed. He had come so close to giving in and having sex with the girl, it shook him to the core.

He squeezed some shower gel into a loofah and began soaping himself down, trying to focus his mind on what to do next. If he was honest, he knew there wasn't anything more that he possibly could do. At that moment he made a promise to himself, and his daughter, that no matter what, he would not give up his quest. Not until he found her.

Happier with himself, Lee washed his hair, rinsed himself down, grabbed a warm towel from the heated rail and quickly dried his hair, before wrapping it around his waist and padding into the bedroom.

He went to his wardrobe opened the double doors, pulled open a drawer at the bottom and got out a clean pair of boxer shorts and socks. He stepped into the shorts, pulled them up then went across and sat on the side of the bed and began pulling on his socks.

Out the corner of his eye, Lee noticed that his wife's wardrobe door was open and the clothes rail was empty. He went over to it and opened both doors: nothing. Apart from a few formal and dressier outfits all her clothes were gone. One by one, he pulled the drawers below open. Most of her underwear, tops, sweaters, all gone.

Lee fell to his knees and felt his whole life come tumbling down around him. And it was all his *own* doing. He stayed there, on the floor, staring into the sparse wardrobe, his mind swimming in confusion.

Finally, after what seemed like an age, he got to his feet and put on a pair of working jeans. Then went across to the dressing table and sat staring at his refection in the mirror. Tucked into the bristles of his hairbrush was a folded sheet of notepaper with his name written on it. He unfolded it and read. It was all too much for him to take in, and held his head in his hands. He felt as if his right arm had just been amputated: his mind was totally shot to pieces.

Everything that he held dear in his life had gone. His wife. His daughter. Even his friends. He felt totally alone in the world. Nothing in his life would ever be the same again . . . not until he found the answer to his daughter's disappearance.

Unable to cope with her husband's vicious, verbal assaults any more, together with everything else that had happened, Susan had felt she'd had no choice but to get away for a while, for both her own sanity as well as Lee's. She had gone to stay with her brother in Brentford. Lee knew that if he went chasing after her straight away it would only make matters worse. Best to give each other some breathing space for a while. He was certain that Susan still loved him as much as he did her and given time, he was sure that they would work things out.

CHAPTER 9

'We've got a sighting, gov!' DS Frost said, storming into Loder's office waving a disc in his hand.

'Where?'

'Berwick Street.'

Loder got up from behind his desk and followed his DS into the incident room. DS Frost sunk his heavy bulk onto a swivel chair in front of a monitor, slid the disc into the machine and pressed the play button.

Tanya walked across from her desk and joined them. They both leaned over DS Frost's shoulder and waited anxiously for the tracking to settle on the grainy picture.

All three of them watched silently as the picture settled showing a view looking down onto the junction where Berwick Street crossed Broadwick Street, in the heart of London's Soho district. The date displayed at the bottom of the screen read 29/09/06, the same day as Donna disappeared, and the time ticking away on the bottom right of the screen showed 21:16.

The picture was grey and fuzzy in the evening haze of the streetlights. The road was choked with taxi cabs and cars moving slowly down Berwick Street towards Shaftsbury Avenue. The streets were busy with suited office types who'd stayed up town after work and weekend revellers out for a good time. Throngs of camera-clicking tourists wandered aimlessly around. Overzealous, punchy-looking doormen fronting the plethora of lap dancing clubs and peep show joints, coaxed people as they walked past with promises of delights beyond their wildest dreams: the reality was usually a disappointment and expensive.

All three of them watched intently not taking their eyes off the monitor for a second. After several minutes, Loder barked, impatiently. 'Fast forward it.' DS Frost hit the search button and the picture speeded up. People darted around the screen like a madcap silent movie.

'There, stop!' Tanya pointed. 'Go back a bit. That should be enough, now play it.' Thick lines descended horizontally down the screen until it settled and began to play.

'Bollocks! It's another back view of the little bastard,' Loder snapped.

Tanya turned towards her boss in astonishment. It was very rare that he swore. In fact, she couldn't remember the last time he had sworn in her company.

Loder was preoccupied with his eyes firmly fixed to the screen, completely unaware of what he had just said.

The traffic came to a halt at the traffic lights. Jason grabbed Donna around the small of her back, turned her to the left and led her across the road. She looked to be walking unsteadily as he helped her off the kerb. As they stepped out into the road a sudden gust of wind blew Jason's hood off his head, revealing a profile of him on the screen. Then for a fleeting moment, Jason turned his head left and very nearly looked directly at the CCTV camera.

'Freeze the picture!' Loder snapped, slipping on his specs to get a clearer look. He studied the still picture for a moment then stood back, replacing his specs back into his shirt breast pocket. 'Still a bit vague. He looks like he's been captured in an infrared night-sight with those little black dots for eyes. At least we've got a better idea of what the little bastard looks like. See if forensics can work on the film, they might enhance a clearer image to work with.'

Tanya leaned over DS Frost's shoulder and asked him to restart the disc. Suddenly, she caught a whiff of baby's sick coming off his jacket. The pungent, stale, milky-smell caught in her nostrils and the back of her throat, taking her breath away. So much so, she had to take a step back and stand next to her boss.

She cleared her throat and blinked trying to clear her watery eyes. Loder's eyes didn't move away from the screen, but a wry smirk spread across his face as he sensed Tanya looking at him.

'Look at Donna, sir. She can hardly stand on her own two feet,' Tanya said.

'Probably pissed,' DS Frost said, not taking his eyes away from the screen.

'She could be drugged?' Tanya countered.

'Could be?' My guess is that he took her into a couple pubs to impress her. When I was his age and wanted to get into a girl's knickers, getting them pissed was the best way about it. Besides, in my experience, they gave in easier after a few slurps of "Easy Rider,"' he said, conceitedly.

Tanya couldn't believe what she was hearing and was just about to tear into her colleague, when Loder made a gesture with his hand behind his DS's head, intimating that it was all talk. It was enough for Tanya to take stock and hold her tongue, but she would file it away for another day.

Tony Frost was an inconsiderate, chauvinistic moron as far as Tanya was concerned. But for all his faults, he was a damned good police officer. He had an unrelenting, dogmatic approach to getting to the bottom of things and had a nose like a bloodhound for sniffing out the obscure. His wilfulness had gotten him into hot water on many occasions, especially his wasteful use of departmental resources. Nevertheless, invariably his hunches were justified.

As a family man and father to three young children and a new-born daughter, nothing was too much trouble. He absolutely embraced everything about family life. And was never happier than being at home with his family around him, and living in what seemed to everyone outside, in a state of perpetual chaos. He loved his wife unconditionally, even though they seemed to bicker and argue with each other most of the time. She always looked tired and haggard, but to him she was a star. She always had time for people, even after being run ragged by the kids all day long.

When Loder's wife had died, Tony Frost's wife, Jean, had been a source of constant support for him. He couldn't have got through it all had it not been for her. Loder liked nothing better than when he joined the family for Sunday lunch. Jean always made Loder feel part of their family: even the kids called him Uncle John.

None of the other pedestrians crossing the junction took a blind bit of notice of Donna wobbling across the road. It was Friday evening and most of the people were two sheets to the wind themselves. Come midnight, most of them would be wobbling from pub to club: it was conditional.

The three detectives watched as Jason and Donna disappeared out of view. Just to be certain that they didn't return, DS Frost, fast-forwarded the tape to the end, but there was nothing more.

'Right, get that disc over to forensics, Tony. And see if we can retrieve any more CCTV footage following them up *that* street, or anywhere else around Soho for that matter,' Loder said.

He straightened his back and rolled his head on his shoulders. Then glanced up at the clock hanging on the wall above his office window. 'Not doing anything special tonight, are you, Tanya?'

'Well, I was supposed to be having dinner with David.'

'I need you with me, tonight.'

'Why, sir?' she asked, but knew that there wasn't an option here. She sensed the mention of David's name, sealed her fate in any case.

'We're going uptown. Have a sniff around, hit a few pubs and rattle a few old cages. It's Friday today and most people who drink in the area are regulars who stay late after work every week. Maybe we'll be able to jog a few memories.'

'Oh, I see. Right, sir.'

'It's after five, now. I'll pick you up around sevenish. Will you be at home or—'

'Yes, sir. Home.' Came the terse reply.

Loder and David Riordan – Davey as he was known around the manor – had a lot of history. Davey was a player: had been for as long as Loder could remember. Although on the face of things, Davey Riordan was a reputable company director who owned a successful freight business. He had served time in the early seventies for his involvement in a bullion robbery at Heathrow Airport.

Nowadays, he tended to take a back seat from the day-to-day running of his company and concentrated his efforts in property developing. He was well connected with many very influential people, all seemingly quite legit. Although he wouldn't admit to it, Loder had a grudging respect for the man; but they both knew where they stood with each other. Loder's biggest regret was when Tanya had got involved with Davey Riordan: he blamed himself for that.

Davey's daughter was brutally murdered and before they eventually arrested and convicted the perpetrator, Loder misguidedly thought that Davey had got himself into something way above his station and that his daughter was murdered in the process.

Loder had assigned Tanya to keep close eye on Riordan, to curry favour with him in the hope that she would overhear something that would implicate him. As the investigation unfolded, it became clear that Loder was barking up the wrong tree. It turned out that a sadistic serial killer had murdered Riordan's daughter. In the meantime, Tanya had gotten too close and fell for Riordan, big time.

When one of his trucks was found to be loaded with cocaine, the Customs & Excise arrested Riordan. He denied all knowledge of anything to do with the drugs. He was convinced that others using his freight business as a drug-trafficking operation had set him up. Loder, for what it was worth, believed that Riordan had no knowledge of what was going on behind his back. And when there was an attempt on Riordan's life by a gunman, Loder's thoughts were confirmed.

To get himself an out, Riordan came to Loder with evidence of corruption of two senior police officers, which had occurred many years earlier. One was Loder's immediate boss, the other a Chief Superintendent. Loder despised corruption within the force, it undermined everything that he had worked and stood for. He acted upon the evidence given to him by Riordan. Both officers were quietly pensioned off. As part of the bargain, Riordan was exonerated of all charges.

It still grated on Loder that it was he, his doing that Tanya had got involved with Riordan in the first place. And when it all came on top, she had been prepared to put her whole career on the line for Riordan. But to be fair to Davey Riordan, he looked after Tanya and treated her well. Tanya's daughter, Katie, looked upon Riordan as a second father. As for Davey Riordan, he would have never been able to come to terms with his daughter's death if it hadn't been for Tanya, and having Katie around was just the icing on the cake; he loved the pair of them to destruction. It gave his life purpose.

Loder couldn't put a finger on it, as to why every time he heard Davey Riordan's name come up in conversation – especially when Tanya spoke of him – it just set something off in his head. But if he was honest with himself, though he was loath to admit it, Loder was envious of them both.

*

It was getting on for eight o'clock when Loder parked up on a meter at the Oxford Street end of Berwick Street. It was a clear evening with a slight chill on the soft breeze.

Tanya hadn't conversed very much with her boss on the journey up to the West End. She could think of better ways of spending a Friday night. With a bit of luck she hoped that she'd be back at Davy's before closing time. She was dressed in a short, black crepe skirt, a matching waisted jacket over a white cashmere V- neck sweater and black tights. In her heeled shoes, Tanya stood very nearly six foot tall. Her get-up was definitely not for running after criminals. Loder didn't get to see Tanya in her civvies much these days and was bowled over with the way she looked. Secretly he felt quite flattered to have such an attractive woman on his arm, metaphorically speaking.

As they strolled down Berwick Street deeper into the heart of Soho, the atmosphere began to change. The aroma of coffee and barbequed food wafted from the busy cafes and restaurants. Brightly coloured awnings with chrome, tubular tables and chairs lined both sides of the street. Umbrella gas-heaters blasted continuous warmth onto the tables. Loder was surprised at how much heat they churned out, and the throngs of people sitting under them certainly seemed comfortable enough.

It was now after ten o'clock and it had been drizzling for over an hour. Feeling the cold and dampness whistling through her thin attire and biting into her body, Tanya was beginning to get fed up and was itching to get back home and to snuggle up in bed next to Davey.

They had been in half-a-dozen or so pubs in the side streets off Berwick Street but so far had drawn a blank. Now standing on the corner of the junction where Donna had been captured on CCTV, Loder looked at his watch and sighed despondently. He could see that Tanya was completely pissed off with it all, as she stood under an awning with her arms wrapped tightly around herself, sheltering from the cold, hazy drizzle.

Loder did a 360 degrees scan of the junction, paying particular attention to the offices and dirty windows of the prostitutes' working rooms above the shops and cafes. A flashing neon sign advertising "models" in a window above a Bureau de Change caught Loder's eye. He thought about going up there and shaking down a couple of the girls, but knew that it would be a waste of time. The working girls around this area were a close-knit community and most were under the cosh of a pimp. Even if one of them did see Donna, he doubted that they would say anything; it was more than their lives were worth.

Burying his hands deep into the pockets of his overcoat, Loder crossed the road and joined Tanya. 'Let's just try that pub over there and then we'll call it a day,' he said, pointing to brightly lit façade on the next corner from where they were standing. Tanya didn't get time to answer; Loder was already striding off in front of her. She rolled her eyes and cursed under her breath as she tailed behind.

The Blue Post stood on the corner of Berwick Street and Broadwick Street. From the outside, the pub looked very pretty with rows of hanging baskets fixed high above the windows and entrance along the front. Purple and white trailing petunias spilled over between thick, green foliage. Large green, folded parasols protruded up from the centre of a few wooden bench-tables on the pavement outside. Dark puddles that had formed on the uneven pavements shone with bright reflections from the neon "Bass" sign in the pub window. Together with the spot lighting pointing up at the hanging baskets, the whole scene looked very inviting. One could be forgiven for thinking that they were in a country village, not central London.

Loder was already at the bar when Tanya entered the pub. She walked over and joined him, and said, 'No one could ever accuse you of being a gentleman, could they, sir?'

Unbuttoning his overcoat and shaking the excess rain from it, Loder smiled, and said, 'I'm sorry, Tanya. I didn't think to—'

'I'll have a large brandy, please.' Tanya cut him short.

'Are you sure?' Loder took a step back in surprise. He'd never seen her *once* drink spirits, all the time she had been on the team.

'Absolutely! I'm cold, wet and frankly completely pissed off, so I might as well *get* pissed,' she sniffed.

'Why don't you grab that table over there?' Loder nodded to an empty space set back adjacent to the entrance.

'I need to find the toilet and see if I can dry myself off,' she said, brushing herself down with the back of her hand

Loder stood tall and looked around over peoples' heads for the toilets. 'Over there, look,' he said, pointing to a sign hanging from the ceiling at the far end of the bar.

Tanya nodded and manoeuvred her way through the busy bar in the direction of the toilets.

Loder watched her as she disappeared through the crowd. An effeminate voice asking him what he wanted to drink caught him unawares. He looked at the smiling, blue-eyed, tanned, bleached-blonde man behind the counter with contempt. It wasn't that Loder was homophobic, he just didn't feel comfortable with gays. In his experience, their patter was always loaded with sexual innuendo and he didn't know how to take it, especially, when it was aimed in his direction.

He ordered a pint of bitter for himself and a small brandy for Tanya; he doubted if she'd know the difference anyway. The barman served the drinks and Loder paid him. When he returned with his change, the barman dropped it into Loder's open hand, rolled his eyes, wet the tip of his finger and wiped his eyebrow, then cocked his head and shuffled away.

Maybe he was anti-gay.

After about five minutes, Tanya appeared through the crowd and slid in on the green, leather-studded bench seat next to Loder. 'Lively pub, isn't it, sir?' she said, holding up her glass of brandy and scrutinising it suspiciously before taking a sip.

'Seems to be,' he said, scanning around the bar. 'Pubs like this are few and far between these days.'

'What do you mean, sir?'

'Look around the place: breathe in the atmosphere.' Loder gesticulated. 'It's tatty, it's got outdated sleazy lighting and the clientele stretch across the whole spectrum of life. Class barriers don't exist in places like these. Professionals mix with eccentrics and oddballs. The unctuous creeps that Soho attracts by the shed-load stick to their own. But they *are* a sponge of information; they don't miss a thing.' Loder took a long swallow of his pint. 'And they serve a damn good pint,' he said, licking the froth from his top lip.

Tanya said nothing as her eyes followed a man sporting a wide-brimmed, floppy fedora with a pink silk band trailing behind and a candy-stripe boater's jacket, breeze through a crowd of noisy office girls, out on the razzle after work.

Tanya took another sip of brandy and emptied the glass. Miffed that she had finished the drink so quickly, she reached into her jacket pocket and pulled out a single ten-pound note. 'Can I get you another, sir?' she asked, getting to her feet.

Loder looked at his half-empty glass. 'You driving?'

'It's your car, not mine. Besides, I'm probably already over the limit. Anyway, when did you suddenly develop a conscience?'

'Better not. It'll be just my luck to get a pull: but don't let me stop you.'

'So kind of you, sir. I might as well have the other half,' she said, with a wry cynicism.

Out the corner of her eye, while waiting to be served at the bar, Tanya caught sight of Loder rushing towards the toilets.

The barman shuffled over as if he had something uncomfortable wedged between the cheeks of his arse.

She ordered a brandy and a packet of salted peanuts to soak up the alcohol. While the barman went to fill her glass she pulled out a manila envelope from her shoulder bag and slid out the pictures they had printed off from the CCTV discs.

Distracted by the grainy pictures pushed under his nose, a man wearing an expensive chalk-stripe suit averted his lascivious stare away from the barman's arse as he stood at the optics and took a furtive glance at the top picture.

'Ever seen them before?' Tanya said, turning to face him and flashing her warrant card.

The man tightened his lips and pensively shook his head.

Tanya flipped the picture over then slowly one-by-one she went through the rest. Curious, or just plain nosey, the barman came over and joined them and began looking at the pictures from an upside position.

'The girl in the photo is thirteen years old and has been missing for nearly two months, after making a meet with that lad,' she said, placing her finger on the grainy picture of Jason.

'Hold on a minute!' the barman said, picking up the picture. He studied it closely for a moment. Then picked up a colour photo of Donna. 'I can't be absolutely certain, but I think she was in here some weeks ago.' He slid the picture to his side of the counter, cupped his elbow in the palm of his hand and tapped the side of face with the other. 'Yes, I'm sure it's them. I'll tell you how I know. I had to throw them out.' He rolled his eyes, combed the side of his hair with his fingers and shook his head – all very theatrical, like he was playing to an audience. 'The poor girl could hardly sit upright for flopping all over the seat,' he said, in a high-pitched shrill. 'They were sat just there,' pointing to the spot where Loder and Tanya had been sitting. 'I mean, we can't have that behaviour in here, this is a respectable establishment. And we do *not*, under any circumstances, allow drug addicts in here.'

'So you think she was drugged?'

'Look, darling. I've seen enough people under the influence around here to know the difference between whether, it's chemical or alcohol induced. 'You get my drift?' He nodded, sagely. 'And that poor girl was definitely not drunk, believe me.'

'Have you seen him in here before?'

The barman pursed his lips and shook his head. 'I can't be certain, but his face is mildly familiar. Let me ask, Chrissy,' he said, picking up a couple of pictures and walking to the end of the bar.

Chrissy was a tall, slim, blonde-streaked man with perfectly applied make-up, false eyelashes that fluttered in Tanya's direction, and a bottom that any woman would die for. He studied the pictures for a moment and shook his head. The barman shuffled back and handed the pictures to, Tanya. 'Sorry,' he said.

She gathered up the rest of the pictures, put them back in the envelope and smiled. 'Thank you very much for your help . . . um, I didn't catch your name?'

'Georgina. But you can call me, Georgie,' he said, mocking a limp hand at Tanya.

She reached inside her jacket pocket, produced a card and slid it across the counter to Georgie Girl. 'If you remember anything else, no matter how insignificant it might seem, or if the lad comes in again, call me. Anytime, day or night,' Tanya said, picking up her glass of brandy and packet of peanuts.

'Of course, officer. Glad to be of help. I do hope you find her: such a pretty girl, it's so sad,' he said, looking askance at the suited man. 'In your dreams!' Georgie said, cocking his head haughtily and shuffling away to serve another customer.

Tanya slid back into her seat, opened the packet of peanuts, tipped a few into the palm of her hand and ate them. What the hell was Loder up to, she cursed under her breath, glancing impatiently at her watch.

Loder dried his hands under the hot air drier for the third time since entering the toilet. He was waiting for the middle door of the block of three cubicles to open. There was someone in there he wanted to speak to and he was taking an extraordinary amount of time. Loder felt increasingly uncomfortable with the funny looks he was getting from some of the people entering the toilet.

  A young lad maybe early twenties with a severe acne problem came in and eyed Loder suspiciously. Loder watched the lad as he went to the urinals pulled down the front of his designer tracksuit bottoms and began to pee. He winced at the sight of a cluster of angry-looking spots around the back of the lad's neck and under his chin where his shaver had taken the heads off them. The skin on the side of his face was a mass of potholes and scars from where old spots had not healed properly.

  The lad sensed Loder eyes bearing into him from behind and smiled to himself. He finished his pee, tucked his penis back into bottoms, walked over to the vanity unit and turned on the tap. Loder was now drying his hands for the fourth time. The lad turned on the tap, pressed the soap dispenser, and began washing his hands.

  Looking into the mirror above the sink, he nonchalantly said, 'You looking for business, mate?'

  'Pardon!' Loder managed, taken by surprise.

  'I can see that you like me. Otherwise you wouldn't have been eyeing me up and down when I came in.'

  Loder was struck dumb. For the first time in over thirty years on the force, he was stuck for something to say. He had been compromised countless times by hardened criminals with offers of money and wealth in return for turning a blind eye or suppressing evidence. But never had he been compromised by a spotty kid with offers of sexual favours.

  'I give fantastic head. Only twenty quid to you, mate. We could do it in that cubicle if you like, long as you're quiet. What do you say? Come'n, you know you want to. You couldn't take your eyes off me when I came in,' he said, turning his head towards Loder and rolling his eyes directly at his crotch.

Loder flashed his warrant card under the lad's nose and his smile instantly turned to a groan. 'I think you and I should have a little chat,' Loder said, taking out a couple of photos from his inside his overcoat. 'What's your name, laddie? And don't give me any bullshit, otherwise I'll have you banged up in a cell for soliciting. Got me?' Loder growled.

The lad nodded. Standing bolt upright, quaking from head to foot, he said, 'Jamie . . . sir. Jamie Murphy.'

'Bet your dad'll be very proud of you when I tell him what his son's been up to?'

'Haven't set eyes on him since I was a toddler,' Jamie said, staring down at the floor. His face was so flamed with embarrassment that his spots looked ripe to explode at any moment.

Loder held up a picture of Donna in front of the lad's eyes. 'Ever seen this girl before?'

The lad shifted uncomfortably from one foot to the other, wiping his wet hands down the side of his bottoms. 'No, inspector. Never seen her before in my life.'

'What about this lad?' He said, holding up the grainy picture of Donna and Jason together.

He squinted at the picture long and hard to focus better, and said, 'No. I don't recognise either of them.'

But there was something about the way the lad's demeanour suddenly stiffened that told Loder he was lying.

'You sure?' he said, in a deep intimidating tone, putting the fear of god into the lad.

'Honestly. I've never—'

Suddenly, Loder flew across the room as the cistern flushed in the middle cubicle and the lock released. As the door opened Loder swung around and stood in front of the man, preventing him from leaving the cubicle.

'How you doing, Ricky? Long-time no see. What you up to these days?' Loder smiled menacingly.

The tall, slim-built, shovel-nosed man stood rooted to the spot. His eagle eyes darting from side to side for an escape route. Realising there was no way out, he acquiesced, 'Eh . . . Mr Loder. What are you doing in this neck of the woods?' he said, unconvincingly upbeat.

'Might ask you the same thing?'

The pot-faced lad stood by the vanity unit confused as to what to do for the best. Suddenly the entrance door banged open against the back wall and a man rushed in wrestling with his zipper.

'Out!' Loder barked.

The man didn't look twice. He just pivoted on his heels and did an about turn without saying a word. Jamie sensed his opportunity and made a dash for the door. Loder made a grab for his collar as he shot past on his left hand side, but he was too fast and couldn't manage to get a firm enough grip on it. 'It's your lucky day, laddie. I'll be back for you another time,' he shouted after him.

Loder walked forward into the cubicle. Ricky stumbled backwards and sat on the toilet. 'Well, well, Ricky Boy. You're looking flush.'

'Is that supposed to be a joke, Mr Loder?'

'Don't know what you mean.'

'What with me sitting on the carzi, an'all.'

Loder chuckled. 'Oh, I get it. Very good. So what are you up to these days, Ricky?'

'Nothing much, bit of this, bit of that,' Ricky sniffed.

'Don't piss me around, Ricky. You still dealing?'

'No, Mr Loder. Honest. I haven't touched a bit of smack for eighteen months, not since I got out on license. I keep well away from it all.'

'That's nice to hear. So, what are you doing up this neck of the woods? Shepherds Green is your manor?'

'Nothing. Just out for a drink.'

Loder moved into the cubicle and bore down on the man. He narrowed his eyes, and said, 'why is it, I don't believe you, Ricky.'

Ricky looked up at Loder and ran his hands through his slicked-black, waxed dark hair in panic. He'd been on the wrong side of Loder before and didn't relish the prospect of going there again. 'Look, Mr Loder,' he said, holding his hands up. 'All I'm doing is a bit of touting . . . nothing illegal.'

'Touting?'

'Yeh, you know, I tout around for punters – tourists mostly – and recommend certain clubs for them to visit. It's all above board, legal like.'

'I'm sure it is, Ricky. What sort of clubs?' Loder said, closing the cubicle door and leaning back against it.

'You know—'

'No, I don't know. That's why I'm asking.'

'Lap dancing clubs . . . mostly.'

'Mostly! I've already told you once,' Loder said, moving towards the man menacingly.

'Alright, alright, Mr Loder,' He said, holding his hands up to protect his face from the slap that he thought he was about to receive.

Loder stood off.

Ricky lowered his hands and sighed. 'I give the punters an introduction card. The more that turn up at the door the more commission I get,' he said, reaching inside his jacket and handing Loder a wad of complimentary cards.

'So what's the angle, Ricky? It's all a little bit too neat and tidy for you.'

'Angle, Mr Loder?' Ricky answered, averting Loder's hard stare.

Loder sensed Ricky was hiding something. After all, he had known him since he was a ten year-old kid, running dope deliveries on his bicycle around the Commonwealth Estate. The proceeds he made used to keep his mother supplied with smack. That was best part of fifteen years ago. When Ricky's mother died of blood poisoning from using infected needles, Ricky was taken into care. While he was there, he was raped and abused by certain members of staff, most of whom, had never been brought to justice. The authorities closed ranks and secreted the victims away to other homes.

Ricky was bounced around from pillar to post until he reached sixteen, he was then allocated a one bedroom flat back on the Commonwealth Estate. It wasn't long until he fell in with all his old contacts and started dealing crack cocaine and anything else he could get his hands on. He didn't stand a chance: didn't know any other way life. Didn't occur to him that most people did an honest day's work for a living. He'd never been in gainful employment in his life. Since then Ricky had spent most of his time in and out of prison. To Ricky, prison was looked upon as a temporary obstacle that he readily endured as part and parcel of his lifestyle.

'You dealing drugs again?' Loder said.

'No, no, honest, Mr Loder. I'm out of all that shit. I promise. I haven't been near any crack or smack for eighteen months, not since the SS put me through rehab. I'm clean, look,' Ricky said, pulling up the sleeves of his jacket to show Loder his arms. 'See, Mr Loder. Smooth as a baby's arse,' He said, holding them up for inspection.

'Okay, Ricky.' Loder softened.

Ricky pulled down his sleeves and smiled inwardly. Then a feeling of horror followed by abject fear filled his clouded mind as he looked up to find Loder bending forward with his hands on his knees and his face three inches from his own.

'Shall we start again, Ricky?' said Loder, softly.

Ricky sighed, like a deflated balloon. 'Okay, okay, Mr Loder.' He leaned back against the cistern to get away from Loder's face. 'I do a bit of touting for some of the brasses around the area.'

'That's better.' Loder leaned back against the door and folded his arms.

'I steer punters in the direction of certain brasses, same as the clubs. The difference is the girls pay me more than the clubs. That's it, Mr Loder. Straight up. It's the best job I've ever had. The girls reckon I'm a natural – I keep them well supplied.'

Intrigued, Loder asked, 'so, how do you go about it?'

'Easy, Mr Loder. I target tourists mostly. Japanese are the best. I show them a picture of a stunning looking young model, and tell them that she's waiting for them right now and that she'll be the answer to all their fantasies. Most of them have never seen a naked European woman before, never alone shagged one. The rest is easy; lambs to the slaughter. By the time they come face to face with the girls and realise that they looked nothing like the picture, it's too late, they've already been had over.'

'What about rent boys? Do you supply any punters to them?'

'No, I *do* not,' said Ricky, taking offence.

Loder knew he'd hit on a raw nerve and could have kicked himself for his insensibility.

Ricky had endured more than his fair share of abuse. He had been a sexual plaything to a mountain of faceless perverts, assuaging to their filthy needs just to get by in life.

'But you are acquainted with some of them that operate around here?'

'Yeh, why d'you ask?'

Loder knew it was a long shot, but pulled out the picture of Donna and Jason. 'Ever seen this lad in the picture?'

Ricky took the photo and studied it for a moment, then handed it back. 'No. Never seen him before,' he said shaking his head.

'What about the girl?'

'No. Sorry, Mr Loder, never seen either of them.'

'Are you sure?' Loder said, holding the photo up in front of his face.

'No, honest. Look, that kid could be one of a hundred dressed in a hooded top like that, and his "boat race" ain't all that clear, is it?'

Loder hated to admit it, but Ricky was right. Half the teenage kids in London wore hooded tops, it seemed to be a regimental uniform for them these days.

'Okay, Ricky. Mind how you go,' Loder said, pulling the door open.

Tanya was finishing her drink when Loder emerged through the crowded bar towards the table.

'Are you alright, sir? I was going to send out a search party you were gone so long.'

'I saw a face that I knew and thought that he might be able to help us.'

'Any luck?'

'No. Zilch,' said Loder, picking up his pint.

'Well, I have.' Tanya beamed.

'Oh, yes. What's that then? I could do with some good news.' He slid into the seat next to Tanya.

'I showed the barman the photos and he was positive that Jason and Donna were in here the night she disappeared. Said that she was all over the place.'

'What do you mean?'

'He reckons that she was out of her brains, drugged up to the eyeballs. He had to throw the pair of them out. He said that Donna could hardly stand up.'

'Is that so?' Loder said, finishing his pint. 'Rohypnol?'

'My thoughts exactly, sir. Donna wouldn't have known what day it was, never alone worrying about the time and getting back home.'

'Officer!' The barman called across to Tanya from behind the bar. 'That lad over there could probably help you more,' he said, pointing at Ricky as he made his way towards the door. 'Hey, Ricky,' he called. 'You remember those two people you helped out of the pub a few weeks ago, well some police officers here are asking about them.'

Ricky stood stock-still, like a fox trapped in a car's headlights, not knowing which way to run. He looked at Loder, then the door.

'Outside, Ricky. Now!.' Loder bellowed, flying up from his seat and grabbing him by the scruff of his collar. Tanya grabbed her shoulder bag and tailed him up.

Loder pinned Ricky up against the wall outside the pub. He had his hand around his throat and was about to give him a slap with the other, when Tanya grabbed his arm.

'Sir!' She said, in earnest.

Loder's eyes met Tanya's and he let go of Ricky's throat. 'Right, spill,' Loder said, pointing a finger in front of his nose.

Ricky's shoulders sunk as if he had the weight of the world bearing down on them. 'What can I say, Mr Loder?'

'Who is he? What's his name?'

'Eh . . . Ryan . . . I think. I've seen him around a few times, that's all. He asked me to help him out of the pub with the girl. I thought that there might be something in it for me so I agreed to help.'

'Where did you take her?'

'Nowhere. I helped him with her up the road a bit then he got hold of her and said that he had a car around the corner and that he could manage. He made a joke of it all. Said that she'd had too much to drink and with a bit of luck he'd get a jump out of her.'

'Was she drunk, or drugged?' Tanya asked.

'Could have been either; I don't know.' He shrugged. 'But she was well out of it.'

'When's the last time you saw this, Ryan, about?' Loder said.

'Ain't seen him since that night. That's the god's honest, Mr Loder.'

'If you're lying to me Ricky, I'll have you banged up back inside quicker than you can make a trick. Do you understand?'

'Absolutely, Mr Loder.'

'Where does Ryan hang about?' Tanya asked.

'All over really. He spends a lot of time mixing with the rent boys round in Old Compton Street. That's all I know.'

Loder straightened his arms and rested his palms against the wall, trapping Ricky between them. He leaned downwards bringing his face in front of Ricky's, and said. 'If I find out you're holding anything back from me, I'll come down on you like a ton of bricks, Ricky. You know what that'll mean,' Loder said calmly, lowering his arms and taking a step back. 'Right, on your way.'

Ricky licked his dry lips. 'If I find out anymore, I'll be straight on the blower, Mr Loder.'

'What do you think, Tanya?' Loder turned and asked.

'I think that I'm bloody freezing, sir,' she said, stamping her feet on the pavement and wrapping her arms around her waist.

'You wait here. I'll go and get the car,' he said, sounding upbeat. Pleased with their night's work

Tanya stood on the corner outside the pub skipping from one foot to the other trying to get some warmth into her. In hindsight, it was probably a mistake to wear a thin jacket on such a miserable night and her tights were not much help – her legs were freezing. 'God, hurry up Loder,' she said, under her breath, crossing her arms and rubbing her shoulders.

The street was busy with processions of tourists mingling with late night revellers. Suddenly a crowd of Japanese men surrounded her, pointed their cameras at her and began clicking away furiously.

They reminded her of little kamikazes darting around all over the place with their florescent duffle bags strapped across their backs.

One of them – no taller than five foot and wearing thick-framed glasses with lenses denser than the bottom of milk bottles – came up to her and said, 'Hooker. How much money you want?'

'Oh, p-l-e-a-s-e,' Tanya sighed, looking to the heavens for strength. 'Why me? What have I ever done to upset you?'

She got out her warrant card and flashed it at the little man in front of her, and said, 'Police!' Though she doubted if he could read it through his bottle-thick glasses.

'Ah, so!' he said, bowing his head furiously with his hands in the praying position in front of him, and backing away. 'So sorry. My mistake,' he said, joining the rest of his crowd and rattling on in some incomprehensible language. 'Ah,' they all said, nodding their heads in harmony.

Out the corner of her eye, she saw Loder pull up in the car. 'Thank Christ,' she sighed, and hurried over to the kerbside, got in and slammed the door.

'What's the matter with you?' Loder said.

'Don't ask. Just get me home. And turn the heater up I'm freezing my tits off here,' Tanya barked.

'Pardon!' Loder remarked.

CHAPTER 10

Tucked under the eaves on the top floor of the House of Commons, Sir Edward Marston MP stood gazing out of the small dormer window of his poky office. The single window overlooked the River Thames and on a bright sunny day like today, it was a view he never tired of. The Marston's were blue-blooded, old stock aristocracy, their family tree could be traced back many generations. The countryseat they hailed from was a twelve-bedroomed mansion on the outskirts of Warwick, known locally as Marston Hall.

Teddy – as he liked to be called by friends and the public alike – was a flamboyant, high-flying Conservative Member of Parliament and close advisor to the leader of the party. His tireless work behind the scenes promoting his leader's public persona was perceived as loyalty beyond the bounds. Moreover, it was made known to Teddy from certain quarters that his work would not go unrewarded should they win the next election.

To everyone that knew him, Teddy Marston was a confident self-assured negotiator who had a talent for being in the right place at the right time. However, he had a secret weakness – a predilection for teenage boys. It was a weakness that had consumed him for many years, and no matter how many times he'd tried, he just couldn't free himself from the overwhelming sexual desire that a fresh-faced, blonde-haired, young teenage boy stirred up inside him. He just couldn't help himself. The old school that he was party to just closed ranks: that's what the nobility did. Most just shrugged it off like it was the norm: an irritating habit. Like an itch that had to be scratched.

The loud shrill of the telephone ringing broke the contemplative tranquillity of the room. 'I'll be down right away,' he enthused.

Standing in front of the mirror, hanging on the back of his office door, he straightened his tie and combed his fingers through his silvery-grey, wavy hair. Fluffing out his silk, breast-pocket handkerchief in his suit jacket, he stood for a moment inspecting his attire. Stature and presentation was paramount in Teddy's books. Never let the defences down. A bright outgoing, confident smile at all times was his motto. Never let the bastards know what you were really thinking behind the façade.

Although privately he knew that he was living dangerously, he just couldn't help himself. His little "weakness" as it was referred to by certain members of his family, all began when he had a fumbling affair with a fellow student while at public school when he was fourteen. Now a forty-seven year old high-flying MP at the pinnacle of his political career, he had to guard his inveterateness more fervidly than at any time in his political life.

Teddy had worked hard at burying his skeletons away from the media and prying colleagues. As far as he was aware, no one suspected or had anything on him and as long as he continued to be discreet, where was the harm? He knew that if the media got wind of his little "weakness" he would be finished in public life. Nevertheless, it was a price he had to pay, he couldn't help himself. It was an addiction. Like a junky succumbs to the smouldering fumes of a foil of crack cocaine, refusal wasn't an option. Tomorrow was another day.

Teddy was a master negotiator, a man who got things done; he got results where others had failed. And when Teddy held court, people listened, they hung on his every word: more importantly, they believed him. For a politician that was a rare gift indeed. It was the mettle that future leaders were made of.

His long suffering wife was well aware of his, *little infidelities,* as she referred to them. She had suspected, soon after they had married, that Teddy was gay. Her suspicions were confirmed, when she unexpectedly turned up unannounced at a hotel where Teddy was supposed to be canvassing potential financial backers one weekend and found him in bed with a teenage boy. For the sake of their three children, the family and his career, she agreed to keep quiet about his sexuality as long as he kept his sordid little indiscretions away from the home. She daren't leave him, because in their world, it wasn't the done thing. Besides, she had nowhere to go.

Down in the main lobby Teddy made his way towards the reception area and saw his little prize patiently sitting on a long, leather-studded bench. The boy's jaw was almost on the floor as he looked in awe around the tall vaulted ceilings.

Teddy crossed the expansive, chequered, marble floor to where his little prince was sitting, looking a picture of beautiful innocence. 'Impressive isn't it, Daniel?' Teddy always addressed him by his full name. Never Danny, as the boy preferred.

'Cor! I'll say, Teddy.'

Teddy put his finger to his lips. 'Mr Marston in here please, Daniel. Right, come with me young man and we'll get you processed, shall we?'

Danny got to his feet and followed Teddy to the reception desk, completely mesmerised by the tall statues peering down all around him.

'If anyone asks, you're here as part of a school project, Daniel,' Teddy said, over his shoulder.

Danny nodded, completely engrossed.

At the desk, Teddy quickly filled out the necessary paperwork and obtained a visitors pass. He pinned it to the front of Danny's sweater. 'What would you like to see first?'

'I don't really know, Ted . . . sorry, Mr Marston. How about you show me your office?'

'I tell you what, Daniel, why don't we pick up some sandwiches and pop from the canteen first and then go up to my office. How does that sound?'

'Yeh, brilliant.'

Back in Teddy's office, they both sat on a small sofa and Teddy watched as Danny tucked into a platter of smoked salmon, potted shrimp, roast beef and horseradish triangles.

'Never had scrum as posh as this before Teddy,' Danny said, through a mouthful of food.

'Take your time, Daniel. We don't want you choking do we?' Teddy said, rolling his eyes suggestively. Here, have a drink,' he said, handing him a glass of lemonade.

'Rather have a beer – you got any?'

'I'm afraid not, Daniel,' Teddy said, running his fingers through the boy's silky fair hair.

'Ah, well. Suppose this'll do,' he said, looking up at Teddy with gorgeous blue eyes.

Danny's blue eyes, his fair hair and lithe lightly tanned body was everything that Teddy craved for in a boy. Ever since he had been introduced to Danny by Harry Delaney, at one of Jonnie James's little private soirees, he hadn't been able to get enough of the boy. It had come to a point that Teddy missed him immensely when he wasn't around. He found Danny insatiable, and most of all accommodating to his every desire.

Feeling Teddy's hand tickling the nape of his neck, Danny looked up lovingly. He knew what Teddy wanted – after all, even at the tender age of fifteen, he was a seasoned professional at the game – and he didn't mind delivering as long as Teddy kept buying him all those little gifts. As long as Harry Delaney didn't get wind of their extra-curricular assignations, where was the harm? Besides, he had his future to consider and Teddy Marston was going to be his meal ticket out of this shitty way of life, whether the old nonce was aware of it, or not.

'I had better lock the door, we don't want to be disturbed, do we?' Teddy said, getting up from the sofa.

No sooner had Teddy secured the latch and turned around, Danny had stripped down to his Calvin Klein's and lay sprawled on the sofa with a teasing smile on his face. Teddy stood in front of the sofa looking down at the boy's beautiful nakedness, completely besotted. 'You don't waste much time, do you, you cheeky monkey?'

Danny's sultry blue eyes looked up innocently at Teddy and he said, fluttering his long eyelashes, 'I don't know what you mean, Sir Edward.' He then swivelled his legs off the sofa, leaned forward and unzipped Teddy's flies. 'We know what you want, don't we?' he said, sliding his hand into Teddy's trousers.

Closing his eyes, Teddy let all his doubts, his fears, his guilt, drift away on a wave of ecstasy. He couldn't stop himself even if he wanted to: and why should he, he wasn't harming anyone. Nevertheless, deep in the back of his mind, he knew that to the outside world he would be perceived as nothing more than a pervert, a deviant, a sexual predator who corrupted innocent young lives. They didn't understand . . . He had needs like any normal person: but his needs could only be fulfilled from the Dannys' of this world. All his doubts just melted away like a soft breeze on an ocean as he felt the soft touch of Danny's hand working expertly on him.

Danny knew that he had Teddy right where he wanted him. All he had to do was come across with the goods, stroke the posh-nosed poof's ego and he was putty in his hands. If his little plan worked, Teddy Marston was going to set him up for life. No more giving himself to fat, old poofs for a pittance, while Harry Delaney pocketed all the profit. No, *siree*. He was going to take Teddy fucking Marston to the cleaners, and then disappear away from London. Perhaps he would go to Spain.

A friend once showed Danny some holiday snaps and he couldn't believe his eyes. Blue skies, topless girls frolicking on sandy beaches, people eating huge platters of weird-looking sea creatures. It was a world away from his shitty existence. He had made a solemn promise to himself that one day he would go to Spain and never return. And if Teddy, complied – he wouldn't have any choice – that's exactly what he was going to do.

Fumbling in his shirt pocket, Danny brought out a small digital camera. 'D'you know what, Teddy?' Danny said, focusing Teddy in the LED viewfinder. 'I love this camera you bought for me.'

'I'm pleased you like it, Daniel.'

'Yeh, I mean, it's so simple to use. Smile,' he said, capturing Teddy unawares.

'Now, now, Daniel. Don't be naughty,'

'Aw, come on, Teddy. It's only a bit of fun. Come and sit down.' Danny patted the cushion next to him.

'We have to be careful, Daniel. I have my position to think of – you know that.'

Danny sidled up next to Teddy and showed him the picture on the LED. 'Takes brilliant pictures don't it?' he enthused. 'I've got a great idea!' he said, finding the intermittent timer mode. 'Let's have one of us together.'

'Oh, I don't really think that's a good—'

Danny was already off the sofa and positioning the camera on the edge of the desk. 'Come on, Teddy. It'll be fun,' he said, quickly jumping back onto the sofa and swinging his legs over Teddy's lap and wrapping his arms around his neck. 'Smile!'

Teddy wasn't sure, but before he knew it, the camera clicked into action. Danny buried his face into the nape of Teddy's neck. Click. Danny then slid his hand into Teddy's open flies and pulled out his penis. Click. Danny kissed Teddy full on the mouth. Click. Danny stood up on the sofa and dropped his underpants so that his penis was right next to Teddy's mouth. 'Go on, Teddy. You know you want to.'

'That's enough, Danny!' Teddy said, getting to his feet. His trousers fell to his ankles. Click.

'Spoil sport,' Danny said, grabbing the camera before Teddy could get his hands on it. 'Why don't I download the pictures onto your computer, Teddy? That way you'll be able to look at them when I'm not around and remind yourself of what you're missing. What do you think?'

'I think that you had better delete those pictures right *now*, Daniel.'

'Okay. Are you sure?'

'Positive,' Teddy said, pulling up his trousers and zipping his flies.

Surreptitiously, Danny slipped out the memory card, tucked it into his shirt pocket, and replaced it with another. He then made a show of fiddling with the buttons on the back of the camera for a moment. 'There you go,' he said. 'All done, look.'

Teddy sat back down next to Danny and watched as he went through the preview mode. Satisfied that all the pictures had been deleted, he relaxed. 'That was very naughty, Daniel,' he berated.

'Only having a bit of fun. No harm done, Teddy,' he said, planting an affectionate kiss on his cheek.

'I have to attend the house shortly so we best be getting you on your way, Daniel.'

'House? What house? Are you going home?' Danny looked confused.

'The House of Commons, Daniel. The place from which, government is run . . . where members of parliament are allowed to bitch at each other like spoilt children, all in the name of politics.'

Danny looked even more confused.

'Don't you bother your pretty little head with it all. Let's get you dressed, shall we?' He said, ruffling Danny's hair.

'Are you sleeping at the flat tonight, Teddy?' said Danny, buttoning his shirt. 'I could come over, if you want.' He teased.

'Yes I am. I don't know what time I'll be able to get away. Do you have your mobile with you?'

Danny reached into his jeans pocket, pulled out a small cell phone and flipped the top open. 'Yeh, plenty of juice left in the battery,' he said, tucking it back into his pocket.

'Good. I'll telephone you when I get home. Should be sometime after six.'

CHAPTER 11

It was getting on for midnight and Lee Carlin was sitting in the Admiral Duncan Pub in Old Compton Street nursing a pint of lager. Earlier he had traipsed around Trafalgar Square handing out photocopied pictures of Donna to anyone who would hold out their hand. Afterwards he had made his way up Shaftsbury Avenue, pasting fresh pictures of Donna over the torn faded ones on lamp posts.

Lee had spent so much time up and around Soho since Donna's disappearance, that many of the local café owners, local residents and even some of the late night dustmen, knew him by name. Sometimes, usually when the weather was bad, he found himself ringing on Donna's – the prostitute's – bell, and if she wasn't busy with a punter, he would go up and they would share a coffee together.

He had grown to like Donna and over the weeks the two of them had swapped many secrets about their private lives. He had told Donna things about himself that he'd never told a living soul: not even his wife. And for all the grief Lee had unloaded onto her, she never once wanted anything in return. Lee thought that Donna was a sad statistic of modern-day life: she was someone who had never been given a fair chance.

She knew exactly what she had descended to and how helpless her miserable existence had become. She had to earn to keep her pimp happy. If she didn't turn over enough tricks to satisfy his greed, then he wouldn't supply her with the smack that she was so completely dependent upon to get her through each day. It was a never-ending treadmill that was impossible to get off. Besides, her pimp wouldn't let her: she was his meal ticket, until she was of no further use. Then he would just toss her out onto the street to fend for herself. Donna was well aware that her drug addiction would eventually send her to an early grave, that's if HIV, or hepatitis didn't claim her first. She welcomed it.

Lee had offered on a few occasions to take her to his home and help find her a rehab unit, but his offer was always met with the same thin-lipped smile and a shake of the head. As far as she was concerned she was beyond repair. It ripped Lee's heart to see such a young – and once, very pretty girl – destroy herself in such a self-destructing, demeaning way. She deserved better.

Donna had said on a couple of occasions that she'd enjoyed their little chats. The best thing of all was that Lee had wanted nothing from her in return, and that alone was a rarity in the orbit of her life.

Lee often brought sticky buns and cream cakes for them both. It brought a twinkle to her lifeless eyes as she happily quaffed down mouthfuls of thick cream and jam like an excited child – which she was really – it always lifted his spirits to watch her actually eat something.

Lee often wondered what people must think of him, accosting them in the street and thrusting photocopies of his daughter into their hands night after night. The truth was he didn't give a flying fuck. He knew his friends and family thought that he was obsessed: some had even said that he had suffered some kind of mental breakdown.

Nevertheless, Lee couldn't just give up on his daughter, even if everyone around him had . . . including the police. He wouldn't be deflected from his pursuit of finding his Donna: not until he knew the truth.

On the steps under the statue of Eros in the centre of Piccadilly Circus, Lee had tried asking some scruffy-looking teenagers who regularly congregated around there, if they recognised his daughter. They had either given him the cold-shoulder or looked at him vacantly as if he was from another planet. They were all too preoccupied with their own agendas – like where their next trick or wrap was coming from – to be bothered with a middle-aged, straight-shot looking for his runaway daughter.

The sea of despair that Lee encountered night after night walking around the scruffy streets of Soho and the West End, had opened his eyes to what an uncaring, selfish, manipulative society we live in. The streets were awash with drugs, and dealers openly touted their evil wares in full view of an unsuspecting public. But for all that, Piccadilly Circus and the surrounding streets were alive, vibrant and bustling with atmosphere. The flashing neon signs that perched high on the facades of every building just added a wonderful vibrancy to the place.

Foreign students, with haversacks strapped across their shoulders, mingled with tourists of all ages from every corner of the globe. Outdated punk rockers with garish spiky hair mooched around scowling at anyone who dared stare at them. While Goths with thick mascara around their eyes and wild dyed hair that was as black as tar, congregated around the statue of Eros, dressed in period get-ups: the whole place was a hotchpotch of different cultures.

The Admiral Duncan had taken the full force of a bomb in 1999. However, terrorists weren't to blame. It was some fucked-up young man with a grievance against gays. It had since been refurbished back to its full splendour, but the few people Lee had spoken to, had said that the place hadn't got the same atmosphere as before. Its soul had been sucked out of it – literally.

It was a Thursday night and the bar was quiet apart from a party of girls celebrating a birthday, or something. Lee wasn't bothered. He was contemplating finishing his drink and getting himself off home. The truth was that he hated going home to an empty house. It had been almost a month since his wife had left and gone to stay with her brother. She had popped back home from time to time to see if Lee was looking after himself, but soon left again. Each time he'd asked her if she was staying, he'd got the same answer. Not until he gave up his mindless obsession, and stopped blaming *her* for everything that had happened.

Lee missed her so much it was as if someone had cut off his arm. He and Susan hadn't spent more than a couple of days apart since they had married. The lonely nights in bed with no one to snuggle up to. The constant nightmares, were at times too much to cope with alone.

Lee hadn't noticed the fair-haired teenager eyeing him up from the end of the bar. He had been too preoccupied with staring at the barman behind the counter, fixing his hair in a mirror. The barman's high cheekbones, flawless complexion, long dark lashes and blonde-streaked, wavy, collar-length hair, gave him the look of a gorgeously attractive female. Lee thought that if he was ever inclined to "swap shirts at half-time," he could quite take a fancy to her . . . him.

The fair-haired teenager sliding in next to him caught Lee unawares and soon brought him back to reality.

'You looking for business?' Danny said. His blue eyes catching Lee's attention.

'Pardon!' Lee said, taken aback at the boy's directness.

'I saw you eyeing up, Cassie behind the jump. Waste of time there, she's spoken for,' Danny, nonchalantly said, taking a swig from a bottle of lager.

'I wasn't doing any such thing,' Lee said, defensively.

'Come on, mate. I could almost hear what you were thinking. Cassie's nice, but she's too old. I'm younger and fitter. And I give very good head, at a price, you understand?' he said, with a wink and a twitch of his eyebrow.

Lee composed himself. He couldn't believe what he was hearing. He was actually being compromised by a teenage kid. It was true, the boy had read his mind. 'Look, son. I can assure you that I'm not looking for a blow-job, or any other job come to that,' he said, now smiling at the boy's barefaced audacity.

'Oh,' said Danny, miffed.

He was after a few quid to buy some puff. Teddy had phoned earlier to tell him that his wife was in town and that he had to meet her for dinner. Danny was put out because he was skint: it had slipped his mind to tap Teddy for some money earlier that afternoon: he'd been too preoccupied with more important things. Teddy always saw him right for money – conscience money.

'How about a beer then?' Danny said, holding up his empty bottle.

'I suppose I could stretch to a beer,' Lee said, getting to his feet. 'Although I doubt you're old enough to drink.'

'Course I am, mate,' Danny shrugged, full of indignation.

While Lee was at the bar, Danny's eyes honed in on a black, canvas shoulder bag lying on the seat next to him. Gingerly, he shifted across the seat, unzipped the top and slid his hand inside. He rummaged around hoping to get his hand on something solid, like a wallet or a camera, but all he could feel was a wad of paper and something that felt like a notebook. He cursed under his breath, zipped the bag up and shifted back along the seat.

Lee brought the drinks over, a pint for himself and a bottle of lager for Danny, and settled back down next to his shoulder bag.

'Cheers, mate,' Danny said, lifting his bottle to Lee before taking a swig. 'So, what you doing around here?' He narrowed his eyes suspiciously. 'Not Old Bill, are you?'

'No, you can relax. I'm looking for someone.'

'I knew it! What you after? Young, old, boy, girl . . . both? I can sort you out, no problem.' Danny rattled off with a spiel that belied his years.

'No, I'm looking for information,' Lee said, unzipping his bag and taking out a picture of Donna.

Danny took the sheet from Lee and gave it a cursory glance. 'What– she gone missing? London's full of runaways, mate. And most of us don't *want* to be found,' Danny said, his tone full of indignation.

'No. My Donna didn't run away . . . she was taken.' Lee then run the whole sorry story by Danny. He was just thankful for the company, whether they wanted it or not.

Lee hadn't really opened up to anyone about his daughter's disappearance, except what he unloaded on Donna. He'd obviously spoken to the police during the course of their investigation and to his wife, but more often than not, that had just disintegrated into all-out war with her. He knew that he was to blame for his wife packing her bags: he should never have taken all his frustrations out on her. After all, it wasn't her fault that Donna had gotten herself involved in an on-line chat room. But he did blame her for not keeping a closer eye on what Donna was up to when spending all that time upstairs in her bedroom, supposedly doing homework.

Now, here he was, sitting in a gay pub pouring his soul out to a complete stranger young enough to be his son: on top of that the little sod had already tried to compromise him. If the situation wasn't so ridiculous, it would be hilarious.

Danny just sat with his feet up on a shelf under the table, thinking. *What the fuck have I let meself in for here.* But he bided his time in the hope that he'd be able to con a few quid out of the sad bastard pouring his heart out next to him. At worst he'd be good for a couple of beers.

Twenty minutes and another refill later, Lee had now turned his attentions onto the police's complete disregard in pursuing his daughter's abductors, and how it was up to him alone to find her.

Danny had endured just about as much as he could take for one night, but his eyes couldn't help straying to the picture of Donna lying on the table in front of him. He couldn't swear to it, but he seemed to remember seeing a girl that resembled her, somewhere, but for the life of him he couldn't recall where.

He finished his bottle of lager. Then held it out, and said, 'Any chance of another one, mate?'

'Yeh, go on then. You could probably do with one after me bending your ear for the last half hour. Same again?' Lee said, scooping up the empties and taking them back to the bar.

Danny picked up the picture of Donna from the table and had a good look at it while Lee was at the bar. Suddenly, the penny dropped. The smiling happy girl in the picture resembled a girl who was at one of Jonnie James's little party's.

The girl he remembered, was very subdued and had said nothing the whole time she was in the MPV on the way to James's house. He remembered the glazed look in her eyes. Doped up to the eyeballs, just like he was the first time Harry Delaney had paraded him in front of all those filthy old pervs. What became of her afterwards, he didn't know. But at a guess, he knew that she'd be working somewhere. Probably at one of Delaney's more discreet establishments, the one's that he never got to see but had heard about through the grapevine.

Lee returned with their drinks and Danny quickly put the sheet back on the table. He was more or less certain, the girl in the picture and the one he saw at Jonnie James's house, were one and the same. And if he played his cards right, he could make a nice little earner out of this situation. He smiled to himself.

'Something amusing you?' Lee said, sitting down.

'What makes you say that?' Danny replied.

'Well, you look like the cat that's got the cream.'

Danny picked up the bottle of lager, took a swig and then placed it gently on the table in front of him. Pensively, he began making small circles with his finger on the wet table. Droplets of condensation from the chilled bottle had made the table top a wet mess. He took another swig and wondered how he was going to play it.

He knew that if he told Lee he'd seen his daughter at Jonnie James's house, he would want to know everything: names, places, the lot, and he couldn't do that. It was more than his life was worth. It would only be a matter of time before it got back to Harry Delaney. Any whiff of a scandal, or people gossiping out of school always found its way back to him, sooner or later. He had eyes and ears looking out for him everywhere. It was uncanny that Delaney knew first-hand every whisper on the street.

It was made plain at the very beginning to everyone, that if they ever breathed a word of what went on at Jonnie James's house, it would be their last.

Danny knew that Harry Delaney was an evil bastard and what he was capable of. At least three of his mates had seemingly vanished off the face of planet in the last two years. One of them, Micky Murphy, had been found washed up in the Thames down at Woolwich Pier with half his arse hanging out. He knew that it would only be a matter of time before he came gunning for him. But what the fuck, he had Teddy Marston now and *he* was going to be his meal ticket out of all this shit. Anyway, when Delaney found out that he'd been having extra-curricular activities with Teddy, he be dead meat for sure.

Ah, fuck it. He thought to himself. He might just as well nick a few quid off of this mug to tie him over, while he set the wheels in motion for Teddy's demise.

'That girl in the picture . . . your daughter?' Danny said.

'Yeh?' Lee replied, taking a long swallow from his glass and wiping the froth from his upper lip with the back of his hand.

'I might be able to help you there.'

'What do you mean? Have you seen her? Do you know where she is?' he rattled off.

'Yeh, I've seen her. But it was weeks ago.'

'Where?'

Just then, "Frankie" blasted out of the juke box. One of the girl's from the party at the end of the bar jumped up and started dancing, thrusting her hips back and forth. Her friends egged her on with wolf-whistles as she hoisted up her short skirt, moved across to where another girl was sitting, stood astride her and pulled her face into her crotch. They both lost their balance and fell onto the floor in an hysterical laughing heap.

'Now, that piece of info will cost you,' Danny said, full of nonchalance. His eyes distracted by the two girls rolling about on top of each other with their skirts half way up their waists and their stringy thongs winking at him.

The barman, busy filling a couple of glasses at the optics, spun around on his heels wondering what all the commotion was. 'Darling!' He feigned, holding his hand against his heart. 'I'd simply die for an arse like that.'

They all screamed with laughter as the two girls uncoupled each other and got to their feet. One of them poked her arse out at him and gave it a slap on the side with her hand. 'In your dreams, Cassie.'

They all screamed with laughter. The girl clearly enjoyed being centre stage.

'Have a look at them, will ya?' Danny whooped.

'Fuck them!' Lee snapped. 'Where did you see her? How much do you want?' he said, reaching into the back pocket of his jeans for his wallet.

'Two hundred quid.'

'I don't carry that sort of money with me,' Lee said, flipping open a small leather wallet.

'How much are you holding,' Danny leaned over to look what notes were inside the sleeve.

Lee pulled out a small wad of twenty-pound notes. 'That's all I've got on me. You can have that.'

'How much there?'

Lee quickly counted the money under the table. 'There's hundred and forty here. It's all yours, just tell me what you know,' he said, biting his lip nervously.

What Lee really wanted to do was drag the money-grabbing little shit outside and beat the information out of him. But he would probably do a runner as soon as he got him outside the door.

Danny ruminated for a moment. 'Okay. That'll do. Pass it under the table, he said, looking around warily.'

'Right, tell me what you know. And if I find out you're spinning me a line, I'll hunt you down and kick the fucking life out you. Do you understand?'

'Yeh, yeh.' Danny shrugged with indifference, dismissing the comment out of hand, and took another long swig from the bottle of beer.

'Come on then, spit it out,' Lee said, agitated.

'Look, I think I saw the girl in that picture at a house, but it was weeks ago.'

'What do you mean, you think? What house? Where?' Lee said, losing his patience.

Danny picked up the sheet and looked at it again. 'Yeh, it was definitely her.'

'Where is this house? What's the address?'

'I don't know the address. All I know is that it's a big old house with a gravel driveway, and great big glass lights outside. What do you call them?' Danny scratched his head, trying to think. 'Oh, yeh! Victorian . . . antique lanterns that's what I heard them called. It's a big, scary old house from the outside. It faces onto Barnes Common and it's owned by some shit-stabbing poof pop star, that's all I know.'

'What's his name?'

'Jonnie James.'

'What, *the* Jonnie James? The old-looking guy with the long, blonde hair, is that who you mean?' Lee said, narrowing his eyes at Danny in disbelief.

'Yeh that's the geezer. But you didn't hear it from me, alright?'

Lee couldn't believe what he was hearing. 'Right, you're coming to the police with me,' Lee said, grabbing Danny's cuff.

'I fucking ain't!' Danny pulled his arm away. 'If you call the Old Bill I'll deny everything. I'll tell them you was after me arse.'

Lee closed his eyes and sighed. His mind was in a quandary.

'Is there anything else you can remember? What sort of state was my Donna in . . . was she okay? Who was she with? Was she with a lad named Jason?' Lee fired off question after question, without pausing for breath.

'She was fine. I only saw her for a moment and I don't remember seeing her with anyone,' Danny said, shaking his head and scratching his chin pensively. *Who the fuck was Jason?*

'You absolutely certain there's nothing else you can tell me?' He looked at Danny in earnest.

'Like I said, I only saw her for a moment. But she was definitely the girl in that picture,' he smiled. He felt sorry for the geezer. If someone had bothered to care about him when he was younger, maybe he wouldn't have gone off of the rails and ended up on the streets.

With a hundred and forty quid burning a hole in his pocket, Danny was itching to get away. Suddenly, he sat bolt upright awash with fear, as Harry Delaney entered the pub with a couple of pals in tow. Luckily, they all went straight up to the bar.

Danny seized the moment and whispered to Lee, 'Got to go.' Then darted out of the door.

It happened so fast, Lee couldn't quite comprehend what was going on. But armed with the information that Danny had given him, he wasn't all that concerned.

Lee crossed his legs and took a swallow of beer in quiet contemplation as to what to do next. Elated, that finally his doggedness had paid off. Donna was alive. Everyone around him had thought that he'd lost a screw, and that his unflinching obsession with pounding the streets night after night was a result of some kind of mental breakdown. Lee was well aware of the fact that everyone close to him thought that he'd lost the plot. Wasn't the full ticket anymore: not the return journey.

But Lee knew that he was always in control of his faculties. He couldn't just give up on his daughter and sit by and wait for a body to turn up. Besides, he always believed that Donna was alive, she called out to him every night to come and rescue her. It was the same nightmare he had night after night. Donna reaching out and calling for her daddy as she slowly faded away into the distance. Her voice was so unequivocal, he carried it with him every day. It had given him the strength to carry on, when everyone around him had given up.

Now, his mind was in a quandary as to what to do for the best. Should he keep the info to himself and go over to Barnes and try and find this, Jonnie James's house on his own, or should he go to the police and let them deal with it all.

As Lee put the picture of Donna back into the shoulder bag, Harry Delaney turned around. Resting backwards with his arm on the counter, his dark, beady eyes scanned around the bar and stopped in Lee's direction. Lee zipped up the bag and caught Delaney's stare. They both locked on to each other for a fleeting moment, neither of them backing down. Then one of Delaney's pals put a drunken arm around his shoulder and asked him what he was having to drink. Delaney laughed and turned around and joined in with the merriment.

Lee had the strangest feeling that he had met the man before. For the life of him he couldn't recall where or when. The man's cold stare had sent a shiver down his spine like no other. It was an unnerving feeling that he hadn't experienced for many years. Lee shrugged it off, finished his drink, picked up his bag, slung it over his shoulder and left.

As he made his way towards the door, Delaney turned on his heels and watched Lee pull the door open and leave. He was well aware of who Lee was, he'd seen him on the television appealing to the public for information about the disappearance of his daughter. Delaney smiled inwardly. His pretty young Donna was safe enough with him: one thousand five hundred miles away.

Nevertheless, he wondered what Donna's father was doing up in Soho. What business could he possibly have up here.

Delaney ordered up another round of drinks. When the barman gave him his change he pulled him aside, and asked. 'The man who was sitting over there,' he pointed to where Lee had sat. 'You seen him in here before?'

'What am I, a detective or something? What man?' the barman said, cocking his nose in the air.

'The man wearing the bomber jacket who just left, you seen him before?'

'Oh, him! The dirty bastard who was doing business with one of those despicable little rentable whores that you surround yourself with,' the barmen said, looking down his nose at Delaney with a detestable sneer.

'Doing business? . . . No, I don't believe it,' Delaney said, scratching the dark stubble under his saggy chin.

'I'm not fucking blind, love,' said the barman indignantly, running a finger through his hair and cocking his head. 'I saw money change hands under the table,' he shuddered.

'What did he look like?'

'Who?'

'Come on, Cassie. Nothing gets passed you,' Delaney ingratiated. 'The lad. Is he a regular?'

'Oh, I don't know, let me see,' Cassie said, rolling his eyes to the heavens, irked. 'He was about five-five tall, skinny, short blonde hair, and he had the most beautiful of blue eyes . . . shame he was a whore, really.'

Delaney knew it was Danny as soon as Cassie mentioned the eyes. If there was one thing that Danny had going for him, it was his eyes.

One flash of those alluring, azure eyes and any one of his clients would gladly empty their bank accounts to get at Danny.

The annoying thing was that Danny was at an age now, where he knew how to use his talent to his own advantage. Delaney knew that Danny done business behind his back. He cut him a bit of slack because he was such a prolific little earner for him.

Now that he had Teddy Marston besotted with Danny, Delaney knew he couldn't let Danny do as he pleased anymore. He'd have to reel him and remind him who was boss. He couldn't let anything get in the way of Teddy Marston's relationship with Danny, because he was going to take the man to the cleaners: when the time was right.

But why was Danny having cosy little chats with Lee Carling, and more to the point why was Lee Carlin giving Danny money. He knew Danny only too well, he didn't do anything for anybody unless there was something in it for himself. And it was a cast-iron certainty that Lee Carlin wasn't paying Danny for sex. So why were they in here together.

As sure as night followed day, Delaney wouldn't let anyone compromise his operation. People had tried, all had failed. He would do whatever was necessary to eliminate the threat as soon as it became apparent. He had done it many times before and had no qualms about it again.

Delaney had no scruples whatsoever when it came down to profit. All the kids he had under his control were nothing more to him than a commodity that he traded to the highest bidder. And when they had passed their sell by date – reached an age that they were no longer desirable for his discerning clientele – they were discarded like yesterday's news to fend for themselves.

Most, usually ended up on the streets selling tricks to anyone who'd have them. Delaney had instilled such fear into them all as to what would happen if they ever breathed a word about him and his operation, that they spent the rest of their miserable existence totally traumatised, petrified of their own shadow.

With every single drop of self-esteem sucked out of them and their minds totally fucked up by their experiences, most turned to hard drugs. With no self-preservation it became a matter of time before getting infected with hepatitis or HIV. Very few came through the nightmare and lived to tell the tale.

CHAPTER 12

It was Friday lunchtime and Lee had finished work earlier than he had anticipated. He'd been on the job and hard at it since 6:30 a.m and had done everything that he needed to do by mid-morning. The four, three-bedroom flats he had on sub contract from Metro Housing Trust were ready for second-fixing, so there wasn't much more he could do until the plasterers had finished putting their final spread on the walls and the decorators had made a start.

Now Lee was driving across Hammersmith Bridge and heading towards Barnes. He had a thing about this bridge, he couldn't put his finger on it, but it always lifted his spirits whenever he drove across.

When he was a boy his dad used to bolt a seat and footrest onto the frame of his bicycle and often would cycle across the bridge to the Boileau Arms pub with Lee perched on the crossbar.

Going over the Thames was like a gateway into the countryside for young Lee. The moment he reached the other side it was like a whole new world had opened up in front of his eyes. Leafy lanes, open spaces and huge imposing Victorian houses. It was a million miles away from their two bedroom flat on the Commonwealth Estate.

Lee and his dad would sit outside on the terrace gardens of the pub, and watch gentlemen dressed in white slacks and shirts playing bowls on the green. His dad would often have one-too-many drinks and on the odd occasion – well, quite regularly really – they had fallen off the bicycle on the way home. Lee often arrived home with a grazed knee or a bump to his head. His mother always quizzed him as to what had happened, but his father swore him to secrecy. It was a wonder that Lee didn't end up, "dolly-dimple," the amount of lumps and bumps he had suffered from the mishaps on that bicycle. But he figured that the fun he had on their escapades outweighed the pain.

On a sunny day like today, the view along Thames was magnificent. In the distance on his left Fulham Football Ground could be seen, just before the river snaked around to the right towards Putney Bridge. Across the river on the far bank was the beautiful old Harrods Depository, now converted into trendy expensive riverside apartments.

Lee glanced over to the bank on the right-hand side and saw throngs of people sitting outside The Rutland and The Blue Anchor enjoying a drink in the warm sunshine. It reminded him of happier times when he and his mates used to go on pub crawls at weekends, visiting the numerous watering holes that were dotted along the banks of the river, right up to Chiswick and beyond.

Once over the bridge, everything seemed to step up a gear. The affluence was apparent by the huge double-fronted Victorian houses hidden behind tall hedges and electric gates that lined both sides of Castlenau Road; even the name of the road sounded posh..

Lee drove along Castlenau for about three quarters of a mile until he reached a junction. Right would take him into the centre of Barnes, and straight over the lights would take him through Barnes Common. He decided to press on ahead. Half a mile further the Common opened up on both sides of the road. It was a strange feeling to be driving in the middle of London and yet one could be forgiven for thinking that one was in the middle of the countryside: had it not been for the traffic.

As Lee followed the car in front it, became clear that he wasn't going to find any large houses like Danny had described to him, along this stretch of the road. Just before he reached Barnes Station he swung a right into Station Road. On his right was dense scrub and a small wooded area. To his left was a cricket ground surrounded by tall, silver birch trees. After about two hundred metres he turned left into a narrow lane. This looked more promising. On his right, set back off of the road, hidden behind tall hedges, was a line of imposing detached houses that looked out over the wooded common.

Lee slowly cruised along the quiet lane for about three hundred metres then turned the car around and parked up. He sat for a moment in quiet contemplation, soaking up the ambience of the surroundings.

He got out of the car, crossed the road and strolled back in the direction he had just come and stopped outside the first property he came to. Peering through the tall gates at the immaculately landscaped lawns, fronting a huge red-bricked house, he noticed a couple of kiddies cycles laying on the lawn and a 4x4 on the drive in front of a garage. Disheartened, he carried on walking. He had passed three houses and none of them fitted the description that Danny had given him. He began to wonder if he was wasting his time, maybe he was in a completely wrong area. In the back of his mind he knew that he should have gone straight to Detective Loder and let him deal with it all.

 Lee's mind was in turmoil as to what to do for the best, when suddenly, as he was about to step off the kerb he heard a loud clunk followed by the buzz of an electric gate sliding open. He looked up and just caught the back-end of a silver Mercedes saloon going through the entrance. Its heavy tyres crunched on the shingle driveway as it came to a stop in front of a double garage. The metal shutters cranked up and over automatically and the Mercedes went in, coming to a halt alongside an old E-Type Jaguar.

 Keeping out of sight behind a brick pillar, Lee waited until the gate slid back into its housing. Tentatively, he peered around the pillar and watched as four teenage lads jumped out of the car and started chasing each other around the lawn. The driver's door opened and out stepped a curly, blonde-haired man wearing dark shades, a baggy yellow tee shirt and tight, brightly coloured jeans and pumps. Lee caught sight of his face as he turned and walked across the drive towards the steps up to the front door. The man was tall and skinny and looked like he'd spent more years under a sun lamp than his wrinkled skin could tolerate – his face looked like a dried prune. When he took off his shades and slipped them into his breast pocket, there was no mistaking the man. It was Jonnie James. Lee's first thought was what a mess he looked. His hair was thin and straggly and tied back in a ponytail with tight ringlets hanging down his back. His honey-blonde hair was obviously permed and dyed and his chin sagged like a turkey's.

Peering around the pillar, Lee looked on as Jonnie James called to the boys. They ran across and two of them slipped in either side of him, the other two tailing up behind. With his arms around their shoulders they walked across the driveway and climbed the steps to the arched porch of the red-bricked house. Jonnie James reached into his jeans and pulled out a small bunch of keys, he opened the door and stood aside as the lads all piled in laughing and joking. Jonnie James followed behind, but as he was about to close the door he suddenly shot a glance in Lee's direction. Caught like a fox in the beam of a vehicle's headlights, Lee froze. Too late, he ducked back behind the pillar as Jonnie James eyed him warily, before closing the door.

With his back tight up against the wall, Lee cursed, before breathing a sigh of relief. He wasn't cut out for all this malarkey and now regretted not going straight to Loder. Gingerly, he peered back around the pillar and caught sight of the two glass lanterns that sat perched on thick brick piers either side at the foot of the steps, just as Danny had described to him.

Breathing heavily, Lee was in a quandary as to what to do for the best. Should he just go in and confront Jonnie James, or should he go to Loder. 'Fuck it!' He said, under his breath and launched himself over the gate, and darted up the shingle drive into the open garage.

Composing himself, he closed his eyes and took a few deep breaths. Noticing a door in the sidewall, he made his way towards it. 'Shit!' he yelped as he tripped over a box of empty wine bottles, sending him careering into the wall and hitting his head. Dizzy, he bounced backwards smashing his arse on the wing mirror of the Mercedes, snapping it into pieces onto the concrete floor. It was like a scene from an Inspector Clouseau movie.

Gathering his thoughts, Lee shook his head and made his way towards the door again. He turned the handle and as luck would have it, the door opened. He poked his head around and up to the top of the staircase to where there was another door. He didn't really know what to do for the best. But something drew him to the door above and before he knew it, he was gingerly making his way up the stairs. He reached the top and tentatively, he turned the door handle. No one was more surprised than he, when he found it was unlocked. Lee's first thought was that people like these, deserved to be burgled leaving doors open all over the place.

   He closed his eyes tightly, cursing under his breath when the hinges squeaked louder than an infestation of starved rats, as he slowly, painfully, pushed the door open. Hiding behind it, he waited silently to see if anybody had heard him.

   Nothing.

   He slipped around the door and found himself in a big modern kitchen. Facing him was a long bay window, under which was a long black granite worktop. Below was a row of shiny claret cupboards that stretched the length of the room. Straight ahead was a door, he guessed, that led out to the hallway. In the corner was a circular glass-topped table with six chairs neatly positioned around. In the middle of the table was a thick wax candle enclosed in a tulip-shaped glass vase. Against the wall directly behind him was a huge, metallic-silver, American style fridge.

   Lee crept across the slate floor towards the open door and stood with his back against the wall craning his neck around to get a view along the long hallway.

   Hearing music and boisterous laughter coming from a room at the end, tentatively, he crept around the door and along the hallway hugging the wall as he went. His trainers sank into the soft, deep-pile of the carpet as he moved straight ahead towards the wide entrance area where the street door was. Directly opposite him was an oak panelled wall; above it was a wide staircase with a beautiful, baroque style banister ascending to the floor above. Set in the panelled wall under the stairs was a door leading down to the basement. It was almost undetectable, but for the small brass lever catch that opened it.

   Lee continued along the hallway until he was almost level with the foot of the staircase. To his left was an open, wide, heavy oak door. Bright sunlight spilled into the entrance hall from the tall bay windows inside the room.

   The laughter emanating from the room straight ahead on Lee's right, was now louder: he felt like he had aged ten years by the time he reached it. The door was only slightly ajar, making it impossible to see inside. He held his breath and leapt across to the other side so that he could get a better view.

Inside, he saw Jonnie James sitting in a high-backed armchair smoking, what looked to be a spliff. One of the boys ran past him wearing nothing but a pair of boxer shorts, grabbed it out of his hand and stuck it in his mouth, laughing. Unsteadily, Jonnie James got to his feet and tried to grab it off the boy. The boy teased him by holding it out of reach as he repeatedly tried to grab it from him. Each time he made a grab, Jonnie James's hands seemed, intentionally or not, to brush the boy's crotch or buttocks. Suddenly, he whipped down the boy's shorts, made a grab at his penis and laughed, 'Is that all you've got, Andy?' The boy quickly pulled up his shorts, embarrassed.

'Who the fuck, are you? What are you doing in here?' Came the voice from behind.

Lee spun around. Rooted to the spot his eyes darted towards the front door, then back along the hallway from where he had just come. The rest of the lads piled out into the hallway and wrestled Lee to the floor as he tried to make a dash for the kitchen. Kicking wildly, he tried to fend them off, but one of them had his arms around his throat in a tight headlock. He could hardly breathe. Then two others each grabbed a leg and pinned down his kneecaps so hard it almost dislocated them. Exhausted, he gave up the struggle and lay prone on the deep-pile carpet with each lad taking a thigh to sit on and the other holding his head in a tight headlock.

'Well, who have we here?' Jonnie James said, standing over him.

'Bollocks!' Lee said, struggling to breathe. 'I'm Donna Carlin's father. Ring any bells, you filthy fucking pervert?'

'What on earth are you going on about? Am I missing something here?' He said, shaking his head, confused.

'She was here, at one of your little get-togethers. What have you done with her, you dirty fucking bastard?'

'Who?' His eyes narrowed, suspiciously.

'My daughter, who else. Let the fuck go of me,' Lee struggled. 'I can hardly breathe, here,' Lee strained, trying to pull the boy's arms down from his throat.

Jonnie James nodded and the boy slacked off a little. 'Who told you that your daughter was here?'

Lee thought for a moment. 'Wouldn't *you* like to know,' He bluffed.

Jonnie James tapped his chin with his fist, contemplating for a moment. He knew that Lee was bluffing, nevertheless, no one in their right mind would break into his house and start throwing wild accusations around without talking to someone first: but who? That was the poser. His little soirees were top secret, known only to a privileged few. People who wouldn't breathe a word about the antics that went on within the confines of these four walls. So where did this man hear it from. Jonnie James decided to front it out and go on the offensive.

'Well, the situation as I see it. We have an intruder in my house throwing wild accusations around. Why shouldn't I just call the police and have you arrested for breaking and entering? For all I know you might be an escaped lunatic: a stalker, or something.'

'You know why,' Lee spat, casting Jonnie James a baleful look. 'My guess is that you've got too much to hide, to have the police crawling all over you. I saw what you were getting up to in there. I don't think the police will look too kindly upon your perverted little games with rent boys.'

'Rent boys! Is that what you think?' Jonnie James said, looking around. 'Did you hear that, lads. He thinks that you lot are all paid for by the hour.'

Lee's accusation was met with belly-loads of laughter from them all.

'You don't know *me*, at all.' Jonnie James threatened. 'Or what I'm capable of,' he smiled. 'Now, what to do with you, that's the question.' He pondered.

'Next time I won't make the same mistake, I'll have the Old Bill in tow with me,' Lee strained through gritted teeth.

'Oh! I'm tired of this. Andy, go and dial 999. Tell them we've apprehended an intruder in the process of trying to burgle my home.'

'You're having a laugh. The Bill will never swallow that one,' Lee said, pulling at his restraints.

'We'll see. You forget, I'm a famous celebrity. The police will believe anything I tell them.'

'In your dreams. You're nothing but a washed up seventies pop star who sang crappy songs dressed as an old queen to hide that ageing ugly boat race of yours.'

Jonnie James leaned down to within an inch of Lee's face, and smiled. 'Made me a very rich "Old Queen," though.'

CHAPTER 13

Stuck in a claustrophobic interview room that reeked of stale cigarettes and bad air, Lee had time to reflect on his actions. He had been carted off to Richmond Nick and grilled at length by a couple of over enthusiastic, young, live-wire Detective Constables.

They had accused Lee of almost every crime in the book, from breaking and entering to blackmail, even attempted murder was mentioned. Getting a result from an arrest at a celebrity's home and the undoubted publicity that would accompany it, would be a feather in both their caps. And it wouldn't do their promotion chances any harm either.

Lee had tried to explain the reasons behind why he had entered the property, but it fell on deaf ears. The two officers weren't having any of it. Now sitting alone with nothing to look at but four soulless walls and time to reflect, he knew that it was madness to have gone to Jonnie James's house on his own. He should have gone straight to Loder. What could he have hoped to achieve going it alone: nothing. But just the sight of that flashy, arrogant bastard, James, laughing and joking with those lads was all it had taken. Together with the nagging thought that his daughter *might* have been held at the house, was enough for him to see red and go off on one: nothing or nobody could have stopped him. He had to see for himself.

Suddenly, the door banged open and a thickset man with whispery grey hair, brushed back high on his forehead, came into the room. Behind him, peering over the man's shoulder, was Loder.

The heavy man pulled out a chair across the table from Lee, flattened his tie against his rounded paunch and sat down heavily. Loder took the chair next to him.

'My name is Detective Chief Inspector Monahan,' the man said, opening a folder on the table in front of him. 'You're already acquainted with Detective Inspector Loder. I thought that he ought to sit in on the interview.'

Lee nodded, eyeing the two men warily.

'You have made some very serious accusations against, Mr James,' DCI Monahan said, sliding the file across for Loder to read.

'I know what I saw. Those lads were running around his house half-naked. It was obvious what the dirty perverted bastard was up to.'

'We'll come to that later, Mr Carlin,' Monahan said, cutting Lee short. 'I'm more interested in what you said to my DC's, concerning your daughter. And why you took it upon yourself to pursue Mr James alone and not take this information directly to, Inspector Loder?'

Lee sighed, his gaze dropped to the table. 'In hindsight, I suppose it was a stupid thing to do.'

'Wasn't it, just,' Loder said. 'Look at me, Lee. What did you think you could have hoped to achieve on your own, you stupid bastard?'

'It was a series of events that just ran away with me,' Lee said. His face glowing like a Belisha Beacon.

'You do realise that you have probably done irreversible damage to the investigation, don't you?'

'What investigation? You're having a laugh, ain't you? You lot gave up on my Donna weeks ago.'

'Explain yourself,' Loder snapped, impatiently.

'I thought that if I found out where Jonnie James lived. I could monitor his comings and goings. Then come to you with everything that I had on him.'

'Got ourselves a regular little "Sherlock" here, haven't we?' Monahan said, turning to Loder.

Clearly exasperated, Loder slowly shook his head. 'And?'

'When I saw him drive into the house and then leave the garage doors open, curiosity got the better of me and without any thought of the consequences, I jumped over the gate and made a dash across the driveway. Next thing I knew I found myself inside the house. The rest you already know.'

'Luckily, for you, Mr James doesn't want to press charges, so long as you don't go anywhere near his property again,' Monahan said.

'He's scared that his sordid, perverted lifestyle will be plastered all across the Sunday tabloids, more like,' Lee said.

'Be that as it may,' Loder said. 'Which brings me to my second question. What's all this I heard about Donna being at James's house?'

'I told all that to the other two monkeys. It's in my statement,' Lee said.

'We can do without the smartarse remarks, Lee. Now, tell *me*,' Loder said, resting back on his chair and folding his arms.

'It's like I said. I met this lad in a pub, up in Soho. We got talking—'

'This lad, does he have a name?' Loder cut in.

Lee thought about it for a moment. Then cursed to himself.

'Eh . . . no. I didn't get his name,' Lee said, in a mumble. 'But I got the feeling he was known around the area,' he offered enthusiastically.

'And, how did you come to that conclusion?'

'He was a rent boy.'

'And what "pearls of wisdom" made you come to that conclusion?' Loder said, sardonically.

'He asked me if I was looking for business.'

'What do you mean? Loder said.

'Do I have to spell it out for you?'

'If that what it takes.' Loder countered.

'He offered me sex . . . and anything else in between come to that.'

'I see,' Loder said, picking up the file and resting it on his knee. 'You met a known rent boy in a pub who offered you sex in exchange for money. You didn't get his name, and then out of the blue, he says that he's seen Donna at Jonnie James's house. Why would he say that?'

'I don't know. You're the detective, you work it out.'

'How did this lad know what Donna looked like?'

'I showed him a photo of her.'

'Shall I tell you how it looks to me, Lee?'

'Do I have a choice?' Lee said, getting irate.

'You meet a male prostitute in a pub that you haven't been into before. He sees you as easy pickings, and when you refuse his offer of sex he latches on to your sob story about Donna—'

'It's not a fucking "Sob Story," you bastard! It's my daughter. My flesh and blood. My baby, we're talking about here,' Lee spat, stabbing his finger to his chest.

'Let me finish,' Loder said, holding his hand up to quieten, Lee down. You show this lad a picture of Donna and he tells you what you want to hear. That he's seen her, and she's alive and well. Am I correct?'

'It wasn't like that,' Lee shouted, kicking his chair away, sending it spinning across the room.

'Kicking the furniture around the room isn't going to help matters, is it? How much did you pay him, Lee?'

Lee acquiesced and with a deep sigh, he picked up the chair and sat back down. 'Hundred and forty quid,' he said, wearily.

Loder held out his open palms and shrugged. 'Now, you see how it looks in the light of day?'

'How could I have been so fucking gullible,' Lee said, rubbing his aching temple with his hand. Then he sparked up. 'What I saw at that pervert's house. There was definitely something not quite right going on there. I could sense it. I'm telling you, Inspector Loder, that filthy bastard was hiding something.'

'You let me worry about that,' Loder said.

'You going to follow it up?' Lee asked.

'As I've just said, you let me worry about that. I don't want you interfering with my investigation again. Is that clear?' Loder said, with a look that left Lee in no doubt what would happen to him if he didn't comply.

'Crystal!'

'If there's nothing else?' Monahan said, turning to Loder.

'No, I think we're done, for now.' Loder shot Lee a look that would have frozen most mortals to the spot.

'You're free to go, Mr Carlin. And I don't want to see you in this police station again. Do you understand?' Monahan said.

Lee sniffed, nonchalantly. Got to his feet and made his way towards the door.

'Oh! One more thing, Lee,' Loder said. 'I can't stop you going up the West End night after night. But if I get any complaints of you harassing people, I'll come down on you like a stampeding bull. Do you understand?'

'Absolutely! Detective Inspector Loder,' Lee said, in a cynical sneer.

'Another thing.'

Lee turned, before opening the door and said, 'What's that?'

'If you should happen to bump into that lad again, I want you to contact me, *directly*. That means before scaring him off.'

'Rest assured Inspector Loder, if I see him again, he's all yours,' Lee said, with a wry smile.

'You mind he is.'

Outside in the lobby, Loder thanked Monahan for the phone call and said that he'd keep him informed of any developments. He then made his way out through the glass swing doors, down the steps and across the car park in the direction of his car. He strode across the tarmac fiddling in his trouser pockets for his keys, found them and bleeped the car open. He took out his mobile phone from his jacket pocket, and slid in behind the steering wheel.

While thumbing through the phone's memory, he loosened his tie and unbuttoned the top of his shirt. Loder hated wearing a collar and tie; he found it irritatingly uncomfortable and often chaffed his neck. What people must have thought of him constantly scratching at his neck. God only knows: probably that he had some indescribable skin disease. He felt much more at home in a pair of denims and a simple crew-neck sweater. Recently, he'd even taken to wearing tracksuit bottoms, sweatshirts and trainers when he was off duty. The small circle of friends he surrounded himself with – usually down his local pub on a Sunday lunchtime – often mocked that he looked like an athlete that had lost his way to the track. The fact that he was tall, six three and lean, wasn't down to a rigid fitness regime. It was down to too much alcohol and irregular eating habits. Loder had never trained or ran anywhere, not even for a bus. His life was his job, even more so, since his wife had died.

The tiny cell phone looked incongruous in Loder's huge hands, and trying to scroll through the memory list was a tedious task that almost always ended in disaster with him pressing two buttons at the same time. Finally, he found DS Frost's number and made the call.

'Tony, I want you to dig up everything we have on a, Jonnie James.'

'You mean *the* Jonnie James? The old pop star?'

'The very same. Specifically, see if there's any history of sexual abuse . . . underage or otherwise.'

'Onto it, boss.'

'I'll be back in about thirty-five minutes, traffic permitting.'

'Okay. In the meantime, I'll get Tanya to run his name through the computer.'

Loder glanced at his watch. It was 5:37 p.m. 'I'll see you in The Crown.'

The Crown & Sceptre was a quaint little pub tucked away behind King Street, Hammergrove. Across the road from the new Lyric Theatre. It was about a ten-minute walk from the office. Far enough away from the local pub opposite the Police Station, where most of his colleagues frequented.

Loder never was much for propping up the bar with loose-tongued, egotistical careerists with only their own self-interests at heart. He preferred to keep at arm's length whenever possible, and keep his small trusted team close at hand, away from the temptations that went with associating with the "A Team."

He found an empty parking meter bay across the road from the theatre and reversed into it. As he locked his car, he couldn't help glancing across at the Lyric, just to see what was on. It was a play that he had never heard of and the lead role was being played by an actor, whose name he faintly seemed to recall from somewhere. It would probably dance around his mind now until he came up with the answer.

Every time Loder passed by the theatre, it always reminded him of the countless times that his wife was left standing out in the cold, while waiting for him to arrive. She had loved the theatre. He on the other hand, could take it or leave it, depending on what was playing at the time. So invariably, he would always arrive late with the same lame excuses. *Busy at work. Couldn't get away.* He doubted if they'd seen a single performance from start to finish. Now that he no longer went there, he missed it.

The pub was beginning to get busy with people dropping in for a drink after work. Loder went up to the bar and ordered a pint of bitter from a studious looking girl that he hadn't seen behind the bar before. In his experience, novices serving behind the bar, treated the job and the customers with equal indifference. Loder watched her as she slowly drew his pint, and then let it settle for a moment before topping it up. *Rash judgements again, Loder smiled to himself.*

She placed the perfect creamy pint of bitter on the counter and smiled up at Loder as she took his money, and then again when she handed him his change. It was a bright, affable smile that lit up her face. No matter what sort of shitty day one had, one's spirits were lifted by the experience,

Instead of finding a seat, he stood at the bar and engaged the girl in idle chat while there was no one waiting to be served. After a few minutes, he had learned that her name was Stacey. She was from New Zealand and was filling in time working behind the bar, while waiting to take up a teaching post at Canberra Junior School, on the Commonwealth Estate over at Shepherds Green. Loder wished her luck in her new venture. *And boy, was she going to need it, working in that run down deprived area. Loder suspected that she was unaware what she was letting herself in for. And he wasn't going to be the one to burst the bubble for her.*

He was about to take his drink across to a table when DS Frost and Tanya came through the door. He pointed to a table in the corner under a window and they both made their way towards it. He ordered a pint of lager for his DS, a glass of white wine for Tanya. Then wrapped his meaty hands around the three glasses and brought them over to the table. Gently, he placed them down, careful not to spill anything, then slid in behind the table and sat next to Tanya.

'Well, tell me the worst,' he said, taking a swallow from his glass.

'There's nothing to tell. Jonnie James is as clean as whistle,' DS Frost said.

'Typical. Still, I'm not surprised,' Loder sighed.

'All is not lost, though, boss,' DS Frost said, smugly.

'Oh, what's that?' Loder said, resting back into the seat.

DS Frost opened his palm in Tanya's direction and said, 'Why don't you tell him yourself, Tanya.'

'I made a call to a friend who works in the paedophile unit at the yard. She told me that although Jonnie James has never been convicted of any sexual offences against minors, it is common knowledge that he always surrounds himself with teenage lads and always has one or two in tow. And the grapevine is rife with tales of him hosting private parties for a specially selected circle of people, where sex with youngsters is freely available. Apparently, he's been at it for years but no one has ever come forward or complained about any untoward behaviour.

There's a rumour that he's a member of some highly secret circle of well-connected people No matter how hard the paedophile unit has tried to infiltrate this little club, they always end up with a wall of silence. They just shut up shop and go to ground until the threat has passed. The paedophile unit just haven't got the resources to bring these people to account.'

'And listen to this.' The two men leaned in closer. 'About ten months ago the unit launched an undercover operation to try and infiltrate this group. But they were told by someone above, in no uncertain terms to back off. It was rumoured that the original complaint came from someone high up in the judiciary.'

Loder rested back into his seat, and crossed his leg across his thigh. Brushing flecks of imaginary dust from his trousers, he ruminated for a moment, then said, 'Why don't we give Mr James a visit tomorrow? Couldn't do any harm . . . could it?' A wry smile crossed his lips.

'Absolutely, sir,' Tanya enthused. 'We'd just be, diligent police officers following up on the break-in at his house.'

'A public relations exercise,' Loder smiled.

'See how he reacts when we hit him with the allegations Lee Carlin made against him?' Tony Frost, cut in. 'It would send out a clear message that we're on his case. Might even cause him to make a slip?'

'It's a shame we can't put a tap on his telephone,' Tanya said.

'Let's not run away with ourselves, just yet,' Loder said, nursing an almost empty glass. 'Right now, I need another beer,' He said, finishing the contents of his glass and handing it to DS Frost. 'Your round I believe?'

CHAPTER 14

Sifting through the morning post in his office at the House of Commons, Teddy Marston was in a buoyant mood. He had heard from the chief whip that the party leader had been singing his praises. The polls were showing a marked improvement and it had been made known to Teddy within certain circles of the party, that it was largely down to his efforts.

He was happy with his lot, as he deftly made a neat cut under the adhesive flap of each envelope with a silver letter knife. The slim-handled ornate knife was a family heirloom dating back to the late 19th Century. It had been handed down to him by his grandfather, who opened his own mail with it in this very office, when he was the Member of Parliament for Warwick.

As he ploughed through the stack of mail, he allocated each letter to a different pile in order of importance. Urgent, not so urgent, sometime never and shredder. Thus far, he hadn't come across anything of great importance. There was a couple of invitations to some charity functions, which were always good for a bit of publicity. His wife was an absolute star at such occasions. She had a talent for seeking the maximum exposure possible for herself and Teddy, while assuming an air of compassion and sincerity for the particular charity they were fund-raising for at the time. It was a God-given talent that had come from generations of breeding and manipulation of the under-classes. To the unsuspecting public and the media alike, Lady Marston was a tireless campaigner for the under privileged around the globe. In reality she was an insufferable snob that protected her status and position in life, vehemently.

There were three invitations inviting him to give a talk. The WI could wait. And the LSE Students Union was a no, no – he'd been on the receiving end of those egg-throwing lefties before. The last one looked interesting; Conservatives Abroad. He quite fancied a few days down in Marbella, all expenses paid. After all, the expat Tory voting community down there was a rich source of funding to the party and there was no better man than he, to inveigle them into opening up their fat, off-shore bank accounts for the good of the party.

There was the usual constituency stuff. Mostly complaints from the great unwashed. He would get around to dealing with them in his own time. But he would always make a point of dealing with the most genuine cases: he felt that it was in his own self-interest to do so.

Nothing like grandstanding in front of the television cameras with a couple of his downtrodden constituents. Handing the keys over to a brand new apartment to a hard-working young couple was a sure-fire vote winner.

The hand-written scrawl on a white A4 envelope looked incongruous in amongst the rest of the typewritten correspondence. He held it up to the light, but was still none the wiser. He slid the paper knife under the flap and opened the envelope, emptied the contents out onto the desk and almost choked in horror at what was staring up at him.

He just sat there, completely numb. His eyes firmly fixed on the 10"x8" photographs of Danny and himself together. His whole life flashed before him. Everything that he had spent years striving for, his career, his status, the persona he'd spent years cultivating: all snuffed out in a puff if the media got wind. The thought of the scandal it would bring to his family and friends sent a shiver down his spine.

Quickly, he gathered the photographs up and stuffed them back into the envelope. Teddy didn't need to look at them, he knew exactly when and where they were taken. His first thought was, *why*? Had he not looked after the boy. Had he not given him everything he had ever asked for, money, gifts. How could he have been so stupid. How could he have been so naïve to think that Daniel had feelings for him. What a damn fool he had been.

Teddy got up heavily from his chair and went across to a cupboard in the corner of his tiny office. He opened it and inside was a small fridge. He cracked a couple of ice cubes out of a tray, popped them into a cut-glass tumbler and poured a large measure of single malt.

His mind was in turmoil as to what to do. The strong alcohol soothed him as it slipped effortlessly down his dry throat. Pensively, he went over to the window and stood gazing down at the River Thames. The bright winter sunshine danced on the choppy water like twinkling diamonds. There was something about the never-ending ebb and flow of the tide and the way barges chugged lazily upon the water that usually had a calming, almost tranquil effect over him: not today.

He finished his drink and poured himself another, then sat back down at his desk. With a deep sigh, he picked up the envelope and slid out the contents onto the desk. He then turned them over one by one until he came to a single sheet of A4 at the end. He turned it over and read the short note written in small capital letters with a black felt-tip pen.

The demand was for fifteen thousand pounds in cash, or he would send the originals to the press. Teddy put his elbows on the desk and held his head his hands. Question after question flashed through his mind. Why didn't he just stick to the faceless boys that Delaney had readily supplied to him to satisfy his needs? Why did he let Daniel get so close to him? But if he was honest with himself, he knew the answer to that one. He couldn't get enough of Daniel. He had an insatiable desire for the boy that he had never experienced with anyone else before. Every time he saw Daniel naked, his heart skipped a beat. Daniel was blonde, blue-eyed, extremely pretty and most of all, obliging. *You fool. You utter fool. You stupid, stupid, man*, he repeated over and over to himself.

Suddenly his mobile phone sprang to life to the tune of the "Lone Ranger." It was poignant, because that's exactly how he saw himself. The trouble-shooter, the confident, self-assured man who always got things done. Teddy wished that he could "High Ho Silver, Away" and ride off into the sunset at this precise moment: never to return.

He looked at the caller's ID and his heart sank. 'Good afternoon, Daniel,' said Teddy, pensively.

'I take it you've got the photos?'

'I have. So, where do we go from here, Daniel?'

'I'll ring you tomorrow and tell you where to drop the money.'

'I see. Oh, Daniel! How could you do this to me? I thought that we had something special together.'

'Teddy. It's nothing personal. I need the money to get away and make a new start in life. I've had enough of all this shit. I need to get away and sort me head out. And you're the only way I know how.'

'Daniel, why didn't you just ask me for the money? I would have happily given it to you without all this unpleasantness.'

'Teddy you wouldn't have let me go. If I'd have asked you for money, you would have gone straight to Delaney. Anyway, when he finds out that we've been seeing each other on the side my life won't be worth jack-shit. He doesn't take too kindly to those who punt around behind his back. And it would have only been a matter of time before he found out. He's got too many eyes looking after his interests: you of all people, must have known that, Teddy.'

A resigned silence ensued.

'Come on, be honest with yourself, Teddy. If you couldn't have me, you'd have made fucking sure that no one else did.'

'Oh, I don't know, Daniel. Maybe. I just cannot believe that you would do this to me: not without help.'

'You've got it all wrong, Teddy. This whole thing is all my own doing,' Danny said, proudly. 'This is my one-time chance to get out of all this shit and away from Delaney for good.'

'I'll wait for your call. Goodbye, Daniel.'

Teddy placed phone on the desk and sat in stony silence. His mind swimming in a sea of confusion. *Why me?* He said to himself over and over. No matter how he tried to condemn Danny, he couldn't. He saw a way out and grabbed it with both hands. Who could blame the boy.

If there was any chance of saving his career, he knew there was only one course of action for him to take. It pained him to do it, but he didn't have a choice.

Teddy picked up his mobile phone and punched in the number.

Harry Delaney was still in bed when he took the call. Lying next to him was a new spring chicken he had been sent from a Children's Home up north. The thirteen year old boy had travelled down to London with the assistant warden of the home. The man had been on Delaney's payroll for many years and was a vital part of his web of perversion.

It was simply a question of economics as far as Delaney was concerned: supply and demand. His close-knit team supplied the product, he then sold it on for a profit.

Initially, the warden would groom certain children in his care. Experience told him the easiest to cultivate, usually the fragile, kids that had never had any home life, or been shown any love, were the most vulnerable. First he would set out to win their confidence, show them little signs of affection, shower them with little gifts and generally make a fuss of them. Once he had won them over, he would then make his move.

In the beginning it was subtle, a tickle here, a stroke there, all seemingly innocent fun, affectionate even, but each time getting a little more bold, with lots of playful sexual innuendo. Eventually, with their spirit broken and stripped of any self-esteem, he would use and abuse them for his own personal pleasure. Later they were seduced with tales of the high life down in London. Their heads were filled with promises of money in their pockets, freedom to do virtually whatever they wanted. It all sounded wonderful to young ears and most jumped at the chance of freeing themselves from the evil clutches of their, so called, "carers."

The *truth*, was in stark contrast to what they had pictured in their naïve young heads. First, Delaney used them and abused them for his own sexual gratification. And then when he had broken them, mentally as well as physically, he instilled a terrifying fear as to what would become of them should they ever think of betraying him. Fear, was the weapon that Delaney's whole evil network thrived upon.

As Delaney listened to the irate ramblings of Teddy Marston on the other end of the line, his demeanour changed from avuncular Harry to the cold, calculating, cruel, self-protective man that he was, in a nanosecond. He turned towards his new, lean, olive-skinned spring chicken and kneed him in the back. The boy woke with a start, and with a confused look on his angelic face wondered what he'd done to upset Delaney. He'd been warned from a couple of the other lads that he'd talked to, what a nasty bastard Delaney could be if he ever got on the wrong side of him, and he sure as hell wasn't going to put it to the test.

With his hand over the mouthpiece of the telephone, he indicated with a shift of his eyes for the boy to make himself scarce. The boy took the hint, kicked the quilt down and jumped out of bed. Delaney's lascivious eyes followed the boy's lithe body, as he pulled on his underpants and left the room.

'Let me get this straight,' Delaney said. 'My Danny is blackmailing you?'

'Yes, Harry. He took some compromising photographs of us both in my office, but I thought that he had deleted them.'

'How the fuck did you allow yourself to get into this position, Teddy? You know the rules.'

Teddy Marston was full of apologies on the other end of the line.

'You had better let me have the photographs,' Delaney said.

'Not bloody likely! I'm feeding them into the shredder as we speak.'

Delaney rubbed the tension on the back of his dark, hairy neck. 'Okay, Teddy, calm down. I want to know the moment Danny contacts you with the drop instructions. Is that clear?'

'Yes, Harry.'

'Right, don't you worry about a thing, Teddy. Leave everything to me. I'll sort it all out for you,' Delaney placated, ending the call.

Teddy Marston bit his lip nervously, and emptied a large measure of single malt down his throat. He then replenished his tumbler with another from the half-empty bottle on his desk: it wasn't even lunchtime yet.

He wished he shared Delaney's optimism. He wasn't sure that he'd done the right thing by contacting him; perhaps he could have sorted everything out by himself. At the end of the day he knew that he didn't have a choice: there was too much at stake. Not only for himself but for the whole network. Once word got out that he had compromised everything, he would be cold-shouldered and left out to fend for himself. It was the unwritten rule, keep your distance, your mouth shut and most of all, anonymity was paramount.

He took another long swallow of whisky and closed his eyes as the strong alcohol bit the back of his throat. He prayed that no serious harm would befall Danny.

Ryan was sprawled on the settee in the lounge, watching Jeremy Kyle on morning TV when the boy crossed the lounge. He cast him a baleful stare that left him in no doubt whatsoever that the two of them were never going to be bosom-buddies. The boy quickly scampered through the room and down the hall to the kitchen.

It had been nearly three weeks since Gary had arrived and Ryan had been banished to the spare bedroom. Usually he didn't mind. Delaney always broke the new boys in before anyone else got to them. But this one was different, Delaney liked this one. He knew the tell-tale signs, the fatherly affection, and the little gifts. Just like Delaney behaved towards him when he had first arrived on the scene as a fresh-faced thirteen-year-old. Ryan guessed, the new boy infiltrating his domain was about the same age as he had been . . . just breaking puberty. Fresh and clean and untainted. Just how Harry liked them, ripe for the taking.

Ryan wasn't under any illusions: he knew that at seventeen he was too old for Delaney's tastes. He'd seen it coming for a long time, but he was damned if he was going to let the fat greasy bastard discard him like a piece of yesterday's trash. He knew too much about Delaney's little set-up to go quietly away. Shit, he was an integral part of the whole operation: or so he thought. Ryan was well aware of what Delaney was capable of. He knew he made people disappear when the mood took him. And if Delaney had any thoughts in that direction, for him, he had better think again. He had enough on him to put him away for a very long time, and the same went for his treasured list of VIP clientele.

Delaney stormed into the lounge, his hairy, fat body wrapped in a towelling dressing gown and carrying a bottle of mineral water. 'We've got a problem,' he growled.

Ryan looked up from the TV, unconcerned.

'Turn that fucking thing off. Now!' Delaney barked.

Ryan aimed the remote at the screen and the TV blinked into silence. He swivelled his legs around off the settee and sat attentively.

'So, what's got you all rattled, Harry?'

'It's that little shit, Danny.'

'What's he done now?'

'He's been seeing Teddy Marston out of school.'

'So?' Ryan shrugged. 'You want me to give him a slap?'

'It's a bit more serious than that. He managed to take some compromising photos of Marston and himself playing about in his office. Now he wants fifteen grand from him, otherwise he's going to send the photos to the papers.'

'Danny ain't got the brains to plan something like this on his own. He must have been put up to it,' Ryan said.

'Well, it would seem that he has, from what Marston has told me. I knew that I shouldn't have let Danny get too close to him.'

'It's a bit late for that now, Harry. D'you want me drag him in?'

'When's the last time you saw him?'

'Who?'

'Who do you think? Danny of course,' he said, aiming a foot into his shin.

'Alright, keep your hair on, Harry,' Ryan said.

'I don't know . . . week, maybe. Come to think of it, he has been keeping a bit of a low profile lately.'

'Right, I want you to get out and find the little bastard and when you do find him, don't do anything on your own. Ring me. Is that clear?'

'Yeh, yeh. Alright, Harry,' Ryan said, full of indignation. 'I *do* know the rules, y'know.'

'Mind you do,' Delaney said, with a cold stare. 'Now get your arse off of that settee and find him.'

As Ryan made his way towards the door, Gary came into the room munching a sandwich and carrying a can of coke. He tried to stand aside but Ryan still managed to shove him out of the way as he stormed out. Hard enough to let him know who was calling the shots. Who was number one.

Ryan's little show of contemptuousness didn't go unnoticed by Delaney. He knew that Ryan's nose had been put out of joint by all the attention he had lavished upon Gary. Delaney wasn't a fool, he knew exactly what was going through Ryan's mind. That the boy thought that he was getting the heave-ho for a younger model. Younger, smoother-skinned, and most of all, amenable; just like Ryan was when he came to him, a frightened skinny thirteen year-old. The difference was, Ryan soon learnt the rules and turned them to his own advantage.

Delaney had spotted early on, the way Ryan took control of the other lads. A natural leader, who didn't take any shit from any of them. He had a vicious streak that was frightening for someone so young. Over the years, Delaney had let Ryan assume more and more responsibility for the day-to-day running of things. And up to now it had worked out well for both of them. The truth was Ryan was too old for him now, it had all become too routine. There was no spark. No sense of control. He had tired of him.

In the early days, Ryan had been completely dependent upon Delaney and would do anything to please him. And Delaney made damn sure that he did. He knew very well that Ryan looked upon him as a father figure and although he wouldn't admit to it, he relished the role of mentor and surrogate father. Nevertheless, needs must. This lost soul – as Delaney thought of Gary – standing in front of him chomping on a sandwich, was going to replace Ryan in his bed. The question was, how was he going to let Ryan down without causing a storm. One thing was for sure, if Ryan didn't accept the situation and it threatened his position, more to the point his lucrative business, he wouldn't think twice about getting rid of him: permanently, if need be.

A shard of light from the morning sun shon through the tall lounge window, capturing Gary, like a vision sent from heaven. His hazel eyes sparkled like diamonds and his lean olive skin glistened in the bright sunlight. He smiled a bright, innocent smile that aroused a desire in Delaney that he hadn't felt for a very long time. He had to have him. Delaney held out his hand and Gary acquiesced.

Ryan would have to go: and soon.

CHAPTER 15

It was a little after 9:00 am when DS Frost pulled up outside Jonnie James's house. Loder got out the car and pressed the intercom on the pillar by the side of the gate. There was no answer.

He turned to Tanya and DS Frost, shrugged, then pressed it again. After a minute or so, the speaker crackled to life.

'Who is it?' Said a disgruntled sleepy voice.

'Police.'

'What do you want?'

'A word,' Loder said, laconically.

'What's it about?'

'I'd rather we talked inside please, sir.'

Loder heard a voice cursing in the background. Then a loud clunk as the lock slipped its latch and the gate quietly rolled back. He slipped through the opening as soon as it was wide enough, strode up the shingle driveway and up the steps to the front door like a man on a mission. DS Frost pulled the car around, parked up and followed in his wake with Tanya. Loder rang the bell at the side of the heavy oak-panelled door, then turned around and surveyed the manicured lawn and colourful bedding plants dotted around the horseshoe driveway.

'Some place. Must be worth a fortune.'

'Can't have made it singing crappy pop songs, surely,' said DS Frost, cynically, just as the door opened.

'You would be amazed the riches that comes from singing "crappy pop songs,"' Jonnie James said, with a sarcastic smile, as he stood wrapped in a short towelling bathrobe with the initials "JJ" emblazoned on the breast pocket.

Loder wasn't impressed.

Tanya tried to stifle her amusement but her face told a different story as she enjoyed DS Frost's obvious embarrassment.

'Please, come in,' Jonnie James said, standing aside.

Loder led his two colleagues through the door and into a large, marble-floored reception hall. Tanya could not help being overawed at the sight of a marble star carved in the centre of the floor. Each one of its five points was in a different coloured marble, and between each point was an astrological symbol. The whole thing was visually stunning against the ivory surround – truly a work of art.

'Do you like it?' Jonnie James said, modestly, to Tanya.

'Very impressive,' she replied

DS Frost cocked his head and sniffed, preoccupied, like a bloodhound searching for a scent. A work of art to him was glossing his front door without any runs in the paint.

'I saw the original design when I was a guest at Giorgio's house in Miami Beach. I snapped a couple of photographs and commissioned a similar design. I'm sure Giorgio would have been furious if he'd ever found out: sadly he's no longer with us, so it doesn't matter now, anyway.' He shrugged, insouciantly, and led the officers along the hallway and into the lounge.

When they entered the huge lounge Tanya's mouth dropped open at the sight of the tall bay window framed with silk drapes, and the velvet-studded, crescent shaped seat. In the middle of the room on the far wall was a tall open fireplace with a marble surround and mantle, above which hung a huge, ornate gilded mirror. At the other end was another bay window that looked onto landscaped gardens.

Jonnie James gestured with his hand for the three officers to sit on the leather Chesterfield adjacent to the fireplace while he sat on the one opposite, between them was a very expensive looking mahogany period coffee table.

'My name is Detective Inspector Loder, this is DS Frost and DC Reid.'

Tucking his robe tight between his legs, Jonnie James said, 'I apologise for my state of undress, but we had a late night last night: know what I mean.' He raised his eyebrows conspiratorially at Loder.

'We?' Loder asked.

'Oh, just a few close friends. No one of any interest, just boring music people. I'm promoting my new, young band. How rude of me, I haven't offered you anything to drink. What can I get you, tea, coffee?' He said, getting to his feet.

'Nothing for us, Mr James,' Loder said.

'If you're sure,' he said, sitting back down. 'Now, I suppose you're here about that unfortunate incident that happened the other day. There was no real harm done. Might just as well let the matter rest.'

'That's very magnanimous of you, Mr James,' Loder said.

'Well the man was obviously disturbed in some way.'

Loder's dislike of Jonnie James was increasing with every second he had to sit in the same room as the self-seeking tosser.

Tanya was trying her utmost to stop herself staring at Jonnie James's, long, straggly, honey-blonde, thin locks of hair hanging over his shoulders.

'You are aware that Mr Carlin has made some very serious allegations against you, Mr James?' Loder said.

'Allegations! You surely can't believe the rants of a man who clearly is in need of medical help, inspector?'

'Mr Carlin's state of mind is not for me to judge. But you do understand that we have to follow procedures, otherwise we wouldn't be seen to be doing our job diligently,' Loder said.

'Of course. How can I help?' Jonnie James rested back into the settee.

'In Mr Carlin's statement, he said that he saw a number of young lads frolicking around in . . . how can I put it, in a semi-naked state of undress. And drugs were freely being passed around.'

Jonnie James laughed. 'I can't believe what I'm hearing here,' he sighed, tiresomely. 'Look, Inspector Loder, let me put you straight,' he said, leaning forward and resting his elbows on his knees. 'At the time of the incident, I was entertaining members of my new band that I'm promoting. We were celebrating the fact that I had just secured them a new record deal. As to the question of "frolicking" naked. The boys had just been playing around in the pool. That's all there was to it.'

'I see.' Loder said, fixing him a disbelieving look.

Jonnie James looked at Tanya then DS Frost and knew by their demeanour that they didn't believe a word he had said. He shifted uncomfortably on the cushion for a moment, then rested back and folded his arms, and said, 'Look, officers. I can assure you it was just high spirits, nothing more. Okay, I had a spliff on the go, it was nothing more than a bit of fun. Not against the law what I do in the privacy of my own home, is it?'

'These lads of yours?' DS Frost asked.

'What about them?' Jonnie James said, caught off guard by the question.

'They are all over the age of consent?'

'What are you insinuating?'

'Well, are they?' Loder countered.

Jonnie James, unfolded his arms and sat up. Sniffed conceitedly, and said, 'Of course they are. But I fail to see the relevance.'

'We have to ask, Mr James,' Loder said.

'Do I need to phone my lawyer, here?' A questionable brow raised.

'Depends?' DS Frost said.

'On what?' Jonnie James swivelled around on his seat to face DS Frost at the opposite end of the settee, clearly rattled.

'On whether you have something to hide, Mr James.' Loder countered.

'I've had enough of this bollocks. I have done absolutely nothing that warrants your intrusion into my home, or my private life. I'm the *victim* here, or have you conveniently forgotten that fact,' he said, swishing his hair behind his shoulder with a swift movement of his head.

'I apologise if our line of questioning upsets you, Mr James, but we have a job to do. You must appreciate that?' Loder politely said.

'Yes. Well, I suppose.' Jonnie James composed himself.

'Can I use your bathroom, please, Mr James?' Tanya asked.

'Yes, of course. Out the door and down the hallway.'

Tanya smiled, got to her feet and left the room. Jonnie James eyed her tall, slim figure and shapely arse through her black trouser suit as she left the room.

Loder looked at the pathetic ageing specimen opposite with his ridiculous hair, skinny body, veiny legs and was repulsed. He had been in the game long enough to know that the man was hiding something. He was a player, he was certain of that. A corrupter of vulnerable minds, and worse, a user and abuser who had been getting away with blue murder for years. This cretin had used his status and wealth to indulge in "whatever" and worse, whoever took his fancy, most of his adult life. Loder was in no doubt whatsoever: he could almost smell the fear emanating from every pore of his repugnant body.

Jonnie James sensed Loder's eyes boring into him and quickly averted his attention away from Tanya's arse and faced him with a salacious grin on his face. Not that Jonnie James found Tanya desirable: it was just sex. Loder fixed the man a look that almost made him empty his bowels right where he was sitting.

Tanya closed the lounge door behind her and quietly made her way up the hallway to where they had come in. She stood in the middle of the marble star and peered up the wide staircase to the landing above. She went across to the foot of the stairs and gripped the thick, polished wood banister and tentatively climbed the first step. As her weight bore down on the hardwood there was a loud creak. *Shit,* she uttered under her breath and stepped back onto the marble floor. Deciding that she didn't have the time to go mooching around upstairs, she tiptoed across the reception hall, careful not to click her heels on the marble and went through an open door.

The room was of similar size and layout as the lounge, with the exception that above the fireplace, was a full-length portrait of Jonnie James with microphone in hand, clad in a glitzy Lurex cat suit and white, knee-length platform boots. Tanya stood back and took in the garish picture staring down at her with black, heavily made-up eyes and false lashes.

Egocentric wanker, she smiled to herself. Behind the door was a huge glass display cabinet that almost stretched the length of the room. She couldn't help herself having a nose inside. The shelves were stacked with photographs of Jonnie James with just about everyone and anyone. From shaking the queen's hand – Royal Variety Performance 1976 – to posing with The Beatles – Abbey Road Studios 1969. Every bit of available wall space was filled with rows of platinum, gold and silver discs framed in glass. Tanya was fascinated by it all. The room was a treasure trove of pop history: she only wished she had the time to take it all in.

   She left the room and quickly made her way down the hallway to find the toilet. She found it soon enough, or more to the point it found her. The door was ajar and there was light shining out into the hall. She poked her head around the door but there was no one around. The bathroom – it would be an insult to call it a toilet – was of a luxury mere mortals could only read about in up-market glossy magazines. All the walls were mirrored, a double-sink was sunk into a black granite top, and a huge bath that could almost accommodate a football team – and very likely had on numerous occasions, filled half the room.

   Tanya depressed a button in the wall above the toilet and the cistern flushed, then went across to the vanity unit to wash her hands. She looked at her reflection in the mirror, and sighed. She was looking tired, haggard: the crows-feet that appeared around her eyes when she smiled were now becoming a permanent fixture. She made a promise to herself that as soon as she had the time, she would book a facial and get her hair done, perhaps something a little shorter, more fashionable. She dried her hands under the hot-air blower and made her way out. The thought already slipped from her mind.

   As she was about to make her way back to join the others, she heard a noise. She turned and walked towards a closed door adjacent to the bathroom and listened for a moment. She then turned the handle, opened it and peered around it.

   A young lad wearing nothing but a long-peaked baseball cap and a pair of boxer shorts that made his spindly legs look like lollypop sticks was drinking juice from a carton in front of a huge American style fridge.

The sound of Tanya's heels on the terracotta-tiled floor startled the lad so much, he almost drowned himself with the juice. Wiping his mouth with the back of his hand, he slammed the fridge door shut with a swivel of his hip, and said, with teenage indignation, 'Who are you?'

'I might ask you the same,' Tanya replied.

'I asked first.'

'What is this, a game?' Tanya asked, walking towards him and taking the carton from his hand.

Loder handed Jonnie James a photo of Donna Carlin, and asked, 'Have you ever seen that girl before?'

Jonnie James perused the picture for a moment then handed it back to Loder. 'No. Never seen her before in my life. Why do you ask?'

'She's gone missing—'

'What's that got to do with me?' Jonnie James snapped.

'We're just following a routine line of enquiry, Mr James,' Loder said, handing him the grainy picture of Jason and Donna together. 'What about him?'

Jonnie James glanced at it and handed it straight back. 'No.'

'You seem very certain. Loder handed the picture back. 'Have another look.'

Jonnie James pressed his tongue against the inside of his bottom lip. His mouth was dry. He held the picture at arm's length and narrowed his eyes to focus. 'No, never seen either of them before. Wouldn't have any reason to, would I?' His mind was racing. He wasn't quite sure at first, but there was no mistaking the picture of Ryan, even though it was a dark grainy copy.

'I don't know, Mr James. You tell me.' Loder countered.

'Oh! I get it.' He clapped his hands together, leaned forward and rested his arms on his thighs. 'This is all about that lunatic that broke into my house, isn't it?'

'As I just said, we're following a number of lines of enquiry, Mr James.'

'Look, inspector . . . Loder,' Jonnie James said, resting back into the cushion again.

DS Frost observed his nervy demeanour and knew that he was putting up a front. Inside, the man was shitting himself, he'd seen the signs a thousand times over.

'I am a famous celebrity and I get kids camping outside my house all the time. It's something that I have to put up with.' He sighed tediously. 'I don't give them a second glance. Sometimes, I take refreshments down to the gate and sign a few autographs. Maybe this girl was seen among them . . . I couldn't say.'

Self-important, egocentric wanker, Loder thought to himself.

'Our information is that the girl was seen inside *this* house, possibly with the lad in the photograph.'

'Detective Inspector, I've already said that I have never set eyes on those two people in that photo. I have my reputation to think of, so if you want to question me further, then you'll have to go through my lawyer,' he said, getting to his feet and tying his robe tight around his skinny body. 'If you don't mind I'd like you all to leave.'

'Thank you, for your time, Mr James,' Loder said, locking eyes with him as he got to his feet. *Reputation? you cocky bastard! If I find out your lying to me, I will rip your "Reputation" to shreds.*

'Are we leaving?' Tanya said, entering the room. 'Just met your "nephew." Seems a nice *boy*,' she said, her voice full of derision.

Jonnie James said nothing. His face glowering like a traffic light, he strode out of the room, opened the front door and stood aside. 'If you don't mind, officers.'

DS Frost and Tanya went out first with Loder following behind. As he was about to leave he turned, and said, 'We'll be in touch.' Then looking over Jonnie James's shoulder he saw a young, teenage lad standing by the lounge door wearing a pair of boxer shorts and a long-peeked baseball cap. 'Can't say I see any family resemblance,' he mocked.

Jonnie James shot the boy a burning look that said, what are you doing down here. 'Some might say that that is a blessing.' He hit back at Loder as he closed the door.

'I thought I told you to stay upstairs out of sight,' Jonnie James spat, knocking Danny's cap off with the back of his hand, as he walked back into the lounge.

'I was thirsty. I'm sorry, John.'

Clearly piqued, he cast him a condescending look. 'how many times do I have to tell you, my name is "Jonnie," and don't you forget it.'

Danny plonked himself on the settee next to him, and slid his hand under his robe and up the inside of thigh until he found his penis, and teased, 'I'm sorry, Jonnie.'

He slapped his hand away. 'Not now, Danny. Be a good boy and get the phone for me.'

Danny jumped to his feet, went across to a small Regency style table against the wall and tossed over the portable phone. 'I'll go and make us a cup of tea,' he said, disappearing out of the door.

Jonnie James punched in the number that he had engraved on his mind. He relived the last hour while waiting for the phone to answer, until finally he heard, "yeh" on the other end of the line. *Such an articulate man.*

'I've just had a visit from the police.'

'What's that got to do with me?' Harry Delaney replied.

'It's got everything to do with you. They were asking questions about that young girl you brought here. They showed me a picture of your boy, Ryan, with her. It wasn't a good picture. Ryan was wearing a hood, but there was no mistaking, it was him.'

'You didn't tell them anything, did you?'

'What do you take me for? The police have obviously been tipped off, otherwise, how would they have found their way to my house. I think that you have a bad egg in your clutch, Harry. We apprehended an intruder in my house yesterday. And do you know who it was?'

'I haven't got time for amateur dramatics,' Delaney said.

'The girl's father. Someone must have told him. And it must have come from your camp, so deal with it.'

'Don't you dictate to me,' Delaney spat back. 'I'll sort it. Leave it to me.'

'You had better. I do not want the police around here again. After all, I have my reputation to think of.'

Delaney rolled his eyes, *sanctimonious cunt,* but held back from giving the man a volley. 'We'll talk later,' he said, and slammed the phone down.

Standing behind the door out in the hallway, Danny heard everything. He was safe here with Jonnie, as long as Delaney didn't find out. It was more than "darling" Jonnie's life was worth to let on that he was staying here. He would stroke his ego – and his bald wrinkly dick – for a couple more days and then he'd have it on his toes with Teddy Marston's lovely dosh.

*

Delaney stood in his lounge looking out of the window watching an irate motorist giving a black traffic warden a mouthful of abuse. The warden just stood there writing a ticket completely oblivious to the tirade of insults that the motorist was firing at him. To the warden, another ticket issued was another ticket less to meet his weekly target and more importantly, more commission in his wage packet.

Ryan came into the room holding a plate piled with bacon sandwiches. He ensconced himself in the armchair, aimed the remote at the television and settled down to watch the Jeremy Kyle show. 'You want one of these, Harry?' he said, chomping into a doorstep of thick bread.

Harry Delaney turned around and looked down at Ryan tearing into the sandwich as if it was his last meal on this earth. It turned his stomach, seeing the grease and brown sauce dripping down the side of his mouth. 'What's happening about Danny? You heard anything?'

Ryan shook his head, completely entranced with two fat ugly women fighting over the same man on the television. The craggy-faced man was just sprawled on a chair, smiling as proud as punch that he had two women fighting over him.

The sandwiches flew up to the ceiling and the plate smashed into pieces as Delaney's shoe found its underside. 'I asked you a question.'

Ryan just sat in the armchair wide-eyed, open-mouthed, riveted with shock. He wiped his chin clean and looked up at Delaney.

'I asked you a question,' he repeated. His eyes as cold as ice.

'Harry I've been everywhere, honest. Danny has disappeared off the face of the earth. No one has seen him for days.'

'He can't be far away. Someone must be putting him up, somewhere.'

The tension between them was broken by the appearance of Gary entering the room wrapped in a clean, fluffy bath towel. 'Is it okay if I run a bath, Harry?' he tentatively asked, flicking his long eyelashes at him.

'Of course it is,' Delaney melted. 'I'll be in, in a minute to soap you down,' he leered lasciviously.

Ryan saw the look on Delaney's face. It was just how he used to look at him when he was fresh and clean. When *he* was Gary.

He could see now that there was no way back for him, no matter how much he put the frighteners on Gary. All he was to Harry Delaney was a dogsbody who kept the troops in check. Someone who did all the dirty work, while he, the unctuous fat child abuser, reaped all the profits. At that precise moment, he saw the man for what he was, a vicious, vile, paedophile that would stop at nothing to get what he wanted.

Ryan made the conscious decision to get out at the first opportunity. Then he was going to bring the whole pack of cards tumbling down around, Harry fucking Delaney. He would take great pleasure in watching him drown in his own mire.

But first, there was something that he had to do to ease his own conscience of mind.

Gary left the room, closing the door behind him. Delaney gave Ryan a kick in the shin. 'get the fuck up, and find, Danny. And don't come back until you've found the little bastard.'

Ryan winced at the pain shooting up his leg, but refused to show it as he stood up and faced, Delaney. They locked eyes with each other, neither backing down first. Ryan hadn't realised it before but he was taller than the fat bastard. Delaney sensed the boy's hostility and for a fleeting moment felt a rush of fear wash over him. He took a step backwards. Ryan turned and made his way towards the door. 'And clear this mess up before you go,' Delaney said.

'Bollocks! Do it yourself,' Ryan said, without turning.

CHAPTER 16

Loder was out in the incident room striding back and forth along the murder board, like a sentry guarding the crown jewels. Deep in thought, he perused the collage of photos and flow charts searching for something, anything, that would kick-start the investigation.

An air of defeat weighed heavy on his shoulders now that the case had been scaled down. Gone was the hubbub of enthusiasm that filled the room when the investigation got off the ground, and the office was packed with eager young officers sifting through mountains of data.

'There has to be something that we've missed. I can't believe that two people,' Loder pointed to the grainy picture of Jason and Donna, 'Could just disappear off the face of the earth. Where is Donna being held? More to the point, who is this, Jason. Someone must know him. And who is protecting him, or hiding him. People do not just disappear like that.'

'Jonnie James knows a lot more than he's letting on. He is the key to all of this, I'm certain of it. And we need to find that lad, Lee Carlin met in the pub.'

'You don't think that he was winding Lee up, boss?' DS Frost said.

'Can't be sure, but we need to eliminate him from the enquiry.'

Loder stood back and sat on the edge of a desk. He looked at the board and shaking his head, he said, 'Look at all these pictures of Jason.'

DS Frost and Tanya got to their feet and joined Loder, standing each side of him.

'Look at the clothes he wears.' Loder said, scratching the stubble on his chin.

'It's all designer stuff,' Tanya offered.

'My thoughts, exactly. Not many hard-working parents can afford this stuff for their kids.'

'Could be knock-offs?' Tanya said.

'Good point, Tanya. What I'm saying is, look at his demeanour. The way he carries himself,' Loder said, tilting his head to one side and nibbling the inside of his mouth, deep in thought. 'In all the CCTV footage that we've trailed through, Jason comes over as a cock-sure, little gangster. This lad has street cred. And more to the point, he's known.'

'Do you think that it might be an idea to circulate his photo around the local children's homes, sir?' Tanya said.

'Can't do any harm.'

'Might as well have a search through the missing persons' data base while we're at it,' said, DS Frost.

'Good idea, Tony.'

'I think that our Jason has done this sort of thing before. I think that he's an active player on the Internet. He obviously turned Donna's head. Otherwise, why would she have agreed to meet him: a perfect stranger?'

Tanya and DS Frost both nodded.

Loder went across to the board and tapped the picture of Laura Davidson. 'And, I bet on Mother Teresa's virginity, that Jason had something to do with Laura's disappearance.'

'You do know the rumours about Mother Teresa, boss?' DS Frost quipped.

Urgh! How disgusting. You really are a sick-minded pig, Tony,' Tanya said, shaking her head in disgust.

Loder couldn't help a smile.

The phone on the desk behind shrilled, diffusing the atmosphere. Tanya answered it, then offered the receiver to Loder. 'DCI, for you, sir.' Loder took the handset from her, listened for a moment and put it back onto the hook. 'I'm wanted upstairs,' he said, rolling his eyes tediously. 'Right, you know what you have to do. Let's get to it.'

Loder straightened his tie outside DCI Oakwood's office, then knocked and poked his head around the door. 'You wanted to see me?'

'Come in, John. Sit down,' DCI Oakwood said, sitting behind a huge desk that seemed to swallow her up.

Loder ensconced himself in the comfortable high-backed chair facing her and casually crossed his legs.

'How's the investigation going, John? Would you care to update me?'

'We're following a couple of new lines of enquiry,' he sighed. 'Hopefully, we'll get some new leads from them.'

'I hear that you gave Jonnie James a visit?' she said with a wry smile. 'That must have been . . . interesting?'

Loder picked up on her tone of voice and intuitively knew that she was holding the deck of cards. 'Yes, well, what can I say? We were acting on information received, Anne. It's all in the report. I take it you're up to scratch with everything?'

'I'm up to scratch, alright. I've just had a mouthful from, "he who has to be obeyed,"' she said, looking to the heavens for help.

'Oh!'

Anne Oakwood looked over the top of her thin-framed designer spectacles and said, 'Is that all you've got to say? Oh,' she smiled.

Loder knew that she was toying with him.

'Jonnie James's solicitor has been on the phone complaining about everything from harassment to police brutality. As far as he is concerned, it's down to us that his client hasn't had a hit record for the past twenty years.'

'Not guilty. Never touched the repugnant, little creep,' Loder smiled.

Anne Oakwood held her hands up in submission. 'It's not me you have to convince, John,' she said, placing her palms down on the desk and heaving her trim frame up, as if she was carrying the weight of the world on her shoulders. She walked over to a water dispenser in the corner of the office and filled two plastic cups.

Loder eyes fell on her petite shapely bottom as she strode across the room in a pair of black flared trousers that hugged her body like a glove. *Forget it Loder, she's your boss. Nevertheless!*

She went over to Loder, and resting against the front of her desk she handed a cup to him. He held the fragile receptacle between his thumb and forefinger then held it up in front of him, gestured cheers, and sipped at the cool liquid.

'Marvellous! Just what I needed,' he said, with a hint of sarcasm.

'I've been told that we've got to back off where Mr Jonnie James is concerned.'

'Typical. If I had the resources I'd put the sleazy bastard under surveillance.'

'Why?'

'I can't put my finger on it, but there's something about him. He's a self-assured, cocky, manipulating shit, who's been hiding behind a façade for years,' Loder said, handing her the flimsy empty cup.

'What are you getting at, John?' Annie Oakwood leaned back and tossed the cup into the wastepaper bin.

'I don't know . . . it's just a feeling that's been gnawing away inside me. You know, he had a teenage lad in the house with him when we were there?'

'Was he a minor?'

'I don't know, I didn't get much of a look. Tanya bumped into him when she was having a nose around. Said that he was James's nephew and was staying with him for a few days.'

'And?' Anne Oakwood said, folding her arms.

'And, nothing.' Loder shrugged. 'The lad was there on his own accord. Tanya got the feeling that he was spinning her a yarn. Said he was a cheeky, streetwise little urchin.'

'Do you think the boy was a prostitute?'

'Well, Tanya was convinced that he was. But proving it, is another thing.' He shrugged.

Anne Oakwood unfolded her arms and placed her palms down on the side of the desk. As she did so, her breasts rode up, pressing an outline of her small nipples against her silk blouse.

Loder looked, wide-eyed. He couldn't help himself.

She caught his gaze. 'What's the matter? Have I suddenly grown horns, or something?' she said, looking down at herself and realising what Loder was staring at. She couldn't hide her embarrassment and quickly moved behind her desk and sat down.

'I must apologise Anne. I don't know what—'

'Forgotten, already,' she said, composing herself. 'You were saying?'

'Saying? Oh, yes,' he said, picking up the thread. 'It appears that there have been whispers and rumours flying about for years as to Jonnie James's sexual preferences.'

'Is that so?' she replied, now back in control.

'The paedophile unit have had him in their sights for years, but could never get near enough to make anything stick. They reckon that he's a member of some underground network that trades in kids.'

'What!' Anne Oakwood furrowed her brow, uncomprehending. 'Are you saying that he's involved in child trafficking?'

'No. I think it's some kind of paedophile ring. Not young children, but teenagers.'

'Oh! So that makes it acceptable, does it?'

'No, of course not. I was just stating a fact.'

'Sorry, Loder. It's just that I find the whole thing . . . abhorrent,' she said, shaking her head with disgust. 'Please, carry on.'

'And from what I'm led to believe, this ring encompasses some of the highest echelons in society. It seems that whenever the paedophile unit gets a foot in the door, they're always one-step ahead of the game and just close ranks and shut up shop. No one has ever been able to get near any of them. And from what I've been told, this network has been in operation for years.'

'That would account for the way the order to back off came down.'

'What do you mean, Anne?'

'The order didn't come from the Super: it came down from the heavens. Jonnie James's solicitor has connections, very high up the ladder. If you get my meaning, John?'

Loder said nothing. Just a resigned nodded.

'That brings me to the bad news.' She placed her spectacles onto the desk and clasped her hands in a praying position under her chin. 'I've also been ordered to scale down the investigation. The excuse being that resources would be better placed in tackling teenage gun crime on the streets.'

'I don't fucking believe it.'

'Well, I wouldn't put it quite so candid, John. But—'

'I do apologise. Mouth opened before the brain was in gear.'

'You seem to do a lot apologising in my company,' Anne Oakwood, mocked.

'I'm still getting my head around having a woman as my boss, I suppose,' Loder said. Then quickly corrected himself. 'I *do* mean that in a positive way, Anne.'

'Glad to hear it, John,' she teased.

What is going on here? Is she sending out, come on, signs? Or just taking the piss?

Loder crossed his legs and pulled himself back onto a professional plane. 'So, where do we go from here?'

'Your guess is as good as mine?' She shrugged.

'Donna *is* still alive, you know. I'm convinced of it,' Loder said, breaking her train of thought.

'Why are you so sure?'

'Because if she was dead, we would have found a body by now. Someone would have stumbled across her. I think she's being held captive somewhere. And I think that this Jason, or whoever his name is, is just a pawn working for someone a lot more powerful. Furthermore, I reckon that our Jason had something to do with the disappearance of the first girl, Laura Davidson.'

'Let's hope so, John. Look, obviously, I've got to seem to be doing as ordered. Nevertheless, I'll keep the relocation of personnel to a minimum. You and your immediate team carry on as normal, okay?'

'What about the flack?'

'You let me worry about that. You just find that poor girl.'

'If that's all? I'll get back down to it.' Loder said.

'God, Loder, do you *ever* stop thinking about sex?' She said, jumping on the double entendre of his statement.

Loder turned and was about to apologise . . . again. But she licked her finger and struck it in mid-air.

He nodded. One nil to you. Then glanced at his watch. It was 6:28 p.m. 'Do you fancy a drink?' he said, without thinking.

'Yes, why not. I've just about had enough of this place for one day.'

'Okay, meet you down in the compound in five minutes,' he said, disappearing out of the door.

Anne Oakwood was already waiting when Loder burst through the heavy doors that led onto the compound that doubled as a car park. He pulled the collar up of his camel overcoat and buried his hands deep into the pockets to keep out the chill of the damp night air. He made his way over towards his boss and said, 'Shall I drive, save taking two cars?'

'Are we not going to the Crown & Sceptre?' she asked.

'Thought we'd go somewhere away from prying eyes: you know what the rumour mongers are like in this place?'

'Why, are you ashamed of being seen in my company, Loder?'

'Of course not. It's just . . . well, we'll be able to talk.'

'I suppose you're right. Where have you got in mind?'

'Somewhere down on the Thames? What about The Doves?'

'Mmm, sounds good. Make a nice change.'

Loder pointed the remote at his car and the indicator lights flashed, as the central-locking released. He opened the door, took off his overcoat, tossed it on the back seat and slid in next to his boss. He started the engine and made his way out into the evening rush hour traffic.

'Probably be quicker to walk,' Loder said, as the car crawled along bumper to bumper.

'Perhaps, it wasn't such a good idea, after all?'

'Oh well, might as well stick with it now,' Loder said, switching on the radio.

It had taken them nearly twenty-five minutes to travel the mile or so to the pub. The entrance to The Doves opened into a narrow, dimly lit alley, still laid with its original seventeenth century cobbles. On the opposite side, behind a high railing stood a group of magnificent Georgian houses set in beautiful landscaped gardens that bathed in a haze of yellow sodium floodlight. The original glass gas lamp still shone dimly above the pub entrance.

Inside was warm and welcoming, as Loder held the door open for his boss and followed her up to the counter. A coal-fire glowed brightly in the grate in the corner of the snug bar. The pub was reputed to have been a regular stopping off Inn for dignitaries and royalty, when travelling upstream to Hampton Court. And if the sticky, nicotine-brown ceiling was anything to go by, it was probably true. Charles 11 and Nell Gwynne were reputed to have canoodled together in the rooms above on many occasions.

'What can I get you to drink, Anne?' Loder asked.

'A glass of red wine would be nice, thank you.'

He ordered a pint of bitter for himself and a red wine for his boss, and thought about ordering a large malt chaser, but decided against it, given that he had to drive. The pretty barmaid handed him his change and smiled. They then wandered up a creaky, oak staircase and out onto a covered terrace, where they sat at an empty table in the corner overlooking the River Thames. There was an awning stretched across both ends of the terrace to keep out the wind and a gas umbrella heater sent swirls of warmth around the tables, which made it all quite cosy.

Loder gazed out across the dark water towards Barnes – a leafy suburb of South West London. Twinkling coloured lights shined in the distance, as the chilly breeze brushed through the tall, silver-birch trees that lined the towpath on the opposite bank. Less than a mile downstream Hammersmith Bridge stretched across the water, its precarious magnificence, illuminated in the headlights of the constant stream of traffic crossing back and forth. The endless flow of heavy duty traffic over the years had taken its toll on the old bridge, so much so, that it had to be closed on numerous occasions for essential repairs. Now heavy traffic was severely restricted.

The IRA had picked up on its weakness and planted a huge bomb under it in 1997, luckily it failed to go off. It is said that the bridge still drops a couple centimetres every couple of years.

Anne Oakwood unbuttoned her cashmere overcoat and took a sip of wine. Looking at Loder just staring across the dark openness, it suddenly crossed her mind how good-looking he was. There was no doubt that the years had been kind to him. His curly hair had greyed a little and was wearing a little thinner. The lines across his brow and along his jowls were cut deeper with age, but with his strong jaw line, it just served to give him a rugged sort of handsomeness that only came with age. In another world, away from the rigour and stresses of her job, and the fact that they were colleagues, she could quite easily be taken by the likes of John Loder.

'Penny for them?' she said, taking a sip of wine.

'Oh, I'm sorry. I was miles away,' Loder said, taking a long swallow from his glass.

'I was just thinking that Jonnie James lives a stone's throw from here. Perhaps I ought to give him a surprise visit: might catch him at it.'

'I don't think that would be a very good idea, John. Besides, it would be me that would have to pick up the pieces when the proverbial shit hit the fan.'

'I suppose you're right. Still all the same,' he said, with a mischievous smile.

'No! Absolutely not,' she smiled back at him.

'Okay. Cheers!' He said, chinking his glass against hers. 'Let's forget about work for a while.'

'Fine by me. What do you want to talk about?'

'Let's talk about you.'

'Me! I'm just a boring DCI who works all the hours God sends. What's left over, I use catching up on my beauty sleep. Nothing exciting I'm afraid.'

'No, secret lovers on the go?' Loder teased, cheekily. But he was intrigued.

'Oh, come on, John. What do you take me for?'

'You're a very attractive woman. I can't believe that you live a life of solitude. You must have some little secret indulgence.'

'Afraid not. What you see is what you get,' she said, with open arms.

Loder raised an eyebrow at her candour.

'Loder!' she said, sheepishly. 'What are you suggesting?'

'Another drink?' he said, finishing his glass and getting to his feet.

'Why do I get the feeling I might need one,' she said, handing him her empty glass.

While Loder was away, she gathered her thoughts, trying to make out what kind of signals Loder was sending out. Was she completely misreading the signs, or was it just a bit of harmless teasing.

He returned with their glasses replenished, sat down and began drinking his pint when he noticed over the top of his glass that she was looking at him in a funny sort of way.

'What have I done *now*? He said.

'My, you *do* have got a guilty conscience, Loder.'

He relaxed back into his chair, crossed his legs and pulled out a packet of panatelas. Fishing around in his trouser pockets, he finally got his hands on a disposable lighter and lit up. Brushing some flecks of ash from his trousers, he blew a thick cloud of white pollution into the night air, and watched it drift away in the cool night breeze.

Anne Oakwood caught a whiff of smoke as it passed overhead and sniffed deeply, savouring the rich woody aroma. She adored the smell of cigar smoke, even more so, since she gave up the cigs eight months before.

'Do you mind if I have a little smoke of your cigar, please?' she asked.

'Are you sure?' he said, taken aback.

'Of course. I wouldn't ask, otherwise.'

He handed her the long, slim cheroot and she drew on it deeply, blowing half the smoke out immediately, taking the rest down deep into her lungs. Then with a satisfying sigh, she closed her eyes, tilted her head backwards and blew the rest out into the night air.

'Heaven,' she smiled, contentedly.

'I didn't know that you smoked,' Loder said.

'I don't. Well, not for eight months, three days and,' She looked at her watch, 'two hours and twenty three minutes.' She rolled her eyes in frustration.

'I know exactly how you feel, Anne. It's been over twelve months since my last cig, but I just can't quit altogether,' he said, conspiratorially. 'You might as well finish that,' he said, taking out another cigar and lighting it. 'Just don't blame me if you start again.'

Happy and relaxed, for the first time in . . . she couldn't remember how long, she took a sip of wine and then another long drag on the cigar. She started to feel a little light-headed. Maybe, it was the rush of the smoke going straight to her head: or the wine. Drinking on an empty stomach was never the most sensible thing to do, and she hadn't eaten anything since breakfast.

Loder couldn't help looking at her as she happily puffed away in a little world of her own, completely oblivious to his attentions. There was something about this little woman sitting opposite him that he found incredibly desirable. He couldn't put his finger on it: maybe, it was the fact that she was sitting smoking a cigar, which looked completely incongruous, perched between her slim, little fingers. Or maybe the fact that she had an incredibly sexy deep voice and was a stunner to boot. Then it hit him, he had it, he had the answer. It was the fact that she hid her sexiness in a shell of hard-boiled professionalism. Loder suspected that she was unaware of just how incredibly attractive and sexy she really was.

'Are you hungry?' He said, casually, watching the delight suffuse her face as another cloud of smoke drifted away on the night air.

'Famished.'

'Do you want to get something to eat?'

'What you got in mind?'

'Don't know. Curry, Chinese, you choose?'

'I've got an excellent Chinese around the corner from me. Why don't we get a takeaway and I'll open a bottle of wine,' she said, without thinking.

'Sounds good to me. Shall we drink up?' he said, finishing his beer in one long swallow.

'Whoa, tiger! Don't start getting any ideas. It's just *food* on the menu.'

It took just forty minutes from leaving the pub, picking up the food and driving through the impressive entrance to where Anne Oakwood lived. It was a tall private block of flats overlooking Haven Green in Ealing. The cream and green, Art Deco façade was truly impressive, and judging by all the prestige vehicles parked on the forecourt, Loder guessed, expensive, too.

She directed him to her reserved parking space and they got out of the car. Taking the lead, she led the way towards the glass-fronted entrance with the carrier bag full of food while Loder skirted up behind. Once inside, they walked past the empty reception desk, across the polished marble-floored lobby towards the lift. As they waited for it arrive, Loder's eyes drifted upwards. He spun around on his heels and drank in the full splendour of the magnificent fresco on the ceiling with concealed lighting, highlighting the scene.

'Some place, this, Anne.'

'They film quite a lot Poirot, here,' she said.

Loder looked at her, nonplussed.

'The television programme . . . Agatha Christie's, Detective Poirot. Have you not seen it?'

'Well, obviously I've heard of him, but I can't say I've seen it on TV.'

The lift arrived, saving his embarrassment of his obvious lack of television knowledge. Loder didn't watch much mainstream TV. He preferred the sport, the odd movie, documentaries and harboured a secret passion for quiz shows.

Once inside the flat, Anne Oakwood went to the kitchen while Loder waited in the lounge. The room was much more spacious than he imagined. High ceilings with decorative cornicing. Neutral coloured, painted walls, pastel green carpet, black, leather sofa and armchair.

The place looked crisp and tidy, like a show flat that a developer would present to prospective buyers.

Everything seemed to have its own designated spot. Its own small piece of territory. Even the magazines on the glass-topped coffee table were fanned out neatly on top of each other with just the title showing: like in a doctor's surgery. They looked inviting to read, but one was apprehensive about picking one up, in case it disturbed them. The room felt kind of sterile: unlived in. Everything in its place and a place for everything.

Loder wandered over to the window and peered down over Haven Green. Traffic streamed silently around the green, towards the junction at Ealing High Street. On the far left, across from the green was Ealing Underground – still busy with commuters returning from work up town.

'Why don't you put some music on Loder?' she shouted, from the kitchen.

What happened to, John?

Loder turned and went across to a mini HI FI that was on a bookshelf in an alcove adjacent to the fireplace. He sifted through a small pile of CD's on top of the unit, found George Benson's Greatest Hits and slid it into the machine. He then went across to the armchair and sat down. As he relaxed into the chair, the back of it shot downwards and a footrest catapulted up, rendering him almost horizontal.

'Make yourself at home, why don't you?' Anne Oakwood said, walking into the room carrying a tray of food containers and plates. 'Where shall we eat, on the dining table or the coffee table?'

'I don't mind, you choose,' Loder said, struggling to sit upright.

'Coffee table,' she said, setting the heavy tray down.

Loder pushed the footrest back into its housing and the back of the chair righted itself. He then went over to the coffee table, shuffled around behind it and sat down on the sofa. He looked up at Anne Oakwood, who had somehow, miraculously, managed to change out of her work clothes and into a baggy V-neck sweater and jogging pants. Standing on the carpet in her bare feet, she couldn't have gone much over five feet tall. And silhouetted in the soft light from the table lamps in the corner of the room, she looked like a vision sent from heaven.

'Oh, shit! I forgot the wine,' she said, rushing out of the room.

As he waited patiently for her to return, the aroma of the food wafting tantalisingly under his nose began to make his stomach groan with hunger.

She bounced back into the room carrying a bottle of wine and two large glasses and placed them on the table, before settling down cross-legged on the carpet. She poured the wine and proffered a glass to Loder. He took it from her and had a sip. 'Very nice,' he said, picking up the bottle and studying the label.

'It's nothing special, Waitrose best buy,' she said, holding up her glass to, Loder.

They chinked glasses. 'What shall we drink to?' she said, as her head swayed slowly from side to side, in tune with the music.

If he had not known any better, he thought that she was a bit pissed.

'I don't know. Absent friends?'

'Ain't got any,' she said.

'What about to getting a result with the Donna Carlin case?'

'Perfect!' she said, chinking her glass against his again, before taking a long swallow. 'Now, what about this food, shall we tuck in? Smells delicious.'

With a sweep of her arm, she sent the magazines flying across the room and placed two plates from the tray onto the table.

So much for my theory on human psychology.

'Shall I?' Loder said, picking up a serving spoon and burying it into a container of rice.

'Please, do,' she said, drinking another drop of wine.

Loder carefully arranged small portions of beef and black bean sauce, chicken with cashew nuts and rice, neatly around each plate, with a sticky barbequed rib on the side.

'I must say, Loder, you're very domesticated . . . for a man.'

'I don't know how I should take that,' he smiled.

'As a compliment.'

'Do you mind if I get a bit comfortable,' he said, taking off his jacket and loosening his tie.

'Long as you don't intend moving in,' she laughed, taking another sip of wine and missing her mouth, spilling it down the front of her sweater. 'Shit!' she said, wiping the stain away with a paper serviette.

'Here, let me,' he said, getting a clean handkerchief from his pocket.

She stood up on her knees and thrust her chest out at him. It took every ounce of restraint that he could muster to stop himself from ravishing her as he carefully wiped the stain dry. He then kicked off his shoes, and got down on the carpet to join her.

He tucked the handkerchief into the top of her sweater to make napkin and spoon-fed her, a mouthful of chicken. 'Pampering to my needs, Loder. You had better watch out, I could get used to this,' she said, archly.

'My pleasure,' he said, taking a spoonful of food for himself, before delivering another to her, as she leaned forward on her knees from the opposite side of the table.

She topped up their glasses as Loder continued to feed his boss and himself until their plates were almost clean.

Looking into her glass, she said, 'I've got a confession.'

'Oh, yes.' Loder said, intrigued.

'When I took this job, it frightened the life out me being your boss. What with your reputation and everything.'

'Feeling was mutual. You've got quite a rep yourself,' he said.

'Really?' she said, looking up at him.

'I've always worked with men, so I was at a loss to know how I should approach things.'

'Oh, come on, Loder. I'm not buying that,'

'It's true. I promise you, Anne,' he said, taking a mouthful of wine. 'But after working with those other two corrupt scumbags, having you as a boss was like a breath of fresh air. Although, I must admit, I felt as if I was walking on hot coals at first.'

'And now?'

'After you cleared the air, and laid down the rules at our first meeting, my estimation of you increased ten-fold. It took balls to do what you did and I respected you for it.

'Haven't got any.'

'What?'

'Balls,' She giggled.

Loder couldn't help a smile. 'Actually, I think we make a great team. What do you think?'

'As long as you are always straight with me, Loder. I think we're going to be a team to be reckoned with.' She held her glass in the air, and said, 'Cheers!'

They both felt a little uncomfortable in the silence that ensued. Both embarrassed for each other.

'That's enough of confession time,' he said, breaking the atmosphere. 'There you go,' he said, handing her a sticky rib with a serviette wrapped around one end, so that her hands didn't get messy. She took it from him and began nibbling the meat off the bone. He did the same. They both had another, before declaring that they were both stuffed.

'Have you seen the state of your chops,' she laughed, licking the sauce away from the corners of her mouth.

'Why, is it a mess?' Loder said, wiping his hands with the handkerchief.

She shuffled around the table to where Loder was sitting, took the handkerchief from his hand, wet it with a bit of spit, and said, 'Come here.'

He turned towards her and spread his legs. She sidled into the space and slotted her legs each side of his hips, then started wiping the sticky sauce from around his mouth. Loder pulled away, wincing.

'Come here!' she said, shuffling closer. 'There you are, all clean,' she said, planting a playful peck on his lips, without thinking.

They both sat looking into each other's eyes. Loder put his arms around her hips, pulled her into him and kissed her softly. He could taste the Chinese and the wine on her lips as they opened slightly and her tongue probed tentatively around. He lifted her sweater up and she held her arms aloft so that he could slip it over her head. He unclipped her bra while she loosened his tie and pulled it through his collar. She then started on his shirt, fumbling with the buttons as the momentum between them increased. Finally, she managed to get it unbuttoned, and he wrestled his arms out of the sleeves. She let her bra fall into his lap, and wrapped her legs tight around his back, pressing her breasts into his chest. They kissed softly both their tongues interlocked, probing, searching. He felt her nipples pressing into him as he hooked his fingers inside the waistband of her joggers. She lifted her bottom so that he could slip them off, then rolled onto her back and pulled her knees up. He pulled them off and tossed them aside. To his surprise, she wasn't wearing any underwear. She unbuckled his belt, unzipped his trousers, slid her hand in and found his erection. He was caught short of breath as she gently massaged his member. His erection was so hard it hurt. She uncoupled her legs from behind his back and he lifted his bottom off the floor and in one swift movement, she pulled his trousers and pants down and threw them over her shoulder, followed by his socks. As she did so, he rested back on his palms and drank in the shadowy contours of her beautiful, petite body in the dimmed light of the room. Her perfectly proportioned small breasts and most of all the triangle of auburn bush between her thighs.

'What!' she said embarrassed, crossing her arms to hide her breasts.
'You really are, quite stunning,' he said, resting his head to the side.
'Loder, I think you need a white stick and dark glasses.'
'Beautiful, in fact.'

She went all coy. It had been a very long time since anyone had complimented her in such a nice way. Had been even longer since anyone had seen her naked. Her inhibitions thrown to the wind, she crawled towards him on her hands and knees and planted a long soft kiss on his lips, and said, 'I bet you say that to all the women just to get into their knickers, Loder.'

'The last I looked you weren't wearing any,' he teased, kissing the top of her nose.

'Loder!' She said, giving him a playful slap.

She felt his erection hard against her as she wrapped her legs around his back again. She ached to have him inside her. She was wet with anticipation. He pulled her close and kissed her while running his hands softly down her back and around her bottom. The electricity dancing up and down her spine sent a wonderful shiver right through her body, as she felt her juices trickling down the inside of her thigh. Lost on a wave of ecstasy, she said, breathlessly, 'The bedroom's more comfortable.' She indicated with her eyes. 'Besides, I'm a bit too old for rolling about on the floor and getting carpet burns on my knees.'

'Carpet burns! Sounds good to me,' he said, getting to his feet with her still firmly wrapped around him. He then looked around on the floor for something.

'Lost something? She said, concerned.

'Yeh. My white stick,' he mocked.

'Ha, ha,' she said, as Loder carried her out of the room.

It was still dark outside when Anne Oakwood opened her eyes. Disorientated, her first thought was that she must have been dreaming about the wonderful night of lovemaking that she had had. She felt warm and contented. Sleepily, she rolled to her side and felt for Loder's strong chest, but the bed was empty. She wiped the sleep from her eyes. *Maybe, it was all a dream.*

'Morning! Sleepy head,' he said, walking into the room, all bright and breezy, carrying a tray of tea and toast, naked as nature intended.

She closed her eyes and felt the pain in her head begin to thump against the inside of her skull. She sat up. 'What time is it?'

'A little after six,' he said, setting the tray down on the bedside cabinet, and getting back onto the bed.

'Are you insane, or something. It's the middle of the night,' she said, snuggling down and pulling the duvet back over her head. 'I don't feel very well,' she groaned from under the cover.

'Here, have some tea,' he said, picking a mug up from the tray.

She turned and peered out up at him from beneath the duvet. She didn't know what to think as he held out a mug for her. Happy. Sad.

Ecstatic. Fulfilled. Definitely apprehensive. All these emotions raced through her mind as she dreamily looked up at Loder.

In the cold light of day, one thing was certain, things would never be the same between them again. Not now she had let her defences down.

'I know what you're thinking, Anne. I can read your mind.'

She heaved herself up, rested her back on the soft velvet headboard, took the mug of tea from Loder, and almost burnt her tongue in the rush to get the steaming liquid down her parched throat.

Loder teased her with a triangle of hot buttered toast, waving it tantalisingly under her nose. She opened her mouth and caught a bite full as he held it for her. A sip of tea to wash it down, then another bite, more tea, until she had finished.

'Another piece?' he said.

She nodded.

The same teasing routine repeated. Except that afterwards, he gently wiped the dribble of butter from the sides of her mouth with his finger and then kissed her. To her shame, she found herself wishing that he had licked it off. A safe reassuring warm glow enveloped her as Loder put his arm around her. She nestled into his wide chest and then reached up and kissed the nape of his neck. It was so long since she had felt so contented: she embraced it with every beat of her heart.

Smiling down at her, Loder took the empty mug from her hand and placed it on the tray. Without a second thought, she threw her leg across his thighs and sat astride him, letting the duvet fall away. Loder couldn't believe how incredible she looked: every single thing about her screamed of sex.

Suddenly, a heavy feeling of guilt weighed down on him. He felt as if he was betraying the memory of his late wife. Somewhere in his mind's eye he saw her smiling face, saying, you can't grieve forever, Loder: time to move on. He blinked, erasing the image from his mind.

'Penny for them,' she said, stroking her fingers through his curly hair.

'Come here, you,' he said, pulling her close.

She smiled dreamily as she rode slowly on his penis until he was hard. She then lifted her bottom and guided him inside her. He clasped each side her bottom with his hands and pulled himself deep into her. She threw her head back and rode on top of him on a wave of ecstasy, as their momentum built to a glorious climax. Then with a long, deep moan that sounded almost like a cry of pain, she exploded with an orgasm so intense that it sent waves of spasm right down to the soles of her feet. Loder followed immediately afterwards, emptying every last drop of semen that his body could produce deep inside of her. Sweating and panting like a couple of exhausted dogs, they leaned back, Anne on her elbows and Loder against the headboard. They both laughed.

'I'm getting too old for all this,' he said, wiping the sweat from his brow with the back of his hand.

'You are! What about me?' she panted.

They both sat for a moment, each gathering their thoughts. She felt Loder's erection subside and his penis fall out from inside her, leaving a lovely trickle of semen down the inside of her thigh. She didn't want the night, the morning, the day, to end. Nevertheless, she knew that they both would have to face up to the reality of their situation. And soon.

Loder sensed what was going through Anne's mind: he was thinking the same. Whatever happened, things could never be the same, not until they were honest with each other.

She's your boss, for Christ sake. Kept screaming through his mind.

'Loder,' she said, inquisitively.

'Anne.'

'What are we going to do?'

'Don't know. What do you want to do?'

'Don't know.'

They both sighed.

'Look, this isn't getting us anywhere, Loder.'

'Anne, why don't we just put it down to experience? Too much, drink. Two people caught up in the emotions of the moment. No real harm done . . . *Is* there?'

'Absolutely not!' she said, all up beat. Inside she was choked with disappointment. But knew that Loder was giving her an out. An easy closure on last night's . . . and this morning's debacle. She admired him for it. 'No one must ever find out, Loder. We keep this strictly between ourselves.'

'Oh, please, Anne. What sort of person do you think I am?' he said, taking umbrage.

'I'm sorry, Loder. It's my stupid head, it's all over the place.'

With a deep sigh, he said, 'I suppose I had better get myself ready for work. Okay, if I have a shower?'

'Of course.'

She couldn't help herself admiring his tall frame and pert bottom as he leaped out of bed and padded across the carpet. As he opened the door, he turned and said, 'Fancy sharing?'

'Thought you'd never ask,' she said, launching herself out of bed and across the room to take his outstretched hand.

CHAPTER 17

Delaney was in a basement flat just behind Golborne Road. It was a scruffy run down area on the wrong side of Ladbroke Grove. It had been given a body-swerve by property developers. Probably because the area was infiltrated with Moroccan, Algerian and Lebanese immigrants.

To the uninitiated, the atmosphere felt intimidating. Gangs of wary-looking men congregated on the pavements outside coffee houses and cafes, that sold diseased-looking meat that constantly turned around on hot spits. All of them rabbling on in obscure foreign languages at break-neck speed.

The only visible sign left of any cockney influence was the pie and eel shop, which still did a roaring trade, especially on market days. But even that was under threat of extinction, with the infiltration of foreign stallholders selling cheap jewellery and knock off designer-labelled clothes made in their own sweatshops over in North London. But whatever one might think, there was no denying the place had a buzz about it. Dark wrinkle-skinned men draped in kaftans and fez's, cemented deals on nothing more than a handshake. To the perceptive, the unmistakable whiff of corruption was rife.

The flat stank of damp and body odour. Delaney was oblivious to it: he spent most of his working life in places like this. Sitting at a table in the galley kitchen that looked out to a small enclosed concrete yard, Delaney counted a wad of money from a cash-box. He stacked them neatly into fifties, twenties, tens and five pound notes along the table, and entered the details into a cashbook, just as any diligent bookkeeper would do. He then counted out three hundred pounds, put it aside and then a further one hundred pounds, and placed it alongside.

A tall, bald-headed, odious man wearing a grubby tee shirt stretched over a fat overhanging stomach brought over a mug of coffee and placed it on the table. Delaney picked it up and drank a mouthful. ' 'There's some moving about money there,' he said, sliding the three hundred pounds to one side. The man scooped the money up and slid it into his back pocket with the deftness of an octopus's tentacle.

'Cheers, Harry,' he said, with a smile. Exposing a mouthful of yellow, nicotine-stained teeth that were so broken and uneven, they looked like a row of dog-ends.

Delaney finished his coffee, lifted his leather attaché case onto the table and thumbed the dials of the combination lock, until it clicked open. He pulled out a cloth cash bag, put the money into it and snapped it shut. Then heaved his heavy bulk up from the small tubular-framed kitchen chair that had all but disappeared under the weight of his fat, overhanging arse. 'I'll just pop next door for a moment, before I leave.'

There was hardly any natural light in the front room, because the only window was below street level and looked out to a concrete wall and the steep steps that led down from the pavement above. The single light bulb hanging precariously on an ancient strip of frayed cord in the centre of the cracked ceiling gave the room a hue of despair. There were two threadbare settees with a circular coffee table between them. The table was strewn with empty mugs, dented pop cans and a large glass ashtray overflowing with cigarette butts. Perched incongruously in the corner was a huge plasma television, and in the other was a leather armchair.

Huddled on one settee were two skinny-looking lads dressed in shorts and tee shirts and a young girl wearing nothing but a vest and a pair of pants. None of them could have been older than fourteen years of age. Sprawled out on the other settee, watching television, was an older girl, of about sixteen or seventeen. She wore leggings and sweatshirt with a blonde ponytail hanging out the back of a baseball cap.

'Got any room for a small one?' Delaney said. The two lads uncurled their legs from under themselves and he plonked himself down, between them. 'Everything alright?' he said, looking at each of them in turn.

'Yeh,' they all said, not taking their eyes off the TV screen.

'What are you watching?' he said, trying to make conversation.

'Jerry Springer,' the older girl replied.

'Oh, right,' he said, trying to sound interested, but none the wiser. 'I've got something for you,' he said, lifting his attaché case onto his lap and pressing the locks open. He opened the lid and looked around the room for a response. No one stirred a muscle. They were too busy watching four black, burly security guys trying their best to restrain a big fat woman with tattooed arms and neck. She had so many metal rings and studs dangling off her ears that a metal merchant would gladly melt her down for scrap.

Delaney tossed a carton of cigarettes over to the older girl, hitting her on the chest. 'Fucking hell, Harry,' she screamed, before realising what it was. Then sat up, and chirped, 'Thanks, Harry!'

'Mind you share them around, Lara.'

'What about us?' a painfully thin girl on the end of the settee said, sounding miffed.

'Here you are, gorgeous,' Delaney said, tossing a big bag of chocolate bars and sweets into her lap. 'See, your uncle Harry, knows how to look after ya, don't he?'

'Thanks, Harry!' Her eyes lit up at all the chocolate she was going to scoff before the others had a chance to get their hands on any.

'Oh, I almost forgot,' he said, reaching deep into his trousers and pulling out a folded wad of notes. 'There you go, pocket money,' he beamed, handing each of them a twenty-pound note. 'Shall I leave yours on the table, Lara?'

'Not with these thieving bastards about, you don't,' she said, jumping to her feet and snatching it out of his hand.

The sound of Delaney's mobile ringing, resounded off the dirty walls around the room. All eyes glued to the TV, no one took a blind bit of notice. Delaney heaved himself to his feet and went through into the kitchen when he saw who was calling.

'Okay, okay. Calm down, Teddy,' Delaney said, holding the tiny contraption away from his ear, as the diatribe screamed out at him. His attention was averted by the bald-headed man ear-wigging behind him. He turned away from him, opened the back door and went out into the yard. He listened until Teddy Marston had run out of steam. 'Right, leave everything to me. I'll be in touch. And don't you worry, I'll sort it,' Delaney said, cutting Teddy Marston off.

He thumbed through the memory until he found the number he wanted. 'Ryan, that cunning little bastard, Danny, has surfaced. We need to sort something out. I'll meet you over at, Wally's, right away. I don't give a flying fuck what you're doing. Get over there, *now!*'

Twenty-five minutes later, Delaney stormed into the stifling heat of the small front room, and growled, 'Is Ryan, here?'

Wally, "The Weasel" as he was known, said nervously 'He's in the carsi.'

'Get me a drink, Wally. Got any Scotch?'

'Yeh, somewhere,' he said, skulking out of the room.

The weasel looked exactly what his nickname suggested. A small, skinny deadpanned man with little beady eyes that never missed a trick. He did not walk, as such, he skulked, with a permanent stoop that always seemed to make him look upwards at people. He had a disgusting habit of rubbing his hands together like Shylock when something, or more likely, someone, excited him. But above all, The Weasel, was a sadistic violent man, who got his jollies inflicting pain on his victims: be it male or female, he wasn't fussy, as long as he could see their faces racked with pain, he was happy.

Delaney knew he could rely on The Weasel's discretion. They had shared the fruits of their spoils for as long as he cared to remember. The Weasel had also disposed of a few undesirables that failed to come up to scratch and therefore not profitable to Delaney anymore.

These days Delaney tended to throw The Weasel the kids that had gone past their sell by date, or who had crossed him. He let The Weasel do whatever he wanted to with them, and wasn't unduly concerned if he never saw them again: which was sometimes the case.

When Ryan wandered into the room, he sensed straight away that Delaney was not a happy bunny: in fact, he was in a filthy mood.

Nursing a tumbler of Scotch in his hand, Delaney gazed out the window. The view from the sixteenth floor flat was quite something, and under normal circumstances would have lifted Delaney's spirits: not today.

He looked down at the curved, glass roof of Paddington Station and the tangle of railway lines that snaked their way out of London to places that Delaney had only read about or seen on TV. To the right the old GPO Tower protruded up like a giant asparagus spear and further beyond was Marble Arch.

Delaney had been brought up in Kilburn. An only son of Irish parents who settled in London after the war. His father was a navvy and worked long hours employed by a building company contracted to clearing away debris from bomb-damaged buildings. His mother worked in the wash house of Porchester Baths, scrubbing clothes for ten hours a day. His father was a violent drunkard who spent most of his wages in the pubs along the Kilburn High Road with all the other Irish immigrants that had settled in the area. There was so many Irish living around there that the locals had christened it County Kilburn.

Young Harry was always on the receiving end of his father's leather belt when he lashed out in one of his drunken rages. His mother tried to protect him, but she too would be beaten black-and-blue and raped right in front of young Harry's eyes. On Sundays after a session in the confession box and few "Hail Mary's" of penance, the old man was a different person. Refreshed and cleansed of all his sins, he would swagger down to the pub after church without a care in the world. Dressed in his double-breasted worsted suit, heavy brogues, and brown homburg tilted cockily on the side of head, he wouldn't return home until he was completely obliterated. So the whole cycle would start again.

This was *his* manor, his bread and butter, and to think that little fuck, Danny, had the audacity to put his livelihood at risk. The thought that Danny could even contemplate the idea of getting one over on him, especially, after everything he had done for him, riled him. Put money in his pocket, kept him off the streets, that was the way Delaney saw the situation. Not the fact that it was he, who first served him up as a piece of fodder that was passed around for nothing more than a bit of entertainment. That it was *he* who stole his innocence and corrupted his mind so much that, Danny actually thought that his life *was* normal: he didn't know any different. But Danny had dared to commit the cardinal sin: betray him. Put everything that he had strived for at risk, and for that reason alone, there was only ever going to be one conclusion.

'So what're we going to do?' Ryan said, breaking the silence.

'The little fucker took some photos of him and Teddy Marston together. Now he's demanding fifteen grand for them. He wants a bag with the money in, thrown over the fence into the bushes somewhere in Hammergrove Park.'

'Where about, exactly? It's a big park.'

'He's sent Teddy Marston a map with all the details.'

'When's it going off?'

'This evening, 5:30 pm.'

'Doesn't leave us a lot of time. We had better get over there and have a look around,' Ryan said

Delaney turned around, threw the Scotch down his throat in one long swallow, walked across the room and handed the empty glass to The Weasel. 'We'll drop by and pick up the map on our way,' Delaney said, pushing The Weasel aside as he went out. 'We'll bring the little fuck back here. When we've got our hands on him, Wally, you know what to do with him.'

The Weasel rubbed his hands at the prospect of what lay ahead. He knew exactly what Delaney expected of him and he wouldn't let him down. In fact, he relished the thought of what fun lay ahead.

The entrance to Hammergrove Park was half way along South Africa Road; further down was Queens Park Rangers Football stadium. On their right, was the sprawling Commonwealth Estate with its huge five-storey blocks of flats that stretched along the whole length of South Africa Road. Delaney pulled up a little way down from the park entrance, outside The Greyhound Pub. He locked the vehicle and they both walked the short distance back to the park entrance. They went through the gate and along the path. On their left on the other side of a long clipped hedge was the children's play park. Some kids were playing on the swings and in the sand pit. Others were noisily racing around after each other, while being watched over by a gaggle of mothers deep in conversation between themselves. What, or who, was on the receiving end of their vitriolic tongues was anyone's guess, but it was a cast-iron certainty that some poor soul was getting his or her, life ripped to shreds.

Delaney got out the folded sheet of paper from his inside pocket and studied it, trying to get his bearings. He passed it to Ryan and he turned the pencilled diagram on its side to get a better idea of the plan. He then walked back out of the entrance, turned right, went about fifty metres up the road and stopped. 'This is the spot. It's marked with a piece of ribbon, see?' he pointed to a strip of red ribbon tied to the wire fence. Delaney looked at the diagram, then the ribbon and gave an agreeing grunt. He stood back and looked one way then the other.

The two metre high wire fence stretched from the territorial army barracks at the top of the road, where the park began, down to the entrance. In total about a hundred metres in length. Behind the fence was a thicket of overgrown bushes and ferns about four metres deep.

The undergrowth was littered with empty beer cans, discarded junk-food containers, old newspapers, a few stripped down baby-buggies and an assortment of rusty bicycle frames. Beyond the bushes was a tall wire fence, at least five metres high, behind which, was an Astro Turf football pitch.

They walked back through the park entrance, turned left into the football cage and checked along the perimeter fence. There was an access gate in the centre of the fence on both sides of the pitch, both were unlocked. Behind the fence on the far side of the football pitch was more thick foliage and beyond was a dilapidated bowling green.

Ryan knew the layout of the park like the back of his hand. The toilets used to be a well-known haunt for nonces and teenage prostitutes willing to do anything – sexual or otherwise – to anyone who would pay hard cash. Just so they could buy the latest designer fashion accessories and show them off to their friends. Junkies of both sexes, who sold their souls for the price of a wrap, would skulk around out of their brains too.

The police had flushed the place clean, and together with the local residents association, the council bowed to pressure and employed a warden to patrol the park and lock the gates at night. He and Danny used to come here on the quiet when they were short of a few quid and turned over some of the more gullible nonces, relieving them of their wallets.

'So, what do you think?' Delaney said.

'Well, there's only two ways in and out. The gate this end and the one at the other end of the park where the back entrance to the BBC is. I can't see Danny jumping over into the BBC,' he said, pointing to a high wall that ran along the back of the park, beyond the bowling green. 'The security guards would be all over him in a second. He must have planned an escape route, he's not that stupid.'

'He fucking well is, if he thinks he can turn me over,' Delaney growled. 'I'll tear the little fuckers arse out when I get my hands on him.'

Dug deep in the thick undergrowth behind the perimeter fence, Danny listened to everything that was being said. He had to hold his hand over his mouth to stop himself from giggling.

'Right, we'll position two bodies at either entrance, another two here, patrolling around the football pitch and another two outside on the road where the drop is. That should do it. He won't be able to get out without at least one of us getting a hand on him.'

That's what you think, you greasy, fat bastard, Danny smiled to himself.

Delaney looked at his watch. 'What time is the drop, again?'

Ryan unfolded the sheet of paper, and said, 'half-five.'

'It's getting on for half-two now. Doesn't give us much time. Let's get back, it'll be easier to organise from home, besides we need to get the MPV out.'

*

Tanya was sitting at her desk, busy scrolling through the missing persons' database. She had been sitting in front of the monitor for well over two hours and so far had come up with zilch. She could not believe how huge the database was and the deeper she delved into it, the more despondent she became.

Instead of just scrolling through the pictures trying to make a match, she found herself reading each profile. Some of the horror stories that she had come across saddened her so much that she couldn't help shedding a tear. After all, she was a mother herself and could empathise with some of the mothers of these kids. It just gave her the resolve to be even more protective of her own daughter. There by the grace of God.

She stretched her arms and yawned, then kicked her swivel chair away from under the desk, got up and went over to the water dispenser and filled a beaker of cool water. Rolling her head on her aching shoulders, she then went over to the window and looked out at the grey, drizzly afternoon and sighed despondently. Taking a long swallow of the cool liquid, she glanced up at the clock above the window of Loder's office. It was 4:00 p.m. The incident room was desolate apart from a secretary busy entering a mountain of report sheets into a computer. It seemed that everyone had lost interest in the case since the investigation had been scaled down. No one bothered anymore. No, "Dead Body," no interest. Nothing to investigate. Move on. End of story.

Tossing her empty cup into the bin, she settled back behind her desk, and decided to give it a couple more hours then call it a day. Besides, David – the man she loved to destruction – was cooking for them both tonight and she didn't want to be late getting back.

This time she steered herself away from reading each individual profile and concentrated on getting an identikit match. Forty-five minutes later her vision began to blur with the intense concentration, and the fact that she needed to see an optometrist. She rubbed her eyes, blinked a couple of times and ploughed on.

Suddenly, something pricked her memory and she scrolled back through the files and stopped at a picture of a fresh-faced, blonde-haired young lad, with the most amazing blue eyes looking out at her. She rubbed her tired eyes again, and straightened her back to get some distance from the screen and a better focus on the picture. She read the profile again, tilted her head to the side and tried to recall where she had seen this face before.

Then it came to her. She kicked her chair closer to the screen and studied the picture closely. The boy's profile read that he was eleven years of age when the picture was taken, but had been missing since he was twelve, after disappearing from a children's home down in Essex.

There was no mistaking those eyes. The lad she had encountered in the kitchen at Jonnie James's house, and the one on the monitor were the same. She clapped her hands in triumph and printed off the information.

Tanya almost careered into Loder on her way out, as the doors threw open and he strode into the incident room with DS Frost in tow.
'Easy,' he said, resting his hands on her shoulders. 'What's the rush?'
'Think I might have hit on something, sir,' she said, handing him the printout.

He took the sheets from her and began to read as he walked across to the murder board and rested on the desk in front of it. Then holding a sheet in each hand, he shrugged. 'So, who is he?'
'I'm pretty certain that the lad in that picture is the same one as I saw at Jonnie James's house. You remember, sir. He said that the lad was his nephew and was staying with him for a while.'

Loder had another look at the picture, and then handed it to DS Frost. 'Are you certain, Tanya?' he said. 'What do you think, Tony?'
'I can't say. I only got a glimpse of him when we were at the house.'
'Me too,' Loder said.
'I had a little chat with the boy when I met him in the kitchen. And, although he's three or four years younger in the picture, there is no mistaking those eyes. That's what first drew me to him. I'm as certain as I can be, sir, that they are one and the same.'

'That's good enough for me,' Loder said. 'It's just the ammunition we need to put that bastard, James under a bit of pressure. Good work, Tanya. Well done. Let's give him a visit, shall we?'

'Remember, we got warned off the last time we went around to his place, boss,' DS Frost, reminded Loder

Loder thought about it for a moment and the stick Anne Oakwood would get from above if he went in all guns blazing. Under normal circumstances he wouldn't have given a "flying fuck." However, these were not "normal circumstances," not since he had stayed the night with her. Besides, he liked Anne Oakwood more than he cared to admit to himself.

'You're right, Tony. No point in upsetting the applecart. I'll run it by DCI Oakwood, first. See what she says.'

DS Frost cast an eye at Tanya. *What's got into him.* When did Loder ever do things by the book? Tanya knew exactly what he was thinking and offered a wide-eyed, "I know," in response.

Loder straightened his tie and took a deep breath before knocking on the door. He had avoided Anne Oakwood as much as he possibly could since the night they had stayed together. Given that she was his immediate boss, made it very difficult. The brief moments that they had seen each other, they were in the company of colleagues. This was the first face-to-face meeting and he wasn't sure what to expect.

He knocked, poked his head around the door and said, 'Have you got a moment, Anne?'

'Of course. Come in,' she said, taken by surprise.

Loder went in and sat in one of the two high-backed chairs in front of her desk.

'What can I do for you, John?'

Loder looked up and could see by her reddening face that she was as embarrassed as he was. He handed her the couple of sheets of A4 with the picture of Danny on and she began to read. As she perused the text through slim-framed designer glasses, he couldn't help drinking in her attractiveness. She had a slim face, high cheekbones and a small nose with a scattering of faint freckles across the top. Her complexion was smooth and needed little make-up to disguise the few age-lines around her eyes and mouth. She really was quite a little stunner, Loder thought to himself.

'So, do you want to fill me in?' she said, looking over the top her glasses at Loder, catching him off guard.

'Eh . . .' he croaked, clearing his throat.

'What's the matter? Cat got your tongue?' was all she could manage to say, as she felt the heat rise under her collar. 'Look, John, we have to work together. What happened between—'

'I'm sorry. Shall we start again?'

'Good idea.'

'Well, as you can see, the lad in the picture is listed on the missing persons' data base.'

'So, what has this . . .' She pulled her glasses higher up her nose and thumbed down the sheet, 'Danny McKee, have to do with our investigation?'

'Tanya came across a lad when we paid Jonnie James a visit, and she's as certain as she can be that they are one and the same. James said that the lad was his nephew and was staying with him. Obviously, we now know that not to be true.'

'So, what do you want from me?'

'Well, I think we ought to give him another visit. We'd just be following up on a missing person's enquiry.'

'True.' His boss nodded, removed her glasses and placed them on the desk. 'But what has it got to do with the Donna Carlin case?'

'Nothing . . . Yet. But remember, Donna *was* seen at James's house. Whether that's true, or not, remains to be seen. I really think we ought to put this cretin under a bit of pressure. Especially, now that we have a legitimate reason.'

'I agree,' she said, getting up from behind the desk and walking around resting against the edge of the desk in front of him.

'Can I take it that I have your okay,' Loder said.

'Absolutely.'

'What about the flak from upstairs?'

'As I said before, you let me worry about that. But I will say this. I do *not* want you going in there Gung-Ho, all guns blazing. No arms up the back or any rough stuff. It has to be by the book, one hundred percent. Is that clear, Loder?'

'Absolutely. I'll be diplomacy personified. You can rely on me.'

'Then why do I feel a demotion waiting in the wings?' she said, with a wry smile.

Loder got to his feet to leave. As he did so, Anne Oakwood handed him the two sheets of paper. It took all of his resolve not to throw her on top of the desk and take her, right there and then.

She saw that he was flustered. 'What's the matter, now?' she sighed. 'You've got my okay, Loder. Was there anything else?' she said, tilting her head to the side, archly.

'I was just wondering if you would like to—'

'Absolutely! Your place or mine?'

'Yours,' he said, with a sigh of relief. 'I love your takeaways.'

She looked up at him sheepishly. 'Shall we say six-thirty in the pub across the road from my flats?'

'Be there at six,' he said, planting an awkward peck on her cheek.

'What's the matter you in a hurry?'

Loder glanced at his watch. 'It's going to be the longest five hours, forty-seven minutes of my life: don't think I'll last.'

Anne Oakwood smiled. If the truth was known, she couldn't wait either. This man standing in front of her made her feel good. No . . . better than just good. Loder made her feel alive, and spontaneous, and extremely naughty. Six o'clock couldn't come around quick enough for her.

CHAPTER 18

The evening rush hour traffic was heavy as the MPV turned into Wood Lane from Shepherds Green. As they neared White City Station, they slowed to a crawl as hoards of football supporters poured out of the station and across the road. The area was awash with police keeping an eye on the rowdy fans as they made their way along Wood Lane and down White City Road towards QPR football ground.

Delaney banged the steering wheel with his fist in frustration. 'The little fucker isn't that silly, is he? He knew exactly what he was doing picking this place and time for a drop,' he snarled. 'Where the fuck are we going to park?'

'Go across the lights at the end here and there should be an overflow car park on the right,' Ryan pointed, sitting in the front next to Delaney. 'We'll have to walk the rest of the way because they close off South Africa Road to traffic on match days, there's no other way around it.'

Delany nodded grudgingly.

Fortunately, the car park wasn't full and they had no trouble finding a space. The night air was cold as the men huddled in a group, burying their hands deep into their pockets waiting for instructions. Delaney looked at his watch, it was a couple of minutes after five. It had taken them nearly twenty-five minutes to travel the three-quarters of a mile down Wood Lane. He cursed under his breath. 'Right let's hurry. Ryan will tell you where I want you all stationed, on the way down.'

It took them seven minutes to reach the drop point. They walked on and waited by the park entrance. Ryan gave each of them their instructions and they paired off in different directions.

'I'll do the drop,' Delaney said.

'Don't you think it would be better coming from someone else, Harry?' Ryan said.

'Why?'

'If Danny sees you hanging about, he's not likely to go for it, is he? After all, you're not supposed to know anything about all this. Danny thinks Teddy Marston is going to do the drop.'

'Suppose you're right,' Delaney growled, grudgingly. 'You had better do it, George,' he said, handing him the carrier bag with the money packaged up inside.

George Kirkum was a tall, slim man in his early forties and was a serial paedophile who had an insatiable appetite for pretty, young girls. A few years back he had been convicted for abusing his own two daughters and spent a pitiful eight months behind bars. He was a violent man who would stop at nothing to satisfy his perversions. They were now, thankfully, available in abundance since he took up with Delaney. His job was to deliver the girls to wealthy clients living out in the suburbs, make sure that they we're well presented and then wait in the car for an allotted time, before collecting them again. No money ever changed hands, everything was done on credit. The Executive Directors Club, billed the clients on a monthly basis. The company was registered in the Cayman Islands and was administered by nominees. Everything clean, legitimate and above board.

'I'll wait in the pub up the road. Keep me updated by mobile. Is that clear?' he said, fixing them both a look that was pure evil.

'Absolutely, Harry. You can count on me,' George Kirkum said, obsequiously

'What about you, Ryan? Where are you going to be?'

'Think I'll make m'self busy around here mingling amongst the crowds. He's got to make a show, somewhere.'

'Okay. Keep me informed. I'm going for a beer.'

George Kirkum made his way back along the road and passed by where the ribbon was tied to the fence. He walked to the top of the road, turned around and walked back behind a gang of singing football supporters. As he passed the ribbon, he tossed the carrier bag over the fence. It landed deep in the undergrowth out of sight behind the front row of bushes. No one took any notice. By the end of the night there would be a mountain of fish and chip papers and junk food boxes discarded over the fence.

Danny saw the bag land from his dugout under a thick bush, twenty-feet away. He hadn't moved all afternoon. He didn't want to risk being seen. He wouldn't put it past Delaney to have left one of his boy's sniffing around after they had all left earlier in the afternoon. No, he had everything planned down to the last detail; he had even brought sandwiches, pop, and his iPod to while away the time. He had already made up his mind to wait a little nearer to the kick-off time when the crowds were dense and in a hurry to get to the match. He wouldn't be seen by the two goons guarding the gates inside the Astro pitch, because there would be a full-blown kick-about starting shortly, and the touchline would be surrounded with spectators. It was a showpiece that the home supporters always staged on match days before kick-off. He settled down comfortably, ripped open the cellophane seal to his pre-packed sandwich and began munching away, smiling smugly to himself.

*

When Loder arrived at the pub across the road from Ealing Station, it was already busy with commuters diving in for a quick drink after a sardine-packed journey home from work. Together with the assemblage of construction workers from the new apartments development in the High Street, the pub made for a lively atmosphere, so early in the evening.

Loder got himself a pint of bitter at the bar, and then found himself a seat just inside the entrance. He glanced at his watch. He was early. He crossed his legs, took a long swallow of his pint, and looked up at the clock above the bar. *What is the matter with you, man, he smiled to himself.* He felt like a teenager waiting for a first date, not a fifty-three year, old battle-hardened detective inspector.

He picked up an evening paper left on the seat next to him and began to flick through it aimlessly, to pass the time.

'Can I get you another drink?' Anne Oakwood said, tossing a heavy shoulder bag onto the seat.

Loder folded the newspaper and jumped to his feet. 'No, you sit down. I'll get them.'

She slipped off her overcoat and Loder folded it and placed it on the seat. She manoeuvred herself around behind the table and sat down. 'A chilled, large white wine, please. I need it after the day I've had.'

He went to the bar, purchased the drinks and slid in beside his boss.

'Hard day, then?' He said, finishing the dregs of his first pint.

'Just the usual politics. Nothing I can't handle,' she smiled, patting his thigh affectionately.

A bolt of electricity shot up his leg into his groin. *What is it, about this woman?*

'Mmm, delicious,' she said, closing her eyes and savouring the taste of the cold wine. 'Just what I needed.'

Mesmerised by her beauty as she relaxed back into the seat, Loder knew that he was falling for Anne in a big way. He couldn't help himself. Everything about this tough, petite woman screamed sex to him.

She opened her eyes and caught Loder looking at her. Immediately she felt her face begin to flush. 'What's the matter?' she said, defensively.

'Nothing. Just admiring the view.'

Trying to hide her embarrassment, she said, 'What do you fancy to eat?'

'Don't mind. What do you fancy?'

'I asked first, Loder,' she smiled

Let's forget about dinner and get straight to desert, he wanted to say.

'There's a good Indian restaurant around the corner. If you prefer, I have some bolognaise in the freezer. I can defrost it in the microwave and make us quick spaghetti, if you like?'

'Sounds delicious,' Loder said, emptying half the contents of his pint down his throat.

'You in a hurry, Loder?'

'Eh . . . no, not really,' he said, placing his glass onto the table.

'Well, I am,' she said, finishing her drink and shuffling out from behind the table. With a hand on her hip and her head tilted to the side, she said, archly, 'You ready?'

'Is the Pope a catholic?' he said, jumping to his feet.

She had to think about it for a moment. 'Ha, ha. Very funny, Loder,' she said, slipping her arms into her overcoat while he held it up for her.

It was only a short walk across Haven Green to her flat. Once inside, Loder put some music on then went into the kitchen where she was busy cooking pasta.

'Anything I can do to help?' he said.

'Why don't you open a bottle of wine,' she said, pointing to a wine rack in the corner of the worktop.

Loder went across and selected a bottle of Rioja. 'This okay?' he said, showing her the label.

'Fine, yes.'

'Corkscrew?'

'In the drawer, over there,' she indicated with her eyes.

Loder found it, opened the bottle and pulled out two large, long-stemmed glasses from a display cupboard above. He poured the wine and passed one to her. They chinked glasses and a melodic chime resonated around the room.

'Why don't you take this through to the lounge,' she said, handing him her glass. 'I'm about ready to serve up.'

He picked up the bottle, made his way into the lounge and set them down on the dining table. 'Can you get some placemats out of the drawer, on the side,' she called from the kitchen.

Loder went to the sideboard, opened the drawer, took out four placemats and positioned them on the table. As he was about to close the drawer something caught his eye. It was a framed photograph of a much younger Anne on a beach with two small boys and a man, all of them happy and smiling into the camera. He studied it for moment and thought what an attractive girl she was: still is.

'What have you got there,' Anne said, carrying a tray of steaming food to the table.

'I'm sorry. I wasn't prying,' Loder said, putting the photo back in the drawer and closing it.

'It's okay. They're my two boys. Both grown up now, of course. One is a corporate lawyer for a big city firm and the other works for the VSO teaching poor African kids in the Gambia. Chalk and cheese those two, but I could not have been more proud of the way they have turned out.'

'And the man? Your husband?'

'That's a different story. One that I don't want to spoil a nice evening by talking about.'

'I'm sorry.'

'No need to be. Come and sit down, pour us both another drink while I serve up,' she smiled.

They ate sedately, until Anne broke the atmosphere. 'What about you, Loder? You have any children?'

'No. We never got around to it, and before we both knew it, it was too late.' Loder shrugged.

'Divorced?'

'No. My wife died of cancer about eighteen months ago. She battled with it, on and off, for years.'

'I didn't know.' She gently rested her hand on his.

'It's not something I wanted in the public domain. It was a relief when she finally went.'

'Come here, Loder.'

'What?' He turned to face her.

'You're a mess,' she said, wiping a dribble of sauce away from the corner of his mouth.

'Let's make a toast,' he said, replenishing both their glasses.

'To what?' she said, holding hers aloft.

'To the future,' he said, chinking them together.

'Do we have a future, Loder?'

'Who knows? For now, let's enjoy the moment.'

She reached across, held his face in her hands, pulled him to her lips, and kissed him softly. Why don't you take me to bed and make mad passionate love to me?' she said, dreamily.

'That's all I've thought about doing since—'

'Me too.'

*

Danny glanced at his fake Rolex watch and said to himself, *show time*. The football game on the Astro pitch behind was in full swing and he could see that the two goons guarding the gates were totally engrossed in the game. The pavement and road in front was crowded with people all rushing to get to the match before kick-off. Everything was just as he had planned it.

Gingerly he crawled along the undergrowth, reached out and grabbed the carrier bag. Slowly and quietly, he re-tracked back to his lair and inspected the contents. Inside, wrapped in a polythene bag were three of the biggest wads of fifty-pound notes that he had ever seen in his life. He had only ever seen a fifty-pound note once before, and that was when Delaney pushed one across a bar to buy a round of drinks. Now he had a whole bunch of them so thick, he couldn't get his hand around them.

Quickly, he wrapped the polythene around the wads of notes and put it back in the carrier bag. Then wrapped the carrier bag up tight and tucked it under his hooded top. Slowly, he crawled back along the undergrowth towards the gate that opened onto the football pitch.

It took him what seemed to be ages to crawl the thirty metres to where he had a small mountain bike hidden. His legs and arms ached like hell, so he decided to rest up for a moment: no point in rushing. He rubbed his legs to get the blood circulating and after a moment or two the pain subsided. He patted the lump under his sweatshirt top, just to make certain it was still there. Then got in a squat position, picked up the bike and with one hand on the handlebars and the other on the saddle, he gingerly pushed it out of the undergrowth. Just enough to get a view from behind the high fence. Tentatively, he looked in both directions. Directly in front, about twelve feet away, with their backs towards him, the two goons were standing on the touchline watching the game. He slid the metal bolt across as quietly as he could – he'd already lubricated it earlier, to stop it screeching. Then with the speed of a greyhound, he pushed the gate open, jumped on the saddle and peddled away, as if his life depended on it: which of course it did.

He sped out onto the Astro pitch behind the spectators and peddled along the side of the touchline, behind the goal and around the other side. The two goons were so engrossed in the game that they didn't even notice, until Danny stopped to release the sliding bolt in the metal gate directly opposite, on the other side of the pitch. By then it was too late.

Danny jumped off the bike, ran it through the opening and disappeared into the bushes. The two goons gave chase but they knew it was a lost cause. He then burst out of the bushes on the other side, jumped on the saddle and peddled like thunder around the bowling green and out along the side of the tennis courts. The main path that connected the two main entrances of the park ran past the front of the tennis courts and was still busy with fans making their way towards the stadium. He pointed the bike towards a wide lawn and peddled as fast as his legs would go, right across the middle of it in the direction of a thicket of bushes and trees on the other side. It was hard going, peddling on the wet grass, but his adrenalin was pumping ten-to-the-dozen. He dug deep and found a reserve of strength that he never knew he possessed. He reached the other side steered the bike onto the path, almost knocking a couple of people off their feet, and through a narrow, concealed, single-paved path between two overgrown bushes.

Danny saw a flash of white light as something hit him square across the chest, sending him somersaulting backwards off the bike and the carrier bag full of money flying into the air. He landed on the hard concrete paving hitting his head with an almighty thud.

Ryan threw the block of wood into the undergrowth and grabbed the money. His first thought was to do a runner with it, but unless he disappeared off the face of the earth, he knew it would be a waste of time. He decided to bury it the best he could while Danny was sprawled out semi-conscious and see how things transpired later. He got out his mobile phone and called Delaney to give him the good news.

Dazed, Danny sat up and felt the blood trickling down his neck. He felt the bump on the back of his head with his hand and looked at the blood all over it. 'Fucking hell, Ryan. You could have killed me.'

'That's nothing, compared to what's going happen to you when, Delaney gets his hands on you,' Ryan said.

A sudden rush of fear washed over Danny. And the enormity of his crime suddenly dawned on him. He fumbled under his top for the package. It wasn't there. He tried to gather his thoughts. Where the fuck was it? His mind was a awash with confusion and his head was throbbing like a jackhammer trying to break his skull open from the inside. He shook his head to try and clear his mind, but it just made the pain worse. 'Where's the money, Ryan? You've fucking nicked it for yourself, haven't ya, you bastard?'

'I don't know what you're talking about, what money?'

'Don't give me all that shit. Where is it? Come on, Ryan. We can share it. Do a runner together. What d'ya say?'

'And how far do you think we'd get, before Delaney got his hands on us? Besides he's here now,' Ryan said, standing at the narrow gate and waving over to Delaney.

'How did you know?'

'Know what?' Ryan said, walking back and standing over Danny.

'Know that I'd use this escape route?'

'Danny, you silly bastard. We used to use this gate all the time when we were working the carsi's together. There was no way you could have got out of the main gates and jumping over into the BBC wasn't an option. This was the only way out. It was obvious.'

'Danny! Well, well, who's been a naughty boy, then,' Delaney smiled. A cold, cynical smile that sent shockwaves down Danny's spine. He closed his eyes, and resigned himself to the fate that awaited him.

CHAPTER 19

It was a dull overcast morning when Loder, DS Frost and Tanya pulled up outside the gates of Jonnie James's house. Loder got out of the car, pressed the intercom and waited patiently for a response. Nothing. He pressed it again, longer this time. Nothing. Impatiently, he pressed it again. This time the speaker crackled to life and a croaky voice, said, 'What do you want?'

'We'd like to ask you a few questions, Mr James,' Loder, politely said.

'What about?'

'I'm not prepared to discuss it out here, Mr James. Now open this gate and let us in.'

'You got any questions, see my lawyer.'

'Open this gate, right now, or I'll have this property swarming with officers before you've even had time to brush your teeth. I'm sure the neighbours would enjoy the spectacle.'

There was a loud clunk and the gate rolled open. DS Frost swung the car around the shingle drive and stopped at the bottom of the steps. The door was already ajar as they climbed the steps. Tanya pushed it open and the three of them went in.

'Shut the door behind you.' Came a voice from down the hallway.

Loder poked his head into the lounge. It was empty, so they went down the hall and into the kitchen, where they found Jonnie James making a pot of filtered coffee. 'Why don't you sit down? I'll be with you in a minute,' he said, going across to the huge American fridge and getting out a bottle of milk. He filled a china jug with the milk, got four mugs from a cupboard, placed them all on a tray with the coffee, and brought it over to the table. 'Shall we?' he said, pulling out a chair and sitting down. Tanya and DS Frost sat facing him and Loder sat on the end adjacent to Jonnie James.

'Shall I be mother?' he smiled, filling the mugs. 'Milk, Inspector Loder?' he said, holding the china jug over his mug.

Loder dismissed it away with back of his hand, and said, 'Can we get on?'

'Of course. Now, what can I do for you?' he said, pulling his white, bath robe tight across his bony chest.

Tanya looked away and scratched the side of her head to compose herself. She then reached into her shoulder bag, placed a thin manila folder on the table and slid it across to Loder. He opened it and placed the picture of Danny in front of Jonnie James. 'Do you recognise the lad in that picture?'

Caught dumbstruck, Jonnie James's left eye began to twitch as he stared blankly at the picture of, Danny. In an instant, he just shrugged, and said, 'No, I don't think so. Why do you ask?'

'When we visited you before, Mr James, I had a chat in this very kitchen with a teenage lad that looked remarkably similar to the boy in that picture,' Tanya said.

'So.'

'Have another look at the picture, Mr James,' Loder said, sliding it closer.

Jonnie James gave it a perfunctory glance.

'Well, you said at the time that the lad was your nephew,' Tanya said.

'Did I?'

'Where is he now?' Loder said.

'He's not here. I haven't seen him for a couple of days.'

'What do you mean, you haven't seen him for a couple of days?' DS Frost, cut in.

'He comes and goes as he pleases. I'm not his keeper,' he said, licking dry spit from the corner of his mouth.

'He's not your nephew, is he, Mr James?' Tanya asked.

Jonnie James drank a gulp of coffee, leaned back in his chair and gesticulated with his arms. 'Look, officers.' He smiled, nervously.

'Danny is his own person; he's a streetwise kid who has a lot of problems. He shows up every so often when he's down on his luck and I take him in and look after him.'

'How noble of you. A regular knight in shining armour,' Loder said, sarcastically.

'Being a celebrity, I think it's incumbent upon me to help where I can, inspector. I organise quite a lot of funding for the disadvantaged, and work closely with a number of children's homes,' he said, proudly.

'I *bet* you do,' Loder countered.

'What's that supposed to mean?' His eyes narrowed.

'How long have you known, Danny?' Loder said.

'About two years, I suppose.'

'Where does he live, when he's not staying here?' Tanya asked.

'Eh . . . I don't know.'

'Come on, Mr James. You can't expect us to believe that?' Tanya said.

'Look, all I know is that Danny stays at a flat with some other lads in Paddington somewhere. That is all I know. Danny is a chameleon, he never speaks of what he gets up to, or what he does when he's not here.'

'How does he contact you?' DS Frost said, spooning a heaped teaspoon of sugar into his coffee.

'He doesn't. He just turns up on the doorstep whenever the mood takes him.'

Loder's impatience with all this small talk was getting the better of him. So he cut straight to the chase. 'Do you have a sexual relationship with Danny?' he said, looking him straight in the eye.

Tanya cringed at Loder's candour.

'Right, that's it. If you want to interview me further you do it through my solicitor,' he said, getting to his feet. 'Now if you don't mind, I've got a busy day ahead.'

Loder got up and shot, Jonnie James a wry smile. 'Look forward to it. We'll talk later, Mr James. Only next time it will be under caution.'

Tanya scooped up the file, tucked it into her shoulder bag and followed Loder out. DS Frost finished the dregs in his cup. 'Nice coffee' he said, as he skirted up behind them.

Loder opened the street door and stood aside to let Tanya and DS Frost pass. He then turned around and said, 'We'll be in touch.'

Jonnie James wiped his mouth and had a good look down by the front gate to see if there was any paparazzi skulking around, before closing the door.

He went into the lounge, picked up the phone, walked over to the window and dialled a number he had permanently etched in his memory. 'That bloody detective, Loder, has been around here again. You assured me that I would not have any more hassle from him. Sort it.'

CHAPTER 20

Lazing on the deck of his houseboat, engrossed in a novel, Richard Binden didn't have a care in the world. The birds were singing in the trees, his fishing line was cast and the sway of the flowing tide as it filled the tributary, gently rocked the boat, like a mother nursing a baby. His eyelids dropped and the book fell into his lap as he began to doze in the warm hazy sunshine.

Suddenly, a thud against the underside of the bow woke him from his dreamy slumber. He thought nothing of it, probably a lump of driftwood or something brought in with the tide – happened all the time. He heard it again. Annoyed with the intrusion, he eased himself up from his deckchair to take a look.

He peered down over the side of the boat and along the hull, but couldn't quite make out what it was. It looked like a clump of weeds tangled around something. He went along the side of the boat to get a better look. His first thought was that it was a carcass of an animal bobbing around just below the water line. He picked up the long stave with a metal hook on the end and gently pushed the lump away from the boat.

Suddenly, it turned over and a pair of bulbous eyes stared up at him. He threw the stave into the water and scrambled backwards onto the roof of the boat. His heart thumped against his rib cage so fiercely he thought he was about to have a seizure. His head swimming in consternation, tentatively, he peered over the side again, just to be sure his eyes weren't playing tricks on him. There was no mistake . . . it was a body. He jumped off the roof of the boat onto the grass bank, fumbled around in his trouser pockets, found his mobile phone and dialled 999.

Loder was in DCI Oakwood's office briefing her on the outcome of his visit to Jonnie James's house, when there was a knock on the door and DS Frost poked his head in. 'Call has just come in, boss. There's been a body washed up in the Thames.'

'Where?'

'Sunbury.'

'Male or female?'

'Not sure, at the moment.'

'Okay. Bring the car round. I'll meet you downstairs.'

'I'll come with you, John,' Anne Oakwood said, grabbing her coat. 'Better if I make myself scarce for an hour or two. Before the proverbial shit hit's the fan over the Jonnie James affair.'

'See you downstairs in five. Let's pray that it's not Donna.'

DS Frost already had the engine running when Loder and Anne Oakwood appeared through the door and down the steps into the compound. 'Looks like we've got company,' he said, turning to Tanya.

'You got a problem with that?'

'No. Just saying, that's all. They seem to be very pally these days, don't you think?'

'What are you getting at, Tony? God! You're like a gossiping old woman,' she said, shaking her head, tiresomely.

'Well, you know. You don't think that they are—'

'No, I don't think.' Tanya cut him short.

'I was just saying that's all—'

'Don't bother, I don't wish to hear it.'

Loder held the door for his boss and she slid across the back seat. He got in next to her. 'Do you know where we're going, Tony?' he said, slamming the door.

'Yeh. Think so, boss.'

DS Frost turned right onto the main road, around Hammergrove Broadway, along the Great West Road, then over Kew Bridge heading towards Richmond.

Sunbury on Thames was on a quite backwater off the main river. Once they had left the motorway and dropped onto Lower Sunbury, they descended down to the riverside and back in the direction of Richmond. It was a quiet lazy hamlet of a place, with just a couple of waterside pubs, a trendy restaurant and a rowing club. Dotted along the waterside were rows of bungalows and further along was a train of prettily painted houseboats with tubs of potted plants and flowerbeds in front. It was a million miles away from the hustle and bustle of London life.

The crime scene had already been taped off and a small crowd had assembled behind it when they arrived. DS Frost parked the car and they all made their way across the grassy bank, ducking under the tape. A canopy had been erected in front of the houseboat to keep prying eyes out.

A police launch was anchored out in the middle of the water between the two banks and a diver was milling around were the body had been found. White, boiler-suited, scene of crime officers were busy going about their business, dusting and photographing everything. The whole scene was efficiently quiet.

Loder looked around for a moment and then walked across the bank to where a grey-suited, young officer was busy taking notes from a SOCO. Loder flashed his warrant card. Unperturbed, the young detective nodded and carried on taking notes.

'Who found the body?' Loder asked, surveying the scene.

The detective, clearly exasperated, pointed with his pencil to the houseboat. 'He's on there.'

'Sir!' Loder barked.

The detective closed his notebook and nodded to the crime scene offer. 'Sir,' he said, succinctly.

'And your name is, laddie?'

'DC Childs, sir.'

'Where's your DI?'

'Not here, sir. DS Knight is on the boat interviewing the person that found the body.'

Loder walked back across the grassy bank to where his team were milling around. 'Tony you go onto the boat. Their DS, should fill you in with all the details. Tanya see what you can get from the SOCO'S. Right, let's go and have a look at our body, shall we?' he said, turning to DCI Oakwood.

He strode back across the bank to where the makeshift canopy was erected and stood by the opening. DCI Oakwood skirted up behind and joined him.

'Afternoon, Gerald,' Loder said, peering down at a tangled heap laid out on a rubber sheet.

Doctor Gerald Burton the Home Office Chief Pathologist, looked up at Loder from his squat position over the body. 'And good afternoon to you, Detective Inspector Loder,' he said, pulling off his soiled gloves and popping them into a disposal bag. He snapped his tatty attaché case shut, gave a deep sigh, pushed his hands down on his knees and heaved his heavy bulk upright. Struggling to escape out of his paper overalls, he gave a nod to his two assistants. They rolled out a body bag, unzipped it and laid it out next to the body.

He handed one of the assistants his discarded whites and joined Loder and DCI Oakwood. Doctor Burton was the archetypal professor with his gingery beard and curly wild hair pushed back behind his ears. Dressed in a faded corduroy jacket with sagging pockets, baggy matching trousers, that had long since lost any resemblance to corduroy at the knees, and heavy leather brogue shoes, his attire was firmly entrenched in the 1940's.

'So, what can you tell me, Gerald?'

'No need to be so rude, John. We haven't been introduced,' he said, with articulated charm, proffering a hand to Anne Oakwood.

'DCI Anne Oakwood,' she said, shaking his hand.

'Ah! John's new boss?' His eyes danced mischievously.

It was obvious to DCI Oakwood that the two men were firm friends.

'So, to business,' Dr Burton said, combing his fingers through his beard. 'The body is that of a teenage male. Cause of death is hard to determine right now. My guess is that the poor lad bled to death.'

'How?' DCI Oakwood, asked.

'The boy has been the victim of serious sexual assault.'

'Can you be more specific?' Loder said.

'The boy's rectum has been ripped apart by a violent assault.'

'What's that in layman's terms?' Loder said.

'He's been buggered to death by one or more people. My guess at this stage is that he was gang raped. The lad must have suffered extreme pain before dying.'

Anne Oakwood closed her eyes in horror.

'I do apologise for being so candid, but there's no easy way to explain it,' the pathologist said, sympathetically.

'Time of death?'

'Hard to determine, given the amount of time the body was in the water. My guess at this stage is that he has not been dead for longer than forty-eight hours. Of course, I will be able to be more accurate after I have performed a detailed examination of the body. That is as much as I can tell you at this stage.'

'Do you mind if I take a look?' Loder asked.

'Be my guest. We have just about finished up here.'

Loder walked over to the body as the two assistants lifted it onto a gurney. He nodded and they unzipped the body bag. He could be mistaken, given the condition the body was in, but he thought that it was Danny McKee. 'Anne, would you mind getting Tanya. See if she can make a positive ID on the body.'

DCI Oakwood couldn't have left the scene quickly enough. At this precise moment she craved fresh air and sunshine more than an addict craved a fix. No matter how many crime scenes she attended, she never felt comfortable at them, specially where children were involved. Apart from giving devastating news to grieving parents, it was the one aspect of the job that she could never get to grips with.

'So, John! Tell me, what is it like working for a woman; a very attractive one at that?'

'It's fine. We work well together. She's a good detective.'

'Come on, John. You can't fool me. I saw the way she looked at you. I can read the body language between the pair of you. After all it's my stock-in-trade. I have known you too many years John, so don't pull the wool over my eyes.

Loder sighed, defeated. 'Okay, yes. I like her.'

The pathologist narrowed a brow, questionably.

'Okay.' Loder held his hands up. 'We've been out a few times, together. That's all you're getting, Gerald.'

The pathologist rested a reassuring hand on Loder's shoulder, and whispered, 'I'm pleased for you. It's about time.'

Tanya poked her head inside the canopy. 'You wanted me, sir?'

'Have a look at this body. See if it's our boy.'

She walked over to the gurney and took a long hard look at the face. But couldn't be sure. She rummaged around in her bag and pulled out the info on Danny that she had run off the computer. She unfolded the sheets of A4 and thumbed down the text. 'Can you turn him onto his left side, please?' she asked the assistant.

He obliged. The brown birthmark on the right hip was confirmation. Suddenly, a lump of raw bowel fell out into the body bag. Tanya jumped backwards in horror, almost emptying the contents of her stomach all over the tent. She stumbled backwards careering into Loder. He grabbed hold of her and steadied her. 'You, okay?' he said, concerned.

Tanya took a couple of deep breaths to compose herself. 'I'm fine, now. Thank you, sir. It was just a bit of a shock that's all.'

'Is it our boy?'

'Yes, sir. I wasn't too certain to begin with, but the birthmark confirms that it's Danny McKee.'

'When do you think you'll have more for me, Gerald?'

'I'll get to work on him later this afternoon. Give me a ring before midday tomorrow. I should have something for you then,' he said.

'Okay, thanks.' He put a comforting arm around Tanya and led her out into the sunshine. 'Go and see if Tony's finished and we'll get out of here.'

Loder and DCI Oakwood made their way back to the car in silence. She looked up at him and could almost hear his mind turning over ten-to-the-dozen.

'Penny for them, Loder?'

'I was just thinking about Tanya's father. I worked with him, you know?'

'No I didn't. Where, here in London?'

'No. In the early seventies, in Glasgow. I was a DC, he was my DI. He died in my arms. Some tupenny-hapenny villain shot him in the neck. I was the first one to get to him. Never forget it as long as I live.'

'Must have been awful, for you?'

'I'd never forgive myself if something happened to Tanya. I promised her mother that I would look out for her, when she was assigned to my team.'

'She couldn't be in better hands, John. Let's head back to town and go for a drink. See if we can come up with some kind of strategy?'

'Yeh, why not.' He had a quick scan around the scene, saw that no one was looking, and planted a soft peck on her cheek. 'Thanks,' He said, smiling down at her.

'What for? I haven't done anything.'

'You have no idea how much good you have done me. Just wait until I get you home tonight, DCI Oakwood.'

'Ooo! So masterful.'

The more she learned about Loder, the more she was drawn to his magnetism: she couldn't help herself. She knew his persona around the corridors of power was that of a solitary, hard-hitting bastard that didn't suffer authority or fools in equal measures. But crack the hard outer shell and what emerged was a kind, caring man who tried to make a difference. A man that she could not get enough of. A man that she was falling deeply in love with.

Forty minutes later, they were all ensconced around a table in the garden of the Crown & Sceptre. Loder was puffing away on a panatela, contemplating what their next move should be. He rested the half-smoked cigar in the ashtray, and said, 'Let's have a re-cap of what we've got so far.'

Tanya got out her notepad and flipped through the pages. She was meticulous when it came to jotting down little markers in the process of a long investigation. Sometimes you could lose sight of what you were actually trying to achieve and miss vital, small clues along the way. She found it indispensable, when going back over old ground.

'One: we've got a positive sighting of Donna Carlin at Jonnie James's house,' Tanya said.

'Not a reliable source,' DS Frost, countered.

'True.' Loder nodded.

'Has anyone shown Lee Carlin a picture of Danny? It's a long shot, but you never know. Danny may have been the lad in the pub that night,' DCI Oakwood said.

Loder shot Tanya and DS Frost a look that said, "Well has he?"

'I'll get onto it, sir,' Tanya said.

'Two: we know that Danny – a known runaway and probable rent boy – was staying at James's house. Presumably, of his own free will. Three: soon after we visit James's house, Danny turns up dead.' Loder nibbled at his lip pensively.

'Which begs the question, do we think that Donna Carlin is dead?' DS Frost said, knowing that the notion was in the back of all of their minds.

'I think that until we find a body, we proceed on the basis that she is alive.' Loder nipped any doubt in the bud.

All three nodded in agreement.

'Going back to what the paedophile unit told us. It's clear that Jonnie James is into something that is so secret: it's watertight. And clearly, its members – for want of a better word – hold some very powerful positions in society. Possibly, even in our own profession . . . no, quite probably. Otherwise, why would we have been warned off? It's plainly obvious that James – or his brief – know some heavyweight people that can bring influence to bear,' Loder said, looking across at his boss for some reassurance.

'It pains me to say it, but I think, DI Loder is right. I've had the riot act read to me, not once, but twice. I was informed in no uncertain terms after the last visit to James's house that my position might be called into question, if we didn't lay off him. That leads me to believe that someone very high up the ladder is pulling strings. I don't know who, or how we get to him. But it's clear we have to play our cards close to our chests. We can trust no one.'

'Another round,' Loder said, diffusing the tense atmosphere around the table. 'You're not allergic to wood, are you, Tony?'

'No,' he replied, confused.

'Well, get up to the bar and get us all a drink,' he smiled, handing him an empty glass.

DS Frost snatched the glass and set off across the garden to the bar. He returned with a tray of drinks, sat down and rolled a cigarette from a leather pouch. The smoke wafting under DCI Oakwood's nose, together with Loder's cigar smoke, was weakening her resolve by the second. Loder saw the mental torment on her face and handed her his cigar.

'Ma'am!' Tanya said, aghast.

'Don't even go there, Tanya,' DCI Oakwood said, waving a dismissive hand.

'Right, back to business,' Loder said, leaning forward conspiratorially. I think we need to get a warrant to search James's house. We need to shake him down, good and hard. See what it throws up. All we've got up to now are miscellaneous bits of the jigsaw. What we need is the one piece that knits it all together and the rest will just fall into place. And, I'm in no doubt whatsoever that Jonnie James is the man that can supply it. The problem we have, is proving it.'

'Getting a warrant won't be easy, given what we already know, boss' DS Frost said.

'Exactly. We need to approach someone who won't be put off by idle threats. Someone who we can put our trust in. Any ideas?' Loder looked around the table.

'What about the Detective Super?' Anne Oakwood, offered.

Loder sniffed. 'Possible.' But wasn't exactly enamoured with the idea; he was new to the job and Loder felt that he didn't know him well enough to trust him. 'Anyone else come to mind?'

They all shook their heads.

'I think we should go above the DS and go directly to the Detective Chief Superintendent.'

'You sure, boss? That's cutting through a lot of egos,' DS Frost said.

'Listen, when I went to him with evidence of Jack Stamp's corruption, he acted upon it. Didn't bury it away in the archives. He exposed Stamp and the DS for what they were. On that basis, I think he is probably our safest bet. First, I want you, Tanya, to get hold of Lee Carlin. Show him the picture of Danny. If he ID's him as the same lad he met in the pub, then it strengthens our case. He can't refuse us a warrant.'

'What if he does, boss?' DS Frost, put a spanner in the works.

'We'll cross that bridge when we come to it.'

Tanya got out her mobile and found Lee Carlin's number. 'Hi, Lee. Where are you? I need to see you for a moment. Okay, I'll be straight over.' She ended the call and slipped the mobile back into her jacket pocket. 'He's at home, sir. I'll get over there now and phone you when I know something.'

'Another drink?' DCI Oakwood said.

'Not for me, ma'am,' DS Frost said. 'Think I'll get off. If that's okay, boss. It's parents evening at Bradley's school this evening. Have to show willing: responsibilities of parenthood,' he said, pulling on his jacket.

'No, you get off, Tony. Tell that boy of yours if his grades aren't up to scratch, there won't be any Christmas box this year.'

'Brainy little bugger, he is. Don't get it from me that's for sure, must be the wife's side.'

'That's one thing we both agree on, Tony. See you in the morning.'

Anne Oakwood brought fresh drinks to the table and sidled in next to Loder. 'So, you want to form a united front when we go to DCS?' she said.

'Makes sense. Enough of work. I'm famished. Do you want to get something to eat?'

'What have you got in mind?' She teased, raising a brow.

Loder smiled. 'You're incorrigible, do you know that? How about we stop off and pick up a couple of steaks and I'll cook for us, at my place?'

'Your home! I *am* honoured. Drink up, and let's get out of here before you change your mind,' she said, emptying her glass.

Forty-five minutes later, Loder was busy cooking away in his kitchen. Anne Oakwood had made herself busy by tossing a bowl of salad. She replenished both their glasses, rested back against the worktop, and watched as Loder confidently got to work on a red wine and mushroom sauce to go with their steaks.

Watching him standing over a hob wrapped in an apron cooking, was a side she knew few people, if any, had ever seen of Loder. In a strange sort of way, she felt quite honoured to be sharing his private space with him.

Anne knew that being here, in this house, was something that Loder wouldn't have decided upon lightly. She doubted very much – no she knew – that no one, never alone a woman . . . a lover, had stepped foot in this house since his wife had died. 'Smells delicious,' she said, nursing her glass in her hands.

'I'm alright on the basics,' he said, turning a pile of mushrooms into the meat juices, before adding the wine. I enjoy cooking when the mood takes me, but there's not much point when there's only me in the house.'

Suddenly, a mobile chirped to life. 'That's mine. Can you get it?' Loder said, nodding towards his jacket draped around the back of a chair.

Anne put her glass down, walked across to where his jacket was and retrieved the mobile from the side pocket. Without thinking, she answered it.

'Um . . . Eh . . . is that you ma'am?' Tanya asked, tentatively.

Oh, shit! It's Tanya, she mouthed, silently to Loder and handed him the mobile.

'Tanya.'

'Good news, sir. We've got a positive ID. Lee Carlin was in no doubt, Danny was the lad he spoke to in the pub.'

'Yesss!' Loder punched the air with the spatula.

'Where are you?' Tanya enquired, tentatively.

'At home,' he said, without thinking.

'Oh. Right . . . I'll see you in the morning, sir. Goodnight, she said, in a double entendre tone of voice.'

'Sorry. I didn't think,' Anne Oakwood said.

'Don't worry. Tanya's discreet. She isn't the sort of person to go around gossiping. If need be, I'll have a quiet word in her ear. Now why don't you take our drinks through to the lounge and make yourself comfortable? I'm just about ready to serve up.'

She picked up the half-full bottle of wine and their two glasses and wandered through to the lounge. The room was comfortably furnished. It was plainly obvious that it was a woman's taste. In front of her was a cream three-piece suite, squarely situated around a period fireplace. A glass-topped, walnut, oval coffee table stood in the middle. The rich, ruby, deep-pile carpet gave the room a warm hue. Looking around, it was spotlessly tidy. Anne sensed that Loder didn't do much "living" in here.

To her left, was a very expensive looking walnut dining suite with a matching display cabinet along one wall and a tall bookcase on the other. The bookcase was neatly stacked with a full set of leather-bound encyclopaedias, rows of teaching manuals and textbooks. She suspected that Loder's wife must have been a teacher or a lecturer. Nothing was out of place. They were all stacked in height order.

She set the bottle of wine and glass down on the table, kicked off her shoes and let the deep pile tickle her toes. Then wandered aimlessly over to the display cabinet and admired the set of crystal glasses twinkling in the light. A colourful prism shone out onto the carpet in front of her. In the middle of the cabinet was a silver-framed photo of Loder together with a woman. She squatted to get a better look. The photo must have been taken at least twenty years ago. Loder was posing proudly dressed in an immaculate navy suit with his arm around her shoulder. Both were smiling and happy. Her first thought was that his wife wasn't what you would call pretty by any stretch of the imagination. *Me'ow. Bitchy cow.* She chastised herself. But if she was truthful, anyone could see that the woman was incredibly attractive. Loder also, cut a handsome figure with his dark, curly hair and sultry dark eyes – come to bed eyes – she called them. He had an enigmatic look about him that most women would make it their life's mission to get hold of.

An uncomfortable feeling suddenly washed over her as she stood up. She couldn't explain it, but she felt as if she was trespassing on forbidden ground. The whole room screamed of a presence. As if his wife was watching her every move; judging her.

Loder came into the room carrying a tray and set it down onto the dining table. 'Here we are,' he said proudly, pulling a chair out for her.

She walked over to the table and sat down. Loder served up some salad with a wooden fork and spoon. 'Hope it's okay?'

'Looks delicious,' she said, cutting into the tender meat. 'And tastes delicious as well.'

Loder replenished their glasses and tucked in. The atmosphere quickly descended into an uncomfortable silence between them. 'Anything wrong?' he asked.

'No, no. I'm fine. Just a bit tired,' she smiled, half-heartedly. 'Think I'll get off home.'

'Why don't you stay here?'

'No. It's best I go.'

'I'll drive you.'

'No, I'll grab a cab. Besides, you've had too much to drink.'

She looked into Loder's eyes and saw that he was hurt. She leaned across and tenderly stroked the side of his face. Then gave him a soft kiss. 'It's not you. It's me. I need to get my head around things.'

'What things?'

'Nothing for you to worry about, Loder,' she said, giving him another kiss. 'Now phone me a cab and I'll see you in the morning.

CHAPTER 21

Loder and DCI Oakwood were in Detective Chief Superintendent Charles Hatchet's office, briefing him on their situation as he perused through the case file.

DCS Charles Hatchet – Charlie Hatchet as the tabloid press had labelled him – had an affinity to the nickname. So Charlie boy – the peoples friend – had happily milked it for all it was worth. Charles Hatchet was one of the new breeds of copper. A graduate in his early forties who had been fast-tracked up the greasy pole of success. He had never experienced, first hand, real-life on the streets or the violence of an inner city London housing estate. Kensington & Chelsea and weekends at the country estate was written all over him – right down to his trendy designer suits and expensive Jermyn Street leather shoes. But all said and done, Hatchet had reduced teenage knife crime by flooding the estates with officers and pursuing a zero tolerance policy towards stop-and-search. "Hatchet by name, Hatchet by nature" the press had headlined.

Loder and DCI Oakwood gave a tentative look at each other as the DCS closed the file, rested his elbows on the desk and clasped his hands under his chin. 'It would seem that you may be right. Someone could be pulling the strings where Mr James is concerned. You were absolutely right in bringing this straight to my attention.'

'Thank you, sir,' DCI Oakwood said.

'Now, what do you want from me?'

'We'd like a search warrant for James's house, sir.'

'I see,' Hatchet said, peering over his half-moon, gold-rimmed spectacles perched on the end of his aquiline nose. He chewed over their request for a moment. 'How certain are you that the body fished out of the Thames and the lad seen in James's house are the same person?'

'My DC spoke to the boy when were at his place and she is as certain as she can be that they are. I trust her judgement one hundred percent,' Loder said.

'Consider it done.'

'Thank you, sir,' DCI Oakwood enthused.

'One thing, detectives.'

'Sir?'

'You both report to me, directly, from now on. I want to be kept up to date at all times. Is that clear?'

'Absolutely, sir,' Loder said.

'Okay,' he smiled. 'If there's nothing else?'

'No, sir. Thank you, for your support,' Loder said, getting to his feet. He made his way to the door and held it open for his boss.

'Remember, DI Loder, DCI Oakwood, report to me, and only me,' Hatchet said, casting Loder a pointed look over the top of his specs.

'Sir,' Loder said.

Outside in the corridor, Loder punched the air with jubilation. DCI Oakwood looked on, amused at his boyish enthusiasm. He strode along the corridor and down the stairs like a dog that had just been gifted the proverbial juicy, big bone. He was *now* a man on a mission. Anne Oakwood had to break into a trot just to keep up with him.

'I'll get Tony to organise a team so we can hit James's place as soon as the warrant comes through,' Loder said, over his shoulder to his boss as she skirted up behind. 'Think I'll scoot over to the morgue first. See what the pathologist has got for us on the body. Do you want to come with me, Anne?'

'Why not. It's probably better that we make ourselves scarce. I don't particularly want to be around when the DS hears what we've been up to.'

Loder parked his car on the forecourt of the mortuary, known locally as the "Dead Centre." One of the cleaners had coined the phrase, telling everyone that he was proud to work in "The Dead Centre of

Hammergrove." The building was tucked away down by the River Thames, just off Hammergrove Road. It was one of West London's more secretive streets. Few people found themselves around there, and the traffic was intent on being elsewhere. Especially since all the heavy industry that used to be dotted along the banks of the river had long since moved on, leaving behind a tangle of half-demolished buildings and piles of debris. Looking at the huge billboards erected along Wharf Road, most of the prime locations had already been acquired for redevelopment into luxury apartment blocks that no normal working person could ever dream of affording.

As they walked towards the entrance, Loder shook his shoulders in preparation. No matter how many times he visited the morgue, he never felt comfortable with it. The drab dirty building didn't help matters. Rumour had it, that it used to be an old Victorian abortion clinic. The edifice did little to dispel the rumour, with its blackened brickwork and pea-green glazed tiles along the length of the façade.

They identified themselves to the young receptionist and then sat down on a cushioned, wooden bench while she paged the pathologist.

Loder found himself eyeing the receptionist, and wondered why a young girl would want to work in a morbid place such as this. She had a sad, sullen look that fitted perfectly with the surroundings. Just like the professional mourners he had encountered when making the burial arrangements for his wife. She glanced across and caught Loder's stare. He quickly averted his eyes and said to Annie Oakwood, 'Let's hope we get some good news here.'

Even with false ceilings, modern concealed lighting and fitted carpets, they could never get rid of the ingrained smell of disinfectant and formaldehyde: it stuck in the throat and reached right down to the pit of the stomach. The smell stayed in the clothes for days.

The buzz of the electric lock releasing, caught their attention. Dr Gerald Burton appeared, dressed in a white surgical gown, green apron and Wellington boots. 'Come on through,' he said, holding the door ajar.

They followed the pathologist along a long terracotta tiled, narrow corridor. The heavy doors set in arched alcoves on each side, looked more like prison cells than offices. The sparse fluorescent lighting cast dark shadows down the walls onto muddy-brown, glazed tiles. At the end of the corridor, hung two heavy, opaque swing doors. The pathologist held one of them open and the two detectives entered the expansive theatre.

Loder felt the temperature drop, sending a cold shiver down his spine. Evenly spaced in the centre were three stainless-steel tables, each perforated with drainage holes and a trough along each side. Underneath was a collecting tray and gully that led away to a sluice. A worn out oak block used as a headrest rested squarely at the head of each table. Along the far wall, was a row of stainless-steel doors on two tiers, behind which, the cadavers were stored. On the opposite side, a small viewing gallery faced down into the theatre from behind a glass curtain.

Danny lay on the middle table, his eyes closed and blonde hair combed back over the wooden block. Had it not been for the pale grey pallor of his skin, one could be mistaken for thinking that he was asleep. The corner of his mouth had a slight curl upward that gave the impression of a wry smile.

Dr Burton stood over the body, pulled on a pair of examination gloves and said, 'Shall we begin? Firstly, death was not by drowning. Taking into account the stage that rigor mortis was at when we found him and the temperature of the water at the time of discovery, together with fact that the skin on his feet had begun to separate. The best estimate I can give you is that the boy died between twenty-four and thirty hours before he was fished out of the water. That makes it between 9:00 a.m and 1:00 p.m on the Sunday.'

'Cause of death?' DCI Oakwood asked.

'There is a contusion to the back of the skull, he pointed to a small split at the back of Danny's head; probably sustained from a fall or being hit with a blunt flat instrument. But it wasn't the cause of death, that was particularly nasty. In my opinion the boy has been lashed to something, probably a bed and brutally raped, repeatedly, over a period of time.' He pointed to some dark bruise rings around the wrists and ankles. He rolled the body onto its side and went on, 'His rectum has been torn open, as is his lower bowel, which led the lad to bleed to death from the injuries. He pointed to the injuries so that they could see for themselves. He then carefully rolled the body onto its back.

'My God! The poor boy must have suffered, horrendously,' DCI Oakwood said, shaking her head.

'I couldn't agree more. This lad went through an horrific ordeal before being left to die.'

'Any traces of semen found?' Loder asked.

'Toxicology is still testing, but given the length of time the body was in the water, I don't hold out much hope. But you never know we could get a lucky break.' The pathologist held his hands out. 'I'm sorry I can't give you more to go on.

Loder pursed his lips, blew out a puff of air, rubbed his cold neck, tiredly, and sighed, 'Thanks for your help Gerald. Let's hope toxicology come up with something.'

The pathologist nodded to an assistant hovering in the background to say that he was finished, and he and another assistant rolled a gurney across to the body. They lifted Danny onto it and rolled him away back to his slot in the huge fridge. It was all carried out in a matter-of-fact way, as if it was an everyday occurrence, which of course it was.

The pathologist led the two detectives back along the corridor and swiped his ID card in the code box by the exit. The door buzzed as it slipped its latch. Dr Burton held it open for them. 'I'll be in touch when I get the toxicology results,' he said, before disappearing back down the corridor.

Standing on the forecourt outside, Loder took deep breaths of fresh air to get the foul taste of formaldehyde out of his throat. He reached into his trouser pocket for his handkerchief and mopped his sweaty brow, then wiped his clammy hands. Even though the morgue was a temperature-controlled fridge, Loder always perspired when he got out into the open air.

The late morning sun was bright and unusually warm for the time of year, so he took off his overcoat and tossed it onto the back seat of the car. Then loosened his tie a little and undid the top button of his shirt.

'Wasn't very pleasant, was it?' DCI Oakwood said.

'No. Didn't make for easy listening,' he said, scraping his tongue on his teeth, to try to rid himself of the foul taste.

'Where to now?' She asked.

'There's not a lot—'

Loder stopped in mid-sentence to answer his mobile. 'That was quick. Right, we'll meet you over there. I don't want anyone making a move until we arrive. And stay out of sight: I don't want Jonnie James getting wind of the operation. Is that clear?'

Loder ended the call and slipped the mobile phone back into his trouser pocket. He then turned to Anne Oakwood, and beamed. 'The warrant has been delivered.'

'That was quick. Hatchet must have pulled a few strings.'

'Let's get on our way,' he said, sliding behind the steering wheel and turning the ignition. 'I've been waiting for this one,' he said, turning to his boss with a wry smile, as he drove off the forecourt.

*

Ryan walked into Delaney's bedroom carrying a mug of tea in one hand and a half-eaten sandwich in the other. 'Going out,' he said, laconically.

'Where?'

'Thought I might go down the Bush Market, see what's occurring.'

Ryan could see something – no, someone – bobbing up and down under the duvet. He had long since been banished to the spare bedroom, in favour of Delaney's new, fresh, young, and above all, submissive, new edition. He knew that he was just in the way, these days. But he couldn't just move out, besides, he didn't have anywhere to go apart from kipping down in some overcrowded bed-sit with some of the other lads. He didn't give a bollocks, anyway. But in truth, it grated on him that Delaney could just discard him, without a second's thought, as if he was something that he'd wiped his arse with and flushed it away down the toilet; out of sight, out of mind. After all the dirty work he had done for him, practically running the day-to-day business for him. Kept all the kids in check: it was even *his* idea to go searching in internet chat rooms. Now he was yesterday's news.

Ryan had read the reports in the newspapers and watched the TV news about Danny. He knew that it was only a matter of time until he met with the same demise. He had to get out of it. Well away from Delaney and his network of violent perverts.

Delaney closed his eyes and a self-satisfied smile suffused his sweaty, bulldog face. Ryan had seen it a thousand times before: now it made him feel sick to the stomach. Gary's blonde head surfaced above the duvet. He had a dazed look and a spattering of semen dribbled down his cheek. With bewilderment, he looked up at Delaney for approval. Delaney put his arm around him, pulled him close and reassured him. 'That's my boy. You know what I like. He then shot Ryan a vicious look, and growled, 'Why don't you fuck off out of it. Make sure you leave your mobile on, in case I need you.'

Ryan turned and left the room without saying a word. He went into the lounge, ensconced himself in the armchair and flicked the TV remote. He watched the morning news with indifference, not really listening to what the newsreader was reporting. His mind was in a place somewhere far away. A picture of Danny – taken a few years earlier – spread across the screen. He turned the volume up a little, but only caught two words, "gang raped." That was enough.

He knew then that he had to get away, sooner rather than later. The money – fifteen grand – that he had hidden when Danny was captured was still buried in the undergrowth in the park.

It was mentioned by Delaney after the event, but Ryan had just shrugged it off and pleaded ignorance. He'd said that he hadn't seen any packages on Danny when he tackled him and suggested that he must have got rid, beforehand. This seemed to appease Delaney at the time. Besides, Delaney was too wrapped up with catching Danny than to concern himself with the money. In the furore that followed it was never mentioned again.

Ryan made a conscious decision, there and then, to get out. First, he'd go down to Hammergrove Park, recover the money and hide it somewhere more secure. Perhaps in his bedroom, because it was a cast-iron certainty that Delaney would never set foot in there. Not now that he had someone else to satisfy his perverted needs.

Then somehow, he didn't know how yet, he was going to bring the whole thing tumbling down. The secret network, the houses and flats that worked the kids all the hours God sent, and last, but not least, Delaney himself. He was going to serve Delaney up like a kipper on a breakfast plate to the Old Bill, with enough evidence to lock him up and throw away the key.

He finished his tea and sandwich, switched the TV off and jumped to his feet with a renewed fervour. Everything was now clear in his mind: he knew what he had to do.

Ryan couldn't help a little smile as he passed the spot where Danny must have been hiding in the undergrowth, when the money was dropped. It was a good plan choosing a match night, when the area was heaving with football supporters. Danny might well of got away with it, if it hadn't been for the fact that he'd forgotten that Ryan knew of the concealed gate. It was obvious to Ryan that, that was going to be his escape route. It was the only way out.

Now, Ryan felt as if he had betrayed Danny. He would still be alive if it had not been for him. Why did he do it? Why did he give Danny to Delaney? He had asked himself that question many times over, since that ill-fated night. He had searched his conscience repeatedly for the answer and came up with just one, loyalty to Delaney. Misplaced loyalty.

Ryan pushed the thoughts from his mind and concentrated on the present as he went through the park entrance. He broke into a trot as he passed the children's play area. The park was empty, but for a few people walking through to Shepherds Green.

He approached the path hidden between the two overgrown bushes and looked around to see if anyone was watching, then ducked into the undergrowth and scrambled across to where he had buried the money.

He got down on his knees and began digging into the soil with his hands. Frantically, he scooped away handful after handful until he was about ten inches deep. Then panic set in. He was sure that he hadn't buried it so deep. Fuck! He cursed under his breath, as he began digging more quickly.

A sigh of relief washed over him as his fingers found the top of the carrier bag. He scooped away the soil, pulled out the package and unwrapped it. A wide smile suffused his face, as he tipped out the contents and tore open the tightly wrapped cellophane around the money, revealing a thick wad of crispy new fifty-pound notes. His eyes wide, he gasped with amazement. He'd never seen so many fifty-pound notes; in fact, he doubted if he'd ever had a single, fifty, in his hands before. There, on his knees, with all this money in front of him, he made a silent vow to Danny, that he would bring down Harry Delaney: he would do it for him.

Quickly, he wrapped the cellophane back around the money the best he could, popped it into the carrier bag, stuffed it under his hooded top and pulled the drawstring tight around his waist. He then got to his feet, ducked back out onto the path and briskly walked in the direction of Shepherds Green.

*

Loder and DCI Oakwood found DS Frost and Tanya parked up seventy yards past Jonnie James's house. In front of them was an MPV with six uniformed officers and two plain-clothed DC's.

They got out of the car and Loder tapped on the window to DS Frost as he passed by. He and Tanya got out and followed Loder to the MPV. Loder slid the door open and ducked his head inside.
'afternoon lads. Have you been briefed yet?'

'Thought we'd wait for you, boss,' DS Frost said.

'Okay.'

Loder gave them a quick briefing on the background of the case. He told them that they were looking for evidence of James's involvement in underage sexual activity, or anything pertaining to a sexual nature.

He instructed the two plain-clothed DC's to take four uniformed men and cover the back of the house. He instructed the other two to go through the garage and make their way up into the house that way.

They all got back into their cars, did a U turn and drove up to the gate. Loder got out and pressed the intercom.

'What a surprise, Inspector Loder. Have you brought your boys along for a swim in the pool?' Came a smart-arse remark over the intercom as the gate buzzed open.

Loder pulled around the shingle driveway and parked at the foot of the steps to the front door. The other two vehicles stopped behind. The men spilled out of MPV and took up their positions. Loder strode up to the steps and knocked on the door. DCI Oakwood stood next to him with DS Frost and Tanya behind.

Jonnie James opened the door and smiled. 'How can I help you, officers?'

Loder got out the folded warrant from his inside pocket and slapped it in his hand. 'I think you know what that is,' he smiled, and brushed past him.

'Come in, why don't you?'

Tanya made her way through to the kitchen and unbolted the door that led down to the garage. DS Frost found his way through to the back of the house to let the others in. Within minutes, the whole place was swarming with police officers.

Jonnie James was in the lounge on the telephone to his lawyer. He ended the call and turned to Loder and DCI Oakwood. 'Now, officers. If you tell me what it is that you're looking for, maybe I can help you. It would save all this upheaval,' he said, smugly.

'That won't be necessary Mr James. Why don't we sit down and have a chat?' DCI Oakwood said, making herself comfortable on the sofa. Loder stood in front of the tall, bay window with the afternoon sun warming his back. He said nothing. Just stood there observing Jonnie James. It was all pre-planned between him and his boss beforehand that she would start the interrogation with an informal friendly approach and he would try to catch him off guard later with the heavy artillery.

Tanya came into the room with one of the plain-clothed officer's and Loder motioned with his eyes for them to go through all drawers and cupboards.

Jonnie James looked on with an unconcerned smirk. 'My lawyer has told me to tell you that we will be suing for any damages to my personal property.'

Loder didn't bite.

'Mr James,' DCI Oakwood smiled. 'You can rest assured that my officers are very experienced in these procedures.'

'And you are?' Jonnie James asked.

'I'm sorry. We haven't been introduced. I am Detective Chief Inspector Oakwood. I'm in charge of the investigation into Danny McKee's murder.'

'Terrible business. But I fail to see what Danny's death has to do with me? He said, brushing his straggly hair over his shoulder.

'To the best of our knowledge, you were the last person to see Danny. . . alive.'

'What are you getting at?'

'Nothing, Mr James. How long have you known, Danny?' Jonnie James sniffed, tediously. 'Couple of years I suppose.'

'And how did the two of you become acquainted?'

Jonnie James thought about the question for a moment. He already knew the answer. He had it all scripted long before this lot had descended upon him. 'Danny was a fan of mine and used to camp outside the front gates to catch a glimpse of me. He was just another autograph hunter. It's something I have to put up with,' he sighed, tediously again. I have been through all this with Inspector Loder, he said, getting irate.'

'I know, but I'd like to hear it for myself, Mr James,' DCI Oakwood, placated.

'Well, as I've already said. One day he'd been out there for hours in the rain, so I took him out a drink and a signed photo of myself. He was soaked through, so I brought him inside to dry off. That's when I learned that he lived on the streets. I felt sorry for him and took him in. I gave him a room and money in his pocket and helped him back onto his feet. After that, he used to come and go as he pleased. He was a very troubled boy.'

'Very noble of you, Mr James.'

'Well, that's the kind of person I am, Chief Inspector. I knew what Danny was going through; I've been there. I know how unforgiving life is on the streets!'

'And, why is that, if you don't mind me asking?' DCI Oakwood said.

Jonnie James knew that he had her. She had fallen for the sob story, hook-line-and-sinker. He was grandstanding now. 'You see, Inspector. . . I *was* Danny, many years ago. You see I was brought up in a succession of children's homes. I was an orphan, carted from pillar to post, until I ran away. But I got lucky. Lots of Danny's in this world aren't so fortunate.'

Loder rolled his eyes, losing patience. He wasn't buying any of it. Tanya looked over to him and gave a surreptitious shake of her head. Nothing. He motioned for her to have a sniff around upstairs. He then moved over to the sofa behind his boss and leaned forward resting his hands on the back of it. 'So, how do you account for the fact that I've got a fifteen year-old teenager lying in the morgue, who has been so brutally gang-raped that his rectum has been ripped open and it's now spewing out all over the slab, Mr James?'

Jonnie James looked physically shocked. He had guessed that Delaney had something to do with Danny's murder. He had learned through the network that Danny was trying to get one over on, Sir Teddy Marston. But to die at the hands of a bunch of animals. Danny didn't deserve that.

How dare Loder stand here in *his* lounge and insinuate that he could be a party to such an horrific crime was an affront to his reputation. He looked after Danny; loved him even. The fact that he sexually abused him for his own self-gratification never came into the equation.

He saw himself as a role model, who looked after his boys. He showered them with empty promises of riches and stardom and slowly nurtured them along until he got them into his bed. Once he had accomplished that, he had them in his clutches and used their self-deprecation and shame, as a tool to work to his advantage.

He never, ever, saw himself as paedophile – he vehemently abhorred the very idea. His conscience was clear. He was absolutely convinced that he had never done anything to anyone against their wishes.

Jonnie James cleared his mind, then shot Loder a look of indignation, and said, 'What are you insinuating?'

'One day, we see Danny, here, in this *very* house. The next, he turns up dead. You tell me?'

'I've had enough of this. What sort of person do you think I am? Do you honestly think that I could do something so . . .' he closed his eyes and held his head in hands. A vision of Danny screaming for mercy, raced through his mind, while Delaney stood over him with that evil smile across his face.

'Mr James. Can you think of anyone who would want to harm Danny?' DCI Oakwood said, softly. 'Did he say if anyone was after him for any reason?'

Jonnie James lifted his head. With a stream of tears down his face, he shook his head slowly. 'No, he never said anything to me. On the contrary, he seemed upbeat. Said that he was finally back on his feet and was going away for a holiday to Spain.'

'Did he say who with?' Loder said.

'No.'

'Were you having sex with Danny?' Loder changed tact.

'No, I was not!' Jonnie James jumped to his feet, clearly rattled. 'I've had enough of this1' he snivelled, shooting Loder a contemptuous sneer.

'I'll say when it's enough. Not you,' Loder said.

'I'm not saying another word without my lawyer present.'

'We can always do this back at the station.'

Jonnie James shrugged with indifference. 'I've got nothing to answer for. Besides, you know as well as me that my brief will have me out before you've had time to hang your coat up.'

Tanya stood in the doorway and motioned for Loder that she wanted him. He looked at Jonnie James wiping his eyes with his sleeve, then tapped his boss on the shoulder and slipped out of the room.

'What have you found?' Loder asked, out in the hall.

'Not sure really, sir. Come and have a look for yourself.'

Loder followed Tanya up the staircase, right at the top of the landing and left into a room at the end. He looked at the sumptuous, deep settees around the walls, the huge period coffee table in the centre of the room and a cinema screen at the far end, and shrugged. 'So, it's a TV, or movie lounge?'

DS Frost walked to the side of the screen, pulled a curtain cord and a set of velvet drapes slid silently open behind, revealing a one-way mirror that filled most of the back wall. Next to it was a door leading into an adjoining bedroom.

'Well, well. What have we here?' Loder smiled.

'Looks like, Jonnie boy, likes to watch, boss,' DS Frost said.

'So it would seem. Find anything else?'

'Over here, sir,' Tanya said, opening the doors to a tall built-in cupboard in the corner at the opposite end of the room.

Loder crossed the room and looked at the sparse video and DVD rack inside the cupboard. It was stripped bare, but for a few popular movies that would be in any enthusiast's library.

'Looks to me like Jonnie boy knew we were coming.' Loder said, tight-lipped.

'Our thoughts exactly, sir,' Tanya said.

'Anyone come up with anything else?'

'Zilch. The whole place is as clean as a pin,' DS Frost said.

Loder shook his head disconcerted, brushed his fingers through his hair and nibbled at his bottom lip, clearly frustrated at the situation. He took a deep breath. 'Any ideas as to who could of tipped him the wink?' Loder looked at Tanya and DS Frost in turn.

They both shook their heads. Keeping stock of what they both were thinking.

'Could have been anyone,' DS Frost, broke the silence.

'I know what you're both thinking,' Loder said. 'But I trust the DCS. I really can't see it being him . . . no, the very idea is ludicrous. Got to be someone else, who either, came into contact with the warrant, or someone who knew that we were in the process of getting one. One way or another, I'll have him, or her, and when I do . . .' He stopped short. 'How far have you got with the search?'

'Apart from pulling up the carpets, we're just about finished,' DS Frost said.

'Might as well gather the team together and let them get off. I'll see you outside when I'm finished with that cretin downstairs.'

Loder entered the lounge with a wide grin on his face. 'Seems you like to play games, Mr James?'

'What are you getting at?' he spat, raising a suspicious brow.

'We found your one-way mirror.'

Jonnie James shrugged. 'Not against the law, is it?'

'No. But what goes on behind it on that king-sized, four-poster bed might be.'

'Unless you're invited to one of my little soiree's you'll never know, will you, Inspector?' he taunted.

'Don't get smart with me, James. I can make life very uncomfortable for you, if it pleases me to.'

'Look,' he said, holding his palms out like a Jewish trader pleads poverty, "my life." 'So, I like to watch, a little. Everything I do is open and consensual. We get quite an audience at times.' He rolled his eyes lasciviously at, DCI Oakwood. 'Know what I mean?'

She crossed her legs, leaned forward a little and said, in earnest. 'Well, Mr James. We'll have to keep an eye on you, won't we? And when you next have one of your, "little soiree's," maybe we'll give you a visit: when you least expect it.' She raised an eyebrow, and smiled.

Jonnie James squirmed back into the cushion to get away from her stare, which was boring straight through him.

'I think we're just about finished, for the time being,' she said, looking over her shoulder to Loder.

DCI Oakwood got to her feet. 'We'll see ourselves out, shall we?' she smiled.

Loder opened the front door and was faced with a reporter and a photographer standing on the doorstep.

'Where is he? The reporter asked.

'Across the hall and in the lounge,' he pointed.

'Thanks for the nod, Loder,' he whispered in his ear, as he passed by.

'You're welcome, Charlie.'

'I owe you one.'

'Forget it. You can have this one on me.'

DCI Oakwood slid in the passenger seat next to Loder and turned towards him in mock disbelief. 'Loder, tell me you didn't?' she said, trying to suppress a smile.

'That'll teach the self-centred, cretin,' he said, with a wry smile, as he turned the ignition and drove out left onto the road. 'Fancy a drink?'

'Love one,' she said, stroking his thigh as he aimed the car in the direction of Hammergrove Bridge.

CHAPTER 22

Soho was busy with evening drinkers spilled out onto the pavements enjoying the warm night air. The restaurants were busy. A myriad of Japanese tourists wandered around snapping photographs of just about anything that moved. The whole area had a party atmosphere. And when a rickshaw taxi came racing around the corner, peddled by a flamboyant figure dressed in full drag and makeup, all the Japanese tourists looked on in awe. As he drove past, a thousand flashlights lit up the night sky as they frantically clicked away with their cameras. It was like a scene from a Hollywood film premiere.

Completely detached from what was going on around him, Lee Carlin was engrossed pasting fresh pictures of Donna onto lamp posts where the old ones had been torn off or faded by the weather. After making his way down Wardour Street, he turned left onto Old Compton Street and set about replacing some pictures in a row of public telephone booths.

Street flyers constantly stocked every phone booth in the West End with cards and photos of scantily clad girls advertising their wares. They were pinned and pasted in every conceivable space – ceiling, sides, above the telephone, and below – presumably in case someone happened to be tying their shoelaces. Each, seemingly, having something different to offer the prospective punter. Straight, gay, lesbian, S&M, young and old. Every taste imaginable – some not imaginable – were catered for: at a price. The cold realisation of what you actually got, once you handed over your hard earned cash, was in stark contrast to what was portrayed on the flyers.

Lee's biggest problem with the phone booths was that the street flyers kept throwing Donna's picture away and replacing it with their own wares. It was a constant battle of wits between Lee and the flyers.

He finished the booths, glanced at his watch and thought that he might as well call it a night and go for a beer.

  He didn't give a second thought to the teenage lad standing in the darkness of a shop doorway who had been watching him going about his task. He thought that the lad was just another runaway, or rent boy punting for a bit of business. The endless long nights Lee had spent up here in amongst the destitute, the prostitution and the seedy porn cinemas had hardened his outlook on life: nothing surprised him anymore.

  The underbelly of the West End, Soho in particular, was nothing less than a cattle market of human exploitation. No matter how many people gave their time and noble intentions to saving souls, the big wheel kept on turning; when a spoke broke away, another replaced it. Lee had learnt it was a way of life. It was the fabric that Soho was built upon: it was what people ventured up here for – a good time and for some, it was sex. It didn't matter what their particular preference was, as long as they we're willing to pay. It was the simple economics of supply and demand.

  Ryan had ventured up to Soho to put the word about to a few trusted mates that Delaney needed a few extra bodies for a big "soiree" he was planning and if they were clean – free of HIV and any STD's – they were in.

  He had happened upon Lee in Wardour Street and one look at the pictures of Donna on the lampposts told him who the man was. For the past twenty minutes, Ryan had watched Lee going about his task and admired his dogged determination in not giving up on his daughter. A vision of Donna sitting on a bed with her arms wrapped tight around her legs, cold and scared, infiltrated his mind, and a wave of guilt swallowed him up as the enormity of what he had orchestrated hit home.

  If only he'd had a father like Lee Carlin, someone who'd loved and cared for him. Someone who could have spent time with him, taught him the rights and wrongs of life. Maybe his life would have turned out differently. Instead, he got an alcoholic mother who would sell him for the price of a bottle of vodka. And a succession of "uncles" that had done dirty, despicable things to him. What chance did he have.

He pulled his hood down over his head, dug his hands deep into the pockets of his sweatshirt top and followed Lee. He didn't quite know why; his mind was awash with scenarios.

Lee made his way back up Wardour Street, turned left then right onto Berwick Street, to where his car was parked. Seeing a crowd of drinkers sitting outside The Blue Post, he decided to pop in for a quick pint before making his way home.

The Blue Post was a traditional pub that sold decent beer. It hadn't been bastardized into a theme pub – yet. Its tattiness just added to the charm of the place. The only problem was that it could be a bit of a scrum to get to the bar at times. Lee managed to get served without too much trouble and found an empty table just inside the entrance. Most people had taken to being outside which suited Lee.

He sat back and enjoyed the moment, listening to "Long Hot Summer" playing in the background. He felt good about himself, having replaced Donna's pictures. He'd covered a wide area from Piccadilly, right up Shaftsbury Avenue and all around Soho. Going on past experience, the pictures would probably last about three weeks before the weather got to them and the street flyers overlaid some with their own paraphernalia.

He took a long swallow of beer and wiped the froth from his mouth with the back of his hand. Out of the corner of his eye, he caught sight of a young, fair-haired lad looking him over. When he glanced back at him, the lad looked away. *Not again,* he thought to himself. What is it about rent boys and me? Do I look that desperate? Is it the way I dress? He looked down at his loafers, his Levi 501's, polo top, under his Harrington bomber jacket and thought, *Nah.* He dismissed the lad's attentions and carried on enjoying his beer: nobody was going to stop him enjoying the moment. Besides, "The Jam" were now belting out "A Town Like Malice." Someone had excellent taste in music.

Forty-five minutes and another pint later he drank up and left. He strolled back to his car, enjoying the vibrant atmosphere and the balmy night air.

He turned the ignition, switched on the headlights and was about to pull away when there was a tap on the window. He turned and saw the lad that was in the pub standing hunched down under a hooded top peering in through the window. Tentatively he buzzed the window down, just enough to see his eyes peering in.

'Yeh. Something you want?' Lee said, in a threatening tone.

'I've got some info that might be of use to you,' Ryan said.

'Oh, yeh?' Lee said, sardonically.

'About . . . Donna.'

Hearing his daughter's name, was like a thunderbolt hitting him straight between the eyes. His mouth dropped in consternation. 'Wha . . . what do you know?'

'I can't talk out here. Let me in.

His head swimming at the mention of Donna's name, Lee nodded without thinking.

Ryan scooted around the front of the car, opened the door and slid in next to, Lee.

'What do you know about my daughter's disappearance?' Lee said, taking a breath to compose himself.

'Not here.'

'Why?'

'Too many faces. Look, I know a quite pub not too far from here. Do the next right.'

Lee was at odds with himself as to know what to do for the best. Nevertheless, he put the car into gear and pulled away. He followed the lad's directions around a maze of one-way streets and began to think that he was being mugged off. They crossed Oxford Street, onto Wells Street and turned left onto Mortimer Street, and he knew where he was. Ryan directed him right into Great Titchfield Street and told him to park up at the first opportunity.

The Kings Arms was a small pub situated on the corner of Riding House Street and Great Titchfield Street. Ryan went in first with Lee behind. 'Why don't we sit down there?' Ryan said, nodding in the direction of a couple of deep-backed armchairs down the far end of the pub. 'I'll get the drinks. Lager for you, ain't it?' he said. Lee nodded. He was still bewildered by the events of the last fifteen minutes.

The pub was empty but for a few regulars that lived locally. Ryan set the drinks down on the table and sat facing, Lee. This end of the pub could have been mistaken for a cosy drawing room, with its deep-seated easy chairs, rickety bookcases on the walls and table lamps with large lampshades discretely situated in the corners.

'Cheers!' Ryan said, lifting his bottle of Bud.

Lee didn't return the compliment.

'What is it you want?' Lee said, eyeing the lad warily over the top of his glass as he lifted it to his lips. 'I'm not in the mood for Jackanory's. Besides, I've already been mugged off once before by one of your pals.'

'Let me guess. Danny?'

Lee said nothing. He didn't trust the kid one iota.

'Found dead, you know . . . Danny?' Ryan said, sadly, looking towards the bar.

'I know. The police told me. Friend of yours, was he?'

Ryan closed his eyes as Lee's comment screamed through his mind. He couldn't bear the heavy burden of guilt weighing down on him. He was supposed to have been Danny's *friend*. Had it not been for him, Danny would still be alive. He had to make things right, if only for his own self-preservation.

'If I tell you everything I know, I could end up the same way as Danny. So my safety has got to be guaranteed.'

'We'll go to the police. They'll look after you. Keep you safe,' Lee said.

'Don't be so fucking naïve. I can't go to the police they'll lock me up and throw away the key. Besides, they're part *of* it.'

'What do you mean? Part of what?' Lee said, trying to get his head around it all.

'You've got no idea, have you?'

'What are you talking about?

'The whole thing. Danny, Donna, they're just a drop in the ocean. The whole operation is one big secret network. There are some big players involved. High court judges, top old bill, members of parliament, pop stars: you name it they're in it.'

Whatever Lee might have thought about the cocky little shit before, he now had his full attention. Just the mention of his daughter's name, in the present tense and not the former was enough to snare him. He didn't have anything to lose, so he thought that he would drop a name into the conversation, just to see what came up.

'Jonnie James . . . Ever heard of him?' Lee asked.

'That fucking filthy creep. I know him, all too well.'

Aware that the lad could do a runner at any moment, Lee dare not take his eyes off Ryan for a nanosecond.

'One of the main players, that evil dirty bastard. Been at it for years, long before I came on the scene.'

'Been at what?'

'God! You really don't have a clue, do you? Jonnie James has a penchant for young teenage boys. Especially the one's that are on the point of puberty; he pays fortunes for them. Likes to watch as well. He's got a room where he films all sorts of goings on: fuck he's got a cupboard stacked full of movies of his exploits, and others too. Go back years they do. Likes to remind himself of all his conquests. It's food for his ego.'

The abject horror of listening to what his daughter may have been put through at the hands of those perverted bastards, was too much for him to come to terms with. He had blocked his mind to it ever since she had disappeared, but to hear it first hand, was like someone had stabbed him in the heart. It woke him up to reality of it all.

'You mentioned my Donna? Do you know where she is?'

'The last time I saw her she was fine.'

'Where was that?' Lee leaned forward, clamping his hands tight together to stop himself from grabbing Ryan's throat and throttling every last bit of information out of him.

'Look . . . I don't know what your name is, but as—'

'Lee Carlin,' Lee, cut in. 'I'm Donna's father; but you already know that, don't you?'

Ryan nodded. Resigned to the fact that he couldn't back off now: it was all or nothing. He sensed Lee's hostility and sank back into his chair to get out of his face, and out of striking distance.

The high-backed chair swallowed up Ryan's skinny frame and at that moment, he looked what he was, a scared kid, in fear of his life.

Lee finished his beer and stood up. 'Same again?'

Ryan drank the dregs of his beer like a seasoned drinker far beyond his years and handed Lee the empty bottle of Bud. 'Don't you dare move an inch, or I'll break your fucking neck. I'm not finished with you yet.'

Gingerly, Ryan leaned forward under the pretence of tying his lace and felt down his sock for the knife he always kept there for security. If the situation went boss-eyed, he wouldn't hesitate for a second about using it.

His anger in check, Lee brought the drinks back to the table and sat down. 'What's your name?' he said, drinking the froth off the top of his beer.

'Ryan.'

'Right then, Ryan. Why don't you start from the beginning?'

'As I've already said. If I tell you what I know, my safety has got to be guaranteed. I can't go back to where I live. I'll have to disappear off the face of the earth.'

'Why?'

'Because the evil bastard that I work for. The man that has been shagging me since I was a thirteen-year-old kid, is the orchestrator behind the whole setup. If I serve him up to the Old Bill . . . he'll kill me. Just like he did to Danny.'

Lee tried to get head around the enormity of what he was hearing. And all this from a kid no more than a few years older than his daughter. He knew one thing for certain, he couldn't let Ryan out of his sight, not for one second, whatever the consequences. His head was swimming all over the place, and the alcohol racing through his bloodstream was just making him even more paranoid than he already was. Without thinking, he said, 'Look, you can stay with me. You'll be safe there. But only if you tell me everything you know: no bullshit or fantasy stories. We got a deal?'

'Yeh. But you can't let the Old Bill know who I am, or where I'm staying.'

'We'll have to see about that, after you've told me everything you know. You'll have to trust me, Okay?'

'Yeh . . . I suppose so,' Ryan said, tentatively. He didn't really have a choice, now he had started the ball rolling. He'd have to play it by ear, see what fathomed out.

'Drink up and we'll go,' Lee said, finishing his beer.

'I've got to do something first.'

'Don't start pissing me about, Ryan. I'm putting my neck on the block for you.'

'I just need to collect something. Can you give me a lift?'

'Yeh, I suppose so. Where are we going?'

'Not far.'

Madame Tausauds – the famous waxworks – was facing Lee as Ryan directed him left onto Marylebone Road. They drove along until they reached the Paddington Flyover and filtered left, then right under the flyover and along Edgware Road towards Maida Vale. This was an affluent area of North London that Lee wasn't too familiar with. He wondered where Ryan was taking him. It wasn't the sort of area you would associate with the Ryan's of this world. After about a mile, they swung left into Clifton Gardens and as they approached Warwick Avenue Underground Station, Ryan told Lee to park up.

He got out of the car and told Lee to wait. For one panic-stricken moment, Lee thought that Ryan was going to do a runner into the station and jump on the underground. But he bypassed the station and disappeared around a corner.

Lee thought about getting out and following him, but then thought against it. If half of what he had told him so far was true, the kid was putting his in life on the line. He had to start putting some trust in him.

He switched on the radio, rolled a cigarette and opened the window to let the smoke out. His mind was bouncing around all over the place at everything he had learned this evening. He never stopped believing that his Donna was alive, even when everyone around him had given up on her. Even his own wife had given up the fight long ago. Lee knew that she and their friends and family thought that his uncompromising doggedness for the truth, his obsession with plastering pictures of Donna all over the West End, was the result of some kind of mental breakdown. Hopefully, now he was going to prove all the sceptics wrong. He was absolutely certain, now more than ever that his daughter was alive. And with the help of Ryan, he was going to find her and bring her home, even if it meant putting his own life on the line.

The one niggling thought eating away in the back of his mind was *what's in it for, Ryan?* Why should he go out of his way: put his life in jeopardy for him? The one thing that Lee had learned from his time in the bowels of Soho, was that kids like Ryan, don't do something for nothing. There's always got to be a pay-off, somewhere along the line.

Two cigarettes and twenty minutes later, there was still no sign of Ryan. Agitated as to what to do, Lee tapped the steering wheel to a tune on the radio with the band of his wedding ring. *Fuck it,* he cursed to himself and got out of the car. He walked up to the corner of the street where he had seen Ryan go earlier and waited. His mind was all over the place, why hadn't he gone with his first instinct and followed the boy. Maybe something had happened to him.

Suddenly, in the distance he saw a hooded figure running towards him. As Ryan approached, he said, 'In the car, quick.' Lee ran with him around the corner and pointed the remote at the car. The sound of central-locking clunking open echoed like a gun fire in the stillness of the night air. Lee jumped into the driver's seat and started the engine. Ryan threw a small holdall into the back, jumped into the passenger seat and slammed the door. 'Let's get out of here,' he said, breathlessly.

Not sure which direction to go, Lee did a U-turn and went back the way they had come until he reached the A40 flyover. He went under the flyover, doubled back around and joined the traffic at the Paddington intersection, heading out of town on the flyover.

Twelve minutes later, they were in East Acton. Lee pulled up onto the drive at the side of his house and stopped in front of the garage doors.

The estate was made up of clean, quiet, streets of detached and semi-detached houses that reached right up to the A40 at one end and Acton Town main line station at the other.

In the sixties and the early seventies, the Goldsmiths Estate was considered a very desirable area, where many affluent professional people lived. As time went by, the money moved out to the suburbs to places like Denham and Gerrards Cross. Leaving the area to the new generation of Margaret Thatcher's newfound wealthy working class. The estate was still considered one of Acton's nicer places to live – the inflated property prices bore that out. Properties were now in the price range of successful builders and tradesmen, such as Lee. Most of the residents in his street were brought up in and around The White City area, a mile or so away. And moving out to live in this rural setting was like moving into the countryside, for most people.

Lee got out of the car, unlocked the front door and went in, leaving the door ajar. Ryan got his bag out of the car, shut the car door and followed him into the house. Closing the front door behind him, he ventured down the hallway and into the lounge.

Pleasantly surprised at the comfortable furnishings and soft lighting of the spacious through-lounge, he dropped his holdall onto the carpet and sat tentatively on the long, L-shaped settee.

Lee walked into the room carrying two cans of beer, handed one to Ryan and sat down on the end of settee facing him. He pulled the ring on the can and drank a long swallow, then said, 'I'm listening.'

Ryan put his can on the coffee table in front of him and pulled off his hooded top, to reveal a bright-yellow tee shirt. Scrawled across the front of it was a motif in big black letters that read, F**K YOU!

Lee couldn't help smiling. The wording just about summed up Ryan's belligerent attitude to everything establishment.

The atmosphere warmed. 'Drink up,' Lee said.

Ryan opened the can, took a long slurp and burped. 'Sorry,' he apologised. 'Nice drum you've got here,' he said, looking around the room.'

Shaking his head at Ryan's cockiness, Lee walked across the room and placed a reassuring hand on the boy's shoulder as he went out into the hallway. 'I'm going to order some food. What do you prefer, Chinese or pizza?' he shouted, sitting on the bottom of the stairs by the telephone table.

'Pizza for me, please.'

Lee found the menu in the table drawer and ordered a large four season's pizza and fries. Then went back into the lounge to find Ryan holding a framed school photograph of Donna.

He quickly put the frame back onto the sideboard when he heard Lee coming up behind him. Lee picked up the frame and wiped Ryan's smudged finger marks off the glass. Suddenly, a thought came into his head that maybe he should have left the prints on the glass and taken them to Loder.

Ryan eyed Lee warily. He knew whatever the outcome. Lee must never find out that he was Jason. The person that lured his daughter away and gave her up to Delaney. If he did put two-and-two together, Lee would probably kill him with his own bare hands. But he was comforted with the thought that he was making everything right: he just hoped that it wasn't too late.

'What will your wife say when she comes in and finds me here?'

'Don't you worry yourself about her. Besides she's away at the moment.'

'On holiday, is she?'

'Yeh, something like that,' Lee said, guardedly.

'So, Danny was a friend of yours?' Lee changed the subject. His private life wasn't up for discussion, especially with a teenage kid that he didn't know from, Adam. Nevertheless, Lee didn't want to rattle him and thought that the best way around things was to let Ryan talk freely in his own time.

Ryan sat back down on the settee and took another swig of beer. Then staring down at the pattern on the carpet to hide his shame, he nodded. 'Yeh, we were mates. Used to turn a few tricks together. Good team, we were.'

'So, do you know what happened to him?'

'Yeh . . . pretty much.' He wiped his moist eyes with his tee shirt.

'Do you want to tell me about it?'

'No. Believe me, you really don't want to know.'

'But you know *who* killed, Danny?'

'Not specifically. But I know Delaney orchestrated it. It's not the first time that someone has mysteriously turned up, "Brown Bread." The fat greasy bastard would stop at nothing if he thought that his livelihood was threatened. I know, first hand, believe me.'

'Delaney! Who's, Delaney?'

'Harry Delaney is my . . . sort of uncle. I live with—'

The ring on the doorbell spooked, Ryan. 'Who's that? He said, jumping up from the settee. His eyes darted from one end of the room to the other for somewhere to hide.

'Relax. It's probably the pizza delivery man.'

Lee went out to the front door and slid the chain across, just in case. The last thing he wanted, was someone barging their way in. Ryan being spooked had unconsciously put him on his guard. Tentatively, he opened the door a crack. 'You order a pizza?'

Lee breathed a sigh of relief at the sight of the tall, crash-helmeted deliveryman standing on the doorstep holding a box and a small carrier bag containing the fries. He released the chain and opened the door. Then reached into his back pocket for his wallet, slid out a ten-pound note and gave it to the man. He took the food and said, 'Keep the change,' nudging the door shut with his hip.

He set the food down onto the coffee table, sat down next to Ryan and opened the pizza box. 'Tuck in,' he said, tearing a wedge off the huge round slab and handing it to him. Lee opened the fries and grabbed a handful, sat back and watched as Ryan began devouring the pizza as if he hadn't eaten for a week. He tore off another wedge and offered it to Lee.

'It's good,' he said, chomping away.

Behind the hard-shelled façade, Lee thought that Ryan was just a kid: a completely fucked up misguided teenage kid. He wondered when the last time Ryan had sat down to a healthy, home-cooked meal. Still, it wasn't for him to stand in judgement of the lad. He was just ecstatic that Ryan had found him and, maybe, at last he might be able to get some answers to all that had happened. Hopefully, Ryan would cast some light as to where Donna was being held.

He knew one thing, he wasn't going to let Ryan out of his sight. Moreover, he would do everything in his power to protect him from this, Harry Delaney, whoever he was.

Ryan gave out a loud burp and wiped his messy face with a couple of serviettes. He had managed to polish off three-quarters of the massive pizza and best part of a box of fries, in the time it had taken Lee to eat just one slice and a few fries.

'That was great pizza. Believe me, I know, I eat enough of them,' he said, finishing the can of beer. 'Got anymore?' He shook the empty can at, Lee.

'In the fridge. In the kitchen.'

'Shall I get it?' he said, getting to his feet.

'If you like. Kitchen's down the end of the hallway.'

'Can I get you one?'

'Yeh, why not. Here put the empties in the bin,' Lee said, handing him his can.

Lee got up, walked over to the window and stood for a moment gathering his thoughts. His mind was racing with visions of his daughter crying and reaching out for him. He closed his eyes and tried to wash the anguish from his mind. The street outside was quiet. He pulled the curtains and Ryan came padding back into the room holding two cans, a tub of ice cream and a large spoon.

'I found it in the freezer. Is it alright?'

Lee nodded, taking a can from him and sitting back down. He pulled the ring, took a swallow and watched as Ryan began stuffing spoonfuls of ice cream into his mouth.

'You were saying?' Lee said, trying to steer the conversation back on track.

'What?' Ryan said, not looking up.

'Harry Delaney. Who is he? What has he got to do with all this?'

'As I said, I sort of run things for him.'

'What things?'

Ryan pursed his lips and blew out a puff of air. 'Where do I begin?'

'How about at the beginning?'

Ryan then set about telling Lee the whole sorry story of his life. How Delaney found him and groomed him. The rent boys. The flats and houses Delaney kept stocked with young, fresh bodies for the perverted needs of his clients. The upmarket parties where kids were passed around like sweets for the selected few. He dropped a few famous names to Lee. The list was that long, Ryan had forgotten most of them: he'd been at it that long they were just faces that meant nothing. Only money.

It was the early hours of the morning when, Ryan finally went quiet. Lee got the feeling that he had unloaded a huge burden that had been weighing down on him for a long, long time. Once Ryan had started, he couldn't stop. He just poured the whole sick, perverted story out. Lee guessed that it was just the tip of the iceberg. There must be a lot more that Ryan wasn't even aware of. How could he, he was just a kid. A victim. His mind long since corrupted.

Lee had sat quietly listening and taking notes so that he didn't forget anything. A few times, he had wanted to run from the room and throw up in the toilet. But he daren't, for Ryan's sake, he had to be seen to be in control. Ryan had skirted around the subject of Donna throughout the whole story. Lee decided that he couldn't wait any longer he needed to know what had become of her. Whether it be good or bad news, he had to know one way or another.

'Danny told me that he'd seen my Donna at Jonnie James's house. Is that true?'

'Yeh, she was there. Delaney had courted her around like a princess.'

Lee couldn't bring himself to ask what happened to her there. He couldn't bear to think about the ordeal she must have gone through.

'So, where is she now?'

'Spain.'

'What! Are you sure?'

Ryan unzipped his holdall, pulled out a couple of photographs, reached across and handed them to Lee. Lee held one in each hand and scrutinised them for a moment, then shrugged. The photos were of Delaney and a young girl of about Donna's age. The girl was naked, but for a pair of tiny bikini bottoms. Delaney looked like a dark, hairy ape with his fat stomach hanging over the waistband of his baggy shorts. His skinny legs that protruded down like a couple twigs, looked as if they were about to snap under the strain of his huge bulk bearing down on them.

They were posing by the side of a kidney-shaped swimming pool in front of a wide terrace of a large, white-painted villa. Delaney's eyes were hidden behind a pair of pilot's shades. He had his arm around the girl's shoulder and a grin on his face, that stretched from ear-to-ear. She was staring down at the floor.

Lee took a long, hard look at the photo. The man looked faintly familiar to him . . . but he couldn't be certain.

'I take it this is, Harry Delaney?'

'Yeh.'

'And the girl?'

'Laura . . .' Ryan didn't want to give too much away. 'Delaney got hold of her . . . must be over a year ago now.'

His tone was all matter-of-fact, as if it was a daily occurrence.

Lee recalled Loder mentioning something about the disappearance of another girl. Hopefully, the photos would confirm it. First, he would get some copies done for his own reference: he might need them later.

'And you're saying my, Donna is being held at this villa?'

'Yeh.'

'How do you know for certain?'

'Delaney transported her down to Spain in the back of a specially designed truck that belonged to a friend of his. The guy owns a freight forwarding business.'

'What do mean?' Lee's eyes narrowed. It was all so shocking, he couldn't get his head around what he was hearing. 'What friend? What's his name?'

'I only know him as, George. He's got a yard over in Kilburn. He owns a lot of big trucks, does George.'

Lee was just beginning to realise how big this whole evil web of filth was. If Ryan had not told him in his own words, he would never have believed something of this magnitude could ever exist. He'd seen the child trafficking documentaries on TV. Kids being abducted from Eastern Europe and smuggled across the world to work in brothels and the suchlike. But to hear it in his lounge and from a teenage kid was something he found almost impossible to comprehend. He felt like getting up and slamming his fist into Ryan's face. It took every ounce of resolve he could muster not to. Right now, he needed Ryan, more than he needed his wife to come home.

'Do you know where the villa is?' Lee said, placing the photos on the coffee table and clasping his hands together to stop them shaking.

'Yeh . . . Well, sort of. I remember the area. It was below Cordoba up in the hills. I remember the place was set in amongst miles of olive groves, overlooking a small village. The locals think that the villa is an orphanage.'

'Could you find it?'

'I think so. If I see the name of the village signposted, then it's a doddle from there. Why d'you ask?'

'Because I'm thinking that you and I might be going on a little trip.'

Lee glanced at his watch and yawned. It was a little after 4:00 a.m. 'Right I think it's time we got our heads down, it's going to be a long day tomorrow. I'll get you a duvet down from upstairs. You alright on the settee?'

Ryan nodded. 'Yeh, it'll do fine,' he said, kicking off his trainers and throwing his legs up onto the cushion: seemingly without a care in the world.

Lee disappeared upstairs to get some bedding. When he returned, Ryan was curled up fast asleep. He threw the duvet over him. For a long moment, he just stood and looked down at the boy. And that was exactly what he was . . . just a boy. Although, he had the nous of someone far beyond his years, when all said and done, he was just a mixed up kid that had been dealt all the cards from the bottom of the pack. What an horrendous life he must have led, Lee thought to himself. He felt sorry for the boy. At the same time, he wanted to throttle him. With a deep sigh, he shook his head and ventured out to the kitchen.

He filled the kettle, rinsed a mug under the tap and popped a teabag into it. He dare not go to sleep because all he would see would be the recurring vision of Donna, holding out her arms pleading for her daddy to come to her. After everything that he had learned tonight, it would only make the nightmare ten-times worse.

Sitting at the kitchen table drinking his second mug of tea, he tried to rationalise everything. His mind was in turmoil as to what to do for the best. He was aware of what he ought to do, and that was deliver Ryan to Loder. But he'd made a promise to the boy, and he had to stand by that.

If everything that Ryan had told him *was* true – he had no reason to doubt that it wasn't – the whole scenario was too enormous for it not to be, then some serious heads were going to roll. The most gratifying one of all would be that dirty, depraved piece of scum, Jonnie James. He couldn't wait to see that self-satisfied, arrogant, smirk wiped from his face.

The first thing he had to do was give everything over to Loder. He wasn't going to make the same mistake again and go it alone. But his daughter was something completely different. For now, he would just play it by ear and see what unfolded. He finished his tea and went upstairs to run a bath. He thought that the hot suds might relax him a little.

Twenty minutes later, he was in his bedroom stretched out on the king-sized bed, wrapped in a white bath towel. He wished his wife was lying next to him. He missed her to distraction. He missed the way her leg would wrap around him as she nestled into his chest at night. He missed the funny way her lip curled up into a smile as she softly snuffled. He missed the fresh smell of her shampooed hair.

Most of all he needed her to soothe his hurt. She would know what to do for the best.

He closed his eyes and the familiar vision of Donna slowly appeared. He heard her weeping and pleading and saw her reaching out to him. But this time, he just smiled and whispered softly. 'Hang on a little longer, poppet – daddy's coming.' He thought that he detected a faint smile as she disappeared into the distance. Contented, his mind clear, he slipped into a restful slumber.

It was after nine o'clock when, Lee awoke. His eye lids felt heavy from the deep sleep he'd had. He sat up, stretched his arms and wiped the sleep from his eyes. Suddenly, an overwhelming feeling of wellbeing washed over him: he felt fresh and alert, ready to take on whatever the day threw at him. He jumped out of bed with a spring in his step and padded across to the wardrobe. He put on clean boxer shorts and a baggy, white tee shirt – he hated the feel of tight-fitting vests against his skin – a crew-neck sweater and clean denims.

A heavy cloud of pessimism descended upon him. The thought that Ryan might have had second thoughts about everything and had done a runner in the early hours. He dressed as fast as could and bounded down the stairs into the lounge.

His fears were allayed when he saw Ryan curled up fast asleep with the duvet pulled up over his ears. Lee left him sleeping while he went into the kitchen to find something for them both to eat.

The fridge was empty, but for a six-pack of beer, a carton of milk, a wedge of cheese, a few eggs, and some cartons of friendly bacteria yoghurt – his wife was convinced that it was good for the digestion – he was never convinced. He opened the freezer and found some sausages that could be cooked from frozen and a loaf of bread, which he could defrost in the microwave. Sorted! Sausage sandwiches.

He banged the bread into the microwave and got out a frying pan from a drawer under the hob unit, poured some oil into it, ignited the gas ring, ripped open the pack of sausages and emptied the lot of them into the pan. Five minutes later, the sausages sizzling away nicely, Lee set about buttering the bread.

Ryan strolled into the kitchen wearing a pair of Calvin Klein underpants and squinted in the bright morning sunshine blazing through the window. With his ruffled blonde hair, lithe body and smooth skin, Lee could see why all the dirty nonces would go mad for him. He immediately cast the thought from his mind.

'Sausage sandwiches, okay?' Lee said.

'Yeh, lovely! I'm starving.' Ryan saw two mugs on the table with teabags in. 'shall I make the tea?'

'The kettle's over there,' Lee said, pointing to the end of the worktop.

Ryan went across, picked it up and filled it with water, slotted it back into its housing, switched it on and sat at the table.

'We're just about done here,' Lee said, forking the sausages onto a plate and slicing them in half with a sharp knife. 'How many sandwiches do you want?'

'Two please.'

Lee raised an eyebrow at Ryan's politeness.

'Coming up. You want brown sauce?'

'Wouldn't taste the same without it.'

Lee loaded a plate with a heap of sandwiches and brought it to the table. Ryan poured the boiling water into the two mugs and waited until the tea seeped through the bags, then scooped them one by one and tossed them onto the draining board.

It looked like an everyday family scene of domestic bliss that the two of them had carried out many times before.

'Get stuck in, Ryan. You're going to need all the sustenance you can get.'

'Don't need asking twice,' Ryan said, chomping away.

Lee was surprisingly hungry considering all the turmoil of the last twelve hours. Now that he'd had time to decipher everything in his mind, he was clear as to what course of action he was going to take: he felt exhilarated at the prospect of bringing down, Harry Delaney's empire. A lot of serious people were going to get what they deserved. Media assassination and long prison sentences. The former would give Lee the most pleasure, especially where the likes of Jonnie James were concerned. He would take great pleasure in watching him squirm and plead his innocence in front of the TV cameras. It was early days, but Lee was upbeat at the prospect of it all.

Forty minutes later, Lee was in the car and on his way to see Loder. He had left Ryan in charge of the TV remote control and an assurance that he wouldn't give him up to the police. Lee had already phoned Loder to say that he was on his way to see him. He didn't say specifically what information he had for him, he just wetted Loder's appetite a little.

It was impossible to get parked anywhere near the police station, and Lee had found himself caught up in the traffic. He carried right on around Hammergrove Broadway and into King Street, before going into the shopping mall car park. It then took him a brisk ten-minute walk back to the police station.

As he walked pass the boarded up Hammergrove Palais, it saddened him. He reminisced at all the wild nights he'd had there in his past life, when he was a young, twenty-something in his prime. He and his mates used to go there most weekends and on Monday nights it was grab-a-granny night. He smiled as he pictured himself dressed in his mohair suit and leather tasselled-loafers that had steel tips on the heels. He and his mates used to sound like a parading army platoon clopping along the pavement, full of cocky bravado. He remembered asking his mate, Brian Whitfield, why he always went for the fat birds. They give in easier, he had said. Glory days!

Lee climbed the steps to the entrance of the police station, went through the double-doors and into a small lobby. In front of him was a glass curtain with a perforated speaker hole in the middle. Underneath was a stainless-steel drawer where small articles and papers could be passed through. Long gone were the days of the long, open counters and a helpful smiling face behind the jump. Now it was more likely that a terrorist bomb would be tossed through the doors.

The duty sergeant came to the counter and eyed Lee warily and asked if he could be of help. Lee told him that Inspector Loder was expecting him. The officer directed Lee to a bench along the wall and told him to wait.

Lee sat down next to a young girl not much older than his Donna. Sitting next to her waving his little legs back and forth was a scruffy little lad looking for something to amuse himself with. He started picking at a loose thread on his woolly jumper. The girl slapped his hand away. 'Leave it, you little fucker.' She then turned to Lee, rolled her eyes. 'Kids, eh. Who'd have them?'

Before Lee had time to engage in conversation with the girl, he was saved by the buzz of the latch slipping its lock and Loder motioning for him to come through.

'What's so urgent that you couldn't speak on the phone, Lee?' Loder said, climbing the stairs up to his office.

'I've come across some vital information that could blow the whole case wide open,' Lee said, climbing the stairs behind Loder.

'And what might that be?' Loder strode along the corridor to his office, held the door open and directed Lee to a seat in front of his desk.

'Where do I start?' Lee said, catching his breath.

'How about you tell me first, where this information came from.'

'I met a young lad in a pub last night and he—'

'Sounds like we've been down this road before.' Loder cut Lee short.

'This is different.'

'Why?'

'This lad knew Danny McKee. He told me who killed him. And he said that my Donna was at Jonnie James's house the night Danny had said that she was.'

'And what's this lad's name?'

Lee hesitated for a moment. 'Eh . . . Regan, his name is, Regan.' It was the first name that came into his head – his nephew's name.

'Where is Regan now?'

'He's gone into hiding, because he's in fear of his life.'

'And why is that?' Loder said, juggling a pencil impatiently between his fingers.

'Because he thinks he might be next on Delaney's list. Especially after what he told me last night.'

'Delaney! Who is, Delaney?'

'Look, Inspector Loder. Do you want to hear what I've got to say, or are you just going to sit there and humour me, hoping that I'll go away?'

'Okay, Lee. You've got my attention. Why don't you start from the beginning?' Loder put the pencil on the desk and folded his arms.

Lee got out an envelope that he had tucked in the waistband of his jeans. He opened it, unfolded the sheets of notes he had jotted down the night before and began unloading everything he had to Loder.

As the story unfolded, Loder became more and more interested. He leaned to his side and tapped on the window for DS Frost and Tanya to join them. They came into the office, grabbed a seat each and sat to the side of Lee, against the wall.

Loder ripped a page from his notepad and scribbled down, Harry Delaney's name. 'Tanya, run this through the computer see if he's got any previous. Lee, for the benefit of, DS Frost, I want you start again, from the beginning.'

Lee rolled his eyes, annoyed, and began again. With the help of his notes, he hadn't missed a thing that Ryan had told him.

Tanya came back into the office five minutes later and handed Loder a printout. She then sat down and listened to Lee, rattling on at fifty miles an hour, trying to get everything out.

Loder diverted his eyes down to the printout then turned his attention back to, Lee.

'That's quite a story,' Loder said.

'We need to bring this kid of yours in for questioning, Lee,' DS Frost said.

'I've already told you, he's had it on his toes. He said that he couldn't go back to Delaney's.' Lee hesitated for a moment. 'He told me that he was going up north . . . Liverpool, I think.'

Loder gave Lee a look that said he did not believe a word of it.

'It seems that Harry Delaney is a model citizen,' Loder said, picking up the printout. 'He's got nothing more than a couple motoring offences to his name.'

'Oh! I almost forgot.' Lee slid out the two photographs that Ryan had given him and handed them to Loder.

'So, who is this?'

'Don't you know?' Lee enjoyed the drama of the moment: milking it for everything it was worth.

Loder studied the two photos, handed one to DS Frost and the other to Tanya. 'I take it that is Harry Delaney?' he said.

'Correct. Now have a close look at the girl.' Lee was grandstanding now. 'You're still none the wiser, are you?'

Tanya looked closely at the photo. 'It's Laura Davidson.'

'Correct! Now do you believe me?' Lee said, full of bravado.

'When was this taken?' Tanya said.

'I don't know. But I think she's still being held at *that* villa with my Donna. God only knows how many other kids are shut away there.'

'Where is this villa?' Loder said.

Lee hesitated.

'All I know is that it's in Southern Spain somewhere.'

'Are you certain you don't know where it is?'

Loder shot Lee a suspicious look. He knew just by watching him shifting around nervously on his chair, that he wasn't telling them the whole story.

Lee held his hands up. 'Look, If I knew where the damn villa was, I'd tell you.'

'It would be in your own best interest to,' Loder said.

'Look, all I know is what Ryan told me. And that's that the villa is out in the sticks somewhere down in Andalucía.'

'Ryan! Thought you said his name was, Reagan?' DS Frost countered.

'Did I?' Lee shifted uncomfortably on his chair. 'Similar name to my nephew.'

'So, what's it to be, Ryan or Reagan?' Loder said.

'Eh . . . Ryan.' Lee hesitated. He wasn't used to all this subterfuge. Look, I've come here in good faith with vital information on the whereabouts of my daughter, and all you lot can do is question my motives,' Lee said, going on the offensive.

'Okay, calm down, Lee,' Loder said He could see that he was getting rattled. Moreover, he knew instinctively, that he was being economical with the truth.

'I hope you're not contemplating the idea of going it alone on this, Lee? Because you'll feel the full weight of the law down on you if I find out later that you've not told us everything,' Loder said, casting Lee a look that would freeze most hardened villains to the spot.

Lee dropped his gaze. He said nothing. He knew he was past the point of no return. He was going to go after his daughter, come what may. And if that meant crossing Loder, so be it. Besides, misguided or not, he thought that he, together with Ryan, had more chance of finding her than this lot.

'Right, you leave everything to us, Lee. We'll take it from here?' Loder said, getting to his feet.

'Oh . . . and if your, *Ryan* shows up again, I want you to contact me, immediately. If everything you have told us about this Delaney turns out to be true, he'll will be in extreme danger. We need to get that lad in here as soon possible, for his own protection.   Is that clear?'

'Absolutely, Inspector Loder,' Lee said, getting to his feet.

'Take him down and let him out, Tony,' Loder said.

CHAPTER 23

Twenty minutes later, Loder had relayed everything he'd been told to DCI Oakwood. She got up from behind her desk and rested against it facing Loder. 'Explosive stuff. If it's true,' she said.

'But it all gels with what we know about Jonnie James,' Loder said.

'We've got to get our hands on this Ryan.'

'I think Lee Carlin was spinning us a line as far as "Ryan" is concerned. He knows a lot more than he's letting on. I'd bet my life on it,' Loder said.

'Do you think this lad could be our, Jason?'

'Thought crossed my mind,' Loder said, admiring his boss's black, pencil skirt and waisted suit jacket.

Anne Oakwood looked down at herself and flushed. 'Loder keep your mind on the job, please.'

'I was.' He smiled, lasciviously.

'Loder!'

'Dinner, tonight?'

'My place, 7:00 p.m.'

'Can't wait.'

'Counting the minutes.'

'Now can we focus our efforts on the job in hand,' she said, getting herself a beaker of water from the dispenser.

Loder couldn't take his eyes off her pert bottom and the way her jacket fitted snugly over her slim hips, as she walked across the room. He had an insatiable desire to bend her over the desk and ravage her right there and then. She was like a drug to him. He couldn't get enough of her. The most frightening thing about it all was, that when she wasn't around, he missed her. He missed just being next to her and soaking up her fragrance. *Boy, did he have it bad.*

'We have to play this close to our chests. The fewer people that know, the better,' Loder said.

'I agree. We'll have to go to Hatchet and give him everything we've got. Besides, he'll need to sanction some search warrants. We keep everything else between ourselves.'

'When are you going to see the DCS?' Loder said.

'Me! We're together on this, aren't we?'

'Of course.'

'Then there's no time like the present, is there?'

*

It was 7:00 am the next morning. Loder had a small team in place outside Delaney's house. It was cold and damp in the early morning mist. Loder figured that it would be light in about half an hour. The street was quiet, but for a handful of commuters making their way to Warwick Avenue underground. Parking was a nightmare. Vehicles were nose-to-tail on both sides right along the road, so they'd double-parked, blocking one side of the road. All Loder needed now was for some smart-arse to start pumping his horn and the element of surprise would be lost.

There weren't any lights on in the front windows of the three-story, semi-detached house. Loder sent DS Frost and a couple of officers around the side to have a look at the back. A fit, young, uniformed Police Constable vaulted over the wooden side gate as if it didn't exist and opened it from the inside. They went through and around to the rear of the house. Loder's two-way radio crackled to life. 'All quiet round here boss,' DS Frost said.

'Good! He must still be in bed,' Loder said. 'Okay. Let's do it. Tony, you go in through the back. DCI Oakwood, Tanya and myself will go through the front.'

Loder walked up the steps to the front door and rang the bell. Nothing. He rang again and waited, impatiently. Nothing. Not a sound. 'Right, let's have this door opened,' he said, standing aside to let an officer through with the battering iron.

The officer crashed the heavy ram against the door where the lock was but it held. He rammed it again. This time the door splintered and Loder kicked it open.

They spilled into the dark, long hallway and DCI Oakwood found the light switch. DS Frost and his team came rushing in from the other end of the hallway and shook his head. 'Nothing. All quiet back there,' he said.

'Upstairs! Check the loft as well,' Loder ordered.

He and DCI Oakwood went into the lounge and turned the lights on. The room was stifling from the central heating and reeked of body odour and stale cigarette smoke. Loder walked to the end of the room and looked through the tall windows out onto the back garden. The grass had long since disappeared and was now overgrown with weeds. A battered oil drum with holes punched into the sides that was used for burning rubbish, stood in the middle. The earth around it was scorched black from piles of old ashes.

'I've got an unhealthy feeling that Harry Delaney has slipped the net,' Loder sighed, turning around to face his boss.

'It would seem so,' she reiterated. 'But how did he know?'

With his hands buried deep into the pockets of his overcoat, Loder shrugged. 'Right, let's take this place apart. Tanya you have a nose around the ground floor. DCI Oakwood and myself will search in here.'

Tanya left the room, went across the hallway and into a room by the foot of the staircase. Usually it would have been used as a reception room or a dining room, but to her surprise, it was a downstairs bedroom.

A king-size bed was against the far wall next to some tall windows that looked out to the garden. It was unmade, like someone had left in a hurry. At the foot of the bed against the opposite wall was a sideboard with a large, flat-screen TV and DVD player on top. The sideboard had drawers along the top and cupboards underneath; one of the doors was left open. There was a period fireplace in the middle of the room. It housed a nineteen-seventies style gas fire with a ceramic hearth. In front of her was two threadbare sofas; one under the front window the other against the wall.

Tanya went over to the sideboard, squatted down and peered into the open cupboard. Inside, cut into the base and fixed firmly to the floor was a safe about eighteen inches high and twelve deep. The door was ajar, it was empty. She pulled on a pair of latex examination gloves, opened the next cupboard and found that it was stacked with DVD'S, all neatly arranged in date order and referenced with two, single capital letters. She plucked one out with the initials JJ, opened the plastic cover, switched on the TV and DVD player, slid the disc into the machine, pressed play and waited. Thick waves descended down the screen then cleared to reveal Jonnie James lying on a bed naked with his arms around two terrified-looking teenage boys. They were both naked and in the early stages of puberty. He had a grin on his face that stretched from ear-to-ear. Tanya stopped the machine and went to find Loder.

DCI Oakwood and Loder stood in front of the bed, while Tanya switched the play button again. She then stood aside so that they all had a view.

Loder and his boss watched in stunned silence.

'Isn't that the room we found upstairs in James's house, the one with the one-way mirror in?' Loder said.

All three of them took a closer look.

'You're right, sir. It's the same four-poster bed,' Tanya said.

'Okay, switch it off. Get all this lot tagged and bagged,' Loder said. The less people that know about this little cache, the better.'

'Someone must have been behind the camera filming all this?' DCI Oakwood said.

'Not necessarily, ma'am. The camera could have been set to film on auto.'

'I very much, doubt that.' Loder said. 'He's playing to an audience there. You can see it written all over his smug face.'

DS Frost poked his head around the door. 'You want to come and see what we found upstairs, boss?'

Loder nodded and strode out of the room with DCI Oakwood tailing him up. He followed his DS up the stairs and into one of the bedrooms. The room was very neat and tidy and expensively furnished. Long velvet drapes tied back with rope tassels, framed the tall windows. The huge bed was covered with a silk duvet with matching cushions stacked up against the padded headboard, and the deep-pile carpet was lush and springy underfoot.

DS Frost stood aside the open door of a built-in cupboard in the corner of the room, and said, with a sweep of his hand. 'Be my guest, boss.'

Loder and DCI Oakwood peered in to find that it had a false back. Inside was a safe, similar in size to the one found downstairs. Above it, was stacked another pile of DVD'S, all referenced and dated the same as the others.

'He must have left in hurry, because he didn't lock the false panel back up after emptying the safe. He didn't bother scrambling the combination on that either, just had to pull the handle down. Bingo! It opened,' DS Frost, beamed.

'I think you're right, Tony,' Loder said, squatting down to get a better look inside the safe. 'There's a bag of pills in here.' Loder moved them to one side with the tip of his pen. Underneath, was a pile of what looked to be legal documents. He ducked his head down further to see four compact discs tucked into a shallow shelf at the top of the safe. He shuffled them to one side with his pen, inquisitively, then pressed his hands down on his knees and heaved his tall frame up.

'Right, get this lot bagged up.'

'Absolutely, boss.'

'Looking at all this, it's plainly obvious that Delaney has done a runner. Someone must have tipped him the wink,' DCI Oakwood said.

'I agree. But who?' Loder said.

'That's the sixty-four thousand dollar question' DS Frost said.

A young detective constable poked his head around the door, and said, 'sir.'

'What is it, Andy?' Loder said.

'Downstairs in the basement. Think you might want to come and have a look at what we've found?'

Loder strode after his DC along the landing and down the stairs to the ground floor, through a narrow door at the end of the hallway, under the staircase that led down to the basement. His heavy brogues clumped on the steep, bare boards as he descended the dimly lit staircase. DCI Oakwood clip-clopped awkwardly behind, in her heels, gripping the banister for dear life, so as not to go tumbling into the back of Loder. At the bottom, he did a U-turn and followed the dank passageway to the end where a door was open and a small, cell-like room was lit by a single bulb dangling precariously on a frayed cord in the middle of the ceiling. Against the wall was a single, tubular-framed bed and mattress. On it was a crumpled dank smelling duvet and a white cotton sheet with green mould growing in the middle. A small pine cabinet was at the side of the bed with a dirty coffee mug and an empty glass ashtray on top. Its surface was ringed with old tea and coffee stains and cigarette burns around the edges, where stubs had been left to smoulder and burn out. Built into the wall was a single wardrobe painted in white emulsion. The doors were grubby with finger marks. Inside, were two wire coat hangers, hooked over a rail. It was empty, but for a children's duffle-bag on the floor in the corner.

'We found this, boss.' A plain-clothed detective smiled, holding up a transparent evidence bag.

Curled up inside was three strands of long, blonde hair.

'Good work, lads. Let's hope it's Donna's.'

Loder rubbed his hands. He felt good inside. At last, everything seemed to be coming together. One almighty big question kept gnawing away at him . . . who was their leak. Who was the person, or people, that were always one step ahead of them. He'd find out, eventually, and when he did, he would take great pleasure in destroying the bastards: whoever they turned out to be.

'Right, let's get a forensics team over here.'

'Onto it, boss,' DS Frost said, with his mobile already at his ear.

'And get that over for DNA analysis,' Loder said, pointing to the evidence bag. He turned and walked out into the passageway. Suddenly, a thought occurred to him and he spun around on his heels. 'I want you to deliver that evidence to the lab, personally. Do not let it out of your possession: not even to the Commissioner himself. Is that clear?'

'Yes, sir,' said a wide-eyed uniformed constable.

He walked back into the room. 'Anyone got an evidence bag?' A sealed bag was instantly produced from nowhere. Loder pulled the seal apart. 'Scissors, anyone?' DCI Oakwood produced a small pair of nail clippers. 'Will these do?' Loder took them from her, awkwardly. The tiny contraption looked incongruous in his long hands. 'Examination gloves?' A pair was thrust in front of his eyes. 'Put these on and snip a sample of hair, please?' he said, to DCI Oakwood.

'Why?' she answered.

'Insurance.' Loder said. 'It's called covering your arse.' He winked.

She went across to the detective holding the bag with the hair samples in. 'Open it, please.' He obliged. Nevertheless, he knew that what was happening was highly irregular. He kept his thoughts to himself. DCI Oakwood clipped an inch off the tress of hair and popped it into the evidence bag that Loder was holding open. He sealed it tight.

'You've seen nothing!' Loder said, looking at each officer in turn. I take full responsibility. If there are any comebacks, it's my arse on the line. Is that clear?'

They said nothing. Just nodded, with a muted, 'sir,' under their breath.

Loder slipped the evidence into his inside pocket, turned and strode out of the room.

Back upstairs, he gathered his team together. 'I don't need to tell you that we have a serious leak somewhere along the line. So for now, we keep everything that went on here this morning between ourselves. You two can finish up here.' He pointed to DS Frost and Tanya.

As Loder and DCI Oakwood crossed the reception hall, he stopped dead in his tracks. 'I need to have a word with the Evidence Logging Officer.'

'What about?' DCI Oakwood said, following Loder up the stairs.

He found the Evidence Logging Officer in the bedroom on his knees listing all the DVD'S and putting them into a large evidence sack.

'I need a favour, Keith,' Loder said, sitting on the end of the bed.

'What might that be?' the officer said, putting down his clipboard.

'I need you to turn a blind eye until tomorrow before sealing up the evidence bags.'

'What! Are you mad, John? You know I can't do that.'

'You have my word that I won't tamper with any of the evidence.'

'That's not the point.'

'Keith, look, I'm close to unearthing something so big that it's going to explode in a lot of people's faces. My problem is, I've got a major leak and I suspect that it's coming from one of our own. I don't know where, but I – no we – DCI Oakwood and myself, think that's it's high up. So high that it's bloody invisible. Every direction we turn with this investigation someone gets there before us. You've only got to look around *here* to see what we're up against.' Loder gave a sweep of his arm to emphasize the point.

'What has that got to do with me? Here, you don't think it's me, do you, because it damn well is *not*.'

'No, no, Keith. Of course not. I know you *too* well, you could never be part of any of this.'

'Thank God for small mercies,' the officer smiled.

'Look, you can call me "Paranoid from Paddington," if you like, but I think that once this lot gets logged into the evidence store, there's a distinct possibility that it might get corrupted, wiped clean, or worse, disappear altogether.'

'Wouldn't be the first time. What do you want from me?'

'I want to get some of the discs copied for a bit of self-assurance, just in case something does happen to them. Cover all the angles, you know the rules. What do you say? I know it goes against the grain, but I wouldn't ask if I didn't think it vital.'

'You've got two hours. That's all I can cover, not a minute more and I'm coming with you – I'm not letting this lot out of my sight for a second – that's the best I can do, take it or leave it.'

'I'll take it. You don't know how much I appreciate this, Keith,' Loder said, putting a reassuring hand on the man's shoulder.

'Loder, you do realise none of discs will be admissible for evidence if it gets out that you've tampered with them?' DCI Oakwood said.

'At least we'll have something to feed to the media if the case collapses.'

The officer rolled his eyes. 'See you both at the disciplinary tribunal.'

'My thoughts, exactly,' DCI Oakwood said.

Back downstairs, Loder pulled DS Frost and Tanya aside and said, 'It's Saturday tomorrow. There won't be much activity on the upper floors, so it's unlikely that we'll be bothered. An ideal time to view all the evidence. We can set up a TV and DVD player in my office.'

DS Frost turned to Tanya. She said nothing: reserving judgement. She liked to work with everything out in the open, not go skulking behind people's backs. Nevertheless, there *were* special circumstances attached to this investigation. Reluctantly, she went along with it all.

'I'll check with you both later. But if I can't get back to the office today, I'll see you both first thing . . . Okay?'

'Yes, sir,' Tanya said. DS Frost nodded.

Ten minutes later, Loder and the Evidence Logging Officer were racing over the A40 flyover heading out of town. He filtered left at the White City turn-off, swung a right at the traffic lights and back under the flyover into Wood Lane. Three hundred metres up on his left, was a row of shops. Luckily he found a space to park on a yellow line right outside the private hire shop where he was going.

The two men got out of the car and went around to the back. Loder opened the boot and handed Keith one of the bags of discs. He lifted out the other, slammed the lid down and went into the shop with the officer looking warily around in every direction in tow behind.

A thin-faced, goatee-bearded, man was behind the counter. His heart sank when he saw Loder walk into the shop. He swallowed hard and forced a faint smile. 'Inspector Loder. What do I owe the pleasure?'

'I want you to do something for me, Rodent.'

The man physically cringed at the sound of the nickname that he had been saddled with for as long as he could remember. He was oblivious to the reason how, or why, he come to be labelled with the name. But to everyone who knew him, it was plainly obvious. His short, skinny frame, hunched back, long nose and pointed chin gave him the look of a rat. And when he moved around, he scurried at break-neck speed scraping his shoes along the ground. When he looked up at people, his nose had an irritating twitch, as if he was sniffing them out. He truly was an odorous man, but that nose of his could sniff out any bit of skulduggery that was going down around the manor. Nothing much passed him by without him knowing about it. That was why he was one of Loder's best snouts. In return, Loder turned a blind eye to his movie pirating operation, as long as it didn't get out of hand.

'Out the back, now!' Loder barked.

The Rodent lifted the counter flap and led the two men through a set of hanging plastic blinds and into the back of the shop. Keith looked around at the banks of disc copying equipment, stacked floor to ceiling. Turning to Loder, he said, 'You know some low people in some low places, John.'

'Ah, well, you know. I try my best.' Loder gave a wry smile. 'Right, to business. Rodent! I want this lot copied as quickly as you can.'

The man bent over and peered into one of the evidence sacks. 'What are they?' the Rodent said, turning to Loder, nose going ten-to-the-dozen.

'Never you mind. And don't even think about filtering off a set of copies for yourself,' Loder said, walking towards him.

'I wouldn't dare, Inspector Loder.'

'You had better not.' Loder fixed the beady-eyed Rodent a baleful look that left him in no doubt as to what would happen to him if he did. 'Get on with it. Quick as you can.'

The Rodent emptied the discs onto the grubby worn linoleum floor and began slotting them into the equipment.

'Keep an eye on him, Keith, while I go to the café next door and get us both some coffee.'

*

Loder knocked on DCI Oakwood's door and went in. She was sitting behind her desk with a thick file opened in front of her. Her face was solemn.

Loder ensconced himself in the chair in front of her desk.

'I've circulated a picture of Delaney to all UK airports and ferry ports, just in case he tries to skip the country: that's if he hasn't already done so,' DCI Oakwood said, resting against her desk facing Loder.

'Judging by the expression on your face when I came in, you've got some bad news for me.' Loder said.

'I don't know if it's relevant, but I looked at both warrants. Jonnie James and Delaney. They appear to have been signed by the same magistrate.'

'I wouldn't read too much into that. It all depends on who's the duty magistrate at the time. Could be just a coincidence?'

'Where was it issued?'

'Acton magistrates.'

'Acton!' Loder sounded surprised. 'Why not West London, or better still, Hammergrove?'

'My thoughts exactly,' Annie Oakwood said.

'The DCS may have been able to fast track the warrants down at Acton?'

'You could be right,' Annie Oakwood contemplated, sipping her coffee.

'What was his name?'

'Who?'

'The magistrate. Wakey, wakey, Anne,' Loder smiled.

'I'm sorry, Loder. My head's all over the place at the moment. Doctor Clifford Armstrong.'

'Doctor!'

'Yes. He's got a string of letters after his name.'

'I think it's best we keep an open mind at the moment. But I don't suppose it would do any harm if we took a furtive look into his background: just to be sure.'

'Any thoughts on our, DCS?'

'Nothing. But I think we need to find out how and who was authorised to deliver the warrants in the first instance,' Loder said.

'Could have been sent by courier?'

'True.'

DCI Oakwood lifted a mug of coffee to her lips, drank some and gazed into space. Loder could almost hear her brain churning everything over.

'What's on your mind?' He cut the silence.

'Oh, nothing,' she sighed.

'Come on, Anne. I know you well enough by now to know when something's not right.'

'It's just that this whole thing is going to be huge. And very soon it's all going to be blown wide open. My concern is, what if it all comes tumbling down around us both. What are we going to be left with?'

'That's the chance we've got to take. I can't do it without you on my side, Anne.'

'I know. It's just me being silly. All the years I've . . . no *we*, have put on the clock and in the end there might not be anything to show for it.'

'I think that we have to do what is right, Anne. Whatever the cost.'

'I know, Loder.'

'Hold on a minute, I've just had a thought,' he said, fumbling around in his trouser pocket for his mobile. He found DS Frost's number and made the call. 'Tony, can you organise a round-the-clock surveillance on Jonnie James's house? Just over the weekend. I don't want him slipping the net the same way as Delaney. I don't care that we're short on manpower: sort it.' Loder glanced across at his boss for confirmation. She nodded her approval. 'DCI Oakwood has sanctioned the overtime. See what you can do. If need be, I'll do a couple of shifts myself, okay?' He ended the call and slipped the mobile back into his pocket.

'Look, there's nothing much we can do around here. Why don't we make ourselves scarce? Might be better we're not around if anyone starts making themselves busy.'

'You're probably right, Loder. What you got in mind?' He glanced at his watch. 'It's past lunchtime. Why don't we grab a sandwich down by the river?'

'I've got a better idea,' his boss said, with a wicked smile on her face.

'And what might that be?'

'Lunch in bed.'

'Sounds good. Got anywhere in mind,' Loder teased.

She walked over and sat astride, Loder. 'My place, soon as you can get there,' she said, planting a kiss on his lips.

'Someone might come in, Anne?' Loder said, cupping his hands around her bottom.

'Don't give a monkey's crap. Besides, I'll probably be out of a job in couple weeks anyway.' She held Loder's face in her hands and kissed his lips softly. 'You up for it, Loder?'

'No, too busy?'

'Oh,' she said, disappointedly. 'Suppose you're right,' and started to get up.

'But not too busy for you,' he said, pulling her close.

'Soon as you can then,' she said, giving him a peck on the cheek before getting off his lap. Flushed, she waved a hand in front of her mouth, and said, 'Phew! I don't know what came over me.'

'Well don't lose it, whatever it is,' Loder said, getting to his feet and making for the door. As he was about to close it, he poked his head back in. 'Move your arse, please.'

CHAPTER 24

It was a depressingly dull, drizzly Saturday morning, when Loder pulled his car into the police compound. On days like these, he liked nothing more than to study the racing form in the morning paper and settle down in front of the television for the afternoon, with a beer and a gamble on the horses. Today was different. He was sitting on a cache of DVD'S that were potentially explosive. He'd tossed and turned all night long wondering what they would find on them. He'd even thought about getting out of bed in the small hours and previewing the copies that he'd run off to satisfy his curiosity, but had decided against it because it wouldn't be fair on the team. And whatever anyone thought about him, personally, he was a team player. Especially, with the trusted few that was closest to him. The other reason was – though he was loathed to admit it – he was fearful of what he might find.

   Luckily, there weren't too many cars around and Loder had no trouble finding a spot to park just by the foot of the fire escape at the side of the building. DS Frost was already there, sheltering under a brolly smoking a cigarette. He walked out from under the metal staircase and waited by the rear of Loder's car.

   'Been here long?' Loder asked, pulling on his overcoat by the driver's door.

   'No, ten minutes, at most, boss.'

   'All quiet on the "Western front?"'

   'Yeh. It's dead upstairs.'

   'Right, let's get to it.'

   Loder climbed the clanking metal staircase to the first level and keyed in his ID code on the pad by the side of the door. The lock buzzed and he pulled the heavy door open. DS Frost rushed through the open door first to get out of the rain. Loder tailed him up, letting the door clunk back into its housing behind him. They briskly walked along the short corridor and passed the staff notice boards pinned to the walls. On the left was a printout of the league table positions of the forces football, rugby and rowing teams; together with snippets from local newspaper reports on their performances. On the right were union notices concerning Health & Safety. They did a body swerve left past the interview suites then down the stairs to the basement and back along to the end of the corridor to the evidence storeroom. They went in and found, Keith – The Evidence Logging Officer – waiting behind the meshed counter with a clipboard and pen at the ready. Loder signed the sheet and Keith lifted up the two polythene evidence sacks onto the counter.

'Anyone been nosing around?' Loder asked.

'No. Dead as a morgue down here.'

'Where's the regular inventory officer? Haven't done away with him, have you?' DS Frost quipped.

'Sent him up to the canteen for an early breakfast. Mind you, he's spent so many years buried down here he's practically brain-dead anyway.'

'I'll give you a buzz when we're finished with this lot,' Loder said. 'Oh, if anyone comes sniffing around asking for me, you haven't seen me.'

The two men took a sack each and as swiftly as they could they went back along the corridor and up the stairs to the third floor incident room and Loder's office.

By the time they reached the sanctuary of Loder's office, DS Frost's thinning hair was plastered flat on his head both from the rain and from sweat that was beading down the side of his temples. Wheezing like a seventy year old – not a man who had just turned forty – he slumped down onto a chair like a sack of spuds. His lungs felt like they were fit to explode. 'That's it! I've got to give up the fags,' he said, wiping his clammy face with a handkerchief.

Loder couldn't help a smile. 'Too many steak and kidney puddings. That's your trouble, Tony,' he said, pointing to the man's saggy stomach bursting to escape through his strained shirt buttons.

'Me? Never touch the stuff,' he said, sitting upright and holding himself in.

Loder hung his overcoat on the single hanger that was hooked on his office door, then went around and sat behind his desk. Tanya had already set up a TV and DVD player in the corner so that everyone had a view. She went over and switched everything on then broke the seal on the first evidence bag and inserted a disc.

There was a soft tap on the door that sounded like a kick and everybody looked towards it, tentatively. 'It's me. Open the door.' Tanya pulled a face and opened it slightly. 'Panic over,' she said, over her shoulder to the others.

DCI Oakwood was standing cradling a cardboard tray with coffee and sandwiches on. 'Thought you'd all like some breakfast before we got started,' she beamed, setting the tray down onto the desk in front of Loder.

He couldn't help admiring how immaculate she looked, dressed in a simple black, trouser suit, with a fitted jacket that emphasised her pert curvy bottom and cream V-neck cashmere sweater. He hadn't left her place until the early hours, and that was only because he wanted to get a change of clothes. He didn't want to be seen in the same clothes two days running. He knew that his eagle-eyed DS, would have put two-and-two together and came up with five – and no doubt a lot of smutty innuendo – which he could do without, especially where Anne Oakwood was concerned. He suspected that Tanya already knew that he was close to his boss, but how close, he wasn't certain. He knew that she could be relied upon to be discreet: Tanya wasn't the sort of person to swap tittle-tattle; certainly not with likes of DS Frost.

Anne Oakwood distributed the greasy bags of bacon sandwiches and opened the lids to the steaming coffees. The smell of the bacon and fresh ground coffee wafting around the small office was overwhelming. Loder's stomach moaned with anticipation as he tucked in. He hadn't realised how ravenous he was.

The feeling of camaraderie in the room was palpable. He knew that it could all come tumbling down around him at any time. Without any doubt, whatsoever, he knew that he could rely on every one of this little team to back him to the hilt, should the proverbial shit hit the fan. Moreover, he was as certain as night followed day, that it was only a matter of time until all hell was going to break loose.

'Drop the blinds please Tanya, and we'll get this show on the road,' Loder said, wiping his greasy lips with a serviette. 'Tony, lock the door. We don't want any sudden surprises.'

Showtime.

They had been at it for about forty-five minutes, and what they had to endure made them all feel sick to the stomach. Although each disc had a date and a set of initials written on the side, when they were played, the date and time appeared in the top right-hand corner of the screen, and more interestingly, the actual name of the person – or people in some cases – had been edited in and appeared as a title at the start of each DVD. All very professionally done.

Tanya had been sitting with a laptop computer perched across her thighs and meticulously listed all the details of each disc as it was played. They had run through most of the films with the picture search on, because none of them wanted to witness the perverted and depraved abuse that was so flagrantly on display, for any longer than was absolutely necessary. But there were parts where they had to stop and watch, to see if they recognised any of the faces on the film.

They hadn't had any luck, so far. But it would only be a matter of delving into the criminal data base files. If that failed, the Inland Revenue DBF's normally came up tops. Either way it would only be a matter of time before every single one of these perverted shits would be brought to book and made to pay for their perversions: hopefully, with long custodial sentences.

If precedence was anything to go by, most would receive a slap on the wrist and told by a sympathetic judge not to do it again. The courts were notoriously lenient when it came to sentencing paedophiles and child abuse cases. Even faced with public outcries and a vehement press, they still handed down farcical sentences.

Suddenly, there was the unmistakable sound of the incident room door-release buzzing. Tanya switched the TV to standby and Loder turned off his desk lamp. They all crouched low and watched through the small slats in the blinds at the figure mooching around the incident room. It was only when the man turned and faced the window of the office that everything became clear.

Everyone in the office crouched lower as DCS Hatchet peered through the blinds trying to look inside. He then stood back, brushed his fingers through his neatly cut, blonde hair and straightened his tie in his reflection before going back out. Suddenly, the handle of the office door turned and they all hit the floor. Unable to open it, the handle went back to its horizontal position. They all breathed a sigh of relief at the sound of the DCS's heavy footsteps fading into the distance down the corridor.

'Someone tell me, what was that all about?' Loder said, getting back into his swivel chair.

Everyone seemed to shake their head and shrug at the same time. All of them equally suspicious, but apprehensive to be the first to say what each was thinking.

'Could have just been around and thought that he'd look in on us?' Anne Oakwood offered. 'After all, he did emphasise that he wanted to be kept up to scratch with everything. As yet we haven't been anywhere near his office.'

'True.' Loder sniffed. 'Why didn't he just give us a bell, see if we were around?'

'Best not to worry about it now. Tanya switch the TV back on, please. The quicker we get through this lot the happier I'll be,' Anne Oakwood said.

Tanya pointed the TV remote at the screen, then lifted her computer back onto her lap in readiness.

After little over an hour and forty-five minutes, they had managed to work their way through the first of the two evidence bags. Loder had seemed to lose interest in what they were supposed to be doing. He couldn't focus his mind on the job in hand. The vision of Hatchet skulking around in his incident room kept playing on his mind. It pained him to admit it to himself, but a niggling thought kept gnawing away at him.

'Christ! I don't believe it.' DCI Oakwood said, horrified.

'What?' Loder looked up at the screen.

'Look who it is.

Loder rubbed his eyes with his thumb and forefinger and concentrated on the aged man lying on the bed naked with a teenage girl sitting astride his saggy belly and flaccid penis.

'Do you know who he is?' Loder asked, blankly

'If I'm not mistaken, I think it's that High Court Judge . . . what's his name?' Anne Oakwood searched her mind. She was certain that she had clashed with him at the Old Bailey some years earlier when she was a wet-behind-the- ears, Detective Constable. The uncompromising old fart had wiped the floor with her in full view of the jury, when she had stumbled over her evidence in an armed robbery trial.

'Lord Chief Justice Baxter,' DS Frost said.

'That's the man! Who would of believed . . .'

'Didn't he get carpeted for handing down a slap on wrist to a couple of serial paedophiles a couple of years ago?' Tanya cut in.

'Yes. You're right, Tanya. He should have dealt out long custodial sentences, but sent them away for therapy instead. If I remember correctly, his summing up went something like, prison wouldn't serve these men any use and what they needed was intensive psychological analysis to come to terms with the error of their ways; or something along those lines.'

'You can see why the bastard's got off now. He's one of them. Puts a different spin on "Looking after your own," doesn't it? Stick the next disc in the machine, Tony,' Loder said. Now he was sitting up and focused on the task ahead.

DS Frost ejected the disc and slid in the next one from the pile stacked on the floor in the open bag. He pressed play then sat back in his seat, folded his arms and waited.

'Oh my, God!' Came the cry from Tanya. Her hands across her mouth in utter amazement. 'Sir Teddy Marston!' She pointed at the screen. 'And that's Danny with him: don't know who the other lad is though.'

'Now we're cooking,' Loder said.

They quickly searched through the disc to the end, just in case there was any other tasty titbits on it, then DS Frost slid the next one into the machine. All four of them waited anxiously for it to begin.

'His face is familiar.' Anne Oakwood said, screwing her eyes at the screen trying to put a name to it.

'Mad Mike McCann,' Loder said.

'Mad? He'll be bloody livid when we pull him in,' DS Frost quipped.

The tense atmosphere in the room melted into laughter.

'What's his claim to fame?' Tanya asked, naively.

'You're probably too young to remember,' Loder smiled. 'He was a big pop star in the late sixties and seventies. If I remember correctly he got nicked for having sex with an underage girl . . . must be twenty-five years ago.'

'Don't tell me, he got off?' Tanya said.

'Correct! He said that the girl told him that she was of consenting age. It transpired that she was, in fact, fourteen years old. And worse still, her parents knew all about it: encouraged it, so it was thought at the time. It was rumoured, but never proved, that he'd been bedding the girl since she was thirteen.'

DS Frost ejected the disc and slid in another. Tanya pointed the remote at the machine and hit the play button. The grainy picture cleared and the room fell into stunned silence.

Everyone just sat open-mouthed in astonishment.

'That's why he was fishing around the incident room earlier,' Loder spat, vehemently. 'Well, at least we know where our leak has been coming from now.'

'You *do* realise we're sitting on a time bomb here, Loder?' DCI Oakwood said. 'What are we going to do? More to the point where do we go from here?'

'I don't know at the moment. Obviously, we can't go steaming in and confronting "Charlie" boy, saying, 'Oh by the way we've got you on film engaged in sex with two underage girls. What have you got to say for yourself you naughty boy?'

'No need for flippancy,' she rebuked, Loder. A friendly reminder of just *who* was in charge here.

'Sorry. But this whole thing is too much to take in,' Loder said, shaking his head. 'I think for the time being we should sit on this disc until we work out a course of action.'

'I don't think we have a choice,' DCI Oakwood said. 'There's no telling where this lot might end up if we take it to a higher authority.'

'What are you saying, Ma'am?' Tanya said.

'I'm saying, judging by what we've already seen and know about this case, there's a distinct possibility that all this lot might conveniently disappear once it's out of our hands. Then all we'd have is nothing more than hearsay.'

'Tony eject that disc,' Loder said.

DS Frost obliged and handed it to Loder.

'I think it's best if I keep this for the time being. I'll take full responsibility for the consequences. No point in putting all our careers on the line.'

'Very noble of you, Loder. But we're in this thing together. Besides, I'm the senior officer and it's my arse on the line as much as yours.'

'Are we all in agreement?' Loder said, directing the question at Tanya and DS Frost.

They both nodded, but Tanya had her doubts. Naively, or not, she still believed in the due process. Everything out in the open and by the book, otherwise, what were they in the job for in the first place. She kept her misgivings to herself: time would tell.

'Right, let's plough through the rest of this lot and get the hell out of here,' DCI Oakwood said.

DS Frost slipped the next disc into the machine and they all sat back and waited anxiously for the show to begin.

It was early afternoon by the time they had finished going through everything. By which time the list read like a "Who's Who." They had a high court judge, a top serving police officer, two fading pop stars, a prominent MP and at least one backbencher who was known to them, a famous theatre actor, a Catholic Bishop and all number of minor celebrities and socialites not yet identified. The potential damage of the evidence they were sitting on was off this planet.

'This lot is probably just the tip of the iceberg,' Tanya said, packing away the laptop into a carry case.

'I agree. This Harry Delaney has obviously been at it for years. He's bound to have some more of this filth stored away somewhere. We need to find him and bring him in. My guess is he'll trade everything he's got if we put him on a promise,' Loder said.

'Right, let's call it a day,' DCI Oakwood said, getting to her feet. 'Get this lot packed away and logged back into store before we get collared.'

Fifteen minutes later, Loder was down in the compound safely ensconced in his car. DS Frost had already skipped the scene – he was taking his eldest boy to see Queens Park Rangers play Wolves, down at Loftus Road. Tony Frost had been a staunch supporter of QPR for as long as could remember. His own father used to take him to watch them when he was just a snivel of a kid. He had fond memories of sitting on his father's shoulders so that he could get a better view of the game and, afterwards, on their way home, they used to stop off at the pie and mash shop for their tea. He now went through the same regime with his own son.

DCI Oakwood got out of her car and hurried across in the drizzling rain to where Loder was parked and got in next to him. 'We need to talk,' she said, wiping her wet face with a tissue.

'I know. Why don't we make our way to the pub opposite your place? I could do with a beer. I've got a foul taste in my throat.'

'Sounds good to me,' she said, opening the door and racing back to her own car.

Loder switched the ignition on and drove out into the afternoon traffic with his boss tailing him up.

Tanya had opted to stay behind for a while to do some filing, so that she had a clean desk for Monday morning. Busting to go to the toilet, she slipped out of the incident room and along the corridor to the washroom.

After she had finished, she opened the washroom door and stepped into the corridor.

She was stopped in her tracks at the sight of DCS Hatchet peering through the porthole window into the incident room. She dashed back into the washroom, locked herself into a cubicle and fumbled around her trouser pockets for her mobile but it wasn't there. *Shit,* she cursed under her breath, when she realised that she had left it in her jacket pocket, which, was hanging on the back of her chair at her desk together with her bag.

She heard a squeak as the washroom door opened. Quietly as she could, she lowered the toilet seat and stepped up onto it – so that her feet couldn't be seen from under the door. She held her breath . . . and just about everything else, as she heard the sound of heavy heels on the granite floor outside. Then the sound of running water, followed by a paper towel being pulled from the wall dispenser. She breathed a sigh of relief as she heard the footsteps go back across the room and the squeak of the door opening.

She dare not move for fear that the DCS was waiting outside: or worse, inside. After a full five minutes, she quietly got down off the toilet seat and unlocked the cubicle door. Tentatively, she opened it a crack and peered out, Then tiptoed towards the exit and held her ear to it for a moment. She said a quick silent prayer to herself and slowly opened the door, just enough to see into the corridor on her left side. There was no one there. She opened the door a little further and peered around towards the incident room. Nothing. The corridor was empty. She then crept along the corridor and peered through the porthole into the incident room and scanned as much of the office as the small window would allow. Everything appeared to be quiet. She keyed in her entry code, went in, grabbed her jacket and bag and bolted back out to the end of the floor. She banged the bar down on the emergency exit, pushed the heavy door open and descended down the clangourous fire escape as fast as her heels would allow her.

The traffic was surprisingly light, considering Queens Park Rangers were playing at home. Loder reached the bottom of Shepherds Green Road and scooted around the Green and up the Uxbridge Road towards Ealing. Within twenty minutes, he was ensconced in a crescent seat in the corner of the pub with a pint in front of him and a large glass of red wine for his boss, for when she arrived.

His mind was turning ten-to-the-dozen with all the morning's events. He still couldn't get his head around everything that he had seen on the discs.

The sound of his mobile chirping startled him back to the present. He pulled it out of his pocket, read the name that was flashing on the screen and answered it.

'Tanya. What? Shit! You sure he never sussed you? Okay. Thanks for letting me know. Don't you worry about it. Enjoy the rest of your weekend.'

Loder was determined to keep focused and not let Detective Chief Superintendent Hatchet cloud his judgement. If the man had stumbled across Tanya in the incident room, Loder knew that Tanya wouldn't have had a choice. He would have demanded that she tell him everything. If Loder had his way, he would cut the dirty bastard's nuts off and throw him to the mercy of the tabloids. One way or another, he would have his balls in a grinder. He was determined to get maximum exposure from this investigation. All the perverted bastards caught on camera – and the perpetrators pulling the strings – were going to be brought before the courts. He was never more certain of anything in all his years as a copper.

The pub was busy with afternoon shoppers stopping off for a quick drink and something to eat. At the far end of the bar, there was a small crowd of football supporters glued to the enormous television perched high up on wall. All in all, it made for a pleasant atmosphere. Loder relaxed back into his seat content in the knowledge that he was inconspicuous in a pub full of strangers.

He glanced at his watch and wondered where Anne had got to. He'd been waiting for almost twenty-five minutes and there was still no sign of her. She wasn't answering her mobile either: he'd tried ringing it twice already. He didn't like to admit it to himself, but he was starting to fret. His glass was almost empty and he couldn't decide whether to get a refill or wait. The decision was made for him when she came bouncing through the door and pointed at his empty glass on her way to the bar.

Loder's eyes widened at the vision of beauty walking towards him, dressed in a pair of figure-hugging jeans and baggy sweater. The flat shoes she was wearing made her even more petite than usual. Loder hadn't realised before just how tiny she really was, and the pint glass she was holding looked incongruous in her small hands – her little fingers bearly wrapped around it.

'There you go'! She said, with a smile. 'Think we probably both need a stiff drink after the morning we've had.'

'I agree, there,' he said, finishing the dregs and taking the froth off of the fresh one. 'I was beginning to wonder where you'd got to? I tried your mobile twice but it wasn't registering.'

'Ahh . . . were you worried about me, Loder? How sweet,' she said, planting a peck on his cheek and sliding in next to him.

'Well, what with everything that's gone on . . . you know?'

'I thought it best to turn the mobile off: incognito for a while. So have you had any thoughts as to what we should do?' she said, taking a sip of wine.

'Nope. I'm still trying to come to terms with it all.'

'You?'

'No. Me neither,' she said, taking another sip of wine.

'This thing is so huge. The damage it could do doesn't bear thinking about.'

'That's the problem. We've not only *got* to start thinking about it, we've got to plan how we're going to approach it.' She sighed, and took another sip of wine, a longer one this time.

'The way I see it,' Loder said, crossing his legs. 'If we take everything we've got to the very top, I reckon they'll bury it and quietly fritter away all the main players into early retirement, and when they're all safely out of harms reach, they'll bring a diluted case in front of the courts. It's not in the establishment's interest to have this sort of a scandal in the public domain: it's too damaging. That said, there could well be more top brass that are part of all this. Hatchet might just be a minnow in a tank full of piranhas, for all we know.'

'We've got to do *something*, Loder. And fast. Hatchet will be on our cases as soon as we get into the office on Monday, that's if he doesn't come looking for us beforehand.'

'Do you think he will?'

'I don't know, but let's just say, I won't be answering my door to any strangers. I think we have to take the view that Hatchet isn't aware of any DVD evidence implicating him, or anyone else for that matter. For all we know he might still be in contact with Harry Delaney and for that reason alone, it's in his own interest to know everything that's going on with the investigation. Up to now, we've managed to give him a wide berth, but once he finds out about the evidence, he'll have us over the coals at the first opportunity.'

Anne nursed her wine glass in her hand and nodded pensively in agreement as Loder paused for a drink of his beer.

'He's a desperate man who could see everything he's ever strived for go down the drain,' he went on. 'You've got to remember it's not only his career, it's the public humiliation that will go with it all. He wouldn't be able to show his face in public ever again if he gets collared.'

A silence ensued between them and she contemplated what civilian life might hold for her after her demise from the police force. It was a cast-iron certainty, as far as she was concerned, that after everything had come out, she would be out of a job: she had already broken every rule in the book.

She wasn't the type of person who would just sit around and vegetate. She would have to do something to occupy herself. Besides, she needed to earn an income to supplement what would probably be a greatly depleted pension, if she was sacked. Probably go into the private security business. That's where most of the washed up ex-police ended up, she thought to herself. On the bright side, she cheered, won't have to bust her arse working twelve hour a day and play departmental politics with tossers, that think that they are the dog's gonads. Better still, won't have to cowl-tail to over inflated, egotistical, chauvinistic superior officers anymore, either.

A smile crossed her face at the bollocks of it all. She knew that she couldn't live with the guilt if she didn't do what her conscience was telling her. And that was nail the bastards, *long and hard*. Whatever the cost.

'What are you thinking about?' Loder broke the silence.

'What the future might hold when my career is in the dustbin.'

'It won't come to that, Anne.'

'Why are you so sure?'

'Because I'll take all the flak. I'll say I was working alone without your knowledge of anything.'

'That's very noble of you, Loder. But at the end of the day, I'm responsible for *your* actions, whether you acted with or without my express authority. I'm the senior officer. The buck stops with me.'

'Ah, well . . . who gives a toss? We'll set up in business together,' he smiled.

'What, you and me?'

'Why not?'

'I can just picture it . . . a geriatric "Dempsey and Makepiece,"'

'Who?'

'Forget it, Loder,' she said, rubbing an affectionate hand along his thigh.

The feel of her warm hand sent a tingle shooting up his leg and into his groin. He had to cross his legs to stop himself getting an erection.

Taking a swallow from his glass, he contemplated their predicament for a moment. 'The way I see it, if we bypass the DCS and go to someone above him with all the evidence, he's going to smell a rat. And who's to know that whoever we take it to, isn't part of this perverted network? After everything we've had to sit and witness this morning, nothing would surprise me anymore.'

'I agree. So what should we do?'

'I might have an idea. Another drink?' he said, picking up her empty glass.

'In a minute. Tell me what you you're thinking,' she said, grabbing hold of his arm.

'I think we should give everything we've got to the DCS, but hold onto the video with him in. That way he'll be none the wiser.'

'I've changed my mind. I think I'm going to need another drink,' she said, offering Loder her empty glass.

Loder shook his head and smiled. He just adored everything about this little woman. He finished his pint and went across to the bar.

He returned a few minutes later with a self-satisfied smile on his face. He set the drinks on the table and slid in next to his boss.

'Why the smug look, Loder? You spent a fiver and got change for a tenner, or something?'

'I think I might have cracked it.'

'Well, don't keep me in suspense,' she said.

'Where was I . . . oh yes. If we hold onto the DVD with the DCS on, he'll be none the wiser.'

'And?'

'We get all the main players into the nick and under caution without his knowledge. He might not like it, but he wouldn't be able to stop it, because the shit would already be flying. After all, we're just conscientious, hardworking coppers going about our jobs the best way we know how. It would be out of his hands. He couldn't do a thing about it . . . could he?'

'Might work,' she said, unconvinced. 'Who's going to do the dirty work?'

'Ah, that's your job.'

'I thought it might be,' she mocked, sardonically.

'You'll probably get a rollicking about not following procedure and suchlike, but his back will be firmly against the wall. By which time I'll have every available interview room occupied. The station will be in chaos.'

'I don't know, Loder. It's a risk.'

'I can't think of another way around it . . . can you?'

'No. I suppose not.'

'If it all blows up in our faces, there's always the media.'

'What the papers?'

'Why not. If our careers are down the pan anyway, what have we got to lose? We'll feed them the bait, anonymously, of course, and let the Sunday Tabloids do the rest.'

Anne Oakwood made a face.

'What about Hatchet? He can't come out of all this whiter-than-white. I couldn't live with the guilt hanging over me, Loder.'

'I've thought of that. If everything goes to plan and we get to go to court with a cast-iron case – of which, I have no doubt – we can sort of drop the disc of "Charlie Boy" into the CPS'S lap afterwards – anonymously.'

'Suppose they don't act upon it?' She nursed her wine glass in her hands.

'We send a copy to a journalist friend of mine. Throw the bastard to the wolves: trial by media. The CPS wouldn't have an alternative. They'd have to hang him out to dry.'

'What do you say, Anne?'

'Yes. Okay, I suppose so. Let's go with it.' She sighed. Resigned to the prospect of early retirement.

'Great! It'll work, you'll see.'

'I hope so . . . for both our sakes. Come on. Drink up, Loder. I'm famished. Fancy a Chinese?'

'Absolutely! I'm still recovering from the last one,' He said, with a teasing twitch of his brow.

'Loder!' She slapped his arm with embarrassment.

CHAPTER 25

Lee drove down the M20 to Folkestone and followed the signs for the Euro Tunnel Terminal. Once there, he found a parking space away from the central concourse, got out of the car and stretched his legs. Ryan's jaw dropped at the sheer size of the holding park and the huge concourse.

The morning air was damp and chilly from an earlier downpour. A screeching flock of seagulls, gliding effortlessly overhead in the blustery, dull slate-grey sky, caught Lee's attention. He didn't like seagulls. He thought them intimidating. When he was eight years of age, while on holiday down in Devon with his parents, a huge seagull had swooped down and pinched a beak full of his chips as he ate them out of a bag. The shock of it had stayed with him all through his life. To this day he always kept a wary eye when he saw seagulls hovering around. They reminded him of the Hitchcock film, "The Birds." He was convinced the gulls already had him in their sights and would attack at the first opportunity should he drop his guard.

He went around to the back of the car, opened the boot and pulled out the confirmation sheet and his passport from the side pocket of his travel bag. He'd pre-booked the shuttle online, earlier the previous day and managed to secure a midday crossing. The big problem was, Ryan, he didn't have a valid passport. The lad had said that Delaney looked after things like that. He had only ever seen his passport once and that was when he had received in the post.

Delaney had taken it from him, saying that he'd keep it safe. It was clear to Ryan now, the real reason the fat bastard kept it locked away in the safe, was to prevent him from doing a runner. Just like he *was* doing. The difference *now,* was Delaney's days were numbered, given that the Old Bill had acted on the information he had given Lee. He was probably banged up in a cell right this minute, sweating and squirming his innocence.

To Delaney, having sex with kids was the most natural thing in the world: it was the law that was wrong, not him. The fact that he robbed their souls – irreparably in most cases – didn't cross his mind at all. He looked upon himself as a father figure who looked after his flock and kept them sheltered, off the streets.

Lee wasn't sure how he was going to handle the situation, because the booking was for himself and the car. The only thing he could think of was to hide Ryan in the boot and pray to God that the car didn't get searched by the Border Control. If it all went pear-shaped, he would have to throw himself at the mercy of Loder and come clean with everything.

'Wait in the car, Ryan. The less anyone sees of you, the better, especially with all the CCTV about. I'm just going over to the booking-in kiosk. I shouldn't be long. I'll bring us back something to eat and drink.'

'I'll have a burger and fries and a large coke, please,' Ryan said.

'Nothing wrong with your appetite is there?' Lee tried to sound upbeat, but he was literally bricking it. He wasn't used to all this skulduggery. He was just an ordinary "Joe" striving the best he could in life to provide for his wife and daughter. Now, he didn't have either. It all seemed so long ago that his world had fallen apart. Everything he lived and breathed for; snatched away from him in an instant by a vicious, evil predator. But no matter what happened he wouldn't be deflected from what he thought was the right thing to do. And that was to re-unite his family: he just prayed that he wasn't too late.

Lee threw on his leather bomber jacket, slammed down the boot and set off in the direction of the terminal building. The huge holding park was busy with cars and 4x4's, pulling huge trailers and caravans. Some looked like five-star rolling apartments, and probably cost a king's ransom. A few owners had set up tables and chairs outside their colourful, shiny palaces and were sitting down eating breakfast and drinking tea. The one thing they all had in common, was the fact that they seemed to revel in the knowledge that they were the object of people's curiosity – or admiration.

Lee could just imagine the mind-numbing conversations that went on between them over a glass of vino at their holiday parks. It was a million miles away from Lee's idea of the perfect holiday. He preferred a nice cool rental villa, near a beach and a bar, where he could laze around all day. And in the balmy evenings, to eat in waterside restaurants with his family and over indulge himself with fresh seafood and chilled wine. A heavy feeling of guilt bore down on him. It all seemed so long ago.

He passed a group of weary-looking people as he joined the queue at the booking-in kiosk. Their bleary, tired-looking eyes looked as if they had been on the road for days. Luckily, Lee was only a couple of hours away from the terminal up the M20. Even less if the M25 was clear.

As the queue thinned and he got closer to the glass-fronted counter, he felt his stomach dancing hoops. His arse began to flap and he wondered whether to make a dash for the nearest carsi. Too late. It was his turn. He took a deep breath and slid the confirmation under the glass curtain. The young pretty girl behind the counter looked at the sheet and began tapping away at a keyboard. Perched high above looking down at his profile was a CCTV camera. Lee stood straight-backed and fixed his eyes at a spot on the wall on the other side of the glass, but something drew his eyes upwards and he gave a furtive glance up at the camera. Then with a bright smile, the girl slid his documents and boarding pass to him. 'Have a nice trip, sir.' She smiled pleasantly. 'Please make your way over to the departure hanger in about forty minutes.'

Lee picked up the documentation, slipped it inside his jacket pocket, and thanked the girl. He then made his way through the entrance of the terminal building in search of food.

Ten minutes later, he and Ryan were sitting in the car feasting on Big Macs and fries, washed down with a reservoir of Coke. Lee thought the burger tasted like cardboard, but he ate it anyway. He could only manage half of his drink. The gas made him feel bloated. He gave out an almighty burp and handed the huge paper cup to Ryan. 'I've had enough of that,' he said, wiping his hands on a serviette.

He glanced at his watch. They still had a bit of time to kill before having to make their way over to the departure hanger. He rolled a cigarette, switched on the radio and tried to relax. Ryan had chomped through his burger, demolished his fries and a gallon of coke as if it was his last meal on this earth. He put the empty food containers into a paper bag. 'I'll run these over to the bin, shall I?'

'No. I'll do it. Best you stay in the car,' Lee said.

'Ok. Let's have the baccy over and I'll roll meself a fag.'

Lee passed him the leather tobacco pouch and cigarette papers, watching in awe as he expertly rolled the perfect cigarette: better than he could manage and he had at least twenty-five years on him.

'Got a light?' Ryan said, sporting a perfectly rounded cigarette between his lips.

'Where did you learn to roll fags like that?' Lee said, igniting the lighter.

'You know, here and there,' he said proudly. 'Used to roll a lot of joints at one time, but I got out of all that shit: made me paranoid.'

Lee shook his head slowly. Was their nothing that this kid hadn't done in his short life. He'd probably experienced more in his short years than Lee had in all of his forty-six years on this planet. Whether it be good or bad. Just knowing Ryan for the short time he had, it was plainly obvious that he'd had a raw deal in life. He'd been betrayed by everyone that he had placed his trust in. Then he'd had the misfortune of being taken in by Harry Delaney and his mind had been totally corrupted. As God was his judge, Lee was going to make that man pay. On the outside, Ryan was a happy go-lucky lad with an infectious personality. Who knows what demons he was hiding on the inside.

Christ he wasn't even out of his teens yet.

Lee got out of the car, walked over to the bin twenty metres away and dumped the bag into it. The weather was deteriorating rapidly. It looked like there was a storm brewing. Thick black clouds were moving in off of the coast. All the noisy seagulls had disappeared leaving a dark, cold, eerie silence in the air. Maybe the gulls had a sixth-sense and knew that bad weather was moving in: either way, they had all gone.

He made his way back to the car, opened the boot, took out his overnight bag and another holdall with both of their clothes in and threw them onto the back seat of the car. He figured that if he had everything on show, the authorities wouldn't bother looking in the boot. He then laid out a duvet and a pillow to try and make it a bit more comfortable for, Ryan. 'Right, you ready, Ryan?' Lee called.

Ryan got out of the car, walked around and joined Lee. They both scanned around to make sure no one was looking. 'In you get,' Lee said. Ryan jumped into the cramped space and assumed a semi-foetal position. 'There's a bottle of water and a torch in that carrier bag tucked in the corner. I'll let you out for air as soon as I can.'

'Okay. Don't be going over any big bumps. Me stomach's a bit dicky,' Ryan said, as he bedded down.

Lee rolled his eyes and with a slow shake of his head, said, before closing the boot, 'I wonder why?'

Lee hooked the boarding pass on the rear view mirror, started the car and cruised slowly around towards departures and joined the waiting queue of traffic. The rain had started to fall, so he switched the window wipers to intermittent. They moaned and screeched as they laboured on the sticky, insect-ridden windscreen. Lee pressed the screen wash, but all it resulted in was a thick smear that obscured his view even more. With the weather deteriorating by the second, he hoped that the uniformed officers checking everyone's documentation would be less stringent. After all, there can't be many people trying to smuggle someone *out* of the UK; they're all trying to get in.

He followed the line of vehicles into a covered hanger and buzzed the window down. A Border Control officer dressed in a navy parka waved him on. Lee breathed a sigh of relief as he passed through the hanger: only to be hit head-on with utter shock as the car in front was filtered left to a holding area by another officer. He gripped the steering wheel so tightly that his knuckles began to turn white. He glanced over to where the car had stopped and watched as a gang of rowdy lads spilled out onto the tarmac, dressed in England football shirts. He quickly turned his attention to what was going on in front of him. His head was spinning and his heart was pounding against his rib cage like a Salvation Army drum. Everything seemed surreal. All around him everything moved in slow motion as if he was detached from the whole scene. Elvis belted out "Jailhouse Rock" on the radio. Was it a sign for him to get the hell out of here before it was too late.

Someone tapping on the side window jolted him out of his trance. He buzzed the window down halfway. 'Join column "D," please sir,' the officer said, waving him in the direction of a long queue of vehicles. He breathed a massive sigh of relief, skirted up behind the line of cars and followed them around to the Shuttle. Had he not been so panic-stricken, Lee would have enjoyed this whole experience, because he'd never travelled on the Shuttle before.

Two men dressed in yellow, hooded cagoules directed Lee into a long, windowless shiny carriage. From the outside it resembled a never-ending giant metal tube. Slowly he manoeuvred the car into the carriage and along to the end, until a uniformed Eurostar attendant held his hand up for him to stop. Vehicles filed in behind until the carriage was full, then the doors slid across shutting them in.

Lee buzzed his window down to get some air, but the carriage smelled dank and full of catalytic fumes and burnt engine oil, so he buzzed it up again. A few people had got out of their cars and were walking along the elevated walkways down each side of the carriage. Lee didn't like the feeling of confinement: he was claustrophobic and hated being shut in. Even now, he would only venture into an elevator if there was other people in it at the same time. He felt like he was shut in some long metal cylinder. He could have murdered a cigarette, but there was no-smoking signs pasted all along the carriage.

He reached into his pocket and got out his mobile phone, thumbed through the memory and found his wife's number. He ached to tell her everything that had happened. What he was doing. Where he was going. All about his fortunate meeting with Ryan. But instead, he closed the flap and put the mobile back into his pocket. He had to keep everything secret: at least until he knew what was going on. He almost jumped out of his skin as his mobile sprang to life to tune of "Mission Impossible." His first thought was that he'd not turned it off properly. He reached into his pocket, got it out and flipped it open. *Shit*, he cursed under his breath. He let the tune play out until the caller hung up. *The last person he wanted to speak to was Detective Constable Tanya Reid.*

Fifteen minutes later, Lee felt the carriage shunt forwards. Slowly it gathered speed as it descended downwards. It wasn't a very comfortable feeling. The visual display screen read, "arrival in thirty-five minutes." *Amazing.*

   He got out of the car, went around to the rear and stood in front of the boot. The car behind was empty. Lee had seen the two occupants walk past him and disappear through to the next carriage. High above on both sides were CCTV cameras dotted along the length of the carriage. Tentatively, Lee opened the boot just enough to duck his head in. 'You okay?' he whispered.

   'Yeh, no problem,' Ryan said. 'You got anything to eat?'

   'God! What are you like? I'll sort you out something when we get over the other side. Shouldn't be too long.' He closed the boot up and got back into the car.

Fifty minutes later, Lee was on his way out of the Calais terminal. He couldn't believe how easy it had all been and made a mental note to himself that when everything was over, he would bring his family on the Shuttle and they would all have a holiday in Brittany. They had been there a few years before when Donna was ten years old. They all said it was the best holiday they had ever had. The sun had shined every day; their holiday villa was fantastic, the location was superb – right next to a vast sandy beach – and there was loads to do. His eyes began to flood at the memory of Donna and him playing in the pool and teaching her how to dive. A deep lump filled his throat as the stream of tears trailed down his face. He sniffed hard and a big globule of phlegm filled his mouth. He wiped his eyes on his cuff, found a tissue in the glove compartment and spat the foul-tasting substance into it.

He pushed the memories to the back of his mind and tried to focus on the road ahead. Up front was a petrol station. He checked the gauge on the dashboard. It read just under half-full, so he pulled into the expansive forecourt to fill up. It seemed that everyone had the same idea as him, as the place was buzzing with people carrying armfuls of sweets, cans of pop and bottles of water from the supermarket shop.

Lee filled up and went inside to pay. While inside he picked up a couple of two-litre bottles of mineral water, a bag of humbugs for himself and a large bag of crisps for Ryan. He got to the front of the pay-desk then realised that he hadn't got any euros, so he paid by visa. Luckily, there was a bureau de change on the premises, so he changed three-hundred pounds into euros using his card.

He got back into the car, started the engine and drove to a quite spot away from all the activity and CCTV. He backed the car up so that the boot was facing onto open countryside, then got out and had a good look around. Satisfied that he wouldn't draw attention to himself, he opened the boot. 'Lively. Into the car, he said, still looking around to make sure no one saw them.'

Ryan leaped out of the boot, around the side of the car and jumped into the passenger seat. Lee closed the boot, had another look all around and got back into the car.

'Oh shit!'

'What now?' Lee said

'I need a piss. I can't hold it.'

Lee rolled his eyes, tiresomely. 'Quick, round the back of the car.' Ryan jumped out, pulled the front of his trackies and Calvin Klein's down and breathed a long sigh of relief as his bladder began to empty.

The sound of the endless stream of urine hitting the ground, gave Lee an uncontrollable urge to join him – see one, do one. He jumped out of the car and ran round the back wrestling with his fly buttons. Finally, he got them open, breathed a huge satisfying sigh and relieved himself. 'Great, this! All we need is to get ourselves nicked for indecent exposure, the moment we set foot in the country,' Lee quipped, buttoning his flies.

'I heard the "Frogs" piss in the middle of the street behind circular barriers, is that true?' Ryan said, in earnest.

'I wouldn't know, but I suppose we might find out on the way down,' Lee smiled, winding Ryan up.

'Well, you won't catch me getting me dick out where everyone can see, that's for sure.' Ryan sniffed.

Once they were back in the car, Lee started the engine and dumped a thick map on Ryan's lap. 'Your navigating.' He had already downloaded a route from the internet the day before, so he wasn't completely at a loss as to what direction he should be heading.

It was a lot easier than he thought it might be. He just followed the stream of British registration plates until he was on the A16 headed in the direction of the E402. Once he was on that road he virtually stayed on it all the way down to the border.

The weather was still overcast, but the sun was trying its best to peek through the thick scudded clouds that were racing in the direction of Dear Old Blighty. Lee filtered into the middle lane of traffic, eased himself back into his seat and settled down for the long drive ahead.

CHAPTER 26

It was 11:55 am on the Monday morning. Loder and his team had been busy since first thing, rounding up the principle players. He and DCI Oakwood had spent most of the weekend co-ordinating the operation.

Loder had taken great personal pleasure in bringing in Jonnie James kicking and screaming his innocence. DS Frost and Tanya had brought in Sir Teddy Marston. The trusted few detective constables that were in on the raid at Harry Delaney's house rounded up Mad Max McCann and a famous old Theatre Queen, by the name of Sir Richard Baxendale. It was only protocol that DCI Oakwood should bring in, The Lord Chief Justice Baxter.

The station was in chaos. No one could quite believe what was going on. The buzz around the building was at fever pitch. The ground floor corridor where the interview rooms were located, were crammed with faces that read like a listing from "Who's Who."

Loder had disappeared up into his office to let things calm down a bit, and to take stock of the situation by brushing up on notes before going into action. DS Frost knocked and went in followed by Tanya and sat across from Loder's desk.

'How are things downstairs?' Loder asked, with a wry smile.

'Chaos!' DS Frost smiled, relishing the situation.

'Good. Just what I was expecting. Are they all briefed up?'

'Not yet. We're still waiting for Jonnie James's brief. Justice Baxter has refused to have one. He's carping on about his civil liberties being compromised, or something: I didn't understand a word of it.'

The high-octane charged atmosphere in the room evaporated into thin air when Detective Chief Superintendent Hatchet came bursting through the door.

'What in the hell is going on, Loder?' he shouted, gesticulating wildly.

Anne Oakwood poked her head out from behind Hatchet, looked at Loder and with a wry smile, zipped her mouth.

'I take it, DCI Oakwood has briefed you, sir?' he said, getting to his feet.

'She most certainly has. But I want to hear it from you, because none of this charade downstairs is her doing. It's got your name stamped all over it . . . and I'm telling you *now* Loder, that I hold you completely responsible. I will not have the good name of this station dragged through the mire by the actions of an out of control insubordinate. Is that clear?'

'Yes, sir.'

Loder thought that the man was on the verge of bursting a blood vessel, his face was so inflamed.

'Where is all this "Evidence," DCI Oakwood informs me that you have? And, why hasn't it been logged in?'

'It has, sir.'

'When?'

'Friday afternoon, sir. Logged. Tagged. And viewed.' Loder locked eyes with the man.

A momentary tacit stand-off ensued, in the tension filled room.

The DCS blinked, breaking eye contact with Loder. 'Then why wasn't I briefed until this morning? I specifically told you that I wanted to be kept up to speed with this investigation.'

And don't we know just why.

'Are you trying to undermine my authority Loder?' he said, narrowing a brow, suspiciously.

'Absolutely not, sir.'

'Then why wasn't I informed of this . . . this . . . charade, before you took it upon yourselves to take matters into your own hands?'

'We thought, DCI Oakwood and I, given the fact that we've had more leaks than the Thames Water Authority all through this investigation, that the least people knew, the better.'

'And you thought it right that *I* should be included in this veil of secrecy of yours, Loder?'

'Not intentionally, sir. It was just that there was so much to organise in a short space of time, it just slipped our minds.'

Loder was relishing the glowering look of consternation on Hatchet's face. He could almost hear the man's mind turning over like an out of control roller index, spinning wildly, searching for options.

Hatchet took a breath. 'I see,' he said, standing straight-backed, with his hands clasped tight behind him.

'I apologise if our actions might have been misconstrued. But I can assure you sir, it wasn't a reflection on your integrity in any way.'

'I'm *glad* to hear that, Loder.'

'It was my decision to keep everything under wraps, sir.'

'Excuse me, sir,' DCI Oakwood said, squeezing herself around Hatchet and into the office. She walked across the room and joined Loder behind his desk. 'I like to say, for the record, that every action DI Loder has taken in this case, has been on my express authority. Not once has he acted without my express knowledge, sir.'

'A united front. Very noble of you, Oakwood. Let's hope you don't live to regret those words, when you're up before a tribunal. You had better get on with things, now that you have started.'

'Thank you, sir,' DCI Oakwood said.

'And I'm warning the both of you.' He pointed at, Loder. 'One step out of line and I'll have you laid bare. I'll hang the pair of you out to dry. Is that clear?'

'Sir!' they both said in unison.

'And you can rest assured that I'll be watching every move you make.' He turned on his heels and stormed out.

I bet you will.

Loder slumped down in his chair. 'Well, that went easier than I envisaged,' he said, with a wry smile.

'Do you think he suspected anything?' DCI Oakwood asked.

Loder shrugged. 'He knows something isn't quite right.'

'How are we going to go about this?' DCI Oakwood said, rolling her neck on her shoulders and brushing her fingers through her hair, tiredly. She was completely stressed.

'I think Tanya and yourself should tackle, Sir Teddy Marston. He might open up if you nurse him along gently. Give him the sympathy vote. I'll take Jonnie James. Tony can have The Honourable Justice Baxter and we'll leave the rest stewing until were ready for them. Is that okay with you all?'

They all nodded.

'Shall I get Andy West to take Sir Dicky Baxendale, boss? He's a good lad.'

'Aye, why not. The quicker we get through them all the better.'

'What about Mad Max McCann?'

'As you've said before, Tony. He's going to be bloody livid by the time we get around to him.'

There was a muffled laugh amongst them all. The nervous tension in the room was almost palpable.

'Okay. Let *battle* commence,' Loder said, wringing his hands together.

He led the team along the corridor towards the interview suites like a regimental sergeant major. He had a look of a man on a mission, stern and focussed. Each of them were loaded up with files.

A small crowd of shirt-sleeved uniformed officers were huddled around the coffee vending machine chatting and drinking from plastic cups. The banter stopped and they moved aside to let the team pass as they approached.

'Are their briefs all here?' Loder asked.

The custody officer, George Dolan, checked the list on his clipboard. 'The last one arrived a couple of minutes ago,' he said.

Loder nodded, casting George Dolan a wry smirk as he strode pass. DCI Oakwood stopped behind Loder, saw the nameplate card on the first interview room door and went in, with DC Reid behind. Loder walked on to the second door, read the nameplate and took a deep breath.

'Good luck, boss,' DS Frost said, as he passed.

'Luck, doesn't come into it, Tony.'

Loder turned the handle and went in. DS Frost took the next room and DC Andy West took the last, with a colleague in tow.

Loder crossed the stuffy room and sat facing Jonnie James and his solicitor across a grey metal table. The room stank of stale tobacco and body odour. Loder knew that the room was used by some of the lads for a crafty fag, the idea being that the extract fan would draw out all the smoke: it failed miserably. A young DC, Kevin Bishop, who had been drafted in at the beginning of the investigation, was already present. Throughout the investigation, the young DC had stood out to Loder as a bright, capable lad who would go far in the force. Loder had made a mental note, that should an opening in his department become available, he would try and get the lad on-board.

There was a soft tap on the door. A uniformed officer entered and quietly stood just inside with his feet slightly apart, his hands clasped behind him with his back against the wall. Jonnie James gave him a condescending sneer. The officer fixed his eyes on a spot on the wall directly in front of him.

'What is all this bollocks, Loder? Why have you dragged me all the way over here? I've got better things to do with my time than sit in a stinking—'

Loder held his hand up in front of him, saying nothing.

The young DC slid a new audio cassette into a recorder, which was fixed to the wall above the table and pressed the record button. A red light blinked once then stayed on. He voiced in the preliminaries; date, time and persons present. Then Loder asked. 'Please confirm that your name is, Jonnie James and you reside at—'

'You damn well, know it is,' Jonnie James barked. Irked.

'Just answer the question, for the record,' Loder said, calmly.

Jonnie James tutted, tiresomely. 'Yes. Now what the fuck am I doing here? I answered all your questions when you rifled my home.

That's another thing. I want it put on record.' He leaned closer towards the recording machine. 'The police wrecked my home and I'll be seeking compensation.'

The Armani suited lawyer opened an A4 sized notepad and scribbled a note.

Loder rolled his eyes tiresomely. *This is going to be a long day.*

'Shall we press on. Mr James, are you acquainted , or have you ever met a man by the name of Harry Delaney?'

Jonnie James's screwed his eyes, suspiciously. 'No.'

'You have never heard this man's name mentioned in passing?'

'Never. Are we finished now?' His metal-framed chair scrapped across the linoleum floor as he pushed it back and went to get up.

'Sit down!' Loder growled.

The lawyer rested a reassuring hand on Jonnie James's arm and he sat back down.

'So can you tell me how you account for the fact that this was found at Delaney's home?' Loder said, opening the manila folder and sliding a DVD across the table.

The Detective Constable voiced in the particulars. Item one . . .

'I don't know. You tell me,' Jonnie James said, sitting back in his chair, folding his arms and cocking his head to the side, taunting, Loder.

Loder paused a beat. It was taking all of his resolve just to stop him burying his fist under the smug-faced bastard's chin.

'Would you like to hazard a guess how this disc got there, at Delaney's?'

'No, idea.'

'Shall we have a look and see what's on it, Mr James?'

'No point. You lot already know what's on it. Did you enjoy yourselves watching a true thespian at work?' He said, with a smirk.

Loder ignored the smart remark.

'But do *you*? Don't you want to know what's on it?'

Not bothered, either way.' James shrugged, with indifference.

Jonnie James knew that Delaney used to film a lot of the first-timers. The pair of them used to have a good laugh when they watched the replays – usually over a drink and a spliff. They had captured some blistering stuff together over the years. Delaney had always said that the movies were for insurance purposes only. Just in case anyone got a little loose-tongued. They had even made a few quid out of some of them; blackmailing the recipients. Some were posted onto a clandestine website for paying members only. But he was never aware that the cunning bastard had *him* on film.

All he had to do was front it out and let his overpaid, under worked lawyer do the rest. Besides, it was in his lawyers own interest to get him out of here, because his taste for young girls was legendary. And he had the evidence in living colour, captured on film, kept safely out of reach for times such as this.

Sir Teddy Marston was sitting next to his lawyer. His shoulders slumped. His face flushed and clammy. Even his trademark pink silk hankie that always stood up proudly like a beacon to the world, lay drooped and listless from his suit breast pocket.

No one had told him quite what he had been brought in for. It was all a bit of a mystery. He was under the misconception that it must be something to do with Danny.

'I could never have hurt the boy, you know. I was fond of him. He could have had anything he wanted from me. All he had to do was ask.' Teddy Marston said. His eyes dull and lifeless, fixed to a spot on the table.

DCI Oakwood and DC Reid looked at each other, confused.

'Would you care to elaborate, sir,' DCI Oakwood prompted.

His lawyer sensed the detectives' confusion and cut in, 'My client does not wish to elaborate, officers. Can you not see that he is not well. I very much doubt that he is fit enough to answer any of your questions, given his present state of mind. Now will you please get to the point as to why my client is here? Otherwise we are leaving.'

Teddy Marston patted the top of his lawyer's hand. 'It's okay, Julian. I want to tell the detectives everything that I know. It has been too long. I can't keep everything bottled up any longer. That poor boy deserves better.'

'What boy?' DC Reid asked.

'Why, Daniel, of course. That's why I'm here, isn't it?'

'Yes, sir.' DCI Oakwood, lied. 'Please go on. What can you tell us of your relationship with Daniel McKee?'

'Well, it's not a secret in certain close-knit circles that I have a . . . weakness. It's something I have to live with, to my eternal shame. I can't help myself, you see. It's like a drug. Daniel was like a drug. I couldn't get enough of him. We were . . . what you might call . . . in a relationship.'

'A sexual relationship?' DC Reid said.

The lawyer jumped in. 'My client absolutely refuses to answer such a scandalous accusation, detective.'

'Please, Julian. I know that you only want to help. Yes, it was a sexual relationship. I loved the boy. I didn't want any harm to come to him. You have to believe me, officer.'

'Absolutely, sir,' DCI Oakwood said, sympathetically.

'Unfortunately, Daniel tricked me into posing with him in some . . . compromising photos.'

'Where did this occur, sir?' DC Reid said.

'In my office at the House of Commons.'

Tanya raised an eyebrow and shot a glance at DCI Oakwood. The enormity of what this sorry man was confessing to, was explosive.

'Anyway, the upshot was that Daniel went on to blackmail me to the tune of fifteen thousand pounds. I told Harry about it and he said that he would deal with the matter.'

'Would that be Harry Delaney, sir?' DCI Oakwood said.

'Yes, it would be, officer.'

'Please, go on, sir.'

'The next thing I heard on the television news that the poor boy had been found murdered.' He gave a theatrical wave of his hand. 'Oh God! It's all so awful. I would have gladly given Daniel the money if he had asked.'

Tanya changed tact, before the man broke down completely. 'What can you tell us of, Harry Delaney?'

Within twenty minutes, Sir Teddy had laid himself bare. He'd told them of the parties. How, Delaney had supplied a never-ending stream of kids for the entertainment of people such as he. And finally, when he was shown the DVD of him cavorting with Danny and another lad, he just broke down in floods of tears. The one thing that he refused to do was name names. Even after everything that had happened. It was as if he was bound by some secret pact.

Sir Teddy sat at the desk, his head bowed in shame. A broken man. His career, his family life, and most certainly his public life now in ruins.

After he was formally charged, the two detectives looked at each other and both knew what the other was thinking. For some inexplicable reason they felt sympathy for the man.

'Just one more thing, sir.' DCI Oakwood slid the photo of Delaney and Laura Davidson across the table and let it rest under his nose. 'Can you confirm for us that that is, Harry Delaney?'

He lifted his head a little and took a look at the photo. 'Yes, it is. The murdering bastard.'

'Have you ever seen the girl in the picture, sir?'

He shook his head slowly. 'No. Never.'

'Would you have any idea as to where this photo might have been taken, sir?' DC Reid said.

He picked up the eight-by-ten photo and studied it for a moment. 'Looks like it was taken at the *bastard's* villa.' The expletive sounded profound in his plum-in-the-mouth, deep aristocratic voice: completely out of character for the man. He put the photo back down and slid it back across the table. 'I had the displeasure of staying there on occasion.'

'So you know the location of the villa, sir?' DCI Oakwood said.

'Yes,' he sighed, tiredly. 'I have the address somewhere.'

'That would be a great help, sir,' DCI Oakwood softly said, shooting a furtive look at DC Reid. *Bingo! Cracked it!*

Sir Teddy reached into his jacket pocket and pulled out a neat, expensive looking, black leather, gold-edged address book. He thumbed through it until he found the page, ripped it out and passed it across the table.

DC Reid copied down the address. 'Is that the telephone number underneath, sir?'

'Mobile number, detective.'

She copied it down, checked it and slid the ripped page, together with the copy, into the folder.

'I'd like to thank you, sir. For being so co-operative. I know it couldn't have been easy for you,' DCI Oakwood said, getting to her feet. 'We'll get you processed as soon as possible, then you will be allowed to leave.' she smiled, and made her way out.

DC Reid ejected the audio tape from the machine, slipped it into its case, closed her file and followed her boss out.

Jonnie James hadn't given any ground at all. He protested his innocence at every angle. And his smart-arsed lawyer was getting right up Loder's nose.

'Look, Detective Inspector Loder,' James said, pensively. 'As I've already pointed out to you. What I do in the privacy of my own home is my business.'

'Not if it involves underage children, it's not.'

'I have never done anything to anyone against their wishes. Every single one of my . . . episodes . . .' a self-satisfied smirk suffused his face . . . 'has been consensual. Has any single *one* of my lads ever complained?' He paused, waiting for Loder to speak. He wasn't being drawn in. 'No, is the answer.'

'I have *you*, Mr James, on film engaged in sexual activity with two minors. What do you have to say about that?'

'How do you know they're minors? Have they told you so, inspector?'

Loder said nothing. He knew that the sanctimonious bastard was right.

'What you have their on that disc is nothing more than me having a bit of fun with a couple of friends.'

'So you consider having two kids screaming with pain as you bugger them, fun, do —'

'That's enough of that, inspector.' The lawyer jumped in.

'I'll ask you again. Do you know, or have you ever come into contact with that person,' Loder said, pointing to the photo of Harry Delaney.'

'I've already told you.' Jonnie James crossed one leg across the top of his thigh.

'Tell me again.'

'No. Never seen him before.'

'Look, Inspector Loder. We're not getting anywhere here. It's obvious that you haven't got anything that implicates my client in any way. We're out of here.'

'You're client will leave, when I say. Not you. Is that clear?'

'Read him his rights, then charge him,' Loder said, scraping his file up and getting to his feet.

'What with? You can't do that,' Jonnie James, looked up, shocked.

'Try and stop me?' Loder said, making his way towards the door. 'Indecent Assault. Should do for starters.'

'That's bollocks! And you know it, Loder,' Jonnie James, shouted.

'We'll let the CPS decide,' Loder said, over his shoulder as he left the room.

Loder strode along the corridor and went in the observation suite to IR1 where DCI Oakwood and DC Reid where viewing the DVD that had been shot of Sir Teddy Marston's interview. He dropped his file on the desk and joined the two women in front of the monitor.

'How did you get on?' he said, arching his back tiredly.

'Fantastic!' DCI Oakwood, enthused. He held his hands up to everything. It appears that young Danny was blackmailing him, so he went to Delaney for help. The next thing, Sir Teddy hears that the boy has been murdered.'

Loder tightened his lips and blew a short burst of air. 'Well, well. Who'd have thought?'

'There's more, sir,' Tanya said. 'The photo of Laura Davidson with Delaney. We've got the address of the villa in Spain and Delaney's mobile number.'

'Where is it?' Loder said.

DC Reid opened her file. 'On the outskirts of a small village, south of Cordoba, sir.'

'Good work. At last we seem to be getting somewhere.' Loder pulled a swivel chair across to the table and sat down to view the DVD. 'Has Tony been in yet?'

'Not yet,' DCI Oakwood said, pulling a chair next to his and sitting down.

All eyes turned to Tanya's mobile phone, as it sprang to life on top of her file on the desk. She picked it up, flipped the top open and answered it.

Loder turned his attention to the photo of Delaney with Laura Davidson and studied it for a moment. 'We still don't know anything about this evil bastard, you know,' he said.

'We do now, sir. That was the paedophile unit. They've got a match with the picture I sent over to them. Apparently, Harry Delaney's real name is Harry Critchley. He's served two terms in prison. Six months in 1982 and 10 months in 1999. He went on the missing list seven years ago while out on bail for assaulting a twelve-year old boy. They're faxing everything over right away.'

'Marvellous!' Loder gave a deep sigh of satisfaction. 'Today just gets better and better.' He kicked the swivel chair away from the desk and got to his feet. 'Let's get upstairs and wait for the fax. Tanya can I leave Mad Max to you? I don't want him upsetting my day.'

'No problem, sir.'

'I don't want you in there alone. Get hold of Andy, or Tony, if he's finished with the Judge, to sit in with you.'

DCI Oakwood was about to open the door when DCS Hatchet came bounding into the room waving his arms around.

'What do you think you are doing, Loder?'

'I'm not aware that I'm doing anything, sir.'

'I've just had Jonnie James's lawyer read me the riot act. Apparently, you bought it upon yourself to charge him with indecent assault.'

'Correct,' Loder said.

'You said that you were only bringing him in for questioning?'

'Changed my mind, sir,' Loder shrugged, with indifference.

'Don't you dare patronise me, Loder. It's the CPS's job to decide whether any charges are to be brought. So just do your job. And that goes for Sir Teddy Marston as well. Is that clear enough for you?'

Loder was so riled that he was close to letting the cat out of the bag. He bit his tongue, took a breath, and said, calmly, with a smile, 'Crystal. *Sir.*'

Hatchet pivoted around on his heels and stormed out of the room.

'Oh, well,' Loder smiled. I think it's safe to say that we've got him rattled.'

'But he's right in what he says, Loder,' DCI Oakwood said.

'Aye, I know,' he sighed. But look on the bright side, the tabloids will be jumping all over them by tomorrow.' He winked, sagely. 'DCI Oakwood and myself will be upstairs if we're needed. Okay, Tanya?'

'Yes, sir.'

Loder retrieved the fax from the incident room, then went into his office. Seated behind his desk, he began reading the four pages of text. DCI Oakwood came in with two plastic cups of coffee, sat down across the desk from him and handed him a coffee. He gave her the first page to read while he read the second.

'Nasty piece of work, isn't he?' Loder said, taking a sip.

'Makes my skin crawl.'

'What I fail to understand, is how do these evil bastards always seem to manage to get jobs working with children? Look at his history, he's been a Youth Club Leader, Scout Leader, and a Warden at – Loder picked up the sheet – Whitehaven Children's Home.'

'Doesn't bear thinking about what the kids were subjected to at that place,' Anne Oakwood said. 'Says here that he's changed his identity on three known occasions to secure employment and elude the authorities.'

'I know.' Loder shook his head slowly. I just can't believe that someone like him, with his history, could be granted bail in the first instance.'

'You've only got to look downstairs for the answer to that one, Loder.'

'Might be an idea to get some transcripts of his court appearances. See who granted bail. Might tie up with someone we've got on disc?'

'Wouldn't do any harm,' Anne Oakwood said.

Loder opened his file, pulled out the photo of Delaney and Laura and nibbled away at his lip, pensively.

'What are you thinking?' Anne Oakwood asked.

Loder turned a couple of sheets in the file and found Lee Carlin's phone number. 'Just bear with me for a moment.' He dialled the number and waited until the answer phone kicked in. He then dialled his mobile. It rang a couple of times then went to voicemail. 'I don't think that Lee Carlin has been completely straight with us. I've got a hunch that he's taken matters into his own hands and is on his way down to Spain to find his daughter.'

'What makes you say that?'

'Think about it, Anne. When he came to us with all this information, which he said that he got from . . . what was the lad's name?' He thumbed through the pile of paperwork in the file.

'Ryan,' Anne Oakwood said.

'Ryan! That's his name. I was always of a mind that this Ryan was our Jason, the lad that Donna met in the chat room. Anyway, Lee Carlin was a bit too vague for my liking when this villa was mentioned.'

'Maybe he never knew anything about it?' She shrugged.

'Come on, I'm not having that. If I'm right and Ryan is our Jason, then I reckon that he knew just about everything that that man was into. And we know that he has dogmatically pursued a one-man crusade in an effort to find his daughter. He's totally disillusioned with our efforts of finding answers. He thinks that everyone has given up on his daughter: even his wife has left him because of his obsession in finding her. He's got no confidence in us.'

Anne Oakwood made a face. 'Seems logical.'

'I said at the time that I thought that Lee was being economic with the truth. He fed us just enough info to break the case open. But since this investigation started there hasn't been one sighting of Donna, apart from the one time at, Jonnie James's house. At the time, I wasn't convinced, given that Lee got the info from a lad that I thought was only out to take advantage of him.'

'We weren't to know that at the time, Loder.'

'I know. But you see what I'm getting at. Donna hasn't been heard of, or seen since. Now, she's either been killed – which I'm pretty certain isn't the case – or she's been trafficked out of the country. And what better place than Delaney's den of depravation in Spain.'

'We *have* got Laura Davidson pictured down there. That's confirmed by Sir Teddy.' Anne Oakwood offered.

'That's what I'm saying. Perhaps he sends all his girls down there?'

'All! She said, shocked.

'Who knows what goes on down there at that villa. How many kids have we got on the missing persons database unaccounted for? How many have gone missing through internet chat rooms?'

'I think you could be right, Loder. But what can we do about it, apart from going through the correct channels?'

'First, we get in touch with Interpol, I suppose. See if they can hook us up with the local police in Cordoba. Then we'll take it from there.'

'Okay. I'll get onto it,' Anne Oakwood said, finishing her coffee and getting to her feet.

'Not a word to Hatchet about this.'

'Give me *some* credit, Loder,' she said, turning her head over her shoulder as she left the room.

CHAPTER 27

Lee had been on the road for over five hours and apart from a short break for petrol and a pee, it was non-stop. He was dog-tired and ached all over. He'd made good time and was now just south of Tours, in France The journey down had been easier than he had envisaged. The roads for the most part were surprisingly quiet: in complete contrast to the clogged up, nose-to-tail motorways of England. The digital clock on his dashboard read 6:35p.m – 7:35p.m European time – it was dusk. He locked his arms out straight and rolled his head to relieve the ache in his neck. There wasn't any point in killing himself and besides, he wasn't enamoured with the thought of driving on unfamiliar roads in the dark. He saw a sign for a rest area one kilometre ahead and decided that it would be a good idea to get something to eat and rest up for the night. Ryan had been like an over-excited child on a great adventure holiday for most of the journey.

   With the seat fully reclined he was now stretched out, fast asleep. The rapid eye movement behind his flickering lashes gave his face a troubled expression. Every now and again, he mumbled and moaned out aloud like he was calling to someone – trying to warn them to stay away from something. When he settled, he looked a picture of innocence, with his blonde hair, long eyelashes and smooth slightly tanned skin. Lee could see why all the filthy nonce-cases probably climbed over each other to get a piece of him. Lee couldn't even begin to imagine the vileness that Ryan had endured for most of his short years. Only God himself knew what horror stories were being played out behind those eyes.

   Lee approached the exit signpost, indicated right and filtered off the road. Slowly he brought the car around onto a vast tarmac car park and slotted in a space near to the main building. He turned the ignition off, arched his back and gave the longest, widest yawn he'd ever had: at one point he thought his jaw was going to lock, his mouth was so wide. He gave Ryan a nudge to wake him up, but only got a long moan in response. He shook his arm. This time his sleepy eyes peered through tiny slits until he got his bearings. 'Are we there, yet?' he said, wiping the sleep from his eyes. Lee couldn't help a smile. 'Come on, wakey, wakey – that's if you want something to eat.'

Ryan cranked up the seat to the sitting position and looked out of the window at the rows of vehicles all around, illuminated under the yellow haze of the huge vapour lamps. 'Where are we?'

'Just south of Tours,' Lee said, opening the door and swivelling his legs around.

'We got far to go?'

Lee whistled in a mouthful of air. 'About another eight hundred and odd miles, I suppose.'

'Fucking hell! That far!' Ryan shook his head, astonished.

'What did you think, Ryan? Cordoba was a Sunday afternoon jaunt away?'

Ryan said nothing. He got out of the car. His eyes were glazed and a deep frown rested where his brow narrowed, as if his mind was turning a thousand questions over. Lee did some leg-bending exercises to get the blood flowing, closed the door and pointed the remote at the car.

The large cafeteria inside the main building was bustling with bleary-eyed holidaymakers, long-distance truck drivers and haulage removers transporting people's life possessions down to the coast of dreams – or returning from the coast of broken dreams and nightmares. Lee moved between the different food counters until he found the grill bar. He selected a dried-up piece of roast chicken simmering under the hot lamps and passed along the counter to where a chef dressed in whites and a tall hat. shovelled a portion of fries onto his plate and some peas. Ryan had already chosen an enormous pizza and a can of pop for himself. Lee served himself a mug of coffee from a machine and went to the checkout to pay.

They found themselves a table, that a unformed waitress had just finished clearing and sat down. Ryan then set about attacking his pizza as if it was his last meal on God's earth. Lee tried to tell him to slow down, but like a dog guarding his food bowl, Ryan was completely engrossed in his mission of demolishing his food before anyone dared to take it away from him. Lee wondered where the lad put it all – he had seen more fat on a chip, than on Ryan, but he could still eat for two people. Lee cut into his chicken, forked a piece and gave it a tentative look, before popping it into his mouth. He had always been a fussy eater, so his wife would always say. He made an accepting face and tucked in to the rest.

Forty-five minutes later, both sufficiently fed and watered they were back in the car and ready to settle down for the night. Ryan was already reclined and drifting away with the duvet up under his chin. Lee sat with the window down, smoking. He felt completely knackered, but his mind was racing too fast for him to sleep. He couldn't get the image of his daughter out of his head: didn't want to. It was what kept him going when everyone around him had seemingly given up.

   There was still a nagging doubt in his mind whether he was doing the right thing. Should he have left everything to the police? What if it got violent? It crossed his mind that he might even have to kill Delaney: did he have it within himself to do it? He would have to cross that bridge, if and when it came to it. All he wanted was his daughter back in his arms and his family reunited. He was adamant that nothing, or anyone would get in the way of that aim. Blowing a cloud of smoke out into the cold night air he prayed silently to the heavens that Donna was still alive. He then closed his eyes and his mind to the devastating thought that she could be . . .

   He took another deep drag on his cigarette, flicked the butt out of the window and buzzed it up, leaving a small gap for air. Cranking his seat down as far as it would go, he covered himself with the leftovers of the duvet and closed his eyes to try to get some sleep.

It was still dark when the sound of a heavy truck rolling past, nudged Lee out from a deep fitful sleep. He looked across at Ryan who was snoring softly, seemingly without a care in the world. He massaged his thighs to get the circulation going – his legs had stiffened up from being crunched in the same position all night. The inside of the windows were dripping with condensation and the car smelt of stale tobacco, body odour and smelly socks. He cranked up the seat to the sitting position, turned the ignition on and buzzed the window down to get some fresh air into the car.

Blinking his eyes to wake himself up, he glanced at his watch, it was 5:19a.m, 6:19a.m French time. He reached over to the back, grabbed a bottle of water and gulped down as much as could before pausing for breath. He ran his fingers through his hair, rolled his head on his shoulders, got out his tobacco pouch and rolled a cigarette. As he took the first drag down into his lungs, it came straight back out in a fit of coughing. Ryan stirred from under the duvet and murmured, 'What the fuck's going on?' Before turning and going back to sleep, Lee couldn't help having a quiet chortle at the lad's choice of words. Though Ryan was surprisingly polite most of the time, sometimes his conversation was punctuated with more expletives than actual words.

Quietly, Lee opened the door, swung his legs out, slipped on his trainers, grabbed his leather bomber jacket from the back seat and got out. Gently he closed the door and stamped his way around to the boot, trying to get the circulation flowing. He opened it up and got out a canvas toilet bag, then set off across the tarmac, still stamping his feet, in search of the washrooms.

Twenty-five minutes later, he was back at the car; washed, shaved, and loaded with hot coffee and ham sandwiches for them both. He got into the car and slotted the paper cups of coffee into a couple of cup-holders concealed under the central armrest. He pulled the duvet down off Ryan and gave him a gentle shove. There was a moan and then nothing. He shoved him again; this time harder. 'Come on, Ryan. Shake a leg.'

There was a deep sigh. Ryan reached down to pull the duvet back up, but he couldn't find it. He opened his eyes and blinked. 'Are you mad? It's fucking freezing in here,' he said.

'Get up, it's getting late. We have to go soon.'

Ryan wiped the sleep from his eyes and cranked up his seat. 'Coffee smells good. Have you got me one?'

'Here you are,' Lee said, handing him the paper cup of steaming coffee, and tossing the sealed ham sandwich into his lap. 'Get that down you.'

'Cor! Lovely, I'm starving,' Ryan said, slotting his cup into the holder.

Where does he put it all, Lee thought to himself as Ryan tore off the wrapping and began devouring one half of the sandwich.

'You had better go and get yourself washed before we leave. You stink like a "Paraffin Lamp,"' Lee said.

'I don't smell like a tramp, you cheeky bastard.' He lifted his arm and had a whiff. 'Phew, perhaps you're right. He then woofed down the rest of his sandwich, finished his coffee and jumped out of the car. 'It's a bit parky out here, Lee. Can I borrow a soap and towel, please?'

'There's a fresh towel in the bag in the boot. Soap's in my toilet bag.'

'What about a shaver?'

'Shaver! You! A gust of wind would wipe that fluff off your face,' Lee laughed. There's one in the toilet bag if you really want. Be careful you don't cut yourself to pieces.'

Thirty minutes later, fresh, clean and alert, Lee was back on the A10, gunning south towards Poitiers and further beyond that, Bordeaux. Ryan was busy fiddling with the car radio tuner, trying to find a station that played English music: he wasn't impressed with Lee's collection of CD's. He'd said that all his music was crap and old-fashioned, though he was quite kind towards Bruce Springsteen.

Lee thought that he would drive until lunchtime, stop for something to eat, then press on until dusk.

*

Loder was sitting in DCI Oakwood's office drinking coffee and going over yesterday's events. They had got statements from all the people they had brought in and all were now under caution. Sir Teddy Marston had already tendered his resignation from the government. Jonnie James was self-righteously screaming his innocence in any wrongdoing to anyone who'd listen. Loder suspected that he was a principle player in, Delaney's web of depravation. Proving it would be another thing. Sir Dicky Baxendale – the theatre actor – thought it was all part of some huge performance: the man was a confused mess by the end of the interview. The Honourable Justice Baxter repeatedly quoted points of law as he was interviewed. When the DVD of him cavorting on the bed with two little girls was played, he refuted point-blank, and said that the disc must have been doctored somehow. He insisted that the whole thing was a plot to undermine his integrity and good name. He vehemently denied having any involvement in the movie and said that he would be seeking a meeting with The Police Commissioner and the Lord Chancellor to reiterate the same, forthwith. It was a masterful performance and even had Loder convinced when he had watched the DVD of the interview afterwards. But then the Honourable Judge had been a renowned prosecution barrister in his earlier life, so he was used to spewing out rhetoric by the shed-load. Mad Max McCann lived up to his name. He was kicking and screaming his innocence in much the same way as his buddy, Jonnie James.

Loder had thought that once he'd got them all under caution and showed them the DVD'S of themselves, that they would have held their hands up: but nothing could have been further from the truth – apart from Sir Teddy Marston. Loder couldn't understand how they all brushed any guilt aside. Having sex with these kids was the most normal thing in the world to these people. It was a way of life to them all. Each and every one of them failed to comprehend the damage they inflicted on those kids. Stripping them of any self-esteem. Corrupting their minds. Robbing them of any chance of a normal decent life.

All the team could do, was work their way through the discs and as the culprits were identified, bring them in for questioning and gradually build a case against them all. At the end of the day it was the Crown Prosecution Service's decision as to whether there was enough evidence to go to court.

The telephone rang and DCI Oakwood answered it. 'It's, Tanya. Apparently, there's a young girl on the line who wants to speak to you, and only you.' She turned the phone around so it was facing him and pressed the speaker button so that they could both hear.

'Okay, Tanya. What can you tell me?' Loder said.

Tanya said that the girl's name was Lara and she had information concerning Harry Delaney. But would speak only to him.

'Okay, put her through.'

'Hello, Lara. This is Inspector Loder. What can I do for you?'

There was a brief moment of silence, then a voice said, 'What's in it for us if we give you the low-down on, Delaney?'

'I'm sure we can make it worth your while, Lara. Where are you?' Loder asked.

'Don't you worry about that.'

'Okay. So . . . what information have you got for me, Lara?'

'Everything you want. Names, dates – the dirty bastards involved. Between us, we can give you everything you need. But you'll have to protect us, because the evil bastards are everywhere. I know personally of two people that have disappeared without trace.'

'Of course we will protect you. How many of you are there?'

'Five of us.'

'Okay. So, shall I come and get you now?'

'Eh . . . yeh, I suppose,' came a tentative answer.

'Do you want to tell me where you are, Lara? I can send a couple of cars for you.'

'No police cars. You've got to come alone in an unmarked car. Don't want to raise any unnecessary attention.'

Loder scribbled down the address being dictated to him, and said that he would be there as soon as he could.

'What do you make of that, Anne?'

'Sounds promising. But let's try and keep them away from Hatchet.'

'We'll sneak them in through the car park and bundle them straight into the interview suites. I'll give you a buzz when I've picked them up.'

'Don't you want me to come with you?'

'No disrespect, but Tanya's very good in situations like this; she has an affinity, a knack of winning teenagers' confidence.'

'So now I'm a tired old hag. Thank you very much, Loder.'

'I didn't mean it like that. It's just that . . .'

'You had better go,' she said, holding a hand out in front of her. 'Before you dig yourself in any deeper.'

He scooped up his files and smiled. 'See you later,' and made a beeline for the door.

Loder and Tanya found themselves outside a grubby basement flat in Golborne Road. It was less than half a mile away from the affluent, trendy area of Ladbroke Grove.

Loder pressed the small illuminated electric bell push and heard nothing. He pressed it again in case it wasn't working. Out the corner of her eye, Tanya saw the curtains ruffle in the window and a pair of eyes peer around them. She stood facing the street door behind Loder. Not letting on that she had seen anything.

'Who is it?' came a voice from behind the door.

'It's Inspector Loder. Are you, Lara?'

'Might be.'

'Why don't you let us in, Lara? We can't talk through a closed door now, can we?'

The door opened a couple of inches until the deadlock chain became taut.

'Who's that?' A half-hidden girl's face looked up and eyed Tanya warily.

'This is Detective Constable Reid. Now, are you going to open the door?' he said, trying his up-most not to sound as if he was losing his patience.

The door closed, the chain slid aside then opened just enough for the two of them to squeeze through. As soon as they were through the door, the girl slammed it shut and slid the chain back into its housing.

'Through here.' A skinny waif of a girl dressed in black, stretch-leggings that peeled around her long spindly legs, led them along a dark, grubby, narrow hallway and into a sitting room.

Inside, were three lads no more than a couple of years into their teens and a frightened looking little girl of about the same age. Lara was the oldest by a couple of years – at most – and appeared to be their leader. Loder doubted if the girl had reached her sixteenth birthday yet, but her tired, hollow, haggard face told a different story.

Lara kicked one of the boy's off of a grubby threadbare settee and he scampered across the room and joined the girl on another, equally grubby settee. The girl sat between the two boys. Both had their arms wrapped around their legs, their knees tucked up under their chins, staring blankly across at Loder and Tanya.

A flat-screen TV stood in the corner perched on a glass table – it was switched on. Loder glanced across at the other two kids. One was sat with an elbow resting casually on the arm of the chair with his legs tucked under him. The other was sitting cross-legged – both were engrossed with something on the TV. Loder doubted if they even knew that he and Tanya were in the room, they were that unconcerned.

Tanya flashed a friendly reassuring smile across the room and said, 'D you all live here together?'

'Yeh,' Lara sniffed.

'No grown-ups living here then?' Tanya asked.

'Not since the greasy fat bastard had it on his toes: must be nearly a week ago now,' Lara said.

One of the lads watching the TV, said, without stealing his eyes away from the screen, 'Didn't leave us any money, and there ain't been any business since. Not a phone call or a single knock on the—'

'Shush!' Lara cut in.

'What do you mean? What is this place?' Loder said, naively.

'Don't you know? Lara laughed.

'I guess it's a working house,' Tanya said.

'That's a polite way of putting it,' Lara said.

'And would I be right in guessing that Harry Delaney owns it: and all of you, as well?'

'Correct! The penny's dropped. But it's run by one of his cronies, who seems to have done a vanishing act.'

'What's his name?' Loder said.

'We know him as Franny. Don't know his real name.'

'Can you describe to us what he looks like?' Tanya asked.

Lara ushered the two lads off of the settee, then lifted the cushion and pulled out a single 8x10 photo and handed it to Loder. Tanya and Loder studied it for a moment.

'Found it in his bedroom,' Lara said.

The picture showed Harry Delaney and a bald, fat, Mediterranean-looking man with his arm around Delaney's shoulder. The man stood a good six inches taller than Delaney. His dark stubble and cold stare gave him a mean, intimidating look. It was a look that would make people think twice before tackling him.

'Thanks. This will come in very handy,' Tanya smiled, her best mumsy smile; the kind of smile that she reserved only for her daughter, Katie.

'You said that you had information for us,' Loder said, getting straight to the point.

'We have, but we want some reassurances before we trade,' Lara said, like a seasoned campaigner negotiating a deal.

'And what might that be?' Tanya asked.

'We want protection and somewhere safe to stay.'

'That can be arranged. We'll get in touch with Social Services they should be able to provide safe accommodation for you all,' Loder said.

'Social Services! You out for a laugh? If it wasn't for them we wouldn't be in this shit, in the first place,' Lara laughed.

Tanya shot Loder a furtive look that said, leave it to me. 'Let me guess, all of you were at some stage in the hands of the Social Services. Specifically, Children's Homes or Orphanages?'

'Correct!' Lara rolled her eyes, tediously.

The other four all nodded in unison.

'And, Harry Delaney got his claws into you with promises of money and somewhere nice to live. But instead, put you to work in places like this. Am I right?'

'That just about sums it up,' Lara said, lighting a cigarette. 'Delaney's got people working for him in homes all around the country. Once the initial grooming is over and the first dirty deed is done, we get filtered quietly away to shit-holes like this.'

'In the beginning,' Lara went on, in a matter-of-fact tone, 'when we were fresh, undamaged . . . and tight – if you get my meaning?'

Tanya nodded. 'I think I get the picture.'

'We were sent up to the big house: seems a long time ago now.'

'The big house . . . wouldn't be, Jonnie James's place?' Loder cut in.

'Yeh. How'd you know about that place?' Lara shot Loder a wary look.

'We'd like to show you some DVD'S and see if you can identify any of the people in them,' Tanya said.

'What, the ones filmed from the dreaded chill-out room, through the one-way mirror?' Lara laughed.

'You know all about that?' Loder said.

'Of course! We had to be especially nice on those occasions, otherwise, Delaney made our lives hell. If we didn't do as he asked, he sent us to be shared around like sweets to his more . . . discerning clients. The one's with . . . unhealthy tastes, shall we say?' Lara purposely didn't elaborate further.

If Tanya hadn't have been actually sitting in this filthy disgusting flea-pit, listening first-hand, she would never have believed what she was hearing. She wasn't that naïve. She knew the depths that paedophiles sank to satisfy their perversions. But to hear it spoken like it was just another day at the office, by someone so young, was a shocking experience. These kids were nothing more than just goods, commodities to earn a profit for those evil bastards.

'We want somewhere safe to stay, and no Social Services.'

'If we look after you, you'll stand up in court and testify against these people?' Loder asked.

The room went deathly quiet.

'Look, Lara. We can see to it that you all give evidence from behind a screen, or even on video from another room,' Tanya jumped in.

Lara looked along the line of confused faces. 'We can do that. Can't we gang?'

All four of them nodded. They seemed to look up to Lara. Perhaps, because she was the eldest: and the most damaged of them all.

CHAPTER 28

Ryan had proved to be a good navigator and was always one step ahead of Lee, by pointing him in the right direction before the road exits were on top of him. It made his job a whole lot easier. They had been on the road for a little over four and a half hours, and had skirted around Bordeaux without too much trouble. Now they were on the A63 heading towards Cestas. Lee saw an exit signposted one kilometre ahead and said to, Ryan, 'Shall we get off at the next exit and find somewhere to eat?'

'Good thinking, Batman. I could do with a nosebag. I'm starving,' Ryan said, handing Lee a perfectly rolled cigarette.

Lee took the cigarette and admired the work of art for a moment, before putting it between his lips and lighting it. He buzzed the window down a little to let the smoke out and was pleasantly surprised by the warmth of the breeze. But for the occasional scudding cloud it was almost unbroken sunshine. All in all, Lee felt quite good about himself: considering everything.

He indicated and filtered off to the right until he came to a junction about a hundred metres further on. 'Left or right?'

Ryan shrugged. 'Might as well go right.'

They drove for a kilometre or so, along a country road with flat farmland either side of them. Lee drove a little further and as he came around a bend, he went over a hump-backed bridge that crossed a fast-flowing stream. A little further ahead the road opened up onto a village square with a market in full swing. He found a place to park at the back of the square and they both got out of the car and stretched their legs.

They strolled into the square and began to peruse around the myriad of canvas covered stalls. Ryan couldn't believe the huge array of cheeses and fresh fruit that was on offer. The pungent smell was overpowering. He turned to Lee and pinched his nose. Lee just shook his head, smiled and took off in the direction of a café in the corner of the square. He ensconced himself at a table under a parasol and drank in the scene. It was a million miles away from anything that he was used to. Farmers wearing beret's, gesticulated wildly, offering anyone who stopped at their stall a tit-bit before making a purchase. Apart from all the fresh fruit and cheeses, there were pates by the tub load, foie gras, salted fish and legs of cured ham that hung precariously on metal hooks. Unmistakeably French.

   A waiter dressed in a long, starched white apron with waxed black hair, slicked back high over his forehead, came over to his table. Lee ordered a small beer, then sat back and watched, as Ryan flitted from stall to stall completely overawed by the whole scene. He was like a child let loose in a sweet shop, spoilt for choice. Though Lee suspected that Ryan would probably opt for a pint, a fag and a packet of crisps: sad really.

   He took off his leather bomber jacket and hung it over the back of the chair. Then relaxed back, lifted his face up towards the warm afternoon sun and soaked up the heat. For a fleeting moment, he lost himself and actually felt the stresses and strains of the last few months slip away.

   Ryan came over to the table grinning like a Cheshire cat and plonked himself down next to Lee. 'Can you believe the stuff that these "Frogs" eat?' he said, taking a slurp of Lee's beer. 'They've got snails over there,' he pointed to a stall somewhere in the distance. 'They look like bogeys,' he said, screwing his nose.

   'Probably taste like them as well,' Lee said, snatching his glass off Ryan.

   From the corner of his eye, Lee caught the waiter hovering near the table and sensed that he was waiting for him to order. He pointed to a wedged chalkboard standing precariously on the cobbled stones. 'Deux menus du jour, s'il vous plait.' That was about the extent of his schoolboy knowledge of the French language.

An hour later, Lee and Ryan had eaten their way through onion soup with fresh crusty bread, lamb shank braised in thick red wine and vegetables followed by cheese and biscuits all washed down with a carafe of red wine.

It was a bit of a heavy lunch for Lee, given that he had to drive until dark. The heady mixture of the wine and beer and a full stomach, together with the warm sunshine, had made him drowsy. His eyelids slowly closed and he began to drift off.

'Wakey! Wakey!' Ryan said.

Lee jumped, bolt upright. Momentarily confused as to where he was. He rubbed his eyes, combed his hands through his hair, then reached into his pocket and pulled out a wad of Euros. He peeled off two twenties and slipped them under a metal clip holding the bill.

'You ready, Ryan?' Lee said.

'Yeh, just about,' he said, dolloping the last of the brie onto a cracker and stuffing it into his mouth. 'Lovely bit of cheese that,' he said, wiping his mouth with a napkin. 'And that lamb! Well, that was the bollocks that was.'

Lee couldn't help a smile as he got to his feet. It was a constant amazement to him, where Ryan put all his food; he never left a scrap. He couldn't help but like Ryan, and genuinely feared for him as to what the future might hold once all this was over. Perhaps he could put him to work; teach him the electrical game, or something?

As they strolled back towards the car, Lee noticed that all the market stalls had packed up and gone. The square had been miraculously cleaned up and everyone had disappeared. There was hardly a soul to be seen, but for a table of tourists sitting outside a bar and a few, flat-capped old men dotted around the square sitting on benches snoozing. It was no wonder the Germans overran the country in a couple of days: everyone was probably having an afternoon nap, he thought.

At the far end of the square was a tall war monument of an infantry soldier in a combat position thrusting a bayonet in front of him. Lee stopped for a moment and took the time to study the long list of names engraved on the side of the obelisk. Young men most of them, some not even out of their teens. They didn't mean anything to Lee, it was just that his grandfather had died in France, sometime after the D Day landings, and he was buried in a war cemetery somewhere in the north. He didn't know what made him stop and reflect: respect for the fallen . . . perhaps? *Lest we forget.*

A tall official building dominated one end of the square. The baroque façade had two huge, heavy wide doors that were studded with black rivets, and above was a wrought-iron balcony with two long flagpoles protruding out high above the cobbled pavement. Hanging limp in the windless afternoon was the French Standard alongside the gold-starred, blue flag of the European Union. Had it not been for all those brave, frightened young men, it could have easily been the German Swastika hanging up there. Lee pondered the thought for a moment. The front façade was still pocket-marked with bullet holes. And Lee guessed that the French had no intension of ever filling them in. A constant reminder of what might have been.

'Come on, Ryan. Let's get out of this one-horse town,' Lee said, striding in the direction of the car.

Back in the car, Ryan passed Lee yet another perfectly tailored cigarette as he perused the map. He studied the cigarette for a moment before lighting it up and shook his head, dumbfounded.

'What! Ryan said.

'Tell me, how do you manage to roll fags like this,' Lee said, taking a drag and studying it between his fingers in amazement.

'Years of practice,' Ryan said, proudly.

Lee couldn't help but smile. Such an old head on young shoulders.

'It's about two hours drive to the border and about another two and a half, maybe three hours to Burgos,' Lee said, pointing the route out to, Ryan. He looked at his watch. It was 12:47 p.m. 1:47 p.m French time. 'Bit of luck we'll hit Burgos before dark and stop for the night. Okay, with you, Captain?'

'Yeh.' Ryan nodded, studying the detailed computer printout of the route, that Lee had downloaded from the internet before they had left.

'Right, buckle-up.' Lee said, tossing the map onto Ryan's lap.

'Just a small concern, but how are we going to get through the border?' Ryan asked

'Same way we got through the Euro Tunnel. You in the boot, and we take our chances.'

Ryan shrugged. Unfazed by the prospect.

*

Loder had commandeered two interview rooms. At short notice he managed to get hold of a couple of Child Protection Officers to take control of the interviewing process, and a couple of Duty Solicitors; he wasn't leaving anything to chance for some smart-arsed defence lawyer to pick holes in. When it came to child abuse investigations, Loder would be the first to admit that he probably wasn't the best qualified. There were strict rules and regulations in place when it came to interviewing kids and he didn't want to cock it all up.

Everything by the book.

In the down-streaming room, he observed the consummate professional in full swing. Never suggesting or making direct allegations against certain individuals; never putting words into the girl's mind. Just gently steering Lara in the right direction and letting her tell the story in her own words. Loder knew that he would have lasted two minutes before ballsing everything up.

Lara was performing like an absolute star. On the direction of Loder, via an earpiece, the CPO had steered Lara down all the right avenues. She had given them an insight as to what went on at Jonnie James's house, and Delaney and James's role in the operation. She told them everything that went on at the basement flat where she and her little gang worked, in such a matter-of-fact way, that it shook Loder to the core.

Now she was working her way through the DVD evidence and, so far, she knew nearly all the kids on the most recent footage – going back two or three years. She also had a good idea where most of them could be found. And if they were given the same guarantees as her little gang, she was certain that she could get them to come forward.

Tanya slid a new disc into the player and pressed the play button. Lara's head dropped. It featured herself and another girl engaged in sex, with The Honourable Justice Baxter. Softly, almost in a whisper, she confirmed to the CPO that is was her in the film and that she was fourteen years of age, at the time the video was shot. The other girl was thirteen. She couldn't recall the other girl's name and she hadn't set eyes on her since. Gone was the cocky pretence. Now, as she lifted her head, there was a deeply damaged, vulnerable young girl that had been let down by everyone in her short life. She had been serially betrayed by the very people that were supposed to protect her. It was little wonder that she didn't trust a living soul.

    The CPO could see that it was all getting too much for her and suggested they take a break. She'd seen it many times before, the shame, the guilt, the confusion that somehow everything was their fault. And after a while, it all became a natural way of life: like doing a day's work. The difference was that they never saw the fruits of their spoils. They were just machines for other people's pleasure, and when the machines had depreciated beyond repair and were no longer viable assets, they were tossed onto the scrap-heap of life and left to fend for themselves.

    Lara hadn't a clue what it was like to be part of a loving family: to slip between crisp clean sheets at night. Safe in the knowledge that no one was going to come visiting and slip in beside her in the dead of night and make her do naughty things. To wake each morning warm, snug and safe. To wash with perfumed soap and dry herself on fresh, fluffy towels that smelled of lavender. To dress in clean laundered clothes. To watch TV in the morning while gulping down bowls of her favourite breakfast cereal drowned with cold milk, before being dropped off at school. A loving kiss before jumping out of the car at the school gates. Everyday things that normal loving families took for granted. Just one hug, a cuddle, a simple affectionate peck on the cheek without an ulterior motive behind it, was all she ever secretly yearned for. Not a lot to ask.

    Lara looked up towards the dark, screened window and stared straight through it. Her eyes were red and moist. Her face had a blank, vacant look about it; as if everything that she had gone through, had come back to haunt her. She then aimed a thin-lipped, sorrowful smile at Loder, that asked, *am I doing okay*?

Suddenly the door burst open and DCS Hatchet stormed in and shot Loder a look of thunder. He was about to unleash a tirade. The officer recording everything in the interview room looked up from his monitor at Loder. 'Shall we stop running while they have a break, sir?' he asked

Loder nodded.

'So, do you want to enlighten me as to what is going on, *Detective Inspector Loder*?' Hatchet roared. His fists clenched by his side fighting to control his anger.

'We had a call from that young girl, sir. She and four of her friends all say that they were held captive against their will and have been serially abused by Delaney and countless others over a period of years. All of them still are, or were, minors at the time the abuse began. We've shown them some of the DVD evidence we have. And, so far, it's proving to be very useful.'

'I see. Why wasn't I informed? *Again*?'

'Everything has moved so fast, I haven't had the time, sir. We managed to get hold of a couple Child Protection Officers at short notice to conduct the interviews. A duty solicitor was fortunately on hand. We just went straight to it, sir.'

'Everything by the book, I see.' The DCS raised a questioning brow. 'Not like you, Loder.'

'Absolutely, sir. Can't be too careful when dealing with child abuse, sir,' Loder said, patronisingly.

'Good work, Loder.' He almost choked on his words. 'I'll leave you to it. Keep me informed of any developments,' he said, making his way towards the door. As he turned the handle, he spun around, and said with a poisonous look, 'I'll look forward to seeing your *full* report on my desk first thing in the morning.'

'Yes, sir.' Loder locked eyes with the man and smiled.

For what seemed an age the two men stared each other out, until Hatchet licked his lips and backed away. As he opened the door he got the last word in. 'Report . . . my desk, first thing.'

He knows. He damn well knows I'm after him.

'The Chief Super didn't seem all that concerned, if you don't mind me saying, sir. You'd think he'd be jumping through hoops at what we're getting here,' the officer said, looking up from his monitor.

'Oh, he will be, laddie. Sooner than he thinks.'

The officer made a face. Unable to comprehend Loder's cryptic remark.

'I'll be upstairs in my office. Let me know when they resume.'

With that, Loder left the room and strode along the corridor, up the stairs and into the sanctuary of his office.

A few minutes later, DS Frost came in holding two plastic cups filled with coffee and a couple of ham sandwiches.

'You must have read my mind, Tony.'

The DS sat across the desk from Loder and began ripping the cellophane wrapping off the sandwich. 'Things seem to be going our way, at last, boss.'

'If it wasn't so damn depressing listening to these kids recounting every sordid detail of their lives, I'd be dancing on the ceiling with delight. How are you getting on with the young girl?'

'The CPO is trying her best, but the poor thing is terrified, especially without Lara by her side. Tanya is looking for a child psychologist to come and sit in; see if she can open the girl up.'

'And the others?'

'They're okay. A bit subdued. A couple of WPC's are keeping them happy, plying them with pop and crisps. They don't really know what's going on.'

'Better get someone to contact Social Services and the paedophile unit. While we're at it, might be an idea to circulate their details to the relevant agencies. After all, they *are*, presumably, someone's kids. Or foster kids? What do I know?' Loder said, throwing his arms up in frustration.

'I'll get on to it,' DS Frost said.

DCI Oakwood poked her head around the door, came in, and sat next to DS Frost. 'How's it going downstairs?' she asked, grabbing the other half of Loder's sandwich and taking a bite out of it.

'Help yourself, why don't you?'

'Thanks. I will,' she smiled, taking another bite.

'Lara is doing fantastic. I think by the time we're finished we'll have enough evidence to shore-up any loopholes. We should have enough to bring down a lot of people.'

'What about Hatchet?' she said, taking a drink of Loder's coffee.

'He came into the down-streaming room with all guns blazing. The interviewing was already underway, so there wasn't a lot he could do. Especially as it was all being carried out strictly by the book.'

'Bet that pleased him. Wish I was there to see his face.' She smiled, and took another bite from the sandwich.

'I got the feeling that he knows we're onto him. I could almost smell the fear pouring out of him,' Loder said.

'Well, he's not going to like what I've just learnt.' A self-satisfied smile crossed her face.

Both men looked at DCI Oakwood suspiciously.

Enjoying the moment, she popped the last of the sandwich into her mouth, wiped her hands on a tissue, and said, 'Just got a call from Spain . . . Cordoba National Police, to be precise.'

'And?' Loder said, leaning forward, conspiratorially.

'Well, it appears that Interpol passed on the picture of Delaney, together with the location of the villa to them. They sent a couple of their boys down to have a gander for themselves.'

She paused a moment to get maximum effect. 'It would seem,' she smiled, 'that we've got a positive ID. Delaney is there, at the villa, with two unknown males and seven kids; four boys and three girls.'

'Yes!' Loder punched the air.

'What about, Donna Carlin?' DS Frost said.

'I've just faxed them a picture of Donna and one of Laura Davidson. They're going to get back to us.'

'We'll have to get over there right away,' Loder said. 'How do we go about getting flights?'

'Don't jump the gun. Normally, we would have to submit everything upstairs and apply for an extradition warrant . . . I think. Never had a need before. Either of you?' DCI Oakwood said.

Both men shrugged, shaking their heads.

'Applying for extradition could take months. Besides, if Hatchet gets wind of this, he'll warn Delaney and we'll lose him. I say, we get over there and make our presence felt. Oversee, Delaney's arrest – make certain that he's taken into custody – then play it by ear. What do you think?' Loder said.

'I don't know—'

'We haven't got a choice, really, Ma'am. Especially, if Donna and Laura are being held there,' DS Frost cut in.

'Shift your arse, Loder. Let me get on your computer,' DCI Oakwood said.

Loder got up from his chair and stood with his back against the wall while his boss squeezed past and sat herself down in his chair. Her legs bearly scrapped the floor, even in heels, as she swivelled the chair around under the desk. She got on-line and Googled British Airways. The website came up and she set about searching for a couple of flights. Within a few minutes, she had learnt that there weren't any direct flights to Cordoba. Madrid was too far away, so their best bet was Malaga. She keyed in their details and it came back with an afternoon flight for the next day. 'What about this one?' she said, resting back in the chair.

Loder bent forward, straightened his arms on the edge of the desk from behind and looked at the screen over her shoulder. He caught the fragrance of her shampooed hair as he leaned close and paused a moment to take it in. 'What am I looking at?' he said.

'The flights . . . look.' She pointed. Heathrow to Malaga, one-way, leaving 14:30 tomorrow afternoon.

'Oh, right,' he said, still none the wiser. 'How are we going to get to Cordoba from Malaga?'

'I'll give the Cordoba police a ring, see if they can arrange for a car to meet us at the airport. Failing that, we'll have to hire one ourselves and drive up. It's only a couple of hours, tops.'

'Okay. What do we do now?' Loder said.

DCI Oakwood looked to DS Frost, smiled and shook her head at Loder's obvious ignorance of the workings of the internet. She gave an impatient sigh, and looked up at Loder from over her shoulder. 'Am I booking it?'

'Absolutely. Let's get out there,' Loder said.

Anne Oakwood shook her wrists like a concert pianist and began keying in the details.

DS Frost picked up on the vibes between Loder and their boss. It wasn't the first time he'd seen it. Still it was none of his business if Loder was having a trade with his boss. He could keep a secret; it was the people he told that couldn't. *Must tell the wife, tonight.*

Five minutes later the confirmation printed out. Loder picked it up and quickly read through. 'What, that's it? No tickets, or anything?'

'No. That's it. We show the confirmation at the check-in desk and it's matched with our booking reference, simple.' She looked up at Loder and rolled her eyes. 'Better pack your shorts, Loder, it's going to be hot.'

She swivelled the chair around, got up, squeezed back around the desk, and sat back down. 'Not a word to a living soul,' she said, eyeing the two men in turn. 'Not even, Tanya. If she doesn't know anything then she can't answer to the fact, Especially, where Hatchet is concerned. Agreed?'

Both men nodded. But Loder wasn't happy. Tanya was part of *his* team and her loyalty was without question as far as he was concerned.

Loder's desk phone rang, breaking the electric atmosphere in the room. He picked it up and listened. 'They're ready to resume interviewing downstairs. Let's get back to it, shall we?' he sighed.

Loder was tired. Both physically, and mentally. With all the years he had on the clock – over thirty – he had never had a case that had gotten to him so much as this one. He was on familiar ground with petty villains, gangsters and murderers. But kids . . . that was a different ballgame. Something he wasn't comfortable with, and listening to some of them describe in graphic detail what they had gone through, like it was a stroll in the park, was mentally draining. He was in no doubt that these kids were damaged beyond repair and no amount of counselling by psychologists or any number of "experts" would ever make them right: not completely. The horrific details of the abuse they had suffered at the hands of the very people that were supposed to be protecting them, would live with him forever.

'I'll join you later,' DCI Oakwood said. 'I'll just pop upstairs and let the Cordoba Police know our flight details and see if they can organise transport for us.'

'Okay.' He took a deep breath, slapped his palms on the desk and heaved himself up. 'Round two.'

*

In the distance a vivid red sun was fading behind tall sweeping mountains, and darkness was beginning to fall in the purple, cloudless sky. Lee had made good time and was now about twenty kilometres south of Burgos. Apart from the break they had for lunch, he had been behind the wheel for over eight hours and had covered a little over eight hundred kilometres since setting off from Tours this morning. His neck and shoulders were aching from the constant strain and concentration of driving on the European right-hand side of the road. But to be fair, the drive was nowhere near as stressful as charging around the M25 or up the M1, and Ryan's navigating was spot on, which made the journey a lot easier.

Getting across the border point was a breeze: disappointingly so. The central concourse in the middle of the road where the border guards were once housed was now derelict and in a state of disrepair. On each side of the carriageway were the obsolete, rusty, mechanical housings of the road barriers. There wasn't a border guard or any kind of an official to be seen anywhere. In fact, it was that easy, Lee stopped the car in a lay-by on the Spanish side of the border and let Ryan out of the boot. Lee thought it was little wonder there were truck-loads of illegal immigrants and terrorists flooding across Europe.

Lee rolled his head on his aching shoulders, locked his arms out straight on the steering wheel and stretched his back. 'There's a service stop up ahead shall we call it a day?'

Ryan gave a long, wide yawn and said 'Yeh, why not. I'm starving anyway.'

A few minutes later, Lee filtered onto a wide, dusty track. The car bounced over the uneven surface kicking up a cloud of dust in its wake until it flattened out onto a huge transport park. There was a myriad of huge trucks and articulated lorries parked three-deep around the far perimeter. The central area was laid out with rows of low-slung, corrugated roofed spaces that shielded vehicles from the heat of the sun.

Lee swung the car into a quiet spot away from the main huddle and parked up. He switched off the engine, opened the door, got out and stretched his legs. Ryan got out the other side, swung his arms over his head and stretched his back. Lee grabbed his bomber jacket from the back seat, locked the car and they set out across the huge car park in the direction of a cluster of buildings. They walked along the edge of the dusty service road that was shielded from the autovia by a bank of dry scrub, tangled with discarded food containers, bottles, cans and all kinds of unmentionable things in carrier bags hanging precariously from the stark scrubby bushes.

Further along in the distance was a petrol station. A steady stream of vehicles – many with British plates – filtered out onto the autovia. As they walked along, Lee couldn't help noticing the many caravans and trailers with British plates parked up for the night.

As they approached the entrance to the restaurant, an emaciated, mangy-looking dog was being chased from the entrance by a waiter wielding a broom. Lee looked at Ryan. 'Don't exactly enamour you with confidence, does it?'

The waiter fired off a volley of abuse in indecipherable Spanish at the animal as it cowered away from the thrusting broom. Then with a nod and a smile, he held the door open for them both. Lee shrugged, and they both went in.

Inside, the café come bar was comfortably air-conditioned and surprisingly clean. Lee went up to the long counter straight ahead and sat on a stool, Ryan launched himself up next to him. Lee's knowledge of the Spanish language was minimal, to say the least, but he knew how to order a drink and understood some basic words for various types of food from his holidays down on the Costas. Most waiters down there spoke English: some better than the English themselves. Here, out in the sticks, Lee guessed, it would be a different scenario, altogether.

The waiter wiped the counter in front of them with a cloth and said, something that sounded like, "dig-a-me"

Dig him what? Where? Was, Lee's first thought as he sat open-mouthed, looking at the waiter.

'Dos cervezas, por favor.' Ryan came to the rescue.

The waiter smiled and went away; happy with the thought that he wasn't going to have to participate in a game of charades – the British had a habit of gesticulating wildly using sign-language to get understood.

'I knew that, Lee said, swivelling around on his stall.

'Course you did,' Ryan patronised, licking a cigarette paper and rolling up.

The waiter brought two, half-litre jugs of beer and a small bowl of olives and plonked them on the counter. Lee wrapped his hand around the handle and took a long swallow. The cool beer was like nectar as it soothed his parched throat. He took another long swallow and put the empty glass back onto the counter. The waiter breezed past with a tray full of beers and swiftly placed another in front of Lee on his way through.

'Now, that's what I call service,' he beamed, taking the rolled cigarette from Ryan and putting it between his lips.

Ryan was used to it now. He didn't mind rolling Lee's fags for him – enjoyed it, in fact.

Lee looked along the counter at an elderly man with his missus, trying to explain to the waiter in "Spanglish" that he wanted two teas with milk. But all the gesticulating in the world wasn't going to get him anywhere. Ryan poked his head forward and said to the waiter. 'Camarero. Quieren dos tes con leche.'

The waiter threw his arms up in exasperation. 'Si, si.' Then shaking his head, he went away mumbling to himself: probably cursing at the arrogance of the British. The elderly man waved his thanks at Ryan and left the counter to find a table.

'How did you know that?' Lee said, completely in awe of Ryan.

'Oh, you know,' Ryan said, nonchalantly.

'Yes, but . . . that was quite impressive.'

'BBC. Spanish for beginners. I got the videos and textbooks.'

'Well, it works. That waiter understood every word that you said.' Lee picked up a menu and opened it. 'What do you fancy to eat?'

'Dunno.' Ryan picked up a menu and flipped through it. He looked at Lee, who was obviously struggling to understand the wording.

'You would think they'd duplicate the menus in different languages, wouldn't you?' Lee said, thumbing down the list of meat dishes. He knew that Cerdo was pork and Entrecot was a sirloin steak – either would suffice for him.

After serving the elderly couple their tea, the waiter came over to them, and with pen at the ready, he said, 'dig-a-me.'

Ryan took the lead. 'Teines menu del dia?'

'Si, senor.' He looked up at the clock above the door. 'Servimos desde ocho horas. En el restaurante.' He pointed to a table-clothed sectioned off area at the end of the room.

Ryan nodded and closed the menu. 'Dos menus del dia y botella de vino tinto de la casa. Gracias.'

'Sounds good to me,' Lee said, rubbing his hands, impressed. 'I got the gist with the meal of the day. Was it red wine you ordered, as well?'

'Yeh. Is that alright with you?'

'Absolutely!'

'They start serving at eight o'clock, in the restaurant.'

Ryan looked up at the clock. 'Quarter of an hour to go.'

The pair of them feasted their way through a three course meal that would have graced the table of any half-decent restaurant in London. The difference was that the bill came to just thirty euros and that included an excellent bottle of Rioja.

Lee left the cash on top of the bill and the waiter discreetly took it away. He lit a roll-up and relaxed back into his chair. A wave of guilt washed over him. He mentally chastised himself for forgetting why he was here in the first place.

The waiter returned to the table carrying a bottle of red liquid and two large brandy glasses filled with ice. He set the glasses on the table, stood back and with one arm behind him, poured two generous measures. 'Una bebida, de la casa,' he smiled.

'Que es?' Ryan asked, sipping at the red, aniseed liquor.

'Pacharan. Es un digestivo.'

'Ah! Si,' Ryan said, like a native.

Lee was completely taken with Ryan's Spanish. Who knows what he could have achieved in life, had he not been dealt all his cards from the bottom of the deck. It still wasn't too late, if he could free himself from his way of life. Lee made a conscious decision to himself that when this was all over, he would help the lad in any way that he could. Even if it meant putting him to work with him. Could even send him to day college; there must be some kind of government grant available. Lee made a mental note and filed it away.

The restaurant was busy with truck drivers, business travellers and tourists, all of them tucking into the menu of the day. The room was loud with conversations in at least three different languages, as far as Lee could make out. But the most animated of them all was undoubtedly the tables of Spanish, gesticulating wildly with their arms at each other in a bid to be heard.

Lee relaxed back and sipped the cold liqueur through the ice, enjoying the aniseed taste as is slid down his throat. As much as he was enjoying the moment, he couldn't let his mind be deflected from his pursuit of finding his Donna. After all, that was why he was here in the first place: not to have a "Jolly Boys Outing."

'You finished?' Lee said, stubbing out his cigarette in the ashtray.

'Yeh, just about.' Ryan slid the last lump of ice into his mouth from his empty glass.

This boy never leaves a scrap, not even an ice cube.

Outside, the night was dark and starry and silent, punctuated only by the sound of the occasional heavy lorry or car driving past on the autovia. Headlights could be seen bumping off of the uneven road far into the distance.

They walked along the dusty track and across the car park in the direction of the car. As they strolled between the rows of vehicles, both of them stared up, mesmerised, at a flashing neon sign perched high on top of a tubular structure at the far end of the park. The sign was so high that the two pink and blue flashing naked girls could probably be seen for miles. As they got closer, music could be heard drifting along on the warm night air. Before Lee could stop him, Ryan was at the foot of the steps that led up to the entrance. He beckoned Lee over.

'One drink?' Ryan pleaded.

Lee rolled his eyes. 'One drink. That's all. We've got a long drive tomorrow.'

Ryan was already up the steps and holding the door open for Lee, as he tiredly climbed up and followed Ryan in. They walked along a short passageway to a set of double doors. Ryan held them open. 'You coming?' he smiled. Reluctantly, Lee followed him in. The inside was dark and sleazy and smelled dank. The bar stretched along most of the length of the back wall. In front of the bar was a lounge area with comfortable leather settees and low tables slung around an elevated stage. On the stage, two topless girls gyrated awkwardly around a couple of shiny metal poles. Before Lee had chance to escape, a long-legged girl wearing a sequined bra and G-string was leading them to a table. With a forced smile, she asked what she could get them to drink. Lee ordered two beers. Ryan peered over Lee's shoulder as she crossed the room towards the bar. 'Fucking hell! What a lovely pair of pins . . . and get a look at that arse, will ya?' he shouted over the loud music.

Lee looked around tentatively to see if anyone heard. 'Will you keep it down. You'll get us shot.'

'Chill out. That's what they're here for.'

Lee leaned forward, and quietly said, 'Don't you fucking tell me to "chill out." This is a heavy place. I'm getting some serious bad vibes.'

'It's nothing more than a glorified knocking shop.' Ryan sniffed, sagely. 'I've done quite a bit of business in places like this.'

Lee slowly shook his head. *Where's it all going to end?*

Discretely dotted around the walls were heavy-looking guys dressed in tuxedos. The place was empty but for a dozen, or so, men sitting around the foot of the stage leering up at the girls. One of them slipped some money into the dancer's G-string and she gave him a close up of her gyrating crotch. The whole place reeked with the stench of despair, and if the blank looks on the girls' faces was anything to go by, Lee wasn't far from the truth.

The waitress brought a tray with two bottles of Heineken on and made a show of bending forward in front of Lee, so that he got a face-full of tits, as she set the bottles and frosted tumblers down on the table together with a small bowl of salted peanuts, under which she deftly slipped the bill under before leaving.

Lee poured the beer into the tumbler, drank a sip and warily, he looked around over the top of his glass. His eyes stopped at a mean-looking bouncer standing in front of a pair of long drapes. The light from a spot lamp caught the side of his face revealing a long deep scar down his cheek. Ryan rolled a cigarette, lit it and passed it to Lee.

'I've got a bad feeling about this place, Ryan.'

'You're an old fart that's your problem.' Ryan smiled, moving his shoulders in time to the pulsating music. He felt right at home.

'That might be so, but I don't feel too comfortable in here.' He scanned around and caught a bouncer giving him the evil eye.

The bouncer pulled the drape aside as a girl led a man by the hand through the opening. Lamb to the slaughter, Lee thought. The short, stocky man was dressed in jeans, tee shirt and heavy boots. Lee guessed that he must be a truck driver on a rest stop. He doubted that the man would be getting much rest now, and his wallet would be leaving a lot lighter than when it came in. Curiosity got the better of him and he craned to see what was going on behind the drapes. He saw the back of a naked girl sitting astride someone in an armchair. His trousers were down at his ankles and she was riding up and down on him. To the left of them was a couple of girls entertaining a man, also spread-eagled on an armchair. One was giving fellatio, while the other stood on the arms of the chair with her crotch buried into the man's face. The bouncer caught Lee's stare and smiled at him. And with a wave of his arm, he opened the drapes wider and gestured for him to come in. Lee quickly averted his eyes and drank a long swallow from his glass.

'We're out of here, Ryan. Drink up.'

'What! I was just beginning to enjoy myself.'

'You do realise this place is a knocking shop?'

'Is it! Well I never.' he mocked.

Lee picked up the bill and nearly passed out at the amount. The two bottles of beer cost nearly half of what he had paid in the restaurant. He reeled off the cash discretely and finished his drink. No sooner had his empty glass hit the table the waitress was over with a two fresh bottles on a tray. Lee got to his feet, put a twenty euro note on the tray. 'Forget the change,' he said to her, as he made a beeline for the door. Her disconsolate blank expression never altered, even though she had just made over five euros tip on two drinks.

Once outside, Lee breathed a sigh of relief. He honestly thought that the bouncers wouldn't let them go without relieving them of a shed-load of euros.

'You alright?' Ryan said, still bopping away to the music.

'Yeh, I'm fine. Come on, let's get back to the car. We've got a long day ahead of us tomorrow.'

CHAPTER 29

Loder checked his bag in then lifted his boss's case onto the conveyer. The weight of it nearly pulled his shoulder out of joint. 'How long do you envisage staying?' he blinked.

'Well, you never know what might happen, do you? Best to prepare for all contingencies.'

'If you say so. Who am I to argue with the voice of wisdom.'

'No need for sarcasm.'

Anne Oakwood placed her and Loder's passport together with the confirmation sheet on the check-in desk and their details were matched off with the computer. The check-in girl tagged the baggage and handed back the passports together with their boarding passes. With a nice smile, she wished them a good trip.

Once they had passed through passport control to the departure lounge, Loder began to relax. He found the bar and queued for drinks, while Anne Oakwood went in search of a table that wasn't strewn with half-eaten food containers and empty glasses.

Loder saw Anne Oakwood waving to catch his attention as he left the bar with their drinks. He made his way over and sat down next to her.

'How long is the flight?' he asked, drinking the froth from the top of his pint.

'About two and a half hours, I think.' She glanced at her watch then at the flight information monitor. 'We should be boarding soon,' she said, sipping at her wine.

'Have you heard from DCS Hatchet since yesterday?' Loder asked.

'No. Not a sign of him anywhere. Seems to have gone to ground.'

'Worrying, isn't it?'

Anne Oakwood made a face and shrugged. 'As long as he's off our back that's the important thing, surely?'

'I don't know. You should of seen the look on his face when he saw the set-up in the interview suite yesterday, and when he saw Lara, he backed off. I could see it in his eyes . . . the fear . . . he couldn't get out of the down-streaming room quick enough. I'm certain that he knows we're onto him. He must do – he's not that stupid. He's a manipulator just like Jonnie James and the others . . . a predator. '

'In some respects, he's worse. He's in a position of responsibility. People trust and respect him. He's supposed to be beyond reproach.'

'That's a joke,' Loder said, taking a swallow of beer.

'I wouldn't worry too much about him, Loder. With all the evidence we gathered from those kids yesterday, a lot of people are going to go down for a long time.'

'What about, Hatchet? Do you think we should have done things differently?'

'No. We didn't have a choice. He's going to answer for his crimes . . . he is *not* going to walk from all this.'

DCI Oakwood glanced up at the flight information monitor. 'Drink up, Loder. We're boarding.'

The baggage reclaim area at Malaga airport was bustling with tourists tearing around anxiously searching for trolleys, as if their lives depended upon it. While others jostled for pole position to grab their luggage off of the carousels. To the seasoned campaigner, everything was executed like a military exercise. The wife – or partner – commandeered the trolley, while her other half set up position ready to grab their luggage; anyone foolish enough to get in the firing line, did so at their peril.

Loder was positioned on the second row while his boss stood out of the way next to a kiosk selling golfing villas. Standing six-three in height was a great advantage because he could see over people's heads and right along the carousel to where it entered the concourse. Luckily, their bags were only two spaces apart. He reached forward, nudging an angry-looking middle-aged man out of the way and grabbed his bag. The weight of his boss's case caught him unawares and almost had him over onto the concourse floor, before he managed to wrestle it off the carousel. He threw his travelling bag over his shoulder, grabbed the other by the handle and dodged his way through the crowd to where Anne Oakwood was waiting. She pressed a button on the top of her case and pulled out a telescopic handle. 'Shall we go?' she smiled, tilting the case onto its wheels and setting off.

She led the way with Loder shifting his bag uncomfortably on his shoulder on her tail. They went through the automatic doors at the end of the concourse and found themselves hit by a throng of car hire reps and chauffeurs waving sheets of paper with printed names on, in people's faces as they passed through.

Loder tapped his boss on the shoulder to get her attention and pointed to a thin-haired man standing by the entrance holding up a sheet of A4, with Chief Inspector Oakwood printed on it. 'Tell the world, why don't you?' his boss, whispered over her shoulder at Loder.

She approached the man, smiled and said, 'DCI Oakwood, this is DI Loder.'

The man stood dumbstruck for a moment not comprehending what he was seeing. Then with a polite nod, he smiled. 'Forgive me, Chief Inspector. I wasn't expecting a . . .' He left the sentence unfinished. My name is Officer Prieto. Fernando Prieto. My car is outside, if you would care to follow me.'

Loder took the lead and followed the tall, slim, shirt-sleeved man out of the arrivals lounge. As he went through the automatic doors and snaked his way through the myriad of people fighting to get taxis, the stifling heat almost floored him, and he had to fight for breath as the hot arid air found his lungs. They crossed the busy underpass to a waiting car where a uniformed police officer was standing guard over it.

Officer Prieto opened the boot and Loder heaved his boss's heavy case in, followed by his own, and slammed it shut. DCI Oakwood sat in the back, Loder chose to sit in the front. The uniformed officer stepped out into the road, held his hand up to stop the oncoming traffic then waved Prieto out. He eased the car out into the wide underpass and joined the flow of traffic heading in the direction of the exit.

They followed the stream of traffic following the signs for Malaga then swept over a flyover spanning the main N340 highway and down around in a circle, filtering onto the N340 signposted Sevilla and Cordoba.

Already most of the traffic had headlights on as they slotted into the centre lane of the busy four-lane road. Loder glanced at his watch. It was 7:23 pm local time – Anne had told him during the flight it might be best to reset their watches to European central time. 'How long is the drive up to Cordoba, Officer Prieto?' Loder asked, turning to the man.

'Traffic permitting, under two hours, senor. I've reserved rooms for you both at a small hotel in the centre of town. I hope that is acceptable?'

'Very much so, thank you. Your English is very good. Where did you learn it?' DCI Oakwood asked, looking into the man's eyes in the rear-view mirror.

'Fernando, please, madam. I took a year out from university and attended Language College in London, many years ago. I also met a wonderful English girl who later became my wife, so you might say I'm very nearly a native.'

'Is that so!' DCI Oakwood said, with surprise.

'Any news on the two girls whose pictures we faxed over?' Loder asked.

'Yes. We have a positive identification on both girls. And, I'm pleased to say that they appear to be in good health.'

'That's fantastic news,' DCI Oakwood enthused.

'Has there been any visitors to the villa, or any strangers sniffing about?' Loder asked, guardedly.

'Not as far as I know. Are you expecting trouble?' Prieto said, eyeing Anne Oakwood in his mirror.

'We're not entirely sure, but we think that the father of one of the girl's knows the location of the villa and might be on his way down here to take matters into his own hands,' she said, looking out of the window down on the urban sprawl of Malaga and the Mediterranean beyond as they rose up into the hills.

Ten minutes later the road swept around to the right for Granada and straight ahead onto the A45 for Cordoba. Loder looked out at a magnificent viaduct that stretched between mountains carrying the traffic off in the direction of Granada. He craned his neck trying to see how far the arched columns reached down into the deep valley below, but it was impossible to see. The structure truly was a feat of engineering genius.

The night sky was very nearly pitch black as the car wound its way up through the hills and out into the country. As they passed Antequera, the traffic thinned and now there was hardly a vehicle on the road. Loder gazed out on the vast emptiness of the countryside as it stretched away into the darkness. He had never seen such blackness. He was used to the constant yellow haze of the street lighting that rose over London at night like a comfortable warm fog. He could never live out in the wilds; he liked his creature comforts too much. He had to have shops, restaurants and pubs all within easy reach; even if he didn't use them, they were there if he wanted to.

He glanced over his shoulder at Anne Oakwood. She was sound asleep, with her head against the side window and her arms folded in front of her. She looked drained and small and vulnerable. He knew better. She was tougher and more resilient than any woman he'd ever known. And could wipe the floor with most of the chip-on-the-shoulder careerists they encountered day after day. If she was on your side, you had an ally who would back you to the hilt. He knew – he had first-hand experience. He also knew that he hadn't felt so much affection for any woman since his wife died.

'She must be tired?' Prieto said, looking in the rear-view mirror.

'We both are. This investigation has really drained the life out of us.' Loder turned and faced the road ahead, and watched the headlights bouncing up and down on the cats eyes in the darkness.

'I'll drop you straight at the hotel and pick you up in the morning. My boss is anxious to meet you both.'

'Thanks. A good night's sleep will do the both of us good.'

Hotel Plateros was a small hotel down a narrow roadway bearly wide enough for a single car. The entrance opened onto a small cobbled square with a couple of tables and chairs dotted around under a huge parasol. Prieto parked the car by the side door, that was used as a public entrance to the bar, come restaurant. Loder got their luggage out of the boot and Prieto helped him into the hotel reception with it.

Anne Oakwood was already ensconced at a table when they entered and was being served a steaming café con leche in a short glass tumbler.

A dark curly-headed man came out from behind a small reception area – which was a cubby-hole hidden under the steep staircase that led to the rooms above – and beamed a white toothy smile. With his arms outstretched, he went straight to Prieto, gave him a hug and kissed both his cheeks. They stood for a moment jabbering away at ninety miles an hour in Andalucían, which meant absolutely zilch to Loder. He guessed it was the equivalent of a southerner trying to understand a broad-accented Geordie in full swing: forget it.

Prieto turned to Loder. 'Let me introduce my brother-in-law, Jose.'

Loder tried his best at a warm smile and shook the man's outstretched hand. 'John Loder,' he said, retrieving his hand before Jose shook it off his wrist. 'Chief Inspector Oakwood,' he gestured towards his boss who was in the process of receiving a refill.

'Encantado,' Jose said, handing two door keys attached to thick wooden fobs to Loder.

Loder walked through into the small café bar and stood next to where his boss was sitting. A tall slim middle-aged woman came out from behind the counter, went across to Prieto and went through the same ritual as Jose. After the kisses and hugs, they both stood with their arms entwined around each other. 'My sister, Carmen,' Prieto said.

Carmen's tired-looking eyes broke into a smile that was both sincere and warm. 'We hope you enjoy your stay with us, Inspector Loder. Now, can I get you something from the bar,' she said, extricating herself from Prieto.

'Thank you. I think I'd like a coffee and perhaps a cognac to wash it down with.'

'I'll leave you in the capable hands of my sister,' Prieto said. 'Get a good night's sleep, both of you. I'll pick you up around 10:00 am.'

'Thanks for everything,' DCI Oakwood said.

'My pleasure,' he said, giving a wave to his sister as he left.

Prieto stood inside the doorway by the reception and chatted to his brother-in-law for a moment, then waved across at the two detectives before disappearing out through the tall, heavy oak doors of the main entrance.

Carmen came across to the table balancing a tray on the palm of her hand. She set down two half-filled glass tumblers of coffee then topped them up with hot milk from a china jug. The pungent aroma of the freshly brewed coffee was a welcome assault on Loder's senses. She then placed two large-bowled brandy glasses onto the table and poured two generous measures of cognac from a bottle.

'What's this?' Anne Oakwood said, holding up the huge glass to the light.

'Help you to sleep,' Carmen winked, leaving the bottle on the table.

Loder and Anne sat quietly drinking their coffee and sipping cognac. He almost jumped out of his skin, at the sound of his mobile resonating loudly around the cavernous white-washed walls. He rolled his eyes and looked about the room embarrassed. Fortunately, there was only a couple of Scandinavian students sitting at the bar and they were unconcerned. Loder fished it out of his trouser pocket, flipped it open and looked to see who it was.

'Tony. Everything, okay?'

Loder crossed his legs and held the mobile to his ear while looking at his boss. After a minute or so, he ended the call and slipped the phone back into his pocket.

'So, what's going on?' she asked.

'It's Hatchet. He's been having kittens, wondering where we've disappeared to,' Loder sighed.

'He doesn't know that we're over here . . . Does he?'

'Not yet. But it's only a matter of time,' Loder said, opening a packet of panatelas. He peeled the cellophane off one and lit it from an oil lamp that smouldered away in a fluted, crimson coloured glass vase in the centre of the table.

DCI Oakwood took the cigar from between his fingers and took a long drag on it. Blowing a cloud of smoke up towards the glass-domed high ceiling. Calmly, she said, 'What did Tony say?'

'Just pleaded ignorance. Said as far he knew, we were out following up lines of enquiry.'

'Nice, this cognac,' she said, with a slur, emptying her glass. 'Fancy another?'

'Sounds like you might have had enough already,' Loder smiled, and emptied the dregs of his glass down his throat. 'Mmm. It *is* nice,' he said, licking his lips and pouring them both a generous measure from the bottle that Carmen had kindly left on the table.

An endearing smile suffused Loder's face as he watched Anne sway gently on her chair, trying her best to get the large bowled brandy glass to her lips without spilling any. Not that there was much left in the glass to spill.

'Come on. Let's get you upstairs to bed,' Loder said.

'Shush! Someone might hear,' she slurred, swaying forward with a finger in front of her lips. 'I thought you'd never ask,' she winked. 'That's the best offer I've had since . . . the last one.' She burst out laughing, showering Loder with spray.

'Come on. Let's get you upstairs,' he said, helping her to her feet.

She shooed him away with her arm. 'Please yourself,' he said, watching her tottering unsteadily towards the lift. He tailed her up and called the lift, then stood close behind her in case she took a nosedive. The lift door silently slid open and she tottered in with Loder close at hand behind. He looked at the room numbers on the fobs and pressed the button for the first floor. The doors opened, she straightened her back and ventured out into the narrow corridor. Confused, as to know which direction to go in, Loder slipped his arm around her back and led her around to their rooms. He opened her door, took her in and sat her on the bed. Then went next door to open his room. He dumped his bag on the bed, grabbed a carrier bag with a bottle of duty free single malt inside and went back out.

By the time he had used the bathroom and found two clean glasses, Anne was flat out with her legs dangling over the side of the bed snoring like a navvy. Loder stood for a moment looking down at her. He couldn't help having a laugh to himself. Even in her drunken state, she was still incredibly attractive.

He picked up the TV remote lying on a dressing table next to the television, kicked off his shoes, swivelled his legs around onto the bed and sat with his back against the headboard. He pointed the remote at the TV and pressed a button at random. The TV came to life on a Spanish news channel. Loder flipped through the channels until he found BBC World News, then poured himself a small snifter and watched a journalist reporting a suicide bombing in Iraq. Bored, he searched through the rest of the channels but found nothing in English, so he finished his drink and switched it off.

He looked down at Anne Oakwood, she hadn't stirred an inch. He got to his feet, went around to the foot of the bed, squatted down in front of her and gently, he removed her shoes. Then unbuttoned her trousers, lifted her bottom up and pulled them off. She gave out a long moan as he pulled her up to the sitting position and wrestled her arms out of her jacket. He managed to pull her cashmere sweater over her head before she threw her arms around his neck and said lazily, through half-opened eyes. 'Take me, Loder. Make love to me. I'm all yours,' she slurred, nestling into the nape of his neck and kissing him. He breathed deeply drinking in the fragrance of her perfume, then with his arm under her legs he hoisted her up. With his free arm he pulled back the duvet and gently laid her down. She released herself from his neck and rested her head on the pillow. He covered her up and kissed her brow softly. She opened her eyes lazily, smiled and then closed them again. Loder sighed, then left and went back to his room.

Breakfast was a solemn affair due to the fact that Anne Oakwood had a thumping hangover and felt like a bag of shit. Carmen had laid out a platter of cold meats, cheese, wedges of freshly cooked tortilla and toasted bread rolls. Anne had managed to eat a little of the tortilla and toast and was now on her second cup of coffee. Loder on the other hand was bright and breezy – irritatingly so. And he had already devoured most of the platter. Two wedges of omelette and a couple of toasted rolls dripping with butter and marmalade. He had woken early and was showered and dressed before 8:00 am. He had then gone into Anne's room and tried, noisily, to wake her. The room had been in darkness and in her confusion had let off a barrage of abuse at Loder. It was only when he'd pulled back the curtains that she realised to her acute embarrassment that it was daylight outside.

He then filled a glass with water and gave her a couple of paracetamol. With a half-hearted smile, she'd moaned, 'I am *never* touching cognac again as long as I live. Oh . . . thanks, by the way.'

'What for?' he had said.

'For putting me to bed. It was *you*, wasn't it?' she had said, with a look of desperation on her face.

'Of course it was. You don't think I'd have left you alone in that state, do you?'

'Well, thanks. You could have stayed . . . the night. I wouldn't have minded,' she had said, archly.

'What and listened to you snoring like an old navvy.'

'I never was, don't exaggerate, Loder.'

'Don't think it never crossed my mind.' He had winked. 'It was probably one of the longest nights I've ever spent. Lying awake, alone, knowing that you were next door.'

'Then why didn't you come and get in beside me?'

'I don't know. Respect, maybe?' Didn't want you thinking I was taking advantage.

'Oh, Loder. How "old-fashionably" sweet,' she said, stroking the side of his face, affectionately. 'I want you to know, here and now, you have my unconditional permission to take advantage of me any time you like.'

Officer Prieto appeared through the reception and sat down at their table. Carmen came over, gave her brother a kiss on both cheeks and set about clearing the table. 'More coffee?' she asked.

'We got time, Fernando?' Anne Oakwood asked.

'Si, of course. I need to take one also.'

Twenty minutes later, they were in the car and driving along by the walls of the ancient cathedral in the historical old town. Prieto narrated its history like a tourist guide as they slowly passed by. He explained that the cathedral – or mezquita – was originally built by the moors and was the largest mosque in Islam. But when the Christians conquered the city in the thirteenth century, they were so in awe of the structure, that they built the cathedral in the midst of the arches and great columns, which can still be seen to this day. Anne Oakwood was fascinated by it all, and drank in the sights as they drove down to the Guadalquivir river and along by the Roman bridge that was in the middle of being renovated. The tall walls of the old city stood majestically along the right-hand side, which, according to Prieto, used to separate the Jewish quarter from the Arab quarter. The architectural beauty of the place was breathtaking, and in different circumstances she would have simply loved to have stayed to sample the delights of what this city could offer.

The central police station was situated just outside the city walls on a street named, ironically, Avenida Dr Fleming. Prieto aimed a remote at the high gates at the front of the building and they slid noisily apart. He drove into a wide compound and parked up in front of the four-storey building, near to the entrance.

He led them through the automatic glass doors into a wide reception area. A toughened glass curtain stretched across the far end. Not any different to the UK, Loder thought. Prieto punched in a code on a keypad at the side of the reception and the lock buzzed. Leading the way he pushed the heavy door and held it open for DCI Oakwood and Loder. They followed him along a cool, marble-floored corridor until they reached the lift. Prieto pressed the call button and the door immediately slid open. DCI Oakwood tentatively went into the tiny lift, followed by the two men. There was bearly enough room for the three of them, even though the sign above the door read 4 personas. Prieto pressed the button for second floor and the door silently closed. There was a sharp jolt as if the lift was going to plummet downwards before the cable took the strain and it started to ascend slowly. Anne Oakwood didn't like lifts at the best of times, but this stuffy claustrophobic cell was giving her the heebie-jeebies. She grabbed hold of Loder's arm, so tightly that she nearly stopped his blood circulation, as she watched the digital display count the floors from ground to two. When the door slid open on the second floor, she shot out into the sanctuary of the air-conditioned corridor and breathed a sigh of relief: never again. Prieto led them along the corridor and into a cool, neat, uncluttered office and sat them down facing a rectangular metal-framed desk. The chairs were low and leather-cushioned, giving the person sitting behind the desk a psychological height advantage over anyone who sat in them.

Loder immediately felt uncomfortable and got to his feet and walked over to the window. It looked down onto a tree-lined avenue below with heavy traffic spewing exhaust fumes everywhere as it crawled along at a snail's pace. The sky was a hazy shade of blue with an intense white sun burning off the early mist. The digital temperature clock in the street below read 27 degrees and it wasn't even midday yet.

The door opened and a tall slim man came in and went straight to DCI Oakwood with an outstretched hand. 'Detective Chief Inspector Oakwood, a pleasure,' he warmly said.

DCI Oakwood shook his hand and almost melted as his startling, dark eyes looked down at her. The man looked more like Julio Iinglesis, than an officer of the Cordoba National Police Dept, in his crisp, white shirt, slicked black hair, and bright smile. 'My name is, Roberto Garcia, Chief Inspector Serious Crime Unit. You must be Inspector Loder,' he said, walking over and shaking Loder's hand, before settling down behind the desk.

'I trust that your accommodation is acceptable?'

'Yes. It's fine. Thank you for asking,' Anne Oakwood said.

There was a knock at the door and a pretty, uniformed female officer came in carrying a tray of coffee. 'Gracias, Luisa,' the police chief smiled, revealing a deep map of crows-feet around his eyes.

Underneath the Latin charm and infectious smile, he looked middle-aged and tired: a trait most police officers suffered from.

'Black, or with cream?' Garcia said, holding a stainless steel cream jug at the ready.

'Cream, please,' DCI Oakwood said.

'And for you, Inspector Loder?'

'Black will do fine,' Loder said, trying his utmost not to sound surly. He wanted to cut through the niceties and get straight to it.

Garcia poured the cream and handed the china cups in saucers to the two detectives. All very pleasant. Very British. Loder drank the strong bitter liquid and felt it bite the back of his throat as it slipped down.

'Please. Help yourself,' Garcia said, opening a bottle of mineral water and filling a small glass. 'It dilutes the bitter after taste.'

Loder filled a glass.

'Down to the business in hand,' Garcia said, opening a file on the desk in front of him. 'I have had an update this morning and it would seem everything is quiet at the villa.' He slid out the pictures of Delaney and Donna and Laura across the desk. 'We have a positive identification on all three people,' he said, pointing to each picture in turn. 'Would you care to fill me in on the background to this case?' he smiled, at DCI Oakwood. This time it was a smile of a shark before it turned and went in for the kill.

DCI Oakwood told Garcia everything that she dared, without compromising their own investigation. Loder stood by the window taking in the view happy to let his boss take the lead.

Fifteen minutes later, Garcia had been told everything that he needed to know. He got up from behind the desk and walked around past Loder and rested against the edge of the desk, facing DCI Oakwood. He folded his arms and nonchalantly, he said, 'How is it, I get the feeling that you are not telling me the whole story?' The white toothy smile of the shark was back.

She felt the heat rise under her collar, and shifted uncomfortably in her chair. Then shot Loder a look for help. He nibbled at the inside of his mouth, thinking what to do for the best, then said, 'We have a leak . . . our end.'

'I see.' He turned to, Loder. 'That would explain why you turned up here without any official paperwork . . . and I guess, any authority? Am I right?'

'Correct,' DCI Oakwood submitted. He man wasn't a fool. Besides, they needed him on side.

'The two girls are part of a wider ongoing investigation. They have been abducted by Delaney and others.' Loder cut in.

The tentative atmosphere was cut as Loder's mobile sprang to life. He reached into his trouser pocket, fished it out and flipped open the lid. He then looked across at Anne Oakwood and let the call go to voicemail.

'Let me guess?' Your boss? Garcia said, scratching his designer stubble.

Before either of them had time to answer, Anne Oakwood's mobile went off. She reached into her shoulder bag and pulled it out, saw who was calling and looked over at Loder, before switching it off.

'You are very popular . . . no?' Garcia mocked.

'Our leak.' Loder said, ruefully.

Garcia closed his eyes for a moment, and sighed, 'If it is any consolation, I think that maybe we also might have a leak,' he said, apologetically.

'How so?' DCI Oakwood asked.

'It would seem that the local mayor is a regular visitor to the villa. He and this Harry Delaney, are . . . how do you say . . . Garcia searched his mind for the correct pronunciation. They are "bosom buddies." And I think that it goes a lot deeper than just the mayor. It seems that the local people think the villa is a private orphanage and has been operating – if that is the correct phrase – for more than four years. In fact, since the current mayor was elected.'

'I wouldn't dismiss anything where, Delaney is concerned,' Loder said, warming to the man by the minute. He is a serial paedophile who has been preying on kids all his life. He's got his fingers in a lot of important pies.'

'Not only in the UK, it would seem,' DCI Oakwood added.

'I suspect the local mayor is just the . . . how do you say . . . the tip of the iceberg. I would have liked to put the villa under surveillance for a period of time, to gather evidence, but it would be wrong to expose those children any longer than is absolutely necessary.'

'Chief Garcia. You can rest assured that we *are* building a case against Delaney and his accomplices that will put them behind bars for a very long time.'

'I do hope so,' he said. 'So cards on the table. Who is the leak your end? Or would you rather not—?'

'Our boss,' Loder cut in. He couldn't see any point in holding back anything now. The way he saw it, Garcia had two choices, he either helped them, or sent them packing.

'What! A policeman?'

'Aye. We've got video evidence of him with two kids,' Loder said, topping up his glass with water.

'Does he know that *you* know?'

'He knows that we have video evidence. And that we have statements from some of the kids involved. So far, he's been left out of the loop. He's not stupid – he must know that we're onto him. When we get Delaney extradited back to the UK and under arrest, he'll face the courts with the rest of them.'

'Could be months, even years, before Delaney is extradited. You see our judicial system is more corrupt than your own. But I suspect that no amount of money changing hands could prevent him from being extradited once everything is out in the open. Paedophiles are despised just as much in this country as your own. Still, we will cross that bridge when we come to it – I believe that is the correct term,' Garcia smiled, sagely.

'Where did you learn to speak such excellent English, Chief Garcia?' DCI Oakwood asked.

'Roberto, please. In answer to your question,' he paused a moment, 'I spent some time in England when I was a student, before I became a policeman. Now, I watch too much satellite TV. To business. First we will head out to the villa. You can observe Delaney for yourselves, just to be certain he is your man. Then we will plan our strategy for his capture. I trust this meets with both your approval?'

'Absolutely. Loder?' DCI Oakwood looked over to where he was standing as she got to her feet.

'Sounds good. Let's get to it.'

CHAPTER 30

The villa nestled halfway up the side of a valley on the outskirts of the sleepy old town of Montilla. From their vantage point across the valley, the surveillance team had a panoramic view of the back of the property. The pool and gardens were carved high in the hillside. An ornate, limestone block wall about a metre and half high surrounded the rectangular perimeter. The property was relatively secluded, away from any immediate neighbours. Far over to the right stood the Parroquia De Santiago, with its imposing tower overlooking the main town square and higher up the valley were the ruins of the Castillo. Wine and olive groves stretched across the rolling hills, surrounding the old town as far as the eye could see.

Through a pair of binoculars, Loder scanned the villa and the immediate surrounding area. From their position across the valley, Loder looked down at about a twenty-degree angle onto the villa. It was a perfect spot for surveillance.

Delaney was sprawled out on a lounger soaking up the afternoon sun. On a table next to him was an ice bucket crammed with bottles of beer, a pack of cigarettes and a tube of sun cream. Laying there with his fat red stomach and short stubby legs glistening in the heat he looked like an overweight turkey roasting away. Loder handed the binoculars to his boss. She held them up to her eyes and scanned the villa. 'Where are the girls?' she asked, focussing on Delaney.

'They are inside the villa,' Chief Garcia said.

'They keep themselves to themselves. The other children are all Spanish so there is a communication problem, I guess.'

She then spotted a man leading three young boys out onto the terrace. They stripped off their tee shirts, jumped into the pool and began frolicking around. To the untrained eye the scene could have been misinterpreted as a family happily enjoying their holidays. The boys were shouting and laughing, seemingly, without a care in the world. There was little sign they were being held against their will. It wasn't what DCI Oakwood was expecting to see.

Delaney heaved his heavy bulk upright and went over to the side of the pool. He watched for a moment then dived into the water sending a small tsunami crashing over the sides of the pool. He surfaced under one of the boys and lifted him up, launching him high into the air. The others all looked on laughing as Delaney went after them. If it had not been for the fact that he was a serial paedophile, one could be forgiven for thinking that the scene was a bit of harmless fun. A devoted father spending time playing with his children.

'Who are those three kids? Have they been identified?' DCI Oakwood said, handing the binoculars to Loder.

'We haven't been able to put a name to any of them so far. Their pictures have been circulated to the appropriate agencies; as yet we have had nothing back,' Prieto said.

'We think they are . . . how do you say . . . boy prostitutes,' Chief Garcia said.

'They might well be, but you can bet your life that they were groomed by that vicious bastard,' Loder said, trying to see into the villa through the binoculars.

'We've had one lad, who we know was closely associated with Delaney, found washed up in a river brutally murdered. We are certain that Delaney orchestrated the whole affair,' DCI Oakwood said.

'Then the sooner we get this man into custody the better,' Chief Garcia said.

Loder loosened his tie and unbuttoned the top of his shirt. The heat was stifling. His face was wet with sweat and the back of his shirt was beginning to stick to his body. DCI Oakwood on the other hand looked cool and fragrant, but for a slight beading of sweat across the top of her brow. She was wearing a cream, short-sleeved, baggy, thin cotton shirt that was unbuttoned to the cleft of her breasts and a knee-length pencil skirt, no tights and low-slung heels. Her auburn hair was gathered up off her neck and clamped in a scrunchy. She looked cool and casual; in a professional sort of way. Whatever it was, Loder thought that she looked fantastic. He even caught Chief Garcia giving her a furtive once-over behind her back.

'So what's the plan? What do you have in mind, Roberto?' DCI Oakwood said, turning towards him with a smile.

'I suggest we go in early tomorrow morning. First light, when they are all still asleep. I don't think it is a good idea to go crashing around in the darkness. Believe me, you cannot see farther than your nose out here in the country at night. We will have the element of surprise first thing in the morning. Hopefully, we will have everything, how do you say? . . . wrapped up, before they even know what has hit them. What do you think?' Chief Garcia, looked first at, DCI Oakwood, then Loder.

'Sounds okay to me. What about you, Loder?'

'Fine.' He shrugged.

'One thing.' Chief Garcia looked at Loder, earnestly. 'I have no objection to you both joining us tomorrow, but you do so as *observers* only. You do not have any official authority for being here. You must understand my situation. You are welcome to come along, but you keep at arm's length. Is that clear?'

'Absolutely. It's your call.' Loder said. He knew that Garcia was right. He and DCI Oakwood were nothing more than renegades in a foreign country. Though they had the best of intentions, they had no official authority here.

Chief Garcia glanced at his watch, it was 2:36 p.m. 'Now, perhaps, you would like to be my guests for lunch? My men will keep us informed of any developments.'

'That would be very nice, thank you.' DCI Oakwood accepted his invitation on behalf of her and Loder.

Loder wasn't all that fussed. He would have preferred to have found a nice bar back near to the hotel, have a couple of cold beers and then to get his head down for a few hours. But at the end of the day, he was outranked.

*

Lee had slept in fits and starts after the episode in the club the night before. He had roused Ryan early and the pair of them were washed and on the road shortly after 6:00 a.m. It was now mid-afternoon and he had covered just under six hundred kilometres. They'd had two short toilet and snack breaks and were now south of Cordoba travelling on the A45 – Autovia de Malaga. Apart from a slight hiccup on the ring road around Madrid, where Lee had found himself in the wrong lane and no one prepared to give way. Belligerently, he had squeezed in between two cars, making one of them brake sharply. The irony of the situation was that the car involved had UK plates. So much for camaraderie.

The sun was beating down on the windscreen but the air conditioning managed to keep the inside of the car at a comfortable ambience. Lee gave a deep sigh and rolled his neck on his aching shoulders. 'Do you recognise anything about the area, Ryan?' he said, with a deep yawn.

'Eh . . . not sure,' Ryan said, fiddling with the radio tuner.

'What do you mean, you're not sure? I haven't fucking driven over thirteen hundred miles to hear you say, eh . . . I'm not sure.' Lee said, tetchily.

'Keep your wig on. I'll know the place when I see it signposted.'

'Well keep your eyes peeled.' *Keep your wig on.* Lee couldn't help a quiet chuckle.

Ryan rolled a cigarette, lit it and passed it to Lee. Then looked at the road ahead. If the truth was known, he didn't recognise anything at all; the area, the signposted place names and most of all, the road they were travelling on. He hadn't been to the villa for almost two years, and the last time he was there, he remembered the road that he and Delaney had travelled on was more like a dusty two-way track, not this newly-laid motorway. He was just praying that he saw something, anything, that would jog his memory.

A road worker dressed in white overalls and a wide-brimmed straw hat flagged them down and the traffic in front slowly came to a halt.

Lee buzzed the window down to let the smoke out and was assaulted with a blast of heat hitting his forehead. In the distance a white haze sizzled off the tarmac. The aqueous sun was still high in the sky. It was hot and arid and caught the back of Lee's throat as he took a breath.

He pushed his shades up higher on his nose and gazed out across the rolling hills of never ending olive groves. They stretched as far as the eye could see, all laid in neatly spaced rows. Further to his left, were huge plains parched in a fusion of reds and pinks, punctuated with the odd whitewashed farmhouse or crumbling finca.

He dragged deeply on the cigarette, enjoying the consistency at the way it was made – Ryan's roll-ups never went out, and he didn't have to drag the guts out of them just to get a decent smoke. Flicking ash out of the window, Lee happened to glance at the crawling traffic on the opposite carriageway. Suddenly, out of the corner of his eye he had the shock of his life. Travelling in a car on the opposite carriageway, he thought that he saw, DI Loder. He pulled his shades down to get a better look, but the moment had passed; the car had accelerated away. He strained his neck around to get a view through the rear window, but it was no good. All he could make out was the backs of two heads, one lower than the other with reddish hair. He dismissed the thought from his mind. 'Nah . . . can't be,' he said, discarding the butt into the ashtray and buzzing the window up.

'What did you say?' Ryan said.

'Me? Nothing.'

A radio DJ jabbering away at break-neck speed in Spanish was starting to grate on Lee's nerves, so he opened up the centre console, found a CD and slotted it into the machine. He tapped away on the steering wheel in tune with the music as "Hollywood Nights" by Bob Seger burst out through the speakers.

'What is that crap?' Ryan shouted, turning down the volume.

'It's a touch of class. A blast from the past.' Lee smiled and turned the volume back up.

'That's it! Over there – look,' Ryan said, sitting up.

'Where?'

'That sign. Montilla. That's the place . . . I'm sure of it. Next exit.'

Now fully alert, Lee approached the exit, indicated and filtered off to the right. At the bottom of the road he came upon a roundabout, went around it and followed the sign that read Montilla, six kilometres.

Adrenalin was pumping around his veins at an alarming rate. Any feeling of fatigue was forgotten: vanished. He was close. He could just *feel* it. Lee gripped the steering wheel as if his life depended upon it. The tension in his back and shoulders he felt earlier had disappeared. He wound his way through a long valley with olive groves rising high on both sides of the narrow road. As he entered the outskirts of town, the terrain levelled out. On both sides of the road, herds of goats wandered aimlessly around foraging for food in the dry scrub. Dangling from their necks were tinny-sounding bells, tinkling melodically away on the warm breeze

Lee bit his lip nervously. 'Do you know where we're going?'

'It's all different. I'm not sure,' Ryan said, shaking his head with confusion.

Lee said nothing. It was no good shouting at the lad that would only confuse him even more. He just bided his time, hoping, praying that Ryan remembered something, anything that would help him to get to his daughter.

'Follow that sign.' Ryan pointed.

'What sign?'

'That one. The one with the picture of a castle on it. I remember that there was an old ruined castle that could be seen on the hill from the back of the villa.'

Lee followed the rising road as it wound its way up high until he found himself caught up in a one-way system around the Old Town. He just followed his nose snaking slowly through narrow streets that were bearly wide enough to take a vehicle. Fortunately, it was quiet. There was hardly a soul to be seen. He turned right and the road opened up onto a large village square. All the small shops were closed and the only sign of any life was a small group of tourists strolling around. They were snapping pictures of the pretty flowers and plants that hung from the wrought-iron balconies of the whitewashed terraced houses around the square. In the corner was a taperia with tables and chairs set out neatly under brightly coloured parasols advertising Cruzcampo Cerveza. He could just murder a cold beer right now, but decided to press on, given that Ryan had the momentum with him. Lee followed the road around to the right and turned into another impossibly narrow street. His back tyres scrapped against the kerb as he straightened up and slowly accelerated forwards. Fifty metres on, he turned left then hard right and the road opened out onto another square with tall, narrow houses, each with copious amounts of colourful blooms spilling over the balconies. Directly ahead about thirty-five metres, stood the Castillo. Lee parked up on the dusty scrub in front of the derelict building and turned to Ryan. 'Is this the place?'

'I think so, yeh.'

They both got out of the car and walked towards a viewing platform at the side of the Castillo. Lee gave the dilapidated façade a cursory glance as they passed by. The tall turrets at the corners of the building and the high perimeter wall were still intact, though crumbling in places. Protruding up from inside was a tall, pitched roof central building that resembled a huge hall. The Castillo had been partially restored but it was evident that there was still a long way to go to bring it back to its full splendour.

The viewing platform was behind a concrete barrier that prevented people from venturing over the edge of the steep valley below. Lee paused for breath at the spectacular view. The old town of Montilla was below with its church and convent overlooking the village square. A myriad of narrow streets snaked off in all directions behind. The elegant buildings around the main square gave the place a feel of prosperity. Dotted in the hills surrounding the Old Town were brightly painted villas and town houses. In the distance a blue-white haze sizzled off the surface of the autovia like a mirage as it snaked its way down to Malaga. Beyond was nothing but rolling hills of olive groves rising up to the horizon.

'So, Ryan. Any recollections?'

He shook his head and scratched his chin, pensively. 'I don't know. I remember that the Castillo was on the right if you were out on the terrace.' He looked down to his left. 'If we find a way around and down in that direction.' He pointed down the valley. 'I might recognise something.' He shrugged.

Lee stood tight-lipped. He was beginning to lose patience. He took a deep breath. 'Right, let's get back in the car and see if we can find a route down.'

Lee swept the car back and around, kicking a cloud of dust up into the air, then bumped the vehicle over the uneven ground until he got back onto the road. Because of the one-way system, he had no choice than to go right. He followed the direction arrows through the winding narrow streets, all in a gradual descent, until he came to a junction. He hesitated for a moment, not sure which way to go. Then with a big sigh, he turned right, purely because the road was descending and sweeping around back in the direction of the Castillo. Above the road on the left was a development of town houses under construction. On the right, set back was a cluster of expensive-looking villas hidden behind tall walls and electric gates.

'There!' Ryan shouted.

'Where?' Lee looked in both directions while trying to keep an eye on a tractor that was directly in front of him.

'We just passed it. I'm sure of it,' Ryan said, craning his neck around to get another look.

Lee stopped the car and looked out of the rear window at the villa. It was set back from the road and down a shallow slope about fifty metres back. The tractor had descended down the hill far enough for Lee to see that the road ahead widened on one side, enough for him to make a U-turn. He put the car into gear, drove on, made the manoeuvre and was now approaching the villa on his left-hand side.

'What do you think? Is that it, Ryan?'

'Yeh. That red 4x4 parked out front is, Delaney's. He leaves it in the garage when he's not here.

Lee coasted slowly past the railing-gated forecourt and just stared, stunned, mesmerised at the ceramic nameplate on the pillar outside.

He was suddenly catapulted back more than thirty years in time. He stopped the car a little way up the road, opened the door and threw up all over the road.

'You alright, Lee?' Ryan said, concerned.

'Yeh. Just had a bit of a shock that's all.'

From the door pocket, he pulled out a duster that he used for cleaning the windscreen and wiped his mouth and chin. He took a few deep breaths to calm himself. Satisfied, there was nothing else to come up, he got back in the car and slammed the door shut.

'Right,' Lee said, composing himself. 'Any ideas on how we get into the place?'

'Fuck me! You look like you've seen a ghost. You alright?'

'You don't know the half of it, Ryan. I'm ok,' Lee said, with a limp smile. 'Now, how are we going to do this?'

Ryan pursed his lips, deep in thought. 'If we climb over the fence at the front, the side gate hasn't got a proper lock.'

'What do you mean, it hasn't got a proper lock?'

'It's only bolted from the inside. You could give me a leg up and I'll open it from the inside.'

'Let's go and get a drink somewhere. I need to get my head around things,' Lee said, starting the car.

They drove back the way they had came until they found themselves in the main part of town. Here, the streets were wider and busier with traffic. They were lined with orange and lemon trees on both sides. It was a little after five in the afternoon and the shops and businesses were opening up after the lunchtime siesta.

Lee parked the car and they walked across the Paseo de Abajo to where there were a cluster of bars and cafes. They found a table shielded from the hot, late afternoon sun by an oasis of palms and sat down. A waiter came over to the table and Lee ordered a couple of small beers.

Ryan rolled a cigarette, passed it to Lee and then began to roll one for himself. The waiter brought the drinks over, together with a small bowl of olives. Lee took a long swallow of the cool beer, almost emptying the contents of the glass tumbler in one go: it failed to rid him of the foul-tasting bile that stuck in the back of his throat. Ryan popped an olive into his mouth, spat the stone out onto the dusty ground and then washed it down with a drink.

'Good olives, them,' he said, popping another into his mouth.

'Are they?' Lee was still frozen with shock.

'Fancy something to eat?' Ryan said, picking up a laminated menu card from the table.

'Do you *ever* stop thinking about your fucking stomach?' Lee snapped.

Like a recalcitrant child, Ryan slapped the menu back down on the table and popped another olive into his mouth.

Lee sighed tiredly. Brushed his fingers through his hair and said, 'I'm sorry. You go ahead and order what you want. Nothing for me, I couldn't eat a thing, my guts are churning all over the place.'

Ryan called the waiter over and in perfect Spanish, ordered what sounded like a banquet. Lee got the impression that the waiter was impressed, judging by the smile he gave Ryan as he left the table.

'How are we going to do this?' Lee said, turning to Ryan for reassurance.

'I think it's best if we go in after midnight. Probably the early hours, when the greasy fat cunt's asleep.'

'Do you think we'll have much trouble getting in?'

'No. Not if everything is how I remember it. The patio doors at the back should be open. So too, Delaney's bedroom windows. He doesn't like sleeping with the air conditioning on, so the windows and doors are always left open for ventilation. And believe me Lee, that place is stifling at night.'

'You know the layout inside the place then?'

'What do you think? You silly bastard.' Ryan rolled his eyes.

'Yeh, of course. What am I thinking. My head's all over the place at the moment.'

Ryan waved the waiter over and ordered two more beers.

'Have you packed a weapon?' Ryan said, in a matter-of-fact tone, as if it was an everyday occurrence.

'What do mean? A gun?' Lee looked at him, stunned at the thought.

'Well, a gun would get us *right* out of trouble,' he joked. But the underlying message was serious. 'Delaney ain't going to just roll over and let us walk all over him. He's a violent, evil fucker. I know. I've seen him in action, remember. And don't forget, he won't be alone in the villa.'

'What are you saying?'

'I'm saying that he's bound to have someone staying there overseeing the place. The last time I was here the place was run by a Spaniard, an old mate of his and believe me, that man was an evil fucker. Delaney helped him do a runner from a bail hostel. He looked after the place, paid the bills, organised the clients and ruled the kids with a rod of iron. If they didn't do what they were told he'd beat the fuck out of them. That's how he got his "jollies." He was a violent bastard who was never without a blade and believe me, he wouldn't think twice about using it.

Lee closed his eyes and tried to blot out the thought of what his daughter must be going through. His one comforting thought was that he was here now and he was coming for her. If he'd had his way, he would have stormed into the house straight away and fuck the consequences.

'Well, I haven't got anything in the car except, maybe, a tyre lever.' Lee said, taking a drink from the replenished glass.

'We'll have to find a shop or somewhere that sells baseball bats, or something similar' Ryan said. The voice of experience.

The waiter clipped a paper tablecloth over the table, then placed two plates down, a basket of freshly cut bread, two sets of cutlery wrapped in serviettes and a bowl of mixed salad topped with tuna.

'Please, tell me you haven't ordered a full blown banquet, Ryan?'

'No. Just some salad and a bit of tapas,' Ryan said, with an impish grin.

The waiter came over to the table balancing an armful of shallow, earthenware dishes and set them down. 'Albondigas, estofado, magro con tomate y pescados variados ,' he said, pointing to each. 'Bon Apetito.'

'What is all this stuff?' Lee asked, tiredly.

'It looks a lot more than it is,' Ryan said, preparing his eating irons for an all-out attack. 'They're only half rations.' He pointed at each dish with his knife in the attack position. 'Meatballs, beef stew, pork in tomato and fried fish.'

Lee forked a couple of meatballs onto his plate, spooned a little of the stew as well and tentatively he tucked in. To his surprise, his stomach accepted the food obligingly without grumbling.

An hour later, fed and watered, they were ferreting around a garden centre on the outskirts of town for some suitable weapons. So far, they hadn't found anything that was heavy enough to do any serious damage with. 'Over there, look.' Ryan pointed at a rack of gardening tools.

They walked along the rack from end to end and the best that they could come up with was a couple of pickaxe handles. Although not ideal, they did have a bit of weight behind them. If someone was to get a clump across the head with one, they would certainly know all about it. Lee purchased two, one for each of them.

Outside the garden centre in the car park, Lee put the weapons into the boot, got into the car and started the engine. He glanced at his watch, it was 7:45 p.m. 'What now? We need to kill a few hours, any suggestions?'

'It'll be dark soon. Maybe we ought to see if we can get a look around the back of the villa, see if there's anything going on. What do you think?' Ryan said.

Lee didn't care much for Ryan's choice of words. Because if he happened to see *something* going on, he wouldn't be responsible for his actions.

'Okay. Let's see if we can find a vantage point somewhere,' Lee said, putting the car into gear.

Twelve minutes later, they were driving past Delaney's villa. The front of the property was shaded and almost in darkness, but for a single lantern on the wall at the side of the front door. Lee coasted down the hill, then turned right at a junction at the bottom and followed the road around and upwards, until they came to a row of terraced town houses. At the top of an incline, there was a stretch of waste ground that had been levelled ready for development. Lee swept the car onto it, parked up and switched off the headlights. They both got out and walked nearer to the edge of the deep valley so that they could get a better view. It was now almost dark and trying to pinpoint Delaney's villa from the other properties dotted around the valley, was impossible for Lee, but Ryan knew the layout better than him.

'That's it over there, look.' Ryan pointed.

'Where?' Lee said, trying to follow Ryan's pointing finger.

'That one with the outside lights on, see? It's got a white ornate perimeter wall, see?'

'Yeh. I've got it.'

'Looks as though everything's quiet. The patio doors are open, and they should be like that all night. Oh, before I forget, there are mosquito screens across all the windows and doors. Unless you're aware of them, you can't see them until it's too late, so remember to slide them across before going inside.'

The pair of them stood and watched to see if anyone made an appearance out on the terrace. To any passing observers, the two of them could have easily been mistaken for father and son as they stood together.

'Shall we go and find a bar somewhere? There's nothing going on over there, Lee.'

'Yeh. I suppose we need to kill a few hours. Besides, I'm going to need quite a bit of Dutch courage.'

CHAPTER 31

It was dark and quiet as they coasted past Delaney's villa in the early hours of the morning. Lee drove on down the hill, turned around, coasted slowly back up again and came to a stop twenty metres past the villa.

He killed the engine, turned off the headlights, quietly opened the door, got out and went around to the back of the car. The clunk of the boot catch releasing sounded like a minor explosion in the stillness of the humid, pitched black night air. Lee cringed as the tailgate squeaked open and the interior light beamed out like a lighthouse beacon.

He handed Ryan one of the pickaxe handles. Ryan rested it against the bumper, unzipped his holdall and rummaged around deep inside until he pulled out a long sheath knife. He flipped open the leather studded strap and pulled out a serrated six-inch blade with a thick wooden handle. 'In case of emergencies.' Ryan smiled, sliding the blade down the back of his waistband.

Lee was caught dumbstruck. It suddenly dawned on him the seriousness of what they were about to do. And seeing Ryan packing what amounted to a deadly weapon that could actually kill someone, just compounded the whole situation. His arse was flapping and no mistake. Seeds of doubt started to cloud his mind and he began to have second thoughts about it all. Maybe they should abandon everything and telephone, DI Loder. Leave it to the professionals.

Too late. Ryan was sprinting down the road towards the villa. He was already over the top of the railing fence and on his way down the other side when Lee got there. Lee passed his pickaxe handle and torch through the railings and clambered over after him, landing with a thud on the paved forecourt. Suddenly, a halogen floodlight came on and froze them dead in their tracks. Caught like a couple of foxes in a vehicle's headlights, they looked at each other for a second, then Ryan made a dash into the shadows under the side gate. Lee followed and squatted down next to him. Ryan shrugged. 'Don't remember that being there.'

'Let's pray that there's not any more little surprises waiting for us,' Lee whispered, breathlessly.

Ryan trained the torch to the top of the gate: it was higher than he remembered.

'Ready?' Lee whispered.

Ryan nodded.

Lee cupped his hands tightly and Ryan stuck his foot in them. With his hands on his shoulders for balance, Lee launched him up as high as he could. Ryan grabbed the top of the gate and swung his leg over. Straddled on top, Lee handed up the pickaxe handle and Ryan disappeared down the other side. The thump of Ryan's trainers hitting the ground sounded loud enough to raise the dead.

'Shit!' Ryan whispered. 'The door's padlocked. You'll have to climb over.'

'How? I'm not fucking Spiderman.'

'Wait there. I'll be back in a minute.'

'Ryan . . .' Lee called, as loud as he dared. But he was already gone.

Lee crouched low behind a concrete pillar to shield himself from any oncoming vehicles and waited. He shined the torch onto his watch. It was 1:36 a.m. 2:36 a.m local time. The seconds ticked away, turning into minutes. Lee's nerves were like over sensitive circuit breakers; one twitch or sound out of the ordinary and he was sure that his heart would trip out.

Suddenly, the forecourt went into darkness. Lee's heart skipped a beat, sending a shockwave racing through his nervous system. The halogen lamp's sensor control had timed out. He wiped his clammy hands on his jeans and gripped the pickaxe handle as if his life depended upon it: which it might well do if everything went boss-eyed.

Stuck, crouched down, outside a violent criminal's villa in a foreign country with nothing but the haunting sound of an orchestra of cicadas shrilling loudly from the trees for company, Lee began to panic. He shuffled uncomfortably to ease the cramp that was creeping up his leg. Suddenly, the high-pitched shrill stopped dead. The silence was deafening. It was if a thousand eyes were watching his every move.

After a short pause, without notice the orchestra started up again. His mind raced into overdrive and the whole scenario began to play out in his head like a timeline. His daughter's stupidity meeting with a stranger from an internet chat room. His wife's lack of faith in him. His comforting chats with Donna – the young heroin-addicted prostitute in Soho that would stay with him for the rest of his days. The chance encounter with Ryan. His stupidity in not telling the police everything when he had the opportunity. But most of all he questioned his own self-belief. His own tormented childhood: the bolt from out of the blue that was the catalyst. Suddenly, Lee had an overwhelmingly bad feeling about how all this was going to pan out.

How had he got himself into this predicament and how the hell was he going to get them both out of it. For all his cocky bravado, at the end of the day, Ryan was just a kid. He made a conscious decision there and then that, if it meant taking a man's life to save his daughter's, or Ryan's: so be it. Tonight, he would kill, or be killed: no matter what the consequences.

Suddenly a deafening click resonated on the still night air. The loud shrill of the cicadas suddenly stopped again, leaving an eerie quietness as if they sensed something was amiss. Lee looked around in panic as the front door slowly opened.

Rooted to the spot, terrified, he lifted the wooden handle above his head in readiness to crack someone's head open. Ryan poked his head out, smiled and waved Lee over. Lee breathed a deep sigh of relief, straightened up and hurried through the open door. Ryan closed it after him and with a finger in front of his lips, he led the way across a wide reception hall.

'That's Delaney's bedroom,' Ryan whispered, pointing the torch at a half-open door around to the right. 'I'll go and find the girls and get them out.'

Lee nodded. He then tiptoed around the edge of the marble-floored reception hall, past the open door to the bathroom and a closed door adjacent to it. With his back tight against the wall outside Delaney's bedroom, he took long deep breaths trying to compose himself. He pushed the door open with the long handle until it was at ninety degrees and poked his head around. It was too dark inside to make anything out. He switched the torch on and shone it into the room. A king-sized bed was directly in front against the back wall. In the middle, snoring soundly, under a thin duvet was a big bulge. The side of a baldhead could just be seen buried deep into a mound of pillows.

The room was about seven metres across, but it seemed like forty to Lee. He closed his eyes and took a deep breath. Gripping the pickaxe handle tightly with both hands he ran into the room and started clubbing at the shape in the middle.

'Get up you fat bastard!' Lee shouted, as he brought the handle down for what seemed the hundredth time, hitting the man's arm as he held it up to protect himself.

The wall lights above the bed came on and a young, fair-haired, terrified face peeked over the duvet next to Delaney. Distracted, full of consternation, Lee stopped hitting the man and held the club high above his shoulder. Suddenly, he felt a punch in the back of his kidney, he doubled up in pain fighting for breath. A hand grabbed him tight around the neck and as his face was wrenched upwards, he saw a long shiny blade scratching the stubble under his chin. Lee dropped the wooden handle onto the marble floor.

Delaney's bulldog face was racked with pain as he languidly rolled onto his back and pulled himself up. The fair-haired boy just stared blankly straight at Lee.

Out of the corner of his eye, Lee saw a mouthful of stained teeth bearing down on him that looked like a row dog-ends and smelt fifty times worse. The blade was so tight under his chin that it had pierced his skin and blood was trickling down his throat and onto his tee shirt.

'So, what have we here?' Delaney said, inspecting the red marks on his shoulders.

Suddenly, there was a piercing scream as the man holding the blade fell in a crumpled heap onto the floor. Blood pumped out across the marble floor from the gaping wound where Ryan had buried his knife into the side of the man's neck and twisted it for good measure before pulling it back out. The man writhed on the floor clasping the wound trying to stem the fountain of blood pumping out of his severed carotid.

'Hello, Harry.' Ryan smiled.

Delaney swiftly opened the drawer to his bedside cabinet, pulled out a revolver and aimed it at Lee. The fair-haired boy next to Delaney panicked and leapt across him in an effort to get out of the bed. In doing so, he knocked the revolver out of his hand, sending it spinning across the floor. A white flash followed by an almighty explosion resonated around the room.

'Fuck! Lee screamed as he felt a hot searing pain rip through the side of his thigh, sending him spinning to the floor.

Delaney leapt out of bed like a jack-rabbit and made a beeline for the revolver. But, Ryan beat him to it. He grabbed the weapon and aimed it at Delaney's head, stopping him in his tracks.

'Back onto the bed. Now!' Ryan shouted.

Delaney scurried back across the room and onto the bed. A look of horror and fear written across his face.

'Dad!' Donna ran into the room and threw her arms around his neck as he struggled to his feet. She buried her head into his chest and held on to him for dear life. Then she saw the person responsible for the hell she had been put through. 'Jason!'

'What!' Lee spun around towards, Ryan. 'That's the fucker you met on the internet?'

'Oh, dear. Didn't he tell you?' Delaney laughed. 'Jason, here . . . Or Ryan, works for me. We go back a long way together; he's like a son to me.'

'Used to be, Harry. But I got replaced by a younger model, didn't I?'

'Gary, here, means nothing to me.' He shrugged with indifference. 'You've always been my favourite . . . son. You know that.' Delaney ingratiated.

'Yeh. Just like Danny once was. Look how he ended up, you filthy murdering bastard.'

'Danny crossed the line. He betrayed me.' Delaney's demeanour changed to that of the devil incarnate.

The consternation on Lee's face was palpable. He was at a loss as to what to do for the best.

Delaney held out his arms. 'Ryan, we're a team, son. Why are you doing this?'

Lee grabbed the gun off, Ryan. 'Give it here, before you do something stupid. Then he heard someone whimpering from behind him. He turned and saw a tall, tear-stained, blotchy-faced girl standing inside the doorway, wearing nothing but a tee shirt. 'You must be, Laura,' Lee smiled, sympathetically. 'Donna, darling. Take Laura and go and get yourselves dressed.

Reluctantly, Donna let go of her father, went across to Laura, took her by the hand and led her out of the room.

'Put your hands where I can see them,' Lee said, pointing the revolver at Delaney's barrelled, hairy chest.

Suddenly, like a bolt of lightning out of the blue, Lee caught a glimpse of something that he hadn't set eyes on for over thirty years. His legs turned to jelly. He grabbed Ryan's shoulder to steady himself and screwed his eyes, refusing to believe what he was seeing.

Delaney turned his arm . . . there was no mistake. The colours had faded, but the tattoo was the same . . . The Mermaid. Memories . . . awful memories that were buried deep in the abyss of his mind, came flooding back to the surface like a burst dam. A life, Lee had locked away many years ago. Tried to blot out its very existence. And until a few hours ago had managed to. All the guilt. The dirtiness. The disgust. The hurt. The hopelessness. The excruciating pain. Like a festering sore that had burst open, spilling its stinking poison everywhere . . . It all came flooding back as if it was yesterday.

Open-mouthed, Lee aimed the gun at Delaney's head. Delaney saw the menace in the man's eyes and shifted uncomfortably back against the headboard. Lee turned his head to the side and tried to picture the man as he was all those years ago. Now, he was fatter, bald, and the face had drooped and folded into itself, but there was no mistaking those cold evil eyes. The look of the devil itself.

'Harry Critchley,' Lee said, calmly.

Lee smiled. Enjoying the glowering consternation on the man's sweaty, bulldog face. Delaney hadn't heard anyone call him by his real name for years.

'Whitehaven Children's Home . . . 1972.'

'I think you must have me confused with someone else, son.' Delaney sniffed, arrogantly.

'I am not your fucking, *son*.' Lee's hands trembled uncontrollably as he gripped the revolver for dear life. 'I should have cottoned on when I saw the nameplate on the wall outside. Happy memories, were they? That why you named this filthy den of depravity after the Home? Amused you, did it? All those kids' lives you corrupted and ruined. Robbed them of any self-respect. Then – Lee's throat clogged with emotion, and he spat a ball of phlegm onto the floor – without a second's thought, you just tossed them aside. Like pigs with their snouts in a trough, they were nothing more than fodder for all your cronies to feast upon.

'You two know each other?' Ryan said, confused.

'Oh, I know this evil bastard. I've been on the receiving end of his . . .' Lee couldn't bring himself to say the words. He screwed his eyes tightly in frustration, determined not to break down and let the tears that were welling up come out. He wasn't going give this bastard the pleasure of seeing him shrink to a mess. Just like he did all those years ago: never let the bastards see your pain.

Lee could smell the fear dripping off of Delaney, as he shifted uncomfortably on the bed. He steadied his hands the best he could and took aim at Delaney's head. 'This is for all those kids you've ruined,' he calmly said.

Delaney held his hands up in front of his face. 'Now come on . . . Lee, you don't want to do this. I'm not worth doing the time for. What would Donna do with her father banged up in prison for murder.'

'Don't you *dare* take my daughter's name in vain.'

No matter how much Lee tried to pull the trigger it just wouldn't happen. Hastily, he wiped the wet from his eyes with his arm, then as he was about to take aim again, Gary grabbed the revolver, aimed it at Delaney and let fire. The kick of the gun going off sent him flying backwards across the room.

The deafening noise ricocheted off the walls. It took Lee a moment to realise what had happened. It was only when the smoke and the smell of cordite filled his nostrils that the reality of the situation dawned on him. There was blood and bits of bone and brains splattered all over the back wall and on the bed. Delaney's bulldog head was slumped down on his chest. There was small bullet hole in the side of his temple and a gaping hole at the back where the bullet had exited.

Gary got to his feet, looked at the smouldering revolver in his hand, as if it was an infectious disease and threw it on the floor.

'You alright, Gary?' Ryan said, running over to him.

'I think so,' he said, wide-eyed with shock.

'I thought you liked the old bastard,' Ryan said.

'I didn't have a choice. You know that better than anyone, Ryan. If I hadn't given in to him, who knows what might have become of me. I might not have said very much, but I heard everything, especially, where Danny was concerned. All I could do was just bide my time until an opportunity arose to get out.'

Ryan said nothing. He just nodded, sagely. He knew exactly where Gary was coming from.

Donna came running into the bedroom screaming hysterically. Lee scooped her up in his arms and held onto her for dear life. Laura stood behind, waiting by the door. Lee turned towards her and held out a hand. She walked over and nestled into his chest as he put a comforting arm around her.

Relieved to hear the sound of police sirens screaming out in the distance, Lee gave a deep sigh. 'let's get out of here.'

CHAPTER 32

DCI Oakwood and Loder were sitting in an outer office at the Crown Prosecution Service. Both were at a loss as to why they were there. All the evidence gathered throughout the investigation had been handed over and a rock-solid case had been built. More than twenty children had come forward and given statements. They were all now in safe accommodation under the Witness Protection Programme, together with the Social Services. Ryan had been their star witness, and had given the police an insight into the workings of the biggest child abuse network this country has ever seen: names, dates and places where Delaney plied his evil trade were all freely given. He painted a graphic picture of absolutely everything that he knew: including the vicious bastards that allegedly killed Danny McKee. In return for his cooperation, Ryan was charged with conspiracy to abduction. Recommendations would be made on his behalf for leniency.

Lee had received a visiting order from Felcham Young Offenders Unit, where Ryan was now on remand. But he couldn't bring himself to face Ryan. It was all too raw at the moment. One side of him wanted to strangle Ryan for what he had done. The other side couldn't help liking the lad and wanted to give him a break. Perhaps in time, when the court case was over, he might feel differently.

The CPS had more than thirty hours of video evidence from the children and, barring a major catastrophe, the case was sewn up. So far, thirty-four people had been charged, including all the main players. All were out on bail, except for Jonnie James. He'd been arrested at Heathrow Airport trying to flee the country and was now on remand in Wormwood Scrubbs. He was still screaming his innocence to anyone who would listen.

Three Children's Homes had been closed pending further investigation – several staff had already been charged. Clearly what was emerging was that, Harry Delaney over a period of more than thirty-four years, had built the biggest paedophile, child abuse network in British history. And in that time its tentacles knew no bounds, it had wound its evil trade into the highest echelons of the British establishment.

Loder was certain that what they had discovered so far, was just a tip of the iceberg. He was in no doubt that more atrocities would come to light in the months and years ahead.

Thanks to the intervention of the British Consulate in issuing emergency passports for Ryan and the girls. And Chief Garcia's swift action at getting Lee Carlin and everyone else onto a plane and out of the country, no charges were being sought by the Spanish Authorities. It seemed that they had washed their hands of the whole affair. Chief Garcia was actively pursuing his own investigation into events that went on at the villa, and from what he had told Loder, he was having the same conspiracy of silence that Loder had encountered. Every direction Garcia turned he was met with a wall of silence: he was in no doubt that there was a massive cover-up going on. But with DCI Oakwood and Loder's help, he was determined to get to the bottom of things.

A fresh-faced, suited young lawyer came into the room and told the two detectives that they were ready for them. They followed him down a corridor and into an expensively furnished, spacious office. There was three men in the room, all shirt-sleeved and subdued. The main man, Alistair Thorpe-Stewart QC came out from behind his huge desk and shook DCI Oakwood's hand warmly. Then with his palm in the small of her back, he led her through a door and into a small conference room. Loder followed behind in front of the other two lawyers. Thorpe-Stewart sat at the head of the table, Loder and his boss sat together on the far side and the two lawyers sat opposite. Fixed high on the wall at the end was a large flat-screen TV. Thorpe-Stewart played nervously with the TV remote control in his hand, gathering his thoughts. He placed it gently onto the table, and turned to Loder and DCI Oakwood. 'What I'm about to show you is highly sensitive and, *must* not be discussed with anyone outside of this room. Is that clear?'

Both detectives glanced at each other, then nodded.

Thorpe-Stewart picked up the remote control pointed it at a DVD player and pressed play. One of the shirt-sleeved lawyers got up and lowered the blinds. In the darkness of the room, Loder made a face at his boss, indicating, what the hell's going on.

Thick horizontal lines made their way down the screen until the picture settled. Then all became clear. DCI Oakwood shot Loder a poisonous look. He gave a confused shrug.

On the video was Detective Chief Superintendent Hatchet lying naked on a bed with Laura Davidson on one side of him and another girl on the other; both girls were naked and wore thick lipstick and mascara. Hatchet had his arms around the girls and wore a grin that stretched from ear to ear. The audio in the background was instructing the girls what to do. The haunting look on their faces was almost too much for Loder; he screwed his eyes not wanting to watch any more than was absolutely necessary. The video played for about fifteen minutes before, Thorpe-Stewart switched it off.

'You get the picture, detectives. I don't think we need to see the rest. So . . .' Thorpe-Stewart sighed. 'What do you want tell me?'

'Tell you?' Loder said.

'Where do you think this DVD came from?' Thorpe-Stewart smiled.

'No idea. Why don't you enlighten us,' Loder said, sarcastically.

'We received it in the post, yesterday.'

'Where from?' DCI Oakwood cut in.

'Well, that's the funny thing. It was post-marked, Malaga Airport.'

'What's funny about it? Looks positively depraved to me, ' Loder said.

Thorpe-Stewart didn't take kindly to being ridiculed, especially in front of his team. His demeanour changed to that of the haughty prosecution barrister as he shot Loder a look of contempt.

'We know that you two have a . . . shall we say, a close working relationship with a certain, Chief Garcia of the Cordoba National Police.'

'Damn right we do. What's your point?' Loder said sharply, running out of patience.

'My point is, Inspector Loder. I keep asking myself, did all the evidence get logged? And is there any more little gems like this likely to surface in the future?'

'How do *we* know?' DCI Oakwood said. 'Everything we found was tagged and logged. And if you're insinuating that we are part of some sort of conspiracy, then you had better have something to back it up. Otherwise we're out of here, right now.'

Loder turned to Anne Oakwood, then to Thorpe-Stewart and said, 'What do you intend doing with this evidence? I take it that you're going to charge him?'

'Well . . . it's not as simple as that.' Thorpe-Stewart clasped his hands in a praying position under his chin and contemplated for a moment. It was all pure theatre; stage-managed to get the full impact of what he was about to say. We . . . that is the Commissioner and the powers that be, think that prosecuting DCS Hatchet is not in the public interest.'

'The Establishments interest you mean,' DCI Oakwood said.

Thorpe-Stewart ignored the comment and went on. 'It would undermine public confidence in the whole of the police force if this got out. That's why we are relying on your . . . discretion.'

'I get the picture now. You get us here on a fishing exercise to see if we're part of some elaborate conspiracy, then you slap a gagging order on us,' Loder said, full of contempt.

'I wouldn't quite put it like that,' Thorpe-Stewart said, with a smug smile.

'How *would* you put it?' Loder said.

'Detective Chief Superintendent Hatchet is deeply ashamed at what he has done. And has stepped down from his post with immediate effect,' Thorpe-Stewart said.

'On medical grounds, no doubt,' DCI Oakwood said, sourly. 'Come on Loder, let's get out of here before I throw up.' She slung her bag over her shoulder, got to her feet and stormed out of the room.

'I take it we can count on your discretion, Inspector Loder?' Thorpe-Stewart said, as he left the room.

'Don't have a choice, do we? Not if we want to stay gainfully employed.'

Loder put the car into gear and drove out of the car park and into the busy afternoon traffic. 'I could do with a drink. I've got a bitter taste in my throat. What about you, Anne?' Loder said, still reeling from the morning's events.

'Is there something that you want to tell me, Loder?' she said, turning to him.

'No. What do mean?'

'You're telling me you had nothing to do with that fiasco upstairs in that office?'

'Absolutely! I've no idea where that video came from,' he said, straight-faced.

Anne Oakwood fixed him a disbelieving stare.

'Honestly!' Loder said, with a wide grin, holding his hands up in supplication while they waited at the traffic lights.

'Okay. I believe you, Loder. Any ideas as to who it might have been?'

'Nope. Why don't you give Chief Garcia a ring, see if he can shed some light on the situation.'

'Why me?'

'You're the senior officer. Besides, I think he was quite taken with you.'

'No . . . do you think so?' She glowered.

'I caught him eying up your rear end a couple of times, when we were in Spain.'

'Really!' she said, smoothing down the sides of her skirt with her hands. Then reached across and gave Loder a soft kiss on the cheek. 'Not my type.'

Loder barrelled his chest out full of self-assurance. Then turning to his boss, he said, vehemently, 'I'm *damned*, if I'm going to let that dirty fucker get away with nothing more than a slapped wrist.'

'What have you got in mind?'

'I've still got the original Hatchet DVD.'

'And?'

'Well, why don't I give it to my journalist contact at the Sunday papers? He's sound. He'd see to it that we weren't implicated in any way and Hatchet gets plastered all over the front pages of the Sunday tabloids. What do you think?'

'Love it! The CPS wouldn't have a choice they'd have to charge him. And if we can get Laura Davidson to testify against him, his demise would be complete. They would throw away the key.'

'Let's go and find a quiet pub and I'll make the call.' Loder said, putting an arm around her and kissing her tenderly on the side of the head.

'Are you sure you had nothing to do with sending that DVD to the CPS?'

'Absolutely! Would I lie to you?' He smiled, sagely

'Loder!' She slapped his arm.

'What!'

THE END

Lightning Source UK Ltd.
Milton Keynes UK
UKOW04f1122291215

265472UK00004B/451/P